Cinnamon Soul
Quinn Lawrence

Fondence City Press

Cinnamon Soul

Quinn Lawrence

Published by Fondence City Press

Copyright © 2025 by Quinn Lawrence

Cover art by Brenda Failache

All rights reserved.

The characters and events portrayed in this book are fictitious. Any similarity to real persons, living or dead, is coincidental and not intended by the author.

No portion of this book may be reproduced, stored in a retrieval system, or transmitted in any form without written permission from the publisher or author, except as permitted by U.S. copyright law.

Also by

The Cinna and Hokuren Series
Cinnamon Soul

1

Cinna ruined countless evenings in the entertainment district during her chase of Velles's most notorious thief. She barreled through drunken revelers clotting the thin streets with dancing and merriment, not even once thinking to apologize for the mess she left behind her. Threats and shouts rang out in the night from aggrieved carousers as they picked themselves off the cobblestone, covered in the remnants of their ales. Cinna ignored them and maintained her focus entirely upon the man in her sights ahead of her.

Catching him was her job. She would not fail.

Maxwell Barnaby risked a look back at her once they reached a less crowded section of Velles, giving her a chance to enjoy the panic in his face. Her boss had told her desperate men were dangerous. As if to prove her correct, Barnaby reached into the breast of his jacket. He pulled out a knife and flicked it at Cinna in a singular motion. His aim was true, but she saw it coming and ducked. The knife whistled as it rushed over her head. Not bad. Far from good enough, but not bad.

A lack of familiarity with the city's streets hampered Barnaby as he scrambled through the thin alleys and long avenues of the entertainment district. To put an end to the chase, Cinna feinted toward the street to the right in hopes of baiting him toward a dead-end alley on the left.

He went left. Cinna smiled to herself and followed him. She stopped running when she reached the alley's entrance. Barnaby discovered what she already knew: he had nowhere to go. Except through her.

Barnaby's breathing was labored as he stood in the light at the end of the alley. Like so many of the magical lights in Velles, it had degraded to a purplish hue that clashed with his bright red jacket. Cinna approached him with slow, deliberate steps, her hands lifted and open to appear as non-threatening as possible. She hoped her frayed tunic, patched trousers, and bare feet, along with her slight stature, would lull Barnaby into a false sense of security.

Voice cracking, Barnaby said, "Stay back. I don't want to hurt you."

"That explains the knife," Cinna said, her pace unaltered.

"Look, I'm merely into self-preservation, you understand." He reached into his jacket again, and Cinna readied herself for another knife. But this time, his hand went to his hip. He pulled out a small crossbow, bolt loaded and ready.

"Put that down before you hurt yourself," Cinna said. She kept her face neutral even as he brought the weapon up and pointed it at her chest. This was perfect.

Barnaby took the insult as intended, narrowing his eyes. "You don't want me to shoot you."

That was *precisely* what Cinna wanted, but she couldn't say that. He'd suspect she had some trick up her sleeve. "I have to risk it, because I can't let you escape. We get paid extra if we bring you into the City Watch. The boss wants to upgrade the office furniture."

"The boss?" Barnaby scowled. "You're with that woman at the casino, then. Who is she?"

His muscles tensed, and Cinna did the same, readying for the shot. Seconds passed in silence. Cinna refused to give him Hokuren's name out of principle. She took a step toward Barnaby to coax him into firing his crossbow. The sooner he did, the sooner this would be over. "Better shoot me, otherwise I'll send you to prison. With all you've stolen, they'll be itching to throw away the key. We know you're the Master Thief, but we know more than that." She waited for a beat. "Maxwell Barnaby."

"How did you figure it out?" His voice shook at the use of his name, but to his credit, the crossbow never wavered.

"I don't know. The boss handles all the investigations. I'm the assistant." Cinna stood about twenty feet from Barnaby, close enough that even someone as nervous as he could not miss.

She took one more step toward him and saw the change in his eyes. Now he was going to pull the trigger. Time seemed to slow into eons, but it was only a few moments before Barnaby's finger twitched and the bolt launched from the crossbow. It was on target and heading straight for her sternum.

Cinna's right hand whipped in front of her and caught the bolt out of the air, the tip a mere inch from her tunic.

She snapped the bolt in half over her thigh and tossed the pieces over her shoulder with as much nonchalance as she could muster. She relished the way Barnaby's mouth gaped as he took a step back, stunned. Before he could recover, she advanced on him, ready to finish the capture.

Hokuren expected her assistant to drag Maxwell Barnaby through the gilded double doors of the Promenade Casino any moment now. Her eyes darted to the front entrance every few seconds, her unease climbing with every new entrant, each another gambler dressed up with the trappings of wealth.

Any moment now.

Head of Security Planck Dovetree, a small man in an impeccable leather cuirass and matching greaves, cleared his throat. Having failed to assuage the initial casino guards, Hokuren now faced Dovetree and his demands for explanation. If Cinna returned with the thief, she could get the officious security man to let her exit without issue.

Hokuren adjusted the button on one of her coat pockets to give her nervous energy an outlet. "As a guest of the gala, I find this harassment unfair."

To meet the casino's strict dress code, Hokuren wore a fashionable tan coat, which contrasted well with her brown skin, her finest trousers and shiny new boots. Her black hair was pulled back in braids that ended in gold rings behind her shoulders. Not a single strand was out of place.

Despite her unassailable appearance, Dovetree remained steadfast in his insistence that Hokuren be brought up on charges with the Velles City Watch. "We revoked your privileges in this casino when you caused that scene at the gala."

"Scene?" said Hokuren, feigning ignorance. "I only asked Maxwell Barnaby, another of your guests, if he was the one who stole Lady Lucille's pocket watch. You know, the one stolen by the so-called Master Thief?" She flicked her coat button. "He made the scene."

Dovetree scoffed. "So you accosted the 'Master Thief' at the gala? If you could have done that anywhere else, we wouldn't be having this conversation. You encouraged him to run off, and in the process he crashed into multiple patrons. We may have to pay for their treatment if their injuries are serious." He turned away, addressing his security team. "Why is the Watch taking so long to get here?"

"There was a time when the Watch could be trusted to be prompt and effective," said Hokuren, her mouth quirking. "But under the current leadership, those days seem to have passed." Her disaffected amusement masked her swelling panic, for now. Her faith in her assistant held, but the eroding force of creeping doubt threatened from the fringes of her mind as there was still no sign of Cinna with Barnaby in tow.

"I didn't ask you," snapped Dovetree. "That's it, forget the Watch. I'm calling in the Dragon."

Hokuren doubted he meant an actual dragon, but she did not wish to tangle with anyone who earned that nickname. She went on the offensive. "Before you do that, help me understand why you were harboring the most prolific thief Velles has seen in quite some time at your gala. I would very much like to explain to the City Watch why I had to confront him here."

"We did not *harbor* him." Dovetree's rising voice attracted the mild curiosity of a few gamblers at the nearest blackjack table.. The security lead worked to keep his voice down as he hissed, "We had no idea he had stolen anything. No one did! Do you think we would allow a known thief on the premises?"

"Well, if you thought . . ." Hokuren trailed off when Cinna entered the casino, leading a man several inches taller than her. Relief flooded Hokuren. "Look, Maxwell Barnaby is back," she said as they approached.

The thief's hands were tied behind his back with the rope Cinna used as a belt. His red jacket looked wet and ruined, he had the beginnings of a black eye, and he worked his stubbled jaw over and over in obvious discomfort.

"Got him, boss," said Cinna, giving Barnaby a shove.

"I never doubted you for a moment." Hokuren looked up to make eye contact with Cinna's captive. "Mr. Barnaby. Remember me?"

Barnaby's only response was to snort. He had responded more positively to her during the gala when she grabbed his hand and led him onto the dance floor. She had kept her steps slow to stay in time with his tentative dancing. Barnaby had seemed to like the attention until she whispered that she knew he was the Master Thief.

Hokuren held Barnaby's gaze, waiting for him to say something. He gave in and said, "You have the wrong man."

She had to admit he was a good liar. She almost believed him. "I most assuredly do not." To Cinna, Hokuren asked, "Did Mr. Barnaby give you any trouble?"

Barnaby glowered at her. Hokuren answered with a placid smile.

"Well, he tried to shoot me with a crossbow," said Cinna, brushing a stray strand of her untamed hair from her face. "So, yeah. I had to explain some things to him."

Hokuren nodded, taking in the black eye and jaw discomfort. Cinna was well-versed in the art of conversation via fisticuffs. "He must have missed. You seem all right."

"He reacted how I hoped he would." The flecks of blue in Cinna's otherwise brown irises—the only giveaway to her elven heritage with her ears hidden by her headband—shone in the casino's magically produced light.

Nearby activities in the casino had stopped. A small crowd of gamblers had formed around them, gawking at Cinna and Barnaby.

Barnaby gathered as much dignity as he could and said, "I have suffered grave injustice at the hands of this woman, and I will see her punished to the full extent of the law."

Dovetree stepped in, face red. "I will see every one of you punished to the full extent of the law for this farce."

"You'd think a casino would be excited that we captured a thief," muttered Cinna, loud enough to be heard.

"Not when you bring him back inside!" Dovetree glared at Cinna. "And you make a mockery of our dress code. Wild, mange-ridden dogs are more welcome here! At least they would have excuses for looking so shambolic. I'll add trespassing to your list of offenses."

The disheveled Cinna, with her shaggy mop of chestnut hair that framed the light brown of her skin, headband, and well-worn, plain clothing, could not have appeared more out of place compared to the stylish patrons of the casino. Hokuren winced at the dirty bare foot prints her assistant was leaving on the plush cream-colored carpet, hoping she didn't receive a bill of cleaning somewhere down the line.

"This place is for fools," said Cinna, her head high. "We're leaving, anyway."

Before allowing Dovetree to retort, Hokuren said, "We are, in fact, leaving. Come along, Mr. Barnaby."

Cinna and Hokuren each took one of Barnaby's elbows and led him away, drawing stares from the assembled gamblers. Concerned that Dovetree would apprehend them for the Watch, Hokuren glanced back at the fuming head of security. But he seemed eager for them to vacate immediately. She held back a smile. With any luck, this little episode would be the talk of the tea houses the following day.

There was silence on the walk to the City Watch's main office. Hokuren held on to Barnaby tight, worried he might try to free himself. But he did not, casting worried glances at Cinna instead. Cinna, for her part, strode with a relaxed gait, as if leading a major criminal through town with his hands bound was a normal occurrence.

When the trio entered the main office, the clerk was resting his head on the desk. He craned his neck and opened bleary eyes, then jumped to attention when he saw them. Pale and lanky, with a freckled face and cropped red hair, he had been eighteen when he had joined the Watch shortly before Hokuren had left. Tarleton. She remembered him because she had been the same age when she joined the Watch ten years ago.

"Oh, Captain Hokuren, a pleasure," Tarleton said, bobbing his head respectfully.

"Seeker Hokuren, please," Hokuren said, giving her investigator title and smiling to show she was not offended. "I am no longer a captain of the Watch, in case you haven't been told."

He had. Everyone had been told. It had been a year since a spat between her and Lord Commander Doubtwell gave Hokuren the impetus to do what she had wanted to do for a long time: quit and open an independent investigation business.

"Uh, right. Um." Tarleton took in Cinna and Barnaby, seemingly unimpressed with both for very different reasons. "Can you, uh, explain the nature of your visit?"

"A wrongful capture!" shouted Barnaby, wrenching himself free of Hokuren's grasp. He could not shake Cinna's hold on his other arm, but he soldiered on. "I have been accosted, humiliated, and treated as a common criminal, and—"

"You are a criminal," Hokuren interrupted him. "Although there's nothing common about you. You left calling cards every place you stole from." Addressing Tarleton, she added dramatic flair to her voice and extended her hand as if showing off a grand prize. "This . . . is Maxwell Barnaby."

This drew no reaction from Tarleton beyond puzzlement. "Who?"

"You know him better as the one who stole Lady Lucille's pocket watch, among many other valuable items. He is the Master Thief."

"The Master Thief." Tarleton gasped. "How did you find him?" The awe in the boy's voice was not professional, but Hokuren liked it nonetheless.

"Dedication." Hokuren was unwilling to give away her methods to the criminal in her possession.

"Lord Doubtwell will be happy to see the Master Thief in prison," Tarleton said.

The Lord Commander of the City Watch, Edward Doubtwell, was Lady Lucille's husband. Doubtwell treated the theft of his wife's pocket watch not just as the loss of personal property but as an assault on both himself and the institution of the City Watch. Despite Doubtwell's enhanced interest, the Watch could not identify who the "Master Thief" from the calling cards. So although Hokuren's parting from the Watch had been less than amicable, Doubtwell found himself so low on options he had turned in desperation to her.

"He certainly should," said Hokuren. "I have placed Mr. Barnaby under citizen's arrest and brought him here so the wheels of justice might turn."

"We're getting a bonus for this. We need new furniture." Cinna piped up. "Our chairs are uncomfortable."

Hokuren shot a disapproving glance at Cinna. "What we plan to do with the bonus money is irrelevant. Officer Tarleton, are you the only one on duty?"

"I am," said Tarleton. His voice warbled and his eyes were wide with fear.

One of the many things Hokuren had clashed with Doubtwell over was his insistence on cutting the night staff to a single officer. He wanted as many people as possible during the day, when it was busier. To Hokuren, that was putting the night officer in a dangerous position. To staff the night shift with an inexperienced member of the Watch on top of that was unconscionable.

"What are you going to do with the prisoner?" Hokuren said sharply, trying to jar him from his unease.

"Let's put him in a cell, then? Would you, er, help me?"

Hokuren resisted the urge to sigh. Tarleton should not have invited her, no longer a member of the Watch, to assist with putting a criminal in his cell. However, Hokuren acquiesced. Barnaby was too important a criminal to leave in the hands of the quailing boy.

"Get some shackles," she ordered, and Tarleton bounded from the desk to retrieve some for her.

As Hokuren applied the shackles to Barnaby and returned Cinna's rope, Barnaby said, "I wish to file a protest."

"You can protest just fine in your cell." Hokuren pushed Barnaby toward the area behind the desk. "Lead the way, Officer Tarleton."

Hokuren nudged Barnaby in the direction of the cells. When Cinna followed as well, Tarleton said, now authoritative, "You can stay here, young lady. Watch personnel only." He looked at Hokuren and licked his lips. "And former Watch personnel."

"What?" There was a hint of frustration in Cinna's voice. "I'm the one who actually captured him. Sure, the boss figured out who he was, where he lived, other thefts he committed, and that he'd be at the casino tonight. But I ran him down."

Hokuren felt bad for Cinna, but she agreed there was no reason for her to join them in the cells. "It's late and you've done good work tonight, Cinna. Go home, get some rest, and come in late tomorrow."

Cinna's anger turned into a sulk at Hokuren's words. "I'll wait for you outside, boss. Please don't take too long."

Hokuren led Barnaby into the barren cellblock, the only light from Tarleton's torch and the streetlights that filtered through the tiny windows above each cell. The cells were only meant to hold a suspect for a day or two until they were either released or transferred to the secure jail outside of Velles's walls. Most of the cells were empty, save for the one being used to hold a couple of drunks. Their snoring broke up the otherwise dead quiet of the room.

As Tarleton urged Barnaby into a cell, the thief kept his voice low. Hokuren hovered near and caught his words. "Hey, kid, you should know you're making a grave mistake tonight. Let me go and lock up this one instead." Barnaby motioned with a shoulder toward Hokuren, who watched Tarleton's face to gauge his reaction. "This is your chance."

"You're the Master Thief," said Tarleton. "And I trust Captain—Seeker Hokuren."

"Make sure that's locked." Hokuren spoke fast, heading off any further conversation between the two men. She wanted Tarleton to listen to as little poison from Barnaby's lips as possible. Tarleton closed the jail door, yanking it twice to confirm the lock engaged.

"And you. Hokuren, was it? The seeker." Disgust dripped from Barnaby's voice as he emphasized her title. She turned away from him and began to leave. He raised his voice to yell at her retreating back. "When I get out of here, I promise revenge against both you and your friend." She did not deign to acknowledge him further.

Back at the front desk, Hokuren released a deep breath. The Master Thief was behind bars, and his words meant nothing. She shivered nonetheless.

Tarleton asked, "Are you concerned?"

"About Barnaby's threats? No," said Hokuren, trying to convince herself as much as Tarleton. "He has much more serious things to worry about right now than me."

"Uh, do you think having him here will be a problem?"

"I certainly hope not."

Tarleton's face went white. "He's a pretty big deal."

"While his crimes gave him notoriety, he's just like anyone else. His jail cell will hold him fine." Hokuren tried a reassuring smile. "Don't talk to him at all tonight or even check on him. He'll survive. Let him stew until the morning shift arrives. As long as he's in that jail cell, he's no problem."

Tarleton nodded his head up and down. "Thanks for your help, Seeker."

He didn't seem like a bad kid. Leaving him alone on night shift was a poor decision by management, but if he was mentored by someone more experienced, he might turn into a solid officer.

Hokuren was ready to take her leave. She had dedicated much of the last ten years of her life to the City Watch offices, leaving her with few happy memories to recall. "I'll take a receipt for Mr. Barnaby and be on my way."

"Uh, right," said Tarleton. He took out a pad and pencil and scribbled a note, before handing it to Hokuren:

I, Tarleton the Night Clerk, say that Seeker Hokuren provided the City Watch with the Master Thief. -Tarleton, Officer Third Class

It was satisfactory. Hokuren wished him well and stepped outside, where she breathed a long sigh of relief. The tension in her shoulders lessened. After all her planning, the night had been a success. This capture resulted from weeks of hard work pounding the streets and following even the faintest of leads until one finally led her to Barnaby.

Hokuren let herself imagine the incoming accolades, but even more importantly, future business. She could not think of a better way to show her value than by bringing in the Master Thief. This should net her enough new clients so she would stop losing money every month, which her dwindling savings account desperately needed.

Cinna leaned against the office's stone wall beside the door. "Boss," Cinna said. Hokuren had never requested Cinna to address her as "boss," but she did not object.

"Didn't I tell you to go home?" There was little chance of that happening. "You've worked too many hours already this week. Frankly, I can't afford to pay you fairly for the amount you've logged." This was a recurring conversation of theirs. Since her hire, Cinna was all but attached to Hokuren's hip. Only at night, once Cinna had walked Hokuren home, were they separated.

"No such thing as too many hours, boss." Cinna ran her hand through her unruly hair, trying to undo a small tangle under her headband. "It's dark and late. I won't let you walk home alone, not tonight. What if Barnaby has friends running around? If you need to, consider this off the clock."

Hokuren couldn't help but smile. There was no point in arguing with Cinna about this. "I give in. I might be the boss, but I can't tell you what to do."

"You said part of the job was protecting you, boss. Just doing what you asked."

"Did you not say you're off the clock?"

"Off the clock for getting paid. For protecting you, I'm never off the clock."

"Oh, fine." There was nothing for it but to accept Cinna's utter dedication. Hokuren had hired Cinna a little over six months ago to serve as her assistant and got a bodyguard in the process. Hokuren didn't mind the protection. She had been attacked because of getting too close to the truth more than once, and Cinna's constant presence and skill gave her peace of mind.

Despite how recently their partnership had started, neither seemed to remember how they lived without the other.

They traded stories of their individual encounters with Maxwell Barnaby on the walk to Hokuren's house. Hokuren described the dance floor and Barnaby's stilted moves, which earned a rare laugh from Cinna.

On her turn, Cinna told Hokuren how she had apprehended Barnaby. Cinna's retelling was so matter-of-fact that it had a believable quality to it, but Hokuren rubbed her ear, thinking she may have misheard. "You *caught* the crossbow bolt?"

"I learned to do it at the Sanctuary."

"The Sanctuary of the Eclipse?" Hokuren knew Cinna had spent ten years learning the combat arts there, but little else. "They taught you to catch bolts?"

Cinna shook her head. "I learned it on my own. The hardest part is finding someone willing to shoot at you so you can practice."

"Catching the bolts isn't the hardest part?"

Cinna only grinned in response.

They arrived at Hokuren's house, where Cinna would depart for the night to go wherever she slept. Not for the first time, Hokuren wondered what kind of place Cinna rented. She had never been invited over. "This was a long and eventful night. Your bed should look quite inviting," Hokuren said, focusing on Cinna's response.

Cinna kept her face straight, but her eyes danced away and back. "Uh, yeah, it will."

Hokuren didn't need her investigative skills to know Cinna was hiding something. Her assistant always turned evasive when asked about her living conditions. Perhaps she had gotten wrapped up in a bad lease situation. Following up on this was rising to the top of Hokuren's to-do list.

But not at that moment. Exhaustion set in the moment she closed her front door. Hokuren liked to have a small glass of wine to celebrate victories on the level of the capture of Maxwell Barnaby, her reward to herself for a job well done, but it was far too late for that. Within ten minutes of arriving home, she fell asleep, her last thoughts still of Cinna and crossbow bolts.

2

Hokuren's usual routine involved watching the sunrise from her office, in case a client showed up early. But she had spent the night wrangling with Barnaby, so the sun already shone brightly in the sky by the time she arrived. Resigned to a late start to the day, Hokuren told herself she deserved it after capturing the Master Thief.

With the Barnaby case completed, she now had no cases to work. Delivering Barnaby only provided value if it eventually turned into more clients through word of mouth. Until then, hers was just another struggling business in a city that cycled through them.

She entered her simple office, which held a desk and three chairs. Two shelving units behind the desk contained some of Hokuren's favorite knickknacks, books, and old case notes. Her favorite item was an actual functioning timepiece with tiny magical gears that had kept perfect time for over four decades, a gift from someone she had once helped while in the Watch. The furniture was old and uncomfortable, something Cinna harped on. It was not her perfect office, not yet. Maybe one day.

Cinna, already inside, whistled to herself as she swept the floor.

"Didn't I say you could come in late?" Hokuren greeted, clicking her tongue.

"Did you actually expect me to do that?" Cinna twirled the broom in her hands.

"Of course I didn't. What are you even sweeping? This floor is spotless." Cinna didn't answer, so Hokuren grabbed the broom from her and placed it in the corner. "Well, come on. We don't have any clients, so you may as well accompany me to get the bonus the Watch owes us. I can hand over your share right away."

"My share?" Cinna exaggerated the surprise in her voice.

Hokuren fixed her with a stare but couldn't keep the amusement from her eyes. "Stop pretending like you didn't know you were getting part of the bonus."

"You're too good to me, boss." Cinna pointed to the desktop, then picked up one of several scattered envelopes and handed it to Hokuren. "From today's mail. Another rent notice in angry red letters. You already paid this month's rent, though, right?"

Hokuren avoided Cinna's eyes as much as she did the demand for rent. "Must be some confusion at the landlord's. We'll clear it up soon." She cleared her throat. "If we go to the Watch now, we might even catch Barnaby being escorted out to the prison. That would be kind of fun, wouldn't it? If he's already gone, we can pop in, get Lord Doubtwell to pay us, and get out."

"Oh, him. The 'blustering, ineffective man,'" Cinna said, frowning. "He doesn't like me."

Hokuren had called Doubtwell that once to Cinna, in private. "Please don't make a habit of repeating that. I don't want it to get back to Lord Doubtwell. And I'm sorry he ignores you."

"It's fine," said Cinna. "I don't suppose me and him would have much to talk about, anyway."

"Let's go." Hokuren opened the door and yelped in surprise. She found herself in front of a tiny, elderly man with a large mustache and an expensive suit, his fist raised for a knock he had been robbed of making.

"Ah, excellent timing," the man said, his old-fashioned dialect trembling with age. "Am I speaking with Hokuren the Seeker?"

"Yes, I am she," said Hokuren, regaining her bearings. As surprises went, a client ranked among the very best. She gestured into the office, waving him in with the hand holding the rent notice. Her cheeks grew warm as she thrust that hand into a coat pocket, hoping he hadn't taken enough interest in the bright red writing to read any of the words before she'd stuffed it out of view. "Err, would you like to come in?"

"Oh, no. I don't believe that will be necessary. I am Wadsworth, at your service." He bowed, and the effort required to straighten back up left Hokuren concerned he would not complete the process. "Apologies if I skip further formalities, I have brought with me an urgent request. I am a servant of Prince Leopold, who asks that you see him at once regarding a commission he wishes to discuss."

Hokuren put her hand to her mouth to hold back another yelp. The very next day after bringing in the Master Thief, she earned a summons from the prince. She almost couldn't believe the good fortune. Mustering all the calm she could, she said, "We are available, if the prince requests us."

Wadsworth coughed into his sleeve before fumbling in his pocket and pulling out an envelope. His hand shook as he held it out to Hokuren. "Excellent. If you can come at once, I've transportation for you." He waved behind him, where a varnished wooden carriage stood hitched to two horses with pristine coats. "I'm afraid I have no information regarding the specifics. The prince himself will provide those. You can review the contents of the envelope on the way."

"Of course we can come at once," said Hokuren. "Give us a moment to lock up."

Once they had retreated into the office and closed the door, Cinna said, "Boss, did that old guy mean the actual prince?"

"The actual prince, Cinna," said Hokuren, taking deep breaths to steady herself. "I almost can't believe it. A successful commission from him could be what we need to really explode this business and no longer get mail like this." She tossed the crumpled rent notice onto the desk.

"The landlord will stop forgetting we already paid the rent if we get a commission from the prince?" Cinna shrugged. "But what about our Barnaby-wrangling bonus?"

"That can wait," said Hokuren, waving her hand. "The prince takes precedence. Now, I want you to come with me. This will be good experience, but you'll need to at least pretend to be respectful of the prince. We cannot risk offending him."

Cinna looked down at the floor. "I don't know how to act around important people like him."

"Don't worry. I'll explain on the way."

Hokuren locked the door outside and put on her best smile as she and Cinna met Wadsworth at the carriage. "What beautiful horses."

"Raised them myself," said a pleased Wadsworth, tugging his bowtie. "Back when I could do such things."

Cinna and Hokuren climbed into the carriage while Wadsworth took the reins in the front. The carriage had windows, one on each side, covered by curtains. Sunlight filtered through, keeping the inside well lit.

The carriage's wheels ran over the bumpy cobblestone of Velles's streets, softly jostling Hokuren. She closed her eyes to focus on the pleasant clopping of the horses' hooves on the stones.

"I've never had horses carry me around before," whispered Cinna, interrupting Hokuren's repose. "It's like being rich."

"Oh? What do you think?" asked Hokuren.

Cinna held her nose. "Well, horses stink."

"Ride with enough of them, and you get used to it." Hokuren smelled the foul mixture of horse dung and sweat more acutely now that Cinna put the thought into her mind. "Or so they say."

To distract from the horse aroma, Hokuren took some time to show Cinna how to act around the prince in accordance with ancient Vellesian custom. She stressed the importance of the bow, bending at the waist and not the back. Unless specified otherwise, everyone referred to him as "Your Eminence." If he invited you to sit with him, you had to sit up straight and, most importantly, you had to sit still.

This last bit would be the toughest part for Cinna, who was always moving or doing something. Even sitting in the casual environment of the carriage, Hokuren lost count of the number of times Cinna shifted her legs or tugged at loose strands of hair.

"Why does he need all these rules?" grumbled Cinna. "He's not better than us. He just got to be born to the previous prince."

"Stop grousing. Part of coming to meet the prince is following the rules. I've heard he's not intimidating as long as we act properly, and if we don't, we won't get the commission from him. And we need it." Hokuren came close to begging Cinna.

She need not go that far. Cinna said, "Yeah, all right. It's for the business. I'll obey."

With that settled, Hokuren opened the envelope Wadsworth had given her. The only content was a colored drawing of a young elven woman Hokuren did not recognize. She appeared to be in her early twenties, with long blonde hair and pale skin. Hokuren admired the skill of the artist; in the portrait, the woman smiled, but the smile did not reach her eyes. Those eyes were flecked with red, one of the most unusual colors for elves to have. She placed it back in the envelope after memorizing it.

When they arrived at the castle, Cinna pulled back the curtain and stuck her head out the window of the carriage to get a better view. "This is amazing," she gasped.

Hokuren agreed. The castle was enormous, far taller than any other building in Velles, with several spires that rose even higher. Although it was visible from most parts of the city, its enormity was staggering up close.

Reliefs covered the marble walls of the castle, each a scenic view of a waterfall, forest, or other natural beauty. A learned friend of Hokuren's once told her that modern master artisans would have required years to carve each relief. But magic had been more potent when the castle was built, and the artisans had created each relief in mere weeks.

The carriage passed over a lowered drawbridge and came to a stop in front of a set of double doors two stories tall and half as wide. Wadsworth invited Cinna and Hokuren to exit as he went to knock on the door. His feeble knock was equal to a fly landing on a window, but someone on the other side barked, "Who goes there?"

"Wadsworth." The old man's voice strained to be heard.

The doors opened, groaning as their massive weight shifted. Cinna and Hokuren followed Wadsworth into a vast entry where a red-and-yellow carpet ran to a grand staircase at the other end. High above their heads hung an enormous glass chandelier full of magical lights. Bright yellow and stronger than any of the streetlights in the city, they kept the windowless area fully illuminated.

They did not follow the carpet, heading instead to a small room off to the left that Wadsworth referred to as the reception, where the Palace Guard demanded Hokuren fill out paperwork.

Hokuren flipped through the papers. The most ominous section was "Next of Kin." With no better option, she would have to put Cinna's name here. "Prince Leopold invited me. Are you certain I need to do this?"

"The prince likes his visits documented," the guard said, his tone suggesting there was no room for negotiation. Hokuren dutifully filled out the fields.

When Hokuren finished and handed the signed documents back, she and Cinna both had red and yellow ribbons tied around their left wrists. The guards explained that these denoted them as special dignitaries of the prince. Cinna began fussing with hers the instant it was secured to her wrist, only stopping when Hokuren, afraid she would tear it, laid a gentle hand on her shoulder.

Wadsworth left them with a bow and two of the guards escorted them through the grand entry to another room, this one containing an elevator.

"I've never been on one of these," said Hokuren, marveling at the visible pulleys and ropes of the contraption.

"Mules power this elevator by turning a giant gear in the basement," explained a guard. Although she was taller than either Hokuren or Cinna, her helmet was too big for her head, making her appear childlike. "All you have to do is tell them which way you want to go." She pushed a button with a "5" next to it. "That will tell them we want floor five, the top floor."

"This is incredible," said Cinna, and Hokuren thought the awe in her voice was because of the elevator. "The mules can read numbers?"

Hokuren almost laughed, catching herself when she realized Cinna wasn't joking.

The guard cleared her throat. "Uh, an operator directs the mules."

Cinna scuffed her feet and flushed red. "I, um, knew that."

Red-and-yellow carpeting covered the fifth floor, which was filled with so many expensive-looking pieces of pottery that they blurred together in Hokuren's mind as a single, indistinct piece. They walked for a few minutes before being admitted to a small chamber in the back.

"Wait here to be called," the guard with the too-big helmet said. "Refreshments are available." The guards left, closing the door with the distinct click of a lock being engaged.

"You know, I'd almost believe we were being imprisoned here," said Hokuren, shuddering. "Dignitaries or not."

Cinna was already at the refreshments platter placed on the only table in the room. Ignoring the assortment of juices, she dug into the stack of freshly baked cookies. She stuffed her first cookie in her mouth and took a bite. "Could be worse, we get time to eat," Cinna said, spitting crumbs.

Hokuren frowned and wiped sodden bits of cookie off her coat. "Who taught you to eat and talk like that?"

Cinna swallowed. "Pretty much no one taught me anything. Sorry, boss."

"As long as it's not in front of the prince." Hokuren eyed the cookies but refrained from grabbing one. "Okay, let's review. Bow, sit properly, and let me do the talking." She made Cinna demonstrate she could pull off the bow.

As Cinna worked on her second cookie, Hokuren's stomach flipped. Getting the prince's commission rested entirely on her. She envied Cinna, who acted unconcerned, like a tourist on a day trip to the castle. Either she had confidence in Hokuren or she knew nothing of the weight of the looming meeting. This was Hokuren's best chance to keep her business going.

"Look at these paintings," said Cinna, in between bites.

Several paintings mounted on the walls depicted adventurers battling giant monsters that Hokuren believed no one, not even the oldest elf, had living memory of. In one, a wizard shot lightning at a bird the size of a small house, which appeared only to enrage it. A plate under the painting gave it the title "Frying the Roc." Why anyone would want to fight enormous birds that became furious rather than dead when you blasted them with lightning was a mystery.

In another, a taller and more robust version of Prince Leopold stood triumphantly clad in a suit of armor and held up the severed head of a defeated dragon. This was called "Victory." A third showed a pair of wizards blasting fire and ice together at ... something. The incomprehensible morass of tentacles, slime, and oddly shaped pieces of flesh gave Hokuren a headache trying to decipher it. The plate read "Grymxx," a word she had never seen.

"What battles these must have been." Cinna's voice was filled with wonder.

Hokuren grunted. "These are fake, though. In real life, every one of these encounters would have been life or death."

"Imagine getting to fight these things. I would truly get to test my skills." Cinna pointed at the Grymxx. "How do you even start thinking about where to punch that thing? What a challenge."

"I would advise against trying to punch it at all."

Cinna worked her way through cookie number four, examining a painting of adventurers hacking at dire wolves with flaming broadswords, when the door unlocked and an attendant stepped into the room. Wearing a bright yellow robe and matching slippers, the attendant said, "Please, Seeker Hokuren, Guest Cinna. Come with me."

It was a quick trip to the large chamber where Prince Leopold awaited them. He wore royal red-and-yellow silk and sat in a deep brown wingback chair arranged in front of a large fireplace. Leopold was supposed to be in his mid-forties, but he looked younger. A life of comfort and plenty will do that. His hair was perfectly styled, and he adorned himself with rings and bracelets of gold and silver.

No amount of opulence and splendor, however, could hide his cherubic features. Lord Doubtwell once told Hokuren that he found the prince impossible to take seriously as a leader because of his "round, soft, dimply chin." Doubtwell's words were often repeated around Velles, though Hokuren loathed the idea that one could "look like a leader."

His chin *was* quite round, though.

Leopold's voice, light and quiet, had a practiced air. "Greetings, Seeker Hokuren. Please, introduce me to your guest and have a seat."

Bowing from her waist, Hokuren said, "A pleasure to be in your service, Your Eminence. This is my assistant, Cinna." She nudged Cinna to get her to bow. The result was a little too deep, but decent.

"Hello, Your Eminence," said Cinna. The practice had been worth it.

The prince inclined his head, and they both perched on the couch opposite Leopold. The couch was tall and Cinna's toes just reached the carpet. To Hokuren's relief, Cinna remained still.

"I appreciate you coming to see me so quickly," Leopold said. As if there existed a realistic option where Hokuren would have turned him down or put him off until later.

"Of course, Your Eminence."

The prince waved a hand. "Please, Hokuren, none of that here. It's just us. Please call me Leopold."

Hokuren's mind raced and her heart beat faster. She had never spoken to the prince, and yet he immediately asked to be on a first-name basis. Something big was happening, and she was about to be pulled into it.

"Of course, Leopold," she said, testing the name. It felt strange on her tongue. "Can we move on to the discussion of your request?" Leopold's head tipped in acceptance, so she went on. "I was not told anything, only given this drawing of a woman." Hokuren held up the envelope she received from Wadsworth.

"You don't know her? Hmm, I probably should allow her to socialize with the people more often," Leopold mused. "That's my daughter, Nyana."

She should have guessed. Hokuren had indeed never seen the Princess Nyana before, but of course knew of the prince's adopted heir, next in line for the prince's estate and rule over Velles. It had been a shock for the prince to adopt an elven child, as no elf had ever ruled Velles in all its long history. And she was his only child.

"And you gave me a picture of your daughter because . . ." Hokuren already felt sure she knew why she had been brought before the prince, but it was bad business to guess what a client wanted.

"Nyana's missing," said Leopold.

Hokuren nodded. The prince did not appear terribly upset. She searched his face and could not find any physical signs of distress, either. No dark circles under his eyes or drawn lines on his face.

"Understood." She pulled out a small pad and pen. It was useless to Hokuren, as she would be able to recall this entire conversation at will later. But appearances were important. People believed she cared to retain what they told her if they thought she took notes. "Please start with the background."

Leopold launched into his tale as Hokuren made marks on the paper to imitate note-taking. "It all started a few days ago. Nyana came to me, claiming to be unable to find her cat, Smoky. He's a gray cat, with white on his stomach and paws. A charming creature. Useless as a mouser, but . . ." Leopold put his hands up as if in mock surrender. "That morning, he did not show up for his customary meal. Nyana was upset, as you can imagine. She and Smoky have practically been inseparable since we obtained him six years ago. Of course, I forbid her to leave the castle grounds in search of the animal. She's become too adept at shaking her guard escort."

Hokuren suppressed a sigh. He sounded like a classic case of an overprotective parent of an adult child. "You think she snuck out to find her cat?"

"I do. Or rather, I did. That was three days ago. No one has heard from her since. I find it hard to believe that she would be so engrossed in her search for the cat that she wouldn't have returned by now, or at least sent word." The prince waved his hand. "Not to mention that we found the cat yesterday. I am quite worried that something has happened to her."

"So you're hiring me to find Nyana?"

The prince nodded. "Yes."

This was going to be the biggest job Hokuren had ever taken. She took a long, steadying breath. "I'll take the commission. I have one question, though. Why me? Have you gone to the Watch?" She hated to give him a reason to reconsider hiring her, but she expected the Prince of Velles to request help from his own City Watch.

Leopold scoffed. "No one in the City Watch could find their own buttocks if you gave them a book on human anatomy." Next to Hokuren, Cinna snickered. "See how long they've been searching for this Master Thief of theirs."

The news of his capture must not have reached the prince yet. Hokuren knew better than to claim it while still officially unverified. He would find out soon enough.

The prince leaned over in his chair, fixing his gaze upon Hokuren. "I hear you are good at finding people. Not too long ago, I had lunch with a small group that included Lady Appleby. She said you found her grandson when he went missing. Do you recall that?"

Hokuren bit her tongue. Lady Appleby, a kindly woman whose only child never married, called her cat her grandson. But if the prince thought he was a person and that impressed him, she would not correct him.

"Of course," Hokuren said smoothly. "You remember, right, Cinna?" She shot her assistant a meaningful glance that she hoped Cinna would interpret correctly.

Cinna, thus far showing little interest in the prince, said, "Her grandson? He's a—oof." Hokuren's elbow to her ribs cut Cinna off. When glances failed, sometimes an elbow could do the trick. With a look of reproach, Cinna continued, "Er, I was going to say that he's a terror. I had to climb a tree to get him, and then he bit me three times." Cinna rubbed a spot on her arm the cat had sunk its teeth into.

"He's very spunky," said Hokuren, chuckling nervously.

The prince raised his eyebrows, but shrugged. "I had never heard of you before my talk with Lady Appleby, but you come recommended. And while I believe my daughter is too well-behaved to bite, she's proved quite good at hiding. My guards have failed to find her. In fairness, they are ill-equipped for this sort of thing. I came to you because I suspect that if you can't find her, no one can."

"I promise you that Cinna and I will do everything in our power to find your daughter. We will, of course, need to discuss my fee."

Leopold waved his hand airily. "I'm prepared to offer you five times your normal fee now, plus that again when she is found. Additionally, we will cover all of your expenses on the condition that you refrain from accepting any other commissions until you find my daughter."

The offer was so generous that Hokuren was shocked into silence. After a moment, she stammered, "That—that will be acceptable, yes."

"Excellent." Leopold motioned to his attendant, who had been standing off to the side during their entire exchange. The attendant dropped a heavy bag of coins into Hokuren's hands. "This is your initial fee, plus several days' worth of expenses. I trust that will suffice for a start."

"For a start, right." The money weighed on Hokuren's mind as much as her lap. It was an indication the prince expected results. "Now that we're officially on the job, we wish to begin immediately. May we have permission to interview anyone in the castle?"

"Yes." The prince turned to the attendant. "See that Seeker Hokuren has access to whomever she requires."

Addressing the attendant, Hokuren said, "I'd like to start with anyone who serves her in any fashion here in the castle."

The attendant's head bobbed. "I can arrange that. She has five guards who spend the most time watching over her. There's also Anne, her lady-in-waiting."

Hokuren nodded and looked back over at Leopold. "Before I go, is there anyone you think I should suspect? Often in a missing person case, it's someone the victim knows well who is responsible. Who should I pay particular attention to?"

"My Captain of the Guard, Julien Davenport," said Leopold without hesitation. "But you can't interview him."

"Why not?"

"No one has seen him since Nyana disappeared." His lips curled into a sneer. "He's always been difficult to manage, but I thought he liked Nyana. They've spent so much time together of late. However, if it turns out he had anything to do with this, I won't hesitate to dole out appropriate punishment."

Hokuren could guess what that meant. "Of course." She stood up. "We will take our leave unless there's anything else we should know."

"Find my daughter," Leopold said, a note of desperation in his voice that didn't quite ring true to Hokuren's ears. "Please."

3

Hokuren sat on a patio across from Cinna, shaded from the hot afternoon sun, in the middle of a respite following their interviews with members of the palace guard. The plates in front of them contained remnants of the meals provided by the castle chef. Roasted duck, spiced to perfection, with seasoned potatoes and fresh green beans. A small banana parfait ended the meal on a sweet note.

"This view . . ." Cinna rose to lean on the balustrade at the edge of the patio. "I've never seen the city like this. I can't believe the people here can have this view whenever they want." Velles spread out far below them, its buildings and streets bathed in sunshine all the way out to the sea. "When I lived in Velles before, my view was mainly gutters."

Hokuren barely registered the wonder in Cinna's voice, consumed with replaying the interviews in her mind.

She interrupted Cinna's gawking at the spectacle. "Let's see what you picked up from the guards. What stands out to you?" Hokuren wanted to involve Cinna more in their investigations. Her assistant was raw, but willing to learn, and talking over the case helped Hokuren chew through her thoughts while giving Cinna a chance to learn by doing.

Cinna furrowed her brow. "I don't understand a lot of what they said about Captain Davenport. They say he wears a suit of golden armor from head to toe that he never takes off, and that he has a special gauntlet on his left hand where the fingers end in claws." She frowned. "Isn't that impractical?"

"It seems so to me." Hokuren leaned back in her stiff, teak-wood chair and hooked a boot around the table to avoid falling backward.

Cinna gestured at the plates on the table. "They've never seen him eat or drink. He doesn't have any obvious hobbies or interests, and they were all afraid of him. What did they say about the way he talks?"

"His voice is always next to you." Every guard had used the same language to describe it.

"What does that mean?"

Hokuren had her finger on her chin. "I'm not sure. They said it was like he was right in their ear, whether he was right beside you or if he was several paces away. The guards also believed he could see everything you did, even if you could swear on your mother's heart that his back was turned. A person in Davenport's position would want to command fear and respect, but he seems to have only the fear. They're absolutely terrified of him."

"Should we even consider what they had to say?" Cinna tapped her fingers on the balustrade behind her. "What if they were lying?"

"They all told the same story. To me, this seems more like Davenport has crafted his own mythology and coached the guards into repeating it. Not dissimilar to the paintings we saw prior to meeting with Prince Leopold."

"I guess it's easier to make things up about yourself than bother to achieve anything," said Cinna. "I bet half of this stuff isn't even true."

Hokuren nodded. "A decent bet." Curious to separate truth from fiction, she hoped to meet Davenport soon. Changing the subject, she said, "How about Nyana?"

"Nyana's boring," said Cinna. She dropped into a chair across from Hokuren. "She almost never leaves the castle and when she does, it's to go to bookshops and clothing stands. The guards said she gave them the slip sometimes, but they didn't know where she went. And then she'd come back on her own."

Hokuren nodded. "Boring is harsh, but she had a sheltered life. Clearly, she needed to hide something from her watchers. When she struck out on her own, she could have been meeting up with someone."

"Ooh!" exclaimed Cinna. She pressed her palms onto the table and jumped up from her chair. "I bet she's got a secret lover that her father would never approve of. Maybe it's some bard who doesn't have any money! Fathers of princesses always hate that."

"Please, Cinna, that happens in the stories you've been reading much more often than in real life. She also spent a lot of time with Captain Davenport. This confirms what the prince himself said. Davenport never went to town with her, though. I suppose his golden armor would be rather conspicuous." Hokuren tapped her chin. "No one seems to know what Nyana and Davenport did during all their time together."

"It's suspicious," said Cinna, using her fork to play with the crumbs on her plate. "Hey, you don't think—" She suddenly looked embarrassed. "That secret lover..."

"I don't think we can rule out the possibility of some sort of relationship between Nyana and Davenport," Hokuren said dryly. "Although, how would it work if he never takes his armor off?"

Cinna didn't look Hokuren in the face. "Don't think I could say, boss."

"Perhaps Anne will have some insights. Cinna, right now, do you think Nyana was abducted, or that she left of her own accord?"

"Um," Cinna stammered. "Of her own accord?"

"You don't sound confident."

"I really don't know."

Hokuren put her finger up. "If you aren't sure, don't just pick an answer. It's okay to not know. Sometimes, like now, you don't have enough information to go on yet."

"Right." Cinna's head dropped.

"But you did well. You remembered the main points of interest from our discussions with the guards. That's the first step."

"Thanks, boss," said Cinna, head popping back up. Of course, the next step, putting that information to good use, would be much harder, and Cinna was still far from that. But she was doing well despite her lack of experience—and brimming with enthusiasm.

"Having said all that, I plan to engage with Anne as if Nyana decided to leave without coercion." Hokuren met Cinna's questioning glance. "My instinct tells me that Nyana did leave of her own will. If Anne knows anything, she'll be more likely to tell me if she thinks I already know. If she doesn't, or she knows Nyana was forced to leave, she'll try to correct me."

"Ooh," said Cinna. "Devious, boss."

A few moments later, their assigned attendant collected them from the porch and brought them to meet Anne, Nyana's lady-in-waiting. Anne dipped into a curtsy, fingers pinched on her conservative, ruffled dress, when Hokuren entered the ad hoc interview space set up for them by clearing a supply room. It had a table and some chairs, which was all Hokuren needed. She considered the boxes stacked against the far wall to be ambiance.

"Your Grace," Anne said as she came out of the curtsy.

"None of that," said Hokuren, face flushing at being treated like nobility. "I'm no grace and I don't need to be genuflected to. I'm Hokuren, and this is Cinna."

Anne glanced at Cinna, pursing her lips with contempt. "You're supposed to wear shoes in the castle."

"Goodness me," said Cinna, looking down at her bare feet. "Am I not wearing shoes? Boss, you never said anything!"

"Cinna." Hokuren cleared her throat. "Anne, if the prince had a problem with Cinna, I suspect he would have aired it. Now, I'll get right to it. Why did Nyana run away, and how did she get out without being noticed?"

Anne's eyes widened, and Hokuren knew she had gotten it right. Now to draw it out. "I don't know. Her cat . . ." Anne's voice grew too quiet to hear.

"This wasn't about the cat, was it?" Hokuren spoke quickly and decisively to shake the truth out of Anne. "She left for another reason, didn't she?"

"I—I can't . . ."

"You can. I already know she ran away. I need you to confirm it for me."

Anne took a deep breath and looked around the small room. She leaned in toward Hokuren and whispered, "Is there anyone listening? At the door?"

"Cinna, check the door. Clear out anyone within earshot, and make sure no one approaches," Hokuren said. Cinna obeyed, posting herself outside the door. She poked her head in and gave Hokuren an okay signal.

"If His Eminence figures out I said this, he'll have my head, so please don't tell anyone you know this." Anne bit her lip. "It's terrible."

Hokuren softened her tone, now that Anne appeared ready to give her the truth. She hoped that one day, she could train Cinna enough to take on the kind-interviewer role so Hokuren could focus on being the tough questioner. For now, she had to play both. "I won't say a word. Whatever you say, no one will ever know it came from you. I promise. Please tell me. It could help, especially if Nyana is in trouble."

Anne's eyes watered. "His Eminence has been angry with Nyana because he believes she's supposed to be a vessel of some goddess. That was the reason he adopted her to begin with. But apparently she's not."

Hokuren stared at Anne, baffled by this piece of information. "What would being a 'vessel' entail?"

"I don't know!" Anne began to cry. "Nyana was so angry with me when I asked that I never asked again. But whatever it is, I've heard him yelling at Nyana."

"Okay," said Hokuren, handing her a handkerchief. Anne blew her nose into it. "Thank you for telling me." She waited for Anne to compose herself before continuing. "Now, as for how she left. No one saw her leave. Did you? Is this another thing you're keeping secret?"

"No," sobbed Anne. "I don't know how she left, but I knew she was going to. She told me to take Smoky and keep him hidden in my room."

Hokuren crossed her arms over her chest. "So you were her accomplice."

"I thought she was just going to leave for the day. I didn't know she didn't plan on coming back." Anne twisted her dress in her hands. "She only told me to hide Smoky so she would have an excuse to leave the castle. I didn't have any further instructions from her. When she didn't come back, I let the cat out so they could 'find' him."

That made sense. And Anne would feel as if she had to go along with the princess's wishes. "As for how Nyana left the castle, do you have any insight into that?"

"She went into her room, and the guards were outside her door. I didn't know when she was going to leave, so I brought her lunch as I always do and the room was empty." Tears glistened in Anne's eyes. Hokuren hoped she would hold them back. "The guards don't believe me, but I think magic was involved."

Hokuren clicked her tongue in irritation. "Magic? Like what, teleportation? No such magic exists anymore, if it ever did. Are there any other, let's say, more realistic theories?"

"I didn't see her leave. No one did. But it's impossible to leave the castle without being seen, especially for the princess."

Yet Nyana did leave the castle unseen. Hokuren knew how she wanted to pursue that thread, but she wouldn't get the answer from Anne. "Okay. One last subject. What do you know about her relationship with Julien Davenport, the Captain of the Palace Guard?"

Anne shivered. "She spent far too much time with that monster."

"Monster," repeated Hokuren, intrigued. "Why do you call him that?"

Anne's voice grew in intensity and she talked rapidly, eager to get the words off her chest. "I know it sounds rude, but everything about him frightens me. He not only looks like he could kill you in an instant, he acts as if it would mean nothing to him to end your life. And you should see his room. Nyana, the guards, and even His Eminence act like there's nothing strange about him. Nyana chastised me when I suggested there was something wrong about him. She told me not to talk about him, for my own good."

Hokuren furrowed her brow. "Was that a threat?"

"It was strongly stated."

The key to figuring out where Nyana went lay with figuring out *why* she left. All Hokuren might find out here in the castle was the *how*. Though she needed to inspect Nyana's room, she couldn't help feeding her curiosity about what might lie in Davenport's room first.

Guards escorted Hokuren and Cinna to Davenport's quarters on the fourth floor of the castle, which had far less decoration than the fifth. There were no carpets or vases or paintings, only gray stone underfoot and shields and swords covering the walls. Busts of captains past squatted upon pedestals lining the floor's main hall, every one of them posed with a glower.

Hokuren stopped in front of one of the glowering former captains. "Does Davenport have one of these?"

"No," said the guard. "You don't get a bust until you're dead."

"Pity."

Davenport's quarters were behind double doors at the end of a long hall. With the way Anne spoke of his room, Hokuren expected something far different from what she encountered.

A dark, windowless room with a cold stone floor greeted them. Hokuren wished for her lantern, settling for the much smaller light that fit in her coat pocket. Against the far wall sat a bed with a gray blanket and a white pillow, both as clean and stiff as if just starched. A pair of sconces, currently darkened, flanked the bed. On the right side of the room was a wardrobe, a desk on the left. The stained wood of the wardrobe, desk, and accompanying chair remained in pristine condition.

"Boss, check this out," said Cinna, the wardrobe open in front of her. Hokuren joined her and found several pieces of clothing, from formal dresswear to casual attire, but none showed any sign of wear. An entire wardrobe full of brand-new items. Did he truly never take off his armor? Hokuren fingered the fabric of a nightgown made of luxurious satin.

Even to bed?

"Cinna. Thoughts?" asked Hokuren, turning to her assistant.

"This is definitely not normal." Cinna held a silken jacket in her hand. "There are a bunch of shirts and pants in here. But where's the underwear?"

Hokuren paused. "Hmm, that's an excellent question." Hokuren had more on her mind than simple undergarments. Anyone wearing platemail would also wear a full set of padded clothing to protect their skin from the metal. She saw no sign of anything like that.

"Although I don't know anything about wearing armor, you can't go around in it as naked as if you've just been plucked by the midwife, can you?" Cinna screwed up her face. "He's got a dangly bit, right? I mean, I don't have one of what he's got, but I imagine that would hurt."

"Yes, I imagine it would." Unless Davenport owned only one such set of underpadding, which he wore on his way out of the castle. Surely he would have at least one spare, for when the first set needed cleaning?

Further investigation of the room uncovered nothing. There were no notes, personal items, or anything at all. Hokuren closed the last empty drawer of the desk. "There's no sign that he lived here. If you told me the castle kept this room as a memorial to someone who died, that would make more sense." She looked at the guards, who had followed the two of them into the room and appeared dumbstruck as well. "Does Captain Davenport have other quarters? Ones he lives in?"

"No," said one of them. "This is it."

"Does he actually even exist, or is he a figment of some sort of illusion shared between everyone in the castle?" Hokuren had to admit to herself that this question had been born mostly from frustration over how none of this made any sense.

The guards exchanged glances before the same guard stammered, "Umm, the first one, I'm pretty sure."

"I'm not sure that was a fair question, boss," said Cinna.

"A reasonable point, Cinna." Hokuren gestured to the guards. "Show me Nyana's room."

Anne waited for them there, lingering at the doorway along with the two palace guards while Hokuren investigated with Cinna.

Nyana had made a concerted effort toward turning her own stone-walled, windowless room into a cozy space. Artwork featuring fluffy animals and pristine forests hung upon the walls, warm and peaceful, nothing like the action-oriented pieces Cinna had been so impressed by earlier. An enormous bed with soft blankets and the largest pillows Hokuren had seen sat on the far end. Two large bookshelves flanked a vanity on the right side. On the left was a desk, painted red, yellow, and orange, like a sunset.

Hokuren poked through the desk, her heart rate increasing when she found a small book wrapped in leather. Hoping it was a diary, she opened it up to find the pages blank. Perhaps it had been a gift, but Nyana had little interest in jotting her thoughts down.

Disappointed, Hokuren flipped through it to do her due diligence, and a small slip of paper tucked into the back caught her eye. The words "Mud Guard" were written in block letters next to a drawing of a shoe. Hokuren could not make sense of it. She showed it to Anne.

"This mean anything to you?"

Anne shook her head. "Mud Guard? I've never heard of it."

The desk had nothing more. Hokuren's eyes swept the room again. "Cinna, Nyana left this room and she didn't teleport. How would she have done that?"

"Hmm." Cinna glanced around the room. "A loose piece of flooring, perhaps?"

The two of them crawled on the stone floor, checking under the various rugs and running their fingers over the mortar between the stones for any sort of broken seam. They found no issues with the masonry. "Maybe it's something else," Cinna said.

"Yes, seems so. Good idea, though." Hokuren stood up and wiped dust from the knees of her pants. She re-examined the bookshelves. They were identical and aligned with the vanity between them. That had to mean something. "It seems too obvious, but we should rule out the old trick where a book on the shelf is actually a lever that reveals a secret passage."

"That would be obvious?" Cinna scratched her head.

The bookshelves were seven feet tall and stuffed full of literature, leaving no gaps. When Cinna reached from her tiptoes, she could not so much as brush a finger on the highest shelf. Hokuren, who was a few inches taller, could not reach a book there, either.

"Could Nyana reach the books on the top shelf?" Hokuren asked Anne.

"No," Anne said, shaking her head. "She's not much taller than you."

"We can at least rule out that shelf." Hokuren started pulling books at random, but that was a foolish way to go about it. There were hundreds between the two bookcases. It could take them the rest of the dwindling daylight to check each one like that. She eyed the book titles. "Look for something that doesn't fit in," she instructed Cinna.

Cinna stared at the books, overwhelmed. "What would that be?"

"It's hard to say. Any book different from the rest. For example, if the books look well-read, but there's one that seems new and hasn't been opened. Something like that."

Most of the books appeared to be romance novels, some with ribald titles such as *The Promiscuous Rogue Erects a Trap*. When Hokuren scanned the shelves, however, nothing stood out. She glimpsed Cinna check a book's cover, blanch, and shove it back in.

"Anything you haven't seen before, Cinna?" Hokuren teased.

"A lot," said Cinna, as always honest to a fault. Her face was reddening.

"I, uh, don't know all these words. What does 'voluptuous' mean?" Hokuren was about to tell her, but as Cinna tugged at the book, there was an audible click. "It's stuck." She pulled with more force, twisting it, trying to yank it free.

Hokuren rushed over. "Wait. You found something." Examining the book, she read the title. *The Secret of the Voluptuous Paladin*. What was it about this one in particular? There must be a pattern. "I have a thought. It's a silly one, but look at this title. Yes, the paladin has a very large bust. But the word I'm focused on is 'secret.'" Despite the clicking sound, nothing seemed to be different about the vanity or bookshelves. "Maybe there's more than one book."

Hokuren and Cinna scanned the rest of the books but didn't find another with the word "secret" in the title.

"Maybe there's a different word, boss," said Cinna as they stood in thought.

"What goes with 'secret'?" Hokuren tried to think of appropriate words.

"Lair?"

That didn't seem right. Hokuren snapped her fingers. "Of course! I already said it. If there's a way out of this room, we'd call it a secret passage, right? Let's find a book with 'passage' in the title."

Not long after, Hokuren found a book with the odd title of *The Throbbing Passage of Time*. She pulled on it. There was another click, but this time, the clicks continued. The vanity lowered into an opening in the floor, revealing a spiral staircase.

"Gotcha," said Hokuren, feeling a little thrill. She tamped down her excitement. Though they had found Nyana's likely escape route, there was more work to be done.

"Oh dear," said Anne, coming into the room and staring into the dark staircase. "Nyana kept this from me." Her surprise and discomfit appeared to be genuine.

"Are we going down?" Cinna asked.

"Absolutely," said Hokuren.

Hokuren summoned the guards outside of the room and informed them of the secret passage. They grimaced, no doubt thinking that one of them would have to explain to Leopold how apparently no one knew about it.

The two guards accompanied Cinna and Hokuren down the stairs while Anne remained in the bedroom. The narrow staircase descended all the way below ground level. By the time they reached the end, Hokuren's head spun with dizziness. The staircase let off into a long hallway, damp and musty. A hatch on the ceiling at the far end required Hokuren's full effort to fling open. When she poked her head out, she was in the middle of a field right outside the castle walls.

"I think it's clear how she got out of the castle," said Hokuren, climbing from the hatch, careful to avoid staining her clothes from the layer of sod and grass covering it. Once back in place, the hatch blended so well with the rest of the field that it was impossible to see unless you knew exactly where to look.

"We can get you back in the castle if you need," a guard said.

"Not necessary, thank you." Hokuren gazed at the setting sun. "We'll check out the area around this hatch and then finish for the day."

The guards left them to their search. Hokuren spotted a muddy patch nearby with wheel tracks and hoofprints. The wagon's tracks went right to the hatch, then turned around and headed for the gate back into Velles.

"Nyana had a wagon?" Cinna stood next to Hokuren, looking out at the muddy field.

"Someone, or someones, met her here." Hokuren bent down, squinting at the tracks. If she got closer, she worried she would go too deep in the mud. Her boots were new and she had her nicest pair of breeches on. She did not wish to ruin them if she could avoid it. "That hatch was heavy. She may have even needed help to open it."

"Does that mean . . ." Cinna closed one eye in thought. "Davenport?"

"A good guess." Hokuren put her hand on Cinna's shoulder. "I want one of us to inspect the tracks, but I don't want to get my boots muddy. You don't have that problem."

"Say no more, boss," said Cinna. She rolled her pant legs up past her knees and began squelching into mud that came up to the midpoint of her shins. Careful not to walk through the wheel tracks, she stared at them, a frown of concentration on her face.

After following one of the tracks for a couple of minutes, Cinna glanced back at Hokuren. "These look like wheel tracks."

"Great work."

A note of frustration in her voice, Cinna said, "I don't know what I'm looking for."

"Some sort of irregularity," said Hokuren. "Even if it's tiny. Is the wheel straight or is there a slight wobble where the track would wind slightly back and forth? Is there any difference between the tracks?"

Cinna bent down farther, placing her hands in the mud to steady herself as she held her head inches above the ground. Strands of her hair fell around her face and brushed against the mud. She squinted into it, walking on all fours to follow the track. Hokuren would never have put herself in a position to look so ridiculous, but she knew Cinna didn't care. Perhaps it was an advantage Cinna had over her.

With mild excitement, Cinna said, "I think I see something."

"What is it?"

"There's this strange dip in the track that repeats every so often." Cinna pointed with a muddy finger. "Here, here, and here."

Another thrill. "A slight bump on the wheel might cause that. Let's see, that would be the right-side rear wheel. Great find, Cinna."

"How will we find the wagon, though? We can't check the right rear wheel of every wagon, can we?" Hokuren smiled as Cinna's face fell further with each passing second. "Oh. We can do that."

"We can try," said Hokuren. "But first we're going to go home and sleep." As Cinna worked her way out of the mud, Hokuren saw the mess her assistant had become. "Actually, before that, we're going to wash that mud off you. Good thing it's time for our weekly bath."

4

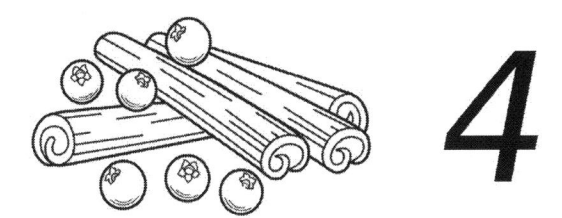

Cinna bobbed in the water at the bathhouse absentmindedly. She was always the first one in the bath, because Hokuren was more deliberate about undressing and hanging her clothes up in the lockers. Hokuren never used the facilities open for all, so they had a private basin to themselves.

The bath's privacy gate opened, revealing Hokuren. As always, she covered herself until she had lowered into the basin, which amused Cinna. They had the same bits, none of them worth being ashamed about.

They shared a bath because Hokuren said it was less expensive this way, and because Hokuren did not trust Cinna to wash herself properly. If she missed a spot or two, she figured she would get it next time, a philosophy incompatible with Hokuren's sensibilities.

But Cinna didn't mind. It was part of their compromise: Hokuren tolerated Cinna not wearing shoes on the job as long as she agreed to the weekly bath. The bath attendants kept the fires under the basins at a steady, pleasant temperature, and getting her back scrubbed felt good, too. This time, Cinna had mud caked on her arms and legs and Hokuren helped her scrape it off, even using the brush to dig between her fingers and toes.

The only downside of baths was that she had to take her headband off and expose her ears. Standard elven ears were long and thin, coming to a point. Cinna's ears were indeed pointy, but short, less than half as long as the typical elf's, and thicker. She grew up listening to Ms. Pottsdam, her caretaker from infancy to the age of ten, tell her that her ears looked squat and "just a little wrong."

Cinna wore her headband almost constantly to keep them hidden. Hokuren never mentioned them. Yet another reason why Cinna liked her.

When they finished washing, they remained in the water as usual, enjoying the warmth of the bath until their time was up. Hokuren sat against a wall of the brick basin, only her head poking out over the surface. Cinna floated on her back, staring up at the ceiling, using her hands to spin slowly in place.

A custom of silence existed during the relaxation portion of bath time, but this was the first moment they had been alone since Wadsworth's arrival. Hokuren had been lost in thought on the way from the castle to the bathhouse, so Cinna let her stew, but there were things she wanted to get off her chest and she couldn't wait any longer.

"Hey, boss," she said, carefully, gauging if Hokuren accepted the interruption.

"Yes, Cinna?" Hokuren's eyes remained closed, but she didn't sound irritated. Cinna took that as a sign to continue.

"Is the business in trouble? Was that rent notice really sent in error?" When Cinna thought about Hokuren going out of business, her stomach knotted and her hands felt clammy.

Hokuren sighed. Not a great sign. "I'll admit, meeting rent has been tight the past couple months. We haven't gotten enough work. I haven't said anything because I didn't want to worry you. The good news is that the prince is paying us enough to make rent. For this month."

"That's good, at least." Cinna considered what she wanted to say next. "I like working for you. I'm not sure anyone else would hire me. I know I'm difficult. Even if they did, I don't want to work somewhere else."

Opening her eyes, Hokuren smiled. "You aren't difficult. I love having you around and wouldn't have things any other way. And . . ." Hokuren paused for so long Cinna thought she wouldn't continue, but she wasn't done. "Whatever happens, I'll help you get through it. The end of the business, should it occur, would not be the end of us, okay?"

The water was cooling down, the fire beneath them burning itself out, a sign their time neared expiration. Cinna switched to treading water to stay warm. "We will keep this business going, boss. We got Barnaby.

Once we find Nyana, you can get the prince to tell everyone how good at investigating you are, and we'll have lots of clients."

"That would be wonderful," said Hokuren. "But we need to find Nyana first. Thinking about the future is important, but it will be meaningless if we disregard the present."

"Right, boss, of course."

Their bath attendant knocked on the privacy screen surrounding their bath. "Five-minute warning," she announced, before moving on.

"Time to dry off and get going," said Hokuren. Cinna jumped from the water, dripping as she bent to help Hokuren out of the basin. The duration of the baths made her skin prune, so she was always ready to leave when they ended.

It was dark outside when they emerged, dried and dressed, from the bathhouse. Cinna still couldn't get used to feeling so clean. Dirt and sweat were natural parts of working and living, and the body was meant to deal with them.

"Home, boss?" Cinna asked, pointing toward Hokuren's house.

"Home."

They walked in companionable silence. When they reached Hokuren's house, Cinna prepared to part, but Hokuren stopped her. "Cinna, I hope you have a good bed to sleep in. Between last night and today, we've been busy. You must be tired."

"It's fine," said Cinna. She kept her face neutral while squirming mentally. Hokuren had been asking about her bed and sleeping arrangements with increasing frequency, and it was all Cinna could do to fend these questions off without looking suspicious. It felt wrong to hide her sleeping arrangements, but Hokuren wouldn't approve of them. "I have a roof over my head. It's all I can ask for. You know me, I can get by with less sleep."

She worried Hokuren would follow up, but she didn't. Instead Hokuren said, "All right then. Have a good night." There was something strange in her voice, but Cinna couldn't figure out what it was. Probably her own mind playing tricks on her.

Cinna walked down the street, checking behind her to make sure Hokuren had gone inside. When she thought she had walked far enough, she turned back in the direction she had come from.

Passing by an uncovered trash bucket in the street, Cinna spotted an apple sitting on top, shining in the light of one of the streetlamps. She ambled over to look more closely. The apple, resting on top of some papers, appeared as clean as if she had found it in a market stall. Maybe cleaner. It made no sense for anyone to throw out such a perfect piece of food. She plucked it from the trash can and rubbed it against her tunic.

How fortunate to find a small snack before bed. The apple's sweetness accompanied her for the rest of the walk back to Hokuren's office.

When Cinna turned down the street where the office lay, her guilt flared up again. Hokuren certainly would prefer Cinna not to use the office to sleep at night. But renting a room meant spending money she would rather save.

The door to the office was ajar, stopping Cinna short. She had watched Hokuren lock it when they left with Wadsworth.

Cinna crept toward the office, steps quiet on the rough cobblestone street. Crashing and banging sounds grew in intensity as she neared.

The first thing Cinna saw when she burst through the threshold into the office was two men swinging clubs at the furniture. Their surprise at her entrance turned to interest within a moment. The men were similar in appearance, both bigger than average, but one had a beard and the other a receding hairline that made his forehead enormous.

The office lay in complete disarray. They had smashed all the chairs, broken the desk, ripped papers, and thrown every object on the shelves onto the ground. The destruction was total.

It was important in these situations to remain calm.

"Hey, this was all our stuff," said Cinna, her voice expressing mild annoyance. She picked up a piece of wood that had, until recently, been a chair leg. One end came to a point. "You won't be leaving until you tell me why you did this."

The men grinned. She knew those looks and enjoyed humbling those who gave them.

The man with the receding hairline answered, "I bet you'd like to know, Hokuren the Seeker. Well, whoever you pissed off, they ain't told me."

"We got our gold, and we don't care who pays us," the bearded man chimed in.

Cinna put a hand on her chin, an emulation of Hokuren deep in thought, constructing a list of potential enemies. No one came to mind.

Perhaps these men knew who hired them, but they would refuse to say without some encouragement. Cinna knew of one way to get them to talk. Neither gave the impression they could use their clubs to strike anything more mobile than office furniture. They were larger than she, as most people were, but their extra bulk mostly comprised useless fat. Nothing to fear.

"I'm not Hokuren. Do I look like I'm a seeker?" She gestured at herself and tugged at a patch on her frayed tunic.

Both men exchanged glances before eyeing her up and down. "Don't know what a seeker's supposed to look like," said the bearded man.

"Hey, this must be the other one," the man with the receding hairline said, pointing a stubby finger at Cinna. "Without the shoes. We're supposed t' beat her up, too."

"A little girl? This isn't going to be fair," said the bearded man, amused.

The "little girl" comment struck a nerve. Cinna rushed the man with the beard without further preamble. He was slow to react, and Cinna went under the swing of his club with ease. It sliced through the air above her head. Circling behind the bearded man, she jabbed the pointed end of the chair leg into his calf. He screamed and dropped his weapon as he fell to the floor.

The man with the forehead swung his club downward, but Cinna dodged the swing while rolling toward him. The club crashed into the floor, creating a small depression, as she sprang up and delivered a punch to his abdomen. He expelled his breath, gasping. As he bent over, clutching his stomach, she finished with a spinning kick that drove her heel cleanly into his temple. He collapsed on the floor, unconscious.

The fight was over. Cinna couldn't help her disappointment, despite the victory. Some challenge wouldn't have gone unwelcome.

Cinna turned back toward the bearded man, who whimpered and pawed at the wood in his calf. "You were right. It wasn't fair at all to fight a little girl, was it?" She grabbed his loose club and held it as if examining it, considering her next move. Hokuren did most of the questioning in their investigations. Okay, all of it. But Cinna had an advantage right now that Hokuren would want her to take. "For the record, I'm almost twenty-five. Now, talk. Who sent you?"

"I—I don't know," he stammered between shallow breaths.

Cinna slapped the club into her palm. She was enjoying this. Hokuren never intimidated her interview subjects. But then, she never started the interview by thrashing them. Perhaps she should.

The bearded man's lip quivered. "I swear! We got the money sent to our door with a note telling us what to do. Whoever it was didn't tell us nothing."

"And you'd go bashing us up without knowing why?"

"Why would I care? The money's good, and it don't mean nothing to me. One job's just as good as the next. But, please, I really don't know who sent us. You can't beat out of me what I don't got."

The man was babbling, and Cinna believed him. According to Hokuren, hired thugs were never truly worth questioning. If she were here, Cinna could imagine her saying, *Why would whoever sent these idiots tell them anything*?

"I think we're done here," said Cinna, still wielding the club. Indeed, why waste time questioning idiots? She needed to get to sleep soon, or she'd miss some exercises tomorrow morning.

She had to get rid of them. Hokuren would want to involve the Watch, but Cinna's only experience with the Watch was during her time as a street urchin, and they had always taken someone else's side.

"Take your friend and go." As if to spur him, she slapped the club on her hand again.

"My leg," cried the man.

"Oh, fine." What a baby. She found the office roll of bandages, flung into a corner of the room, and a large rag. The rag she gave to the man. "Bite this and hold still." Rolling him on his side, she gripped the wood with one hand and yanked it from his leg. He screamed into the rag while Cinna wrapped the wound with bandages. "It wasn't too deep. You're fine. You won't even need a healing potion. Gather up your friend and leave before I decide the wood looked better in your leg after all."

When the two men hobbled out, Cinna cast her glance across the office.

Pieces of wood, shredded papers, and other detritus covered the floor. She set right to work, clearing a small area before yawning. She would get her sleep, then get up in time to do her exercises before Hokuren arrived.

Then she could figure out how to explain what happened without admitting she slept at the office.

Before she could curl up on the floor, Cinna heard more footsteps approaching. She would have thought the one set of thugs was enough. Carefully, she knelt beside the door, fist at the ready.

A hand holding a lantern passed the doorway, then Hokuren's shaky voice rang out. "Cinna, are you here?"

"Boss?" Cinna jumped up in the entry, startling Hokuren. "What are you doing here?"

"I should really ask you the same question." Hokuren poked her head into the office and put her hand to her mouth. "But I have a much more pressing one. What happened?"

Cinna swallowed. It would be difficult to explain her presence here. "It was hired thugs, boss. They said someone sent them. Now one has a hole in his leg and the other a concussion. That's why you hired me." Cinna shot Hokuren a tentative smile, but Hokuren wasn't looking at her.

"Yes, it seems you were quite effective." Hokuren picked up her favorite timepiece, crushed into a jumble of complicated pieces. The magic inside kept moving the internal gears, but these gears now spun in broken circles. The dial would forever read half past ten. "Everything is in ruins. I don't think anything can be salvaged," Hokuren muttered. She placed the timepiece gently on the broken desk and gave it a small pat, as if saying goodbye.

"Can we get the chairs repaired, at least?" Cinna asked, attempting to piece two scraps of wood together like she was working on a three-dimensional jigsaw puzzle.

"I don't think any of them are in fewer than seven pieces."

"Most of this had little value, you said so yourself." Cinna gave up on the pieces and tossed them into a corner. "You kept telling me you wanted to replace all this old stuff."

"Not like this." Hokuren picked up the bloody piece of wood, grimaced, and tossed it into the same corner. She turned toward Cinna, her face drawn. "They wouldn't say who hired them?"

"They mentioned you by name, boss. Even after some threats, they couldn't say who they got their pay from."

Hokuren swiveled in a circle, taking in the entire mess. "I guess I should be glad they came to the office and not my home."

"Good thing I was here," said Cinna, a statement she regretted when Hokuren gave her a sharp stare.

"Yes, but that's the thing. What are you doing here? You were supposed to go home."

Cinna detected frustration, maybe anger, in Hokuren's voice. She worried Hokuren would fire her and panicked at the thought.

"I was just, uh—" The attempt to form a lie died on her lips. Whatever happened, she had to tell Hokuren the truth. She owed her that, at least. Deflection, however, still felt like a viable option. "I'm sleeping here. What brought you back tonight?"

Hokuren's lips were thin lines, and she didn't fall for the bait. "For how long have you been sleeping in the office?"

"For a while," Cinna admitted.

When Hokuren spoke again, she did not sound as mad as Cinna expected. She sounded concerned. "I know I can't pay you much, but you make enough to get a bed somewhere. I don't want you sleeping on a floor." Her face twisted in disgust. "And how often do you eat trash?"

Cinna felt her face flush. She had not noticed that Hokuren followed her here. "It wasn't trash, it was a whole apple! People throw perfectly good food away all the time. I don't want it to go to waste."

"Will you tell me why you're eating out of trash buckets and sleeping on the office floor?" The note of disappointment in her voice stung.

"You pay me plenty, boss. But I need to save it all." Hokuren said nothing, so Cinna filled the silence. "I didn't want to tell you yet, but I want to have enough to hire you. As a seeker. Your fee for what I'm asking for might be a lot, so I was waiting until I had enough saved up."

"What do you want to hire me for?" Maybe Hokuren would not fire her after all, as long as she remained honest.

"I want you to find my parents. My birth parents."

Hokuren paused, putting her finger on her chin. "Sit with me, Cinna.

Let's discuss this." She placed the lantern in the center of the area Cinna had cleared on the floor. The surrounding debris cast eerie shadows on the walls. They sat cross-legged across from each other. "Why do you want to find them?"

"I don't even know who they are. Never did. I was an infant when they left me on the doorstep of Ms. Pottsdam, who was already an old lady. She always told me she did not know who left me, or why."

Cinna swallowed hard. She had given Hokuren the sanitized version. *Your worthless folks saddled me with you in my final days*, she remembered Ms. Pottsdam telling her. The words bubbled up unbidden, and they struck like a knife to the gut as they always did. She shook her head to chase away the memories.

"I need to know why they didn't want me. Ms. Pottsdam never wanted me, but at least she had an excuse. They don't." Cinna could not help the bitterness in her voice. Her parents had gotten away with leaving her behind for too long. "Do they ever think about me?"

"They might not even be alive." Hokuren's voice was softer than normal as she drilled straight to the point, as usual. "Assuming they are, what answer from them would satisfy you?"

"I don't know. There probably isn't one. I want to hear their answer, anyway. It's not fair that they know and I don't, and I want to tell them what I think about them. I want them to have to reckon with their decision, but I don't even know where to start looking. So when I starting working for you and saw how good you were, I figured that if anyone could find them, it'd be you."

"You need not go into flattery. If it's important to you and this is what you want, I'll help you." Hokuren's eyes were kind. "I'll also warn you that the answer you get could be worse than not knowing at all."

Cinna closed her eyes and nodded. "I know. I expect it to. They have to be awful people."

Hokuren drew a big breath. "Perhaps. Many people aren't meant to be parents, and when they have children, they make selfish choices. It's wrong, yet it doesn't make them monsters. I know who my parents are, and I don't speak with my father anymore. My choice." Hokuren met Cinna's eyes. "You want that choice, don't you? Then we'll find them."

"Thanks, boss."

"And keep your money. I can't charge you. I wish, though, that I hadn't found this out right after promising the prince not to take any further commissions."

"Let's find Nyana first." Cinna felt sheepish. "I'm sorry I used the office as a place to sleep."

"Not as sorry as I am. If I had known you curled in a ball on the floor of my office every night, I'd have taken action already." Hokuren took one of Cinna's hands and placed it between both of hers. Hokuren's hands were so much softer. It had been more than six months since Cinna left the Sanctuary of the Eclipse, but her hands still had all their callouses from constant work with her quarterstaff and other weapons. "I will not allow it. Until I help you find a place, you'll sleep at my house on my couch. It's not ideal, but it's not the floor."

"I'm sure it's very comfortable." Cinna didn't believe she deserved Hokuren's kindness, not to the extent given, and would have to determine how she could pay her back. All she could do for now was be the best assistant possible.

Hokuren released Cinna's hand. "I have one condition for helping find your parents."

"Anything."

"No more eating out of the garbage. You will eat healthy, nutritious food that has never been in the trash if I have to feed you every meal myself."

"You won't have to do that." She couldn't ask so much from Hokuren. "I won't eat from the trash. I promise." Hokuren studied her closely and Cinna was glad she meant what she was saying. If she didn't, Hokuren would know.

Cinna walked back to Hokuren's house with her. Something Hokuren said was on her mind. "Why don't you talk to your father?" she asked. A wave of curiosity washed over her. Why would someone who had the means to talk to their parents willingly not? Hokuren seemed startled, so Cinna rushed to add, "You don't have to tell me if you don't want to."

"No, I'll tell you. I was just surprised you asked. We haven't discussed our pasts much." Hokuren seemed to take a moment to gather her thoughts. "Our relationship was never strong."

"What happened?"

Hokuren stared straight ahead. "My mother died shortly after giving birth to me. My father and my two older brothers—I wouldn't say they blamed me, exactly, but they felt she'd still be alive if it wasn't for me."

Cinna was indignant on Hokuren's behalf. "That isn't fair."

"No, it's not. But as a kid, I didn't know that. I carried the guilt for a long time, and I still sort of do. If I hadn't been born, my mother—" Hokuren trailed off, stopping in the middle of the street. Cinna wanted to comfort Hokuren, but she didn't know how. She hid her frustration in silence while Hokuren composed herself and continued. "My father has a business in Fondence, where I'm from. He's a merchant who mostly trades in fabrics and dyes, but he'll peddle anything that he thinks can turn him a profit. I was never involved in his work, even though he included my brothers in the business from an early age."

"Was that because of your mom?"

"Perhaps, but not entirely." Hokuren sighed. "My brothers were twins born twelve years before me. I believe my parents didn't plan or even desire my birth. By the time I came around, my father had already solidified his plans to give my brothers the business." She closed her eyes. "I don't know if that would have been different if Mom had survived, though you can bet I thought about it a lot when I was a kid."

"When I was a kid, I imagined I could be an elven queen destined to be restored to her throne," said Cinna. Then she put her hands over her mouth. "I'm sorry, this is about you."

Hokuren laughed. "It's fine, I needed the levity. As my brothers worked with my father, I was left to my own devices. I read mystery novels, got interested in being like my favorite investigators. I wanted to be a seeker, investigating crimes and putting the bad guys in jail. You know, kid stuff."

"Um, right," said Cinna, who had mainly thought about surviving as a kid.

"But when I was seventeen, my brothers were returning from a trip to pick up a shipment of yarns from the port town of Oro. It was a routine trip, they made it monthly. This time, however, there were bandits." Hokuren seemed lost in the memory. Cinna didn't interject this time, waiting patiently. Finally, Hokuren said, "A man who traveled with them came back to Fondence and told us the wagon had been attacked and my brothers were dead. And suddenly my father was forced to consider handing the business over to me, lest it leave the family."

"I'm sorry, boss," said Cinna. It felt weak, but she did not know what else to say. "Did you leave because he wouldn't?"

"Hah." This time, Hokuren's laugh was harsh. "No. He actually tried to give it to me. But it felt like an obligation. He said that you had to hand your business off to your child, even if you were afraid that child wouldn't be able to handle it."

Hokuren lifted her head to look up into the sky. Cinna stopped next to her. "He tried to teach me for about a year. But the whole time, I couldn't get over the fact that he obviously didn't want me to take over. I came to hate the business. I came to hate him. So I left. I ran away. All the way to Velles, where I thought he couldn't find me. It was a long trip for a girl who'd never left her home city to make all alone. He didn't like me, and I didn't want his damn business."

Cinna twisted her fingers behind her back. "And you don't talk to him?"

Hokuren gave Cinna a wan smile. "That's right. I've never talked to him again because I'm embarrassed. He finally tracked me down a couple of years ago. I received a message from him, telling me he was getting on in years and wanted to retire, demanding I return. The old coot still thinks he can get me to take his business. He sent multiple messages, the last one more than a year ago. I don't know if he stopped because he gave up, or—" Hokuren didn't finish her thought.

Cinna struggled, trying to think of something to say. No one had told her such a personal story about themselves before, and she had no experience to draw upon. After a moment, something popped into her head. She hoped it was appropriate. "Do you know anything about your mom?"

Hokuren answered by reaching into her shirt and pulling out a locket on the end of a necklace. She opened it and showed the contents to Cinna. There was a drawing of a woman, smiling. She was pretty, the lines of aging on her face only making her appear more dignified. Her hair, pulled back and braided, was similar to the way Hokuren wore her own. "This is the only image I have of her. People said she was kind and intelligent. I've always wanted to be like her, make her proud. I wish I knew if I was succeeding."

"She does look kind," Cinna said. "I'm sorry you never got to meet her."

Hokuren took back the locket and, after one last long view at the image inside, placed it back under her shirt. "So am I."

5

Hokuren awoke after a restless night. It had been difficult to revisit those old memories and feelings with Cinna. She alternated between pangs of regret for her role in her mother's death and repudiation of her self-blame. The two competing thoughts, running over and over, kept her awake.

And if she grew bored with that torment, she thought back over her busted office. Even with the prince's pay and the expected bonus from capturing Barnaby, new furniture would eat into the budget. Plus, they now needed to waste precious time cleaning up the mess.

Groggy, Hokuren padded downstairs from her small bedroom loft in her nightclothes to find Cinna fixing breakfast. "What are you making?"

Cinna, focused on a cooking pot in the fireplace, looked up at the greeting. "Oh, morning, boss." She stirred the contents of the pot. "I'm making porridge."

"Porridge," repeated Hokuren, voice flat. "That's, hmm, very nice of you." She disliked porridge, but was not about to be rude.

When she judged the porridge had cooked enough, Cinna ladled Hokuren a bowl. Overcooked, it came topped with half a banana and a far too generous dusting of cinnamon. "Tell me what you think, boss."

"It's great," lied Hokuren, choking a spoonful of oats down. She knew she should say something about the cinnamon, too expensive to use in such excess. But the spice made her think of something else. "That's funny, all the cinnamon. Your namesake."

Cinna, half done with her bowl before Hokuren had taken her second bite, put her spoon down in the porridge. "How do you know my full name? I've never told you."

Hokuren raised her eyebrows. "It's not really a stretch."

"I suppose." Cinna looked upset for a reason Hokuren couldn't quite discern.

"The actual answer is that I did my due diligence. When I hired you, I checked with the city registry. You know, just making sure you didn't have any major crimes in your past."

"Only minor crimes here, boss." Cinna spooned more porridge into her mouth while Hokuren pondered what crimes Cinna might consider minor. "I didn't even know I was in the registry."

"Your Ms. Pottsdam registered Cinnamon Pottsdam as her ward, yes. By the laws of Velles, that was enough to make you a citizen."

"I'm a citizen?"

"You didn't know?"

Cinna shrugged. "Never did me any good."

"Don't be so sure. Hiring you would have been trickier if you weren't." Hokuren jabbed her spoon in Cinna's direction. "If you didn't know about the registry, then you don't know the interesting thing about it. You're listed as a human."

Cinna blinked. "I'm an elf. Right?" She put her hands to her head, feeling for her ears under her headband. "Am I an elf?"

"Of course you are. Ms. Pottsdam cannot change that. Those flecks in your eyes and your ears make it obvious. But I admit I've wondered ever since why she listed you as human."

"She, uh, always hated my ears."

"Mmmm." Hokuren was aware of some sort of complex Cinna had with her ears. Since Cinna never mentioned it, Hokuren left it alone. But that tidbit helped shine some light on where it might have come from.

"As for my name, blame Ms. Pottsdam as well." Cinna stared at the little container of cinnamon, still on the kitchen counter. "She loved cinnamon and said if she was going to be saddled with me, she needed to call me something she actually liked. So, Cinnamon it is." She placed her spoon in her bowl with some force. "I don't like it. The name. I like the spice."

"You still go by Cinna."

"I really was a burden to her in her final years, and she took care of me when I couldn't care for myself. So, she deserves some credit, and I accept the name." Cinna frowned at her bowl. "Well, I'd prefer if you continued to call me Cinna."

"Cinna it shall remain then."

"So, what's the plan, boss?" Cinna finished her porridge and raised her eyebrows at Hokuren's still almost-full bowl. "Are we going to start looking for Nyana?"

"Yes," said Hokuren, taking another bite of charred oats and trying not to grimace. "But first, we'll pay the Watch a visit. We need to report last night's attack on the office and collect our bonus." She sighed. "I don't even know when to fit an office cleanup into our schedule. I'm a little worried that whoever sent those men might send more."

"I won't let them hurt you." Cinna hit the table with her fist. "Until we find out who did this and put a stop to it, I'm sticking with you everywhere."

Hokuren smiled at Cinna's protective instincts. "I think that's pretty much what you were going to be doing anyway, now that you sleep at my house." She set her bowl aside. "I think I've had enough of this porridge, thank you."

The awful familiarity of the Velles City Watch main office washed over Hokuren as she approached. More imposing in the harsh daylight than the moonlit night with its minimalist architecture, the dark blue building dwarfed the surrounding homes and shops.

Watch members milled about outside and a line of petitioners waited for their turn at the clerk's desk. Just a normal day. Hokuren had staffed that desk years ago and knew the reports would primarily comprise minor incidents or thefts. Most would be too trivial, like a stolen shop item or a shove during an argument, to be followed up on unless they involved someone important.

Trailed by Cinna, Hokuren skirted around the line and motioned to the clerk. Someone she didn't recognize, a mousy young woman with a blonde ponytail, had replaced Tarleton. This clerk must have been hired after Hokuren's departure from the Watch.

"Is Lord Doubtwell in?" Hokuren asked.

"He's in a meeting," said the clerk without missing a beat. She had received excellent training. All Watch members were instructed to give that line to anyone asking for Lord Doubtwell.

"So he's in his office," said Hokuren. "Perfect, it so happens he's supposed to be meeting with me. Come on, Cinna." This was a near truth. Doubtwell had asked her only to see him again once she'd caught the Master Thief.

Hokuren went straight to the door leading into the back offices. The clerk found herself trapped with the current petitioner, irate about the interruption. "Don't go back there, ma'am," the mousy clerk called out. Hokuren ignored her.

A sign on the door said, "No Unauthorized Entry Under City Watch Law." It had been there for as long as Hokuren could remember. It was effective, as even the most brazen criminals hesitated at committing crimes in the one place crawling with members of the City Watch.

"There's no such law," Hokuren explained as she opened the door, in case Cinna was concerned.

She was not.

No one stopped Hokuren as she marched straight to the rear of the building, past unoccupied desks for high-ranking officials who came and went at their leisure. She walked as if she belonged, knowing this was enough to cause anyone who could have intercepted her to hesitate until it was too late. She knocked on Doubtwell's door, located at the far wall.

"Seeker Hokuren to see you, sir."

The gruff voice on the other side of the door was muffled. "Enter."

Hokuren made sure Cinna followed her in before closing the office door behind her. "Good morning, sir." Hokuren forced herself to call Doubtwell "sir" because she needed him to provide her with work as she struggled to get her business on steady ground. Still, it rankled.

Lord Doubtwell, Commander of the Velles City Watch, sat in an overstuffed chair behind an enormous and ornately decorated wooden desk. His bald head and white eyebrows gave away his advancing age. Though he had grown soft and didn't fit as well as he used to into his City Watch armor, his mind was still as sharp as ever.

"Hokuren, I'm surprised to see you." He pretended to glance over a sheet of paper in front of him, intended to show his disinterest in her.

This display did not fool Hokuren. There had been a point in time when she had been a fresh-faced recruit to the City Watch and she'd regarded Lord Doubtwell with respect. As she moved up the ranks of the Watch and spent more time with him, that regard had been scrubbed clean away.

"You seem more annoyed than surprised," said Hokuren. She and Cinna remained standing, as Doubtwell did not provide chairs for anyone except himself in his office.

Hokuren caught Cinna gazing at one of the many expensive pieces of pottery on the walls, a tea kettle said to have been used by the very first elves. With such a ridiculous claim it had to be a fake peddled at the Sunday market. Doubtwell maintained an inflated sense of his own intelligence, making him exactly the type to be taken in by the market's grifters.

"Perhaps I am," said Doubtwell.

"I would have thought you'd be more welcoming, considering I brought you the Master Thief, Maxwell Barnaby." She crossed her arms over her chest. "And my office was smashed by some hired thugs."

Lord Doubtwell sat straight in his chair, finally looking up from the paper on his desk. "Forget your office. You brought the Master Thief here? When the flames did you do that?"

"I left him in one of the holding cells here two nights ago. You're telling me you didn't know?"

Doubtwell launched himself from his chair and stalked around his desk. Even though Cinna had her back turned to him, she still deftly jumped aside as he bulled his way to the door. "Why wasn't I told?" he yelled.

"I . . . actually don't know," said Hokuren as Doubtwell exited the office without another word.

Cinna gave Hokuren a quizzical look. "Should we follow?"

Hokuren nodded. "Something's wrong."

The two of them followed Doubtwell back to the clerk at the desk, currently taking a report from a new petitioner, a young man.

"Where's the Master Thief?" Lord Doubtwell shouted, interrupting the petitioner. The young man did not dare to complain, however. Most people in Velles knew who Doubtwell was, and few wanted to confront him when he was angry.

The mousy clerk flinched and squeaked, "I—I don't know. Am I supposed to? No one knows who he is."

Lord Doubtwell raised his voice. It boomed in the small space. "Hokuren says she arrested him and placed him in a holding cell, but you know nothing about this? Which one of you is lying?"

"Neither." Hokuren kept her voice calm, even as her stomach turned at the clerk's confusion. Doubtwell turned to face her, pausing his bellowing to take a breath like a volcano between eruptions. She nodded to the line of petitioners still waiting to be heard. "Sir, we should continue this conversation elsewhere. Shall we take a look at the cells?"

Doubtwell simmered, but agreed. To the clerk, he said, "You, whatever your name is."

"It's—" The clerk was interrupted by another Doubtwell outburst.

"Don't bother, I don't care and I won't remember. You desk clerks are impossible to keep track of and irrelevant until you manage to reach a more senior position. Now, come to the cell area with us," said Doubtwell. The clerk looked as if she would rather set her hair on fire. Doubtwell turned to the line of people hoping to report to the clerk. "Important Watch business. You'll all wait until she's back."

The collective groan from the crowd on the other side of the desk was muted. None of them were going to challenge Lord Doubtwell in his current mood. Hokuren kept Cinna close and followed Doubtwell into the cell area. The unhappy clerk took the rear.

When they entered, Hokuren found the cells all empty. There was no sign of anyone having occupied the cell she placed Barnaby in the previous night. All her work to capture Barnaby undone.

She tried to hide her disappointment, stiffening her back when she felt her shoulders slump. Now was not the time to feel sorry for herself.

Doubtwell rounded on the clerk. "Hokuren says two nights ago she brought the Master Thief here and placed him in a cell. That would have been the night clerk who received him. Tell us exactly what you were told during your handoff yesterday morning."

The clerk quailed under his stare. "I—I got the report when I got in for my shift," she said, her voice shaking. "All I was told was that there were two drunk people. I confirmed their sobriety and let them out. That was all. There was no Master Thief or anyone else."

Lord Doubtwell turned to Hokuren, his eyes narrowed. "I ask again, did you lie to me? She says Tarleton didn't see any sign of the Master Thief."

Hokuren steadied herself. Something had gone wrong here, but the first thing she needed to do was clear her name. She produced the receipt she'd received from Tarleton and handed it to Doubtwell. "Not true. She said Tarleton didn't tell her about the Master Thief. But he went with me to put Barnaby in that cell when I brought him in." Hokuren gestured at the exact cell.

"Suppose I believe this is Tarleton's signature on this receipt. A problem remains. I don't see anyone by the name of Maxwell Barnaby here!" Lord Doubtwell's voice rose to a shout. When he didn't receive any response to this, he lowered his voice. "Hokuren, we've known each other for a long time. Despite the differences we've had, I don't believe you would lie to my face about something like this. But what I want to know is, what happened here?"

"He was here and then he escaped." Cinna's voice was quiet, but her words settled over the room. All eyes were on her as she stood by Barnaby's empty cell. She poked her fingers into the lock on the cell, screwing up her face to focus. "I think this lock could be picked." She pulled out a lockpick from her headband. Her hands maneuvered the tool within the lock as she shook her head. The lock clicked, and the door swung open. Returning the lockpick to her headband, she addressed Doubtwell. "You don't even need to be skilled to pick this."

Lord Doubtwell stared at Cinna as if he had never seen her before, even though she had accompanied Hokuren on multiple visits to his office. "Are you saying our cells are of unusually poor quality?"

"Not unusually so, no," said Cinna evenly.

"You searched him before we placed him in his cell, right?" asked Hokuren.

"Of course, boss. Right when I caught him. I didn't find anything, but I'm not an expert. The best thieves have a spare pick hidden somewhere. Some spots are hard to find, even during a search."

Lord Doubtwell turned toward Hokuren, a pained look on his face as he pointed at Cinna. "Who is this rogue, anyway? And why does she know so much about how thieves act?"

"This is my assistant, Cinna," said Hokuren tersely. "You've met. Instead of worrying about who she is, consider instead what she is telling us. Either he had a spare lockpick, or someone provided him with one." She frowned as another possibility popped into her mind. "Or someone let him out with a cell door key." She waited for Doubtwell to reach the proper conclusion on his own.

The room was silent. After a long moment, Lord Doubtwell let out a reluctant sigh. "The night clerk. Tarleton. He would have to be involved somehow." His shoulders sagged. "I'm not used to being betrayed by members of my Watch."

"It bothers me that Tarleton gave me the receipt and then didn't mention Barnaby at the shift handoff. Surely he would know it would only be a matter of time before everyone realized Barnaby was here and his lie of omission would be exposed. Tarleton is young and new to the Watch, but I don't think he's stupid." Hokuren put her finger on her chin. "There's another possibility, of course. Tarleton may have helped Barnaby and tried to cover it up long enough to escape somewhere, but he also could have been coerced into it. Threatened. I didn't think Barnaby had accomplices in Velles, but if he does, they may have found him."

"Yes," said Lord Doubtwell, grasping at this offered branch of hope. "Of course. Tarleton's still green. He lives with his poor old mother, and he'd be easy to threaten." The aging commander straightened up. "Not that giving in to criminals like that is acceptable, but it's not treason."

"He seemed nervous on shift handoff," said the mousy clerk. "Now that I'm thinking about it. And he didn't show up for his shift last night."

"He didn't?" asked Hokuren, alarmed.

"He was lying," said Doubtwell. "Yes. It all makes sense." He slammed his fist into the wall, a sudden outburst of violence. "Damn! We were so close to putting that menace away forever."

"We know he lied, but we don't know why he lied." Hokuren paced the floor of the cellblock. "With the waters this muddied, further speculation won't help. We need to talk to Tarleton." She had promised the prince to take no other jobs, but this was her capture, and she intended to finish it. "If you would hire me again, I could—"

Doubtwell did not let her finish. "This should be an internal City Watch investigation." His tone suggested he was not interested in negotiating this point. "As for your bonus. Technically, you did as asked. You found the Master Thief and brought him to the City Watch. Our failure to keep him is not your concern. See the controller on your way out for payment. Here." Doubtwell scribbled on the receipt Hokuren had given him and handed it back. Hokuren glanced down to find instructions for her payment, signed by Doubtwell. She had expected him to put up much more of a fight before paying out. "Our business is concluded."

It was as obvious a dismissal as Hokuren had ever received, but she had to make one last attempt. "Sir, I feel responsible and I can—"

"You'll do nothing except take your payment and move on. This is an order from me as the commander of the City Watch. We will handle this from now on, and you will not be involved under any circumstance." He gestured to a cell, his voice dark. "Make no mistake, I'll have you and your rogue tossed into one of these if I find out you talked to Tarleton or investigated this behind my back. And that's a promise."

"Understood," Hokuren said, her voice polite but clipped. "We'll be on our way." With reluctance, she stalked from the room quick enough that Cinna had to trot to catch up.

"We forgot to file the report about the office, boss," said Cinna, soon after they had left the main office.

"I didn't want to stay a minute longer than necessary." Hokuren's lips puckered in disdain. "Anyway, I believe we know who did it."

"Barnaby's the obvious guy, I agree." Cinna pressed her fist into her palm. If she met the thief again, she'd have to give him more of a beating than before.

"Come on, since we can't do anything about Barnaby for the moment, let's do what we're supposed to do and put all our efforts into finding Nyana."

Cinna groaned. "It's wagon wheel time, isn't it?"

"Not quite. First, we need to make some copies."

Cinna didn't understand how the copyit worked at Gerard's Printing and Paper. That put her in good company: no one did. Gerard was an elf who maintained the contraption, a machine said to be over two thousand years old. It contained complicated magic that could no longer be replicated, allowing it to make copies of any image fed into it in mere seconds.

Prince Leopold owned the copyit, much like any item with irreplaceable magic in the city. In the prince's name, Gerard shepherded the machine, making sure the people of Velles could use its features at a reasonable price. Once it ran out of magic, that would be the end of the copyit.

When they bid Gerard farewell it was with ten copies of Nyana's picture. Afterward, Cinna followed Hokuren to a bar on the other side of Velles, The Garrulous Squirrel. Hokuren explained that in its heyday, the bar bustled with adventurers passing through the city. It had fallen on hard times, suffering from the decline of the adventurers themselves.

"Didn't know you were the morning beer sort," said Cinna, unimpressed with the bar from the outside. The faded sign of a chattering squirrel hung in front of a window, long since broken, boarded up with moldering wood.

"I'm not." Hokuren smiled. "Are you ready to meet some old friends of mine who are?"

"Didn't know you were friends with the morning beer sort. How do you know they're there?"

"If they're in town, they're here. And they're in town."

The Squirrel was empty save for a table of four boisterous adventurers playing cards. Set in front of them were empty breakfast plates and cups of coffee. A shifty-looking young boy, probably below the legal age to sell alcohol, stood behind the bar. It smelled of stale ale and something burnt, and dishes from the previous night still lay scattered on unused tables.

Cinna stepped in some sort of liquid and stopped to inspect the bottom of her foot. A quick sniff revealed that it was ale, to her relief.

"It's a bit of a dive," she mumbled.

"More of a plunge," said Hokuren.

One of the adventurers caught sight of them entering. "Well, if it isn't Hokuren the City Watchdog," he said. He had one good eye, the other covered by a patch.

Hokuren snapped back, "Krusk, you know I left the Watch. Keep up."

"The Watch doesn't truly let you leave, does it?"

"Who cares about the Watch?" A short and stout woman with a war hammer leaning against the table next to her turned in her chair to inspect Cinna. "When did Hokuren get a new girlfriend?"

"Don't tell me those flyers I saw a while ago paid off," said the only elf in the group, her blonde hair woven into an intricate series of braids. "I didn't think you would actually get a positive response."

"Hokuren put up flyers for a girlfriend?" said the one Hokuren had called Krusk.

Cinna became overwhelmed by the sudden cacophony from all the strangers and lurked from behind Hokuren. As chuckles filled the air, Hokuren put her hands up to call for silence. "Let me introduce you. Everyone, this is my assistant, Cinna." She pointed out each individual adventurer. "Cinna, this is Krusk, Galina, Lyriel, and Dorben. Like many adventurers, they crack jokes to cover up the existential dread of losing their profession."

Cinna did her best to map each name to an adventurer. Names, especially this many in rapid succession, were difficult. But if she assigned a single trait to each one, she found her odds of memorizing them increased.

Dorben, the last member of the group, was a small man with a brown brimmed hat. "Excellent to meet you, Cinna." He took off his hat and saluted. "I'm sure you and Hokuren have a worthy reason to be hanging around at a bar this morning."

"We're here to see you," said Hokuren.

"I see you do not," drawled Dorben, taking a healthy sip of his coffee. It smelled more of rum than coffee.

"Hokuren graces us with her presence." Krusk, the one with the eye-patch, affected the nasally accent used by longtime residents of the Aviary, the neighborhood of old money in Velles. "For the first time in months, mind you. Let me guess, you have a job for us."

"How do you figure?" asked Hokuren.

"You only come to see us when you need something."

"You've got me there."

"A job would be welcome," said Lyriel, the elf with blonde hair. Her eyes danced with excitement, their yellow flecks a close match to her hair. She stuck her thumb toward the Job Board. "This thing's got nothing but unsuitable thug work, when it has anything." She cast a furtive glance at the young bartender sullenly watching them. "Our bills here are piling up faster than the jobs are, that's for sure. That dread is not as existential as you say. It's quite real."

"It's true. The board's been too dry for a while. Since we won't stoop to those thug jobs, we need work," said Galina, who had the big war hammer. "And we're getting tired of playing cards and drinking." Behind her, Krusk and Dorben shook their heads in disagreement.

Hokuren held up the copies of Nyana's picture. "This job will pay, but it may not be fun."

"Your jobs never are. We're desperate, and we're listening," Dorben assured her. "What do we need to do?"

Hokuren handed out a copy to each adventurer. "The usual tactic when I want someone found. Spread out over the city and show this to anyone and everyone and ask if they've seen the woman in the picture. Also ask about a tall man in golden armor who might be accompanying her. In theory, he should have a difficult time staying inconspicuous."

"Oh, good, another 'go around town and ask everybody if they've seen the person in this picture' job," said Galina, slumped in her chair.

"At least it isn't a cat this time," grumbled Krusk.

6

"They sure were enthusiastic about that job you gave them," said Cinna as she and Hokuren walked back to Hokuren's house to secure the Barnaby bonus once the adventurers started their canvass of the city.

"Like all good investigative work, it's a grind." Hokuren shrugged. "However they may appear, they are diligent and they'll earn their pay."

Cinna grinned and leaned closer to Hokuren. "They called me your new girlfriend. I'm no one's girlfriend, but does that mean you have an old one? Can I meet her?"

Hokuren blanched. "There's no girlfriend to meet anymore."

"Umm—"

"No, no, don't get the wrong idea. She's not dead or anything." Hokuren waved her hands nervously. "She and I had . . . different ideas about what we wanted our future to be." She had a faraway look in her eyes. "It was a year ago, but it's still a bit of a sore spot for me."

"Oh! Sorry, boss." Cinna felt worse than when she stepped in the random liquid at the bar. "I didn't mean—"

"You're fine. One day, I'll tell you about it, if you'll listen. But right now, we've too much to do for me to go down into those memories."

The mood had grown gloomy, Hokuren's head hanging low, and Cinna knew it was her fault. She tried to think of ways to cheer the boss up. Her gaze settled on a bakery, and she stared longingly even as they passed. "You know, a slice of pie might make you feel better."

That always worked for Cinna, anyway. Blueberry pie was one of the few pleasures she recalled from her time living on the streets of Velles as a child, and it remained one of the few extravagances she allowed herself with the pay she earned.

Hokuren eyed Cinna knowingly. "Go ahead and get us some pie." She handed Cinna a few coins from the bonus-pay purse. Cinna murmured in delight and rushed to the bakery, purchased two slices of pie, and returned to give one to Hokuren.

During her trip to the bakery and back, Cinna had come up with a new topic to further distract Hokuren from the disastrous discussion of her prior relationship. "Boss, are we not going to do anything about Barnaby?"

Pie in hand, Hokuren shook her head. "I admit, Barnaby escaping feels like a loose end. And I don't like those. But Nyana has to be our priority, even if that's not very satisfying."

"I hate that Barnaby got out."

"No disagreement here, but I'm more bothered that Tarleton either collaborated with Barnaby or someone coerced him. I fancy the latter, because he didn't seem the ambitious type." Hokuren pulled a face. "But then there's something nibbling at my brain about the way Lord Doubtwell acted. It felt wrong to me, but with the news of Barnaby's escape being so fresh, I think I missed something. Plus, Doubtwell was so emphatic that we stay out of things. It felt like he was too eager to be rid of us. But then, what does he gain from Barnaby's escape? The thief stole his wife's precious pocket watch. He must want to cover up what happened."

Cinna listened to Hokuren's rambling patiently, happy to see a return to normal from the boss. Her monstrous bites covering her lips in blueberry filling. The warm filling was perfect, with just the right level of tart working in concert with the sweet. Swallowing, she said, "Boss, you've said that when people want us to go away, that's when we need to be there the most."

"So you do listen to me sometimes," said Hokuren, taking a dainty nip from her pie.

"I always listen to you," said Cinna, wounded.

Hokuren grinned. "I'm just giving you a hard time. You do listen. I'm never sure what will stick and what I'll need to repeat."

Cinna always tried to remember everything Hokuren told her, but there was so much. "So will we? You know, be where we're not wanted?"

"There's the slight problem of not being paid. I have little enthusiasm for working for free, so—" Hokuren halted, almost causing Cinna to bump into her right as she was about to take her final bite of pie.

"Cinna," said Hokuren, her voice low and tinged with sudden fear. "Up ahead."

Three people lingered outside Hokuren's house. They wasted no time in heading toward Cinna and Hokuren, swaggering with daggers unsheathed and glinting in the late day sun. Their leader appeared to be a burly man with a mustache. Flanking him from a few feet behind were a tall man with a nose ring and a bald woman with a tattoo of an eagle over her scalp.

This group was not here to bust up Hokuren's possessions. These were assassins.

Cinna rushed in front of Hokuren, eager to act the bodyguard she had been hired as. She popped the last of the pie into her mouth. Trouble or not, pie need not be wasted.

"Cinna. Run and get the Watch," rasped Hokuren from behind her.

As much as Cinna loathed to disobey the boss, she would sooner gargle glass than fetch the City Watch. "Get somewhere safe, boss. I can handle this, but I can't protect you at the same time."

"You can't really mean to fight them."

Cinna did mean to fight them—and win. She tried not to take offense at the lack of faith in Hokuren's words. "I won't be long."

Her movements controlled and purposeful, Cinna approached the three assailants, who stopped and waited. Unbidden, she recalled something the Master at the Sanctuary of the Eclipse had said when asked how to fight an opponent with a blade without one of your own.

Run. And if you can't, don't let them cut you.

The trick, then, was to dodge and counter. Always be ready to make her next move. Go for weak spots, never let up, end the fight as quickly as possible. Don't let them cut her.

The mustachioed man in front of the other two said, "We can go easy on you, if you'd like to live. Do just enough to fulfill our job."

Cinna did not want to talk to them. She wanted to get right into the fight. But her training had taught her patience. The chances of winning only increased if she took every advantage offered.

"You'd better not, because I sure won't." She moved closer, staying in the middle of the street. The more space, the better.

"Suit yourself." It would be a joy to knock the sneer from this man's face. "We were given good coin, girl."

Judging from the way he held his dagger, he would swipe across his body to her right, so she would dodge to the left and remove him from the fight to even the numbers. She ran through the motions in her head as she got close enough to make her move. As for the others, she would have to improvise.

Cinna planted her foot on the cobblestone and launched herself at the man with the mustache. He had his dagger up and ready, slashing at her precisely the way she expected. She twisted her body as she jumped to avoid the blade, landing right next to him in perfect position.

Her fist struck the man at the base of his throat. He made a sound like a strangled duck and grabbed at his damaged airway, dropping his dagger. Cinna moved toward her next target even as he fell to his knees on the ground.

The man with the nose ring gaped at his flailing companion, but recovered quickly. He defended his neck with his arm, as if Cinna would ever use the same trick twice. Instead, she grabbed the other arm, the one holding the dagger, and twisted it around his back. He cried out and dropped his weapon.

Movement in Cinna's peripheral vision alerted her to the knife thrown by the bald woman with the eagle tattoo from several feet away. She flung herself away from Nose Ring as the blade whizzed past her shoulder.

Cinna kept Nose Ring, now freed, between herself and Eagle. He tried to grab her, but she slipped back from his reach, brushing against the side of a building.

As she was pressed against the building, her speed and quickness would be less of an advantage against the size and strength of Nose Ring. He took a second dagger out and brandished it. She needed a weapon of her own, and she knew where to get it.

Cinna moved to the right, locking eyes with Eagle. With Nose Ring no longer in the way, the mercenary took the opportunity, flicking her wrist and throwing the knife in her hand.

Cinna ran toward it, past Nose Ring. He slashed at her, but she ignored it, focused on the knife in the air. She swiped with her right hand and snagged it, wrapping her fingers around the cheap leather hilt. Turning to Nose Ring, she grinned at his incredulous look.

A harsh pain in her left arm caused her to wince. Nose Ring's blade had sliced deep into the muscle, and the sleeve of her tunic was already turning crimson.

Cinna had gotten cut, had not followed Master's instructions. Nothing new there.

The wound would heal. She watched Nose Ring wave his dagger, dancing back and forth. Drawing blood seemed to animate him. Dangling her left arm as if it were useless, she transferred the knife to her left hand; the right stanching the bleeding. Breathing heavily, she presented an easy target to him.

Nose Ring took the bait, closing in sloppily, thinking she was weak. Before he could make a move, she came to life, thrusting the sharp blade of the little knife into his side. He grimaced as she ripped the weapon out.

Not giving him a chance to rally, she kicked at his side, aiming for the knife wound she had delivered moments ago. He took a step backward to avoid a direct hit, but she got enough of him that he cried out in pain.

She swung the knife high, and he ducked. As she hoped he would. She had her elbow ready, driving it down on top of his head right as she brought her knee up into the bridge of his nose.

There was a satisfying crunch, and blood spurted from his ruined nostrils. Nose Ring grabbed for his face, twisting in agony.

Cinna left him and moved toward Eagle. The woman had another throwing knife and, seeing Cinna approach, threw it. But she was nervous, having seen her allies fall, and her aim was poor this time. Cinna made no move to evade, letting the projectile fly harmlessly past her ear.

Eagle's eyes shifted, her expression turned to fear. She put her hands up. "Okay. Okay. We're going," she said. "We weren't paid enough for this."

"That's not what he said." Cinna pointed at the mustachioed man.

Nose Ring shuffled back from Cinna, holding a hand over his broken nose, the wound in his side hampering his movement. Eagle gathered the mustachioed man, still in a fit of coughing and wheezing, not yet recovered from Cinna's throat punch.

All three of the mercenaries slinked away down the street. Cinna considered questioning them further, but saw little point. It had to be the now-freed Barnaby harassing them. She stood still and kept her eyes on them, Nose Ring's blood dripping from the knife into the street at her feet, until they turned the corner. Only then did she allow herself to relax.

Hokuren's boots pounded the stone as the boss approached from behind once the danger passed. "Are you all right?"

"I'm fine. I guess the adventurers who answer the thug postings aren't the best." Cinna turned to face Hokuren and saw her boss startle.

"Your eyes," said Hokuren, eyebrows raised. "The blue in them, is it shining?"

Blinking and looking away, Cinna said, "I think it can get like that." She wiped the blood from the knife in her hand onto the edge of her tunic.

"And you're not fine. Let me see your arm."

"Oh, right." The dagger wound. With her adrenaline fading, Cinna felt the sting of the cut. "I let the nose ring guy get me on purpose. He made a mistake, acting as if I'd no longer be a threat with this little wound."

"Little wound?" said Hokuren, grabbing Cinna's arm. "On purpose? I didn't know you were so—'reckless' is the nicest way to put it." She pulled Cinna toward the house. "Come on, let's get you inside. I have bandages. If we have to, we'll take you to a healer."

"No need." Cinna did not resist Hokuren's pull, but she knew the wound would take care of itself. "It'll be good as new in the morning, boss. Not even a scar."

"I don't think you've ever lied to me before, so don't start now."

Following Hokuren into the house, Cinna sat in a chair at the small dining table as instructed. Hokuren prodded the injury and looked confused when Cinna did not react. "Doesn't this hurt?"

"Yes, but not that much. Master at the Sanctuary said I had 'uncommonly high pain tolerance.'" Cinna did not add that the limits of that tolerance were often tested.

Hokuren was staring into Cinna's eyes, and Cinna once again wondered if her boss could read her mind. When Hokuren spoke again, there was distress in her voice. "They didn't do this to you at the Sanctuary, did they? You know, hurt you."

"Injuries happened." Cinna hoped Hokuren would let it go. "I'm a naturally quick healer, boss. I always have been. It comes in handy."

With gauze and bandages, Hokuren treated and wrapped the wound. "I suppose we'll see how natural a healer you are. It doesn't look as bad as I thought it would. But why did you let him cut you?"

"I wanted a weapon," said Cinna. "To get the one that the eagle woman threw, I had to focus on it." She set her chin. "I know what I'm doing."

"It was careless. You're incredible in a fight, but you aren't invincible. That dagger could have hit you somewhere much worse."

"I'm fine," Cinna said in a small voice.

"This time."

Cinna was quiet. Finally, she said, "Sorry to make you worry, boss."

Hokuren sighed. "I just don't want to see you get hurt. It was difficult watching you against those thugs."

"It was Barnaby," said Cinna, her voice hardening. "We can't ignore this."

"I suspect it was. But we have to trust the Watch for now." Hokuren played with a button on her coat. "Now that Doubtwell knows he's escaped, and his identity, I'm sure even they can find him. At the very least, their search should put pressure on him so he can't be hiring more people to come after us."

Cinna trusted Hokuren, not the Watch, but if the boss didn't want to pursue Barnaby, there would be little Cinna could do to convince her. She would have to stay vigilant. "If you say so," she said.

"Now, get some rest. If you're well enough tomorrow, we can start we can start surveying some wagons. Hope you enjoy close inspections of wheels." Hokuren patted Cinna's shoulder.

Cinna yawned, her eyelids heavy. Her body could heal this injury, but its work exhausted her. She drifted to the couch Hokuren made up for her and fell into it.

As she closed her eyes, Cinna's thoughts turned back to Barnaby.

Hokuren took the prince's request to focus entirely on the search for Nyana to heart. Cinna was not concerned about handling Barnaby's hired thugs. Unless he paid out for better quality, what he was sending would be no trouble.

But the Watch had better hurry and recapture him. Or she would have to convince Hokuren that they should do it for them.

The following morning, Hokuren came down to find Cinna once again making porridge, but this time with fewer clothes on. She had shed her tunic and trousers to clean the blood off them and was now clad in her undergarments. It had not taken her long to become comfortable in Hokuren's home.

The loose outfit that Cinna typically wore hid her lithe, muscular body. She had once told Hokuren her training emphasized as much strength as possible without sacrificing her main advantage her small frame offered: her speed. She earned her physique by spending hours on various exercises and routines each day, mostly before Hokuren woke up. Hokuren did not consider herself to be in either great or poor shape, but Cinna made her feel much closer to the poor side of the scale.

"How's your injury doing?" asked Hokuren.

"Oh, great, boss." Cinna held up her her injured arm, unbandaged. "You can barely tell it was ever there, see?" Hokuren was about to demand to know why the bandages were already off, but her protests died on her lips.

The wound was... gone. Hokuren thought for a moment that perhaps it had been on the other arm, but she had dressed the wound herself. Not even a scar remained, the skin as clear as a newborn's. "Did you have a healing potion I didn't know about?"

"I wouldn't hold out on you like that, boss. And even with the savings I have, I couldn't afford one."

"Then how is your wound completely healed? It's been a single night."

"I told you. I'm a quick healer."

Hokuren sat in a chair at her dining table, trying to absorb this new information. No wonder Cinna was so rash. She put her finger on her chin. "You did, but this is something that 'quick healer' doesn't quite get across. I didn't realize the extent of your ability. It's remarkable."

"Yes." Cinna stared down at the floor. "I'm sorry I haven't told you before, but when people find out, they're jealous or think I'm weird." She gave Hokuren an admonishing glare. "Or I'm hiding healing potions from them."

Hokuren had felt the question about healing potions fair, but understood Cinna's objection. "How many people have found out?"

"Almost no one outside the Sanctuary knows, and they don't contact the outside world much. And now, you know. I didn't hide it from you now because it's okay if you know."

"I appreciate your trust. Please remember what I said yesterday, though, about you not being invincible. I'm thankful you drove off the thugs, but I want you to be careful." Cinna gave Hokuren a nod. "I'm glad you're doing well. Looks like we can continue our search for Nyana."

"Let's do it." Cinna rushed to finish her porridge and then took a second helping. "I'm always starving when I have an injury to heal, so I made extra for myself today."

Healing potion use caused enhanced appetites as well, as the body required extra energy to pull off its rapid repairs. Perhaps there was something in Cinna's physiology that emulated a healing potion? No one knew exactly what happened in the body that caused it to heal itself faster when someone drank one. Healing occurred, and that was good enough for most.

The investigation grind began following the porridge clean-up. For the next few days, they scoured the city, checking the wagons that congregated around merchant warehouses and market stalls. Hokuren would ask the proprietors if any wagons had arrived with a specific passenger, flashing Nyana's picture. They also visited the two wagon-rental facilities in the city.

The search got them nowhere. Hokuren checked so many wagon wheels she was sure she would see them in her dreams. The adventurers returned to the Squirrel with complaints about spending an entire day showing people a picture no one recognized.

After four days without success, Hokuren considered trying a different tack as she waited outside the Garrulous Squirrel for the adventurers to return for the usual midday meet up.

Cinna seemed exasperated. "We haven't gotten anywhere, boss," she fumed. "I think we've seen every wagon in Velles already."

"We definitely haven't come close to that," Hokuren said, trying to hide the smile that came on despite her own weariness. "Nor have our adventurers talked to everyone in Velles. It's a big city. This was always going to take some time and effort." She sighed. "We're going to need a little luck, though."

Luck arrived in the form of Galina, the last of the adventurers to arrive at the meet up, joining the rest at the table inside the bar. "Sorry I'm late, but someone recognized your woman."

Hokuren's heartbeat quickened. When investigative grunt work paid out with a lead, there was no greater thrill. Hokuren peppered Galina with questions. "Who? Where? When?"

Galina handled the questions with aplomb. "The clerk at the Library of Reverie. She checked out some books six days ago."

Nyana had disappeared seven days ago, according to the prince. "Which books?" asked Hokuren.

"The clerk wouldn't say."

"Fine. Anyone with her?"

"Do you mean did she visit the library with a man in ostentatious golden armor?" Galina's smile was wide enough to show her teeth. "No, she was apparently alone."

Hokuren placed one of the prince's coins on the table. "It's a lead. Thank you."

"Are we done, then?" asked Krusk, his voice weary.

"No," said Hokuren. The adventurers grumbled, but they still needed the coin. "Now we know she was in Velles, at least. Someone else may have seen her. Give it another day." She stood up and gathered her coat. "Cinna and I are going to the library."

7

The Library of Reverie was both the biggest library in Velles and one of the oldest buildings in the city, built over three thousand years ago to honor Reverie, a mystic figure from Velles's earliest days. Reverie, the person, had written the first story of Velles's founding. Reverie, the library, now held that work within its archive, along with thousands more texts and stories.

On a previous visit, Hokuren had explained to Cinna why the library was one of her favorite places. The musty smell that could only come from a collection of old books. The way the librarians treated every book with reverence. That there was always a book available, no matter the subject, and someone there who knew how to find it.

She had asked Cinna, "What do you like best about the library?"

"I like walking on that big rug in the lobby," came the reply.

The rug led from the massive double doors at the entrance straight to the front desk in the vaulted lobby. The rest of the ground floor lay beyond doorways to the right and left of the desk, full of reading rooms and hundreds of bookshelves. Far to the right was a grand staircase for accessing the two upper floors. Sunlight streamed in from a stained-glass ceiling, depicting scrolls and tomes surrounding the figure of Reverie, a faceless man who shone with what one artist called "the light of knowledge."

Hokuren stole a glance at Cinna as they walked on that enormous rug. There was a small smile on her assistant's face. In boots, Hokuren did not experience the rug the same way as Cinna, and she doubted she would even if she were also barefoot.

The clerk at the desk was Yoland, a tall, pale human with cropped dark hair. He recognized Hokuren and greeted her with warmth, his hands spread from within the oversized green robe worn by all librarians at the Reverie.

"Ah, good to see you, Seeker! What is it today? Need another book on some family history or another? Just so you know, I haven't seen any missing cats lately." He winked to sell the joke.

Hokuren chuckled appreciatively. "Not today, thank you, Yoland." She scooted close to the desk and leaned in. Keeping her volume a notch above conspiratorial, she whispered, "Were you shown a picture of a woman you recognized earlier today?"

Yoland leaned in close as well. "Was that brutish lady with the hammer—?"

"Working for me? Yes. I've been hired to find the woman in the picture."

"I see." Yoland straightened, and his face hardened. "So, I imagine you want to know why she was here."

"Can you tell me what books she was looking at? Did she appear under duress?"

"To your second question, no." Yoland folded his arms across his chest, his body language closing off in a hurry. "She was by herself, and there was absolutely no evidence she was in any sort of danger. As to your first question, also no. She requested and received assistance from the Head Curator. Only he knows what she read or checked out."

Hokuren could not hide her surprise. "She met with the Head Curator?"

"She asked for him by his name, and they seemed on familiar terms."

So Nyana had a relationship with Head Curator Okumak Lire. He was notoriously difficult to meet with. Hokuren had once inquired if she might receive a moment of his time to express her appreciation for the library's continued existence, receiving a terse rejection in response. Being the Princess of Velles perhaps made things easier.

"The Head Curator doesn't help just anyone." Hokuren tapped her finger on the desk. She knew Yoland. Even if the clerk knew something, unlikely as it was, he would consider it his duty to keep the Head Curator's business to himself. She did not want to be stymied by Yoland's ethics. "I will need to meet with the Head Curator and ask him. Is he available? This is a matter of some urgency."

"That will not be possible," Yoland said, running his tongue over his upper lip. "The Head Curator's calendar is occupied for the next fifteen months from today's date."

"Fifteen months!" Hokuren did not have to fake her incredulity. "That's ridiculous." Yoland said nothing.

She had a card to play, one she only played because she was low on options. "I am investigating this woman's disappearance at the behest of Prince Leopold." Yoland's eyebrows rose. Hokuren continued, "If I have to, I'll ask the prince to arrange a meeting with the Head Curator. But that will cost precious time and I'm already behind. The prince will not be pleased to hear the Head Curator delayed things by pretending to be busy." She did not think even Okumak Lire could dodge a meeting requested by the prince.

"The Head Curator's not pretending to be busy. He truly is busy." Offended, Yoland's tone expressed deep disapproval.

Hokuren scoffed at this. If Lire was anything like the typical person in a position of power in Velles, he enjoyed talking about how much he did more than actually doing anything.

Yoland frowned. "Seeker Hokuren, the Head Curator receives a great deal of requests for his presence and my job is to send as many of them away as possible." Now that Hokuren could believe. Yoland sighed with resignation. "But you invoked Prince Leopold, so I will at least ask him. Please wait here."

Hokuren slumped against the desk as Yoland ascended the grand staircase. "He's going to hold this against me every time I visit from now on."

Cinna put her elbows on Yoland's desk. "What if the curator guy won't see us? Are you really going to go talk to the prince?"

"I have little option. If Lire met with Nyana, then he might know something about why she left the castle or where she planned to go. I have to talk to him."

"And what if he doesn't tell you anything?" Cinna had something on her mind, but Hokuren could not figure out what. Instead, she continued to follow Cinna's questions.

"I don't know. I'm hoping he'll at least let us see the record of Nyana's visit. It would have a list of the books she checked out."

"If it's important and you think the curator won't let you see it . . . should we steal it?"

Hokuren didn't expect that response and put a finger to her lips with alarm. "Shh! Cinna, this is a quiet library and sound carries. We are absolutely not going to steal anything."

Cinna lowered her voice, but didn't give up. "Boss, you said it was important to get something out of this trip. Where are the records kept? I have experience with sneaking into places." She gave Hokuren a sly smile. "And sometimes items mysteriously go missing when I'm around."

Hokuren groaned. She recalled Cinna staring at the expensive vases in Lord Doubtwell's office. "You didn't steal from Doubtwell, did you?"

"No, I work for you. I'm out of the thieving game," said Cinna, waving her hands. "When I was on the streets, desperate for food, or money to buy food, I picked a few pockets, stole a few trinkets. Even a few valuables." Cinna was straightforward, neither ashamed nor proud. Hokuren could understand how, when faced with starvation, theft became appealing. "I've stolen things guarded by people much more vigilant than librarians in robes and slippers. I could find that record and bring it to you."

"We don't want to get kicked out and never let back in. I love this place."

"I'll be the one getting kicked out." Cinna's voice rose with her excitement level. "You can tell them I acted on my own and you had no idea. If I get kicked out—well, I'll miss the carpet, I suppose."

"Hmm." This was not how Hokuren wanted to proceed, but Cinna was right. She wanted to get something from this trip. And she suspected that even if she spoke to Lire, the Head Curator would stonewall her. If he and Nyana were friendly, he would have no reason to tell her anything.

And it was unusual for Cinna to push so hard for something. Hokuren almost always decided what to do, and Cinna went along with it. It was encouraging to see her argue for a course of action. She wanted to contribute, and Hokuren appreciated that. However, the only things

Cinna pushed for were to beat people up or, now, commit theft.

"Come on, this could be our only option, right?" Cinna pleaded as Hokuren deliberated with herself.

"You sure you won't get caught?"

"I'm great at being ignored."

Hokuren fought her instinct to say no. That record could be quite valuable. "Okay. Here's what we'll do. We'll give the Head Curator a chance. If he gives me the information I need, we don't need to risk any theft. But if he doesn't, I'll give the sign and leave. And you can do your thing."

"What's the sign?"

"If I get what I need, when I'm leaving with Yoland I'll say 'Good day, and thank you.' If I don't, I'll say 'This was a waste of time.' Got it?"

"Waste of time, got it, boss." Cinna's face brightened. The flecks of blue in her eyes seemed to dance, but when Hokuren blinked and looked again, they were still. "I'll hide myself nearby, and if I get the sign, I'll go steal the record."

"The records room is on the second floor. It should be visible from the staircase, so you can't miss it." Hokuren pointed up past the staircase, and Cinna nodded. "Now, you can't actually take the record. Then it will be obvious we stole it. You need to memorize it."

Cinna looked stricken, as if she had been told to eat the record. "You know my memory. What if I can't? What if there's a whole bunch of books listed?"

"Do the best that you can. Even knowing some books would be better than none." Putting her hand on Cinna's shoulder, she said, "No one other than librarians should ever be on the second floor. If you can't get the record without getting caught, abandon it." When Cinna said nothing, Hokuren pressed her. "Is that clear? I don't want to hear you got in some fight with the battle pages."

"I already said I wouldn't get caught. But okay, if it doesn't seem possible, I'll leave." Cinna tilted her head. "Wait, what are the battle pages?"

"They're a group of—" Hokuren cut herself off when Yoland appeared on the staircase, returning with the Head Curator's answer. He stopped when he was halfway down to the first floor and beckoned.

"The Head Curator has graciously agreed to see you, Seeker," Yoland said, his tone formal.

Hokuren nodded. "Wait for me outside, please," she said to Cinna.

"You got it, boss." Cinna walked out of the library through the front door. Hokuren followed her with her eyes, hoping Yoland noted Cinna leaving as well. Only once Cinna had left did she turn back and climb the stairs.

Lire's office was on the third floor, also home to the library's most prized publicly available books and private reading rooms reservable for a price. Hokuren followed Yoland through a maze of hallways before she found herself in front of a door with "Head Curator" written in large, ornate font.

"This is the office of the Head Curator," said Yoland, apparently in case Hokuren had forgotten how to read. "I'll wait for you outside and escort you back to the entrance when you have concluded your meeting."

Hokuren knocked on the door before entering. Inside, she encountered a mountain of a man, almost seven feet tall and heavyset. Okumak Lire. He occupied an immense chair that appeared custom-made to hold his bulk, and his large glasses with lenses thick enough to magnify his eyes did little to reduce his intimidation factor.

A teapot and two cups and saucers lay on the desk between them. Hokuren was not offered any tea.

Lire stared in stone-faced silence at her. She would start out with a polite greeting, she decided, since it did not appear as if she would receive one from her host. "Good day, Head Curator. Thank you for agreeing to meet with me."

Okumak Lire waved a large hand. He could palm her head like she would an orange if he wanted. "You threatened to bring the prince down on me. I had little choice." His baritone voice boomed in the small office.

"I do apologize, I merely—"

"You merely want me to violate the code of privacy we maintain at our esteemed library because you've been hired to find someone who doesn't want to be found. Do I have the general idea?" Lire regarded her from behind his glasses, looking down. She felt like a bug, here to annoy Lire until he decided he had enough and squished her.

"I don't find your framing—"

"I understand you avail yourself of our collection regularly," Lire went on. Being interrupted once by this man was irritating, but twice was aggravating. It reminded her too much of working with Lord Doubtwell. With the patience learned from that experience, Hokuren kept herself outwardly calm. Lire narrowed his eyes. "Would you like it if we told anyone who asked what you were reading?"

Hokuren needed to avoid getting defensive. "If I was in trouble and someone thought my choice in reading material might help me, yes." There was little point in continuing to play his games. "I'm searching for the prince's daughter, Nyana. You met with her after she left the castle. You're the only person I know of who has done so. I'm worried someone coerced her into leaving, and you might have information I need."

"Nyana is not in trouble, nor was she coerced." Lire continued to stare at Hokuren. He did not blink often.

"How do you know this?"

Lire shifted in his seat. "You know, I am not surprised the prince wants to find her. I am surprised he hired you."

Hokuren was unsure how to take this, ignoring it on the grounds that Lire's opinion of her hire was irrelevant. She refused to let him change the subject. "You seem to know Nyana well, Head Curator. I'm given to understand few do. Do you know why she left the castle and caused her father great worry?"

Lire laughed, a thundering series of deep guffaws. Hokuren resisted the urge to put her hands to her ears. "Great worry? That's a good one. Well, I bet he's worried about something, anyway. Tell the prince that she's fine. It was her decision to leave the castle. She's an adult and can leave when she pleases. You should quit this commission and leave Nyana alone."

Unconvinced by his cryptic responses, Hokuren asked, "Do you know Julien Davenport? Was she with him?"

"Julien Davenport has given Nyana much more support than her father ever will," said Lire, a nonanswer to her question. "And that's all I'll say on that." He stood up. "In fact, that's all I'll say to you at all."

As she feared, Lire was a dead end. "At least tell me what books she was interested in. If I must, I can have the prince fill out an official request with the Watch for a copy of her records, but wouldn't it be easier to avoid all that paperwork?"

"No." Lire moved to the door and opened it. "If the prince wants to, he can file his request. I believe I have given you enough of my time and answered your questions. They weren't the answers you wanted, but they're the ones you'll get."

Hokuren didn't want to stop here. She wanted to keep chipping at Lire, see if something shook loose. But he had all but grabbed her and tossed her out. In fact, that might be what he did next, and it would hardly trouble him to do so. With a terse word of thanks, she left.

Neither she nor Yoland spoke on the way back. When they were on the first floor, in the entry, she couldn't see Cinna. She hoped that meant Cinna had a good hiding spot. "This is a waste of time," she said, hoping Yoland wouldn't wonder why she spoke so loudly. For the first time in their partnership, it would be up to Cinna to salvage something from a library visit.

8

Cinna should have hoped for Hokuren to succeed in her visit with the curator, but when she heard Hokuren declare the visit a waste of time, her heart rate quickened in excitement.

Huddled under the lowest steps of the grand staircase, Cinna hid from Yoland's view at the front desk. The clerk returned to his seat once he escorted Hokuren out, and his position gave him a clear view of anyone climbing the staircase. Cinna needed another visitor to show up to get Yoland out of the way.

A half hour passed in silence. Cinna had become accustomed to sitting in the reading rooms of the library for long periods while Hokuren read. There she could view the colorful book covers, do light exercises on top of the large tables—if no one else was around—and smell the familiar odor of the old books. Nothing fascinating, but it was something.

The lobby, by contrast, was stifling in its sterility. There were no smells nor anything to look at, either. Cinna grew bored, her patience tested. Even the floor, a smooth, chilly stone, was an uninteresting surface to crouch on. She did not know how often the library had visitors, but she needed one to appear soon or she would lose her mind.

How could Yoland sit there at his desk and do nothing for hours each day, surrounded by emptiness? Cinna feared few things, but a life of tedium like his made the short list.

After what seemed like an hour, a new person mercifully entered the library and made his way to Yoland. "Roberto," Yoland greeted him, with the warmth he showed to Hokuren before she gave him difficulties. "Come to continue your look into the Hortic Era?" Cinna had no idea what the Hortic Era was, but she hoped when you studied it, the librarian had to spend a lot of time with you.

Cinna risked peeking out from the staircase. The visitor, Roberto, wore a bright red cloak and spoke in low tones she could not make out. "Come on, move," she muttered to herself as he yammered on.

Finally, Roberto shut up and Yoland bowed and directed him with a hand. "Please, come with me." He led Roberto into one of the branching hallways on the first floor. Perfect. Now was her chance.

Darting out from her hiding spot under the stairs, Cinna leaped over the railing and ran up to the second floor. No one appeared to be in sight as she ascended. The second floor seemed to contain nothing but books. Shelving units full of the things, each twelve feet tall if Cinna's estimate was correct, spread in every direction from the central staircase. The records were on this floor, but she did not know where.

She was about to pick a random path to take when something in the corner of her eye caught her attention. A small room to the right, past rows of shelving units. It could be the records room. Hokuren had told her it would be visible from the staircase.

Cinna crept on her toes, the second floor's wood smooth and well-maintained. The high shelves blocked her sight beyond the narrow corridor of the row she walked through. If someone crossed in the aisle between bookshelves, she wouldn't see them until it was too late.

She could hear them, however, and as she moved down the row, she caught the sound of shuffling feet ahead. Which row the footsteps might enter was an open question.

Glancing around, Cinna found a gap in the books on the lowest shelf nearby. She squeezed into the space without thinking further, folding her torso against her thighs and putting her legs on top of the books stacked upright on the shelf. Her small size often served as a liability, but if she were any bigger, she would not have fit. She shuffled against the back of the shelf, uncomfortable but safe from view unless someone bent down to look. If they did, she would be in a tough position to defend herself.

With her back contorted and head nearly pressed against her stomach,

Cinna held her breath as the footsteps grew louder, headed toward her. A few seconds later, the bottom of a librarian's green robe appeared in front of her.

Cinna grew antsy as the librarian stood still, worried she had been spotted.

"Ah, where does this go?" the librarian muttered.

There was a gentle scraping sound above her, the librarian placing books on the second shelf.

"C-A-F... C-A-G..." the librarian read out letters. "C-A-M... There we go."

Cinna made a small, silent prayer, asking any god listening to make sure the librarian didn't put books on the bottom shelf. She included in her prayers a promise to think later about what the god might gain from such an intervention.

Whether due to the divine or plain luck, the librarian finished filing books without checking the bottom shelf. Cinna didn't dare to so much as breathe until the librarian's retreating steps grew inaudible, even as she started feeling lightheaded. With the coast clear, Cinna wiggled out of the shelf and back onto the wood floor. Stretching her aching back, she hoped that would be the only time she needed to attempt something like that.

Her fortune held, and she made it to the room without encountering further librarians. She opened the unlocked door a crack and slipped inside, shutting it behind her with the faintest of clicks.

The records room was thin, perhaps only ten to fifteen feet wide, but deeper than it seemed from the staircase. Filing cabinets lined the walls and there was a small desk in the center, on top of which sat blank records sheets and quill pens beside an inkwell. Cinna carefully opened one of the drawers of the first cabinet to the left. It overflowed with records. The filing cabinet drawer extended to a distressing length. She couldn't count the number of records in the drawer, but it had to be over one thousand. She surveyed the dozens upon dozens of similar drawers that promised similar amounts and cursed.

There wasn't enough time to search through all the records. Cinna twisted her fingers together, furious to be stymied immediately. There had to be some sort of filing system, otherwise the librarians wouldn't bother storing the records. Cinna examined the cabinets and found letters written on each drawer. Alphabetical order, of course. She slapped herself on the forehead for almost missing something so obvious.

Cinna followed the labels on the cabinets until she came upon the "N" cabinets and, after a couple of missteps when trying to suss out how to spell "Nyana," found the records she was looking for. The princess had only three records in her name. Cinna pulled them all out.

The records contained the books checked out along with dates. Nyana checked out two books three years ago, one last year, and then the final one during her most recent visit six days previous. Four book titles in total to memorize, which at first glance seemed manageable.

Cinna's heart plummeted as she read the book titles. They were written in script. She knew print lettering, and with the practice Hokuren had put her through, her reading and writing had steadily improved. But script, used only in formal writing, comprised an utterly different, more aesthetically pleasing alphabet.

An alphabet Cinna never learned.

Sweat developed on her brow. Hokuren had asked her to memorize the titles, but she only saw loops and scribbles. Her anxiety grew as she weighed her two options, neither of them good. One was to tell Hokuren she couldn't read script and thus had failed the mission. Cinna dismissed this one straight away. Instead, she could take the records, which would give them the information they wanted. But Hokuren specifically told her not to do that.

A pit grew in her stomach, expanding with each passing second. Nervousness was an unusual and unwelcome emotion. Think. There had to be another option. Cinna scanned the room, hoping for inspiration to strike. Her eyes settled on the blank records and quill pens. An idea appeared, struggling to the surface of her consciousness. Maybe . . .

Yes! When Cinna placed a blank record sheet over Nyana's, the ink from Nyana's was visible through the blank record. Cinna smiled. She might not be able to read the script, but she could trace it.

She grabbed a quill pen and the inkwell. Quill pens were out of fashion, and Cinna had never used one. On the rare occasion she wrote, she always used a magic pen. A simple spell caused a pen to dispense ink when pressed against a surface, and they were less expensive than quills.

Despite Cinna's lack of experience with it, she considered the idea of a quill pen rather simple. Dip it in ink, write on the paper, repeat when the ink ran dry.

In practice, this turned out to be more difficult than she imagined. The ink had a tendency to drip off the quill when she did not want it to. And the quill required a specific touch. If she pushed too hard, it made a big blob. If she pushed too lightly, not enough ink transferred to the paper. Cinna messed up the first three new records she attempted. Inky splotches and stains dotted the table as the failures piled up. Her headband grew damp with perspiration as she felt the time ticking, every moment increasing her chances of discovery.

On the fourth try, she got the hang of it. Sort of. The traced copy Cinna made had none of the original's elegance, but when she compared the two records side by side, her little squiggles looked reasonably similar to the squiggles on the original.

With something at least halfway decent, she breathed easier for a moment until she saw the mess around her. Ink blobs and smudges marked the table, the floor, and many of the blank records, not to mention her hands, clothes, and even her toes. Her aborted attempts, which she had crumpled into balls and tossed in frustration, littered the room as well. But her mind's internal clock screamed for her to leave and not worry about cleaning.

Cinna pinched the copy she made between two of her least-stained fingers and blew on it until the ink seemed dry enough. Folding it, she shoved it into the front of her trousers, where she figured no one would search even if they caught her.

She crammed Nyana's records back in the drawer, almost where she found them. Close enough.

As Cinna turned to leave, the door opened. She froze, seeing nowhere to hide in the room. She stood in front of the table and steeled herself for what was to come.

The person who entered was not one of the robe-wearing librarians. This librarian had a dangerous air: tall, broad-shouldered, and clad in leather armor colored white and marked with black horizontal lines.

His movements were smooth enough that Cinna immediately took him seriously as a threat. His helmet didn't cover his face, so Cinna got a good look as his eyes widened before he gave a knowing nod.

"So, the Head Curator was right to suspect you might try this," he said, his hand on his hip where he had a short, thick hand axe hanging from a loop in his belt. "I'm here to escort you to the City Watch, to answer for your crime, Seeker Hokuren."

Once again, she had been confused for her boss. "Hokuren?" Cinna said, attempting to sound confused. "Who's that?"

The man regarded her anew. "Bare feet? Highly irregular. No, you aren't Hokuren. Don't match the description one bit. Who are you? One of the street urchins?" He rubbed his chin. "You'd smell worse, I think."

"Uh, yes, I'm an urchin! And I'm lost," said Cinna, frantically contemplating how to get out of this situation. The man was muscular and wearing enough armor that taking him on in the cramped quarters of the records room would be tricky, and he blocked the only door.

"Lost? Not sure I believe that." The man glancing around the room in disgust. "Did you come here to steal or vandalize? Or both?"

"Er, I thought maybe there would be some expensive books here." Cinna kept her eyes on him, reaching her hand back to search blindly for the inkwell. Made of a precious, delicate glass, it had some weight to it.

The man laughed. "Someone like you wouldn't find any buyers for books." He crossed his arms over his chest. "Assuming that's all this is. Well, come quietly with me to the City Watch. We'll figure out the truth when you're in a jail cell."

"Sorry, but I'm too busy for jail." Her fingers found the inkwell and gripped it. She would fight to the death before ever going back into a cell.

"You may have misunderstood me. I was not making a request."

Cinna tensed as he pulled his hand axe from its belt loop. "I'm not afraid of librarians."

"Librarians, that's a good one," the man said, but there was no conviviality in his words. "The battle pages are not ordinary librarians."

He swung the axe at her, leading with the blunt side. Cinna backflipped onto the table, landing on her feet. Some ink spilled from the well in her hand. She hopped behind the table so it now stood between her and the battle page. He cursed and for a few moments they engaged in a little dance as Cinna's every movement kept the table between them.

"Enough," he said, winding up and putting all of his might into an overhand blow, bringing the axe down on the table with a thunderous crash that broke the virtual silence of the library. The table split down the middle, scattering quills across the room and empty records sheets into the air.

The battle page kicked the pieces of the table aside, giving Cinna her opening. She stepped forward and splashed the remnants of the inkwell into his face as he lifted his axe once again.

He howled and then gargled as the thick black gloop flooded his eyes and mouth. Collapsing to his knees, the battle page rubbed at his face in desperate agony. Cinna dashed to the door past the writhing page, bursting out of the records room.

She made a mad sprint for the staircase, no longer concerned with stealth. Another battle page appeared in the aisle as she ran.

"Stop her!" came a garbled cry from behind her, the first battle page still working on his ink problem.

The second battle page ran toward her, but if he expected Cinna to turn around, he was sadly mistaken. She jumped on the shelves to the right and launched herself leftward, getting enough height to grab the top. Pulling herself up, she continued her escape across the top of the shelving unit, passing the page.

"Tricky," he said, doubling back to follow her on the ground.

When she came to a gap between rows, she judged the jump to be too far, so she let herself fall back to the floor. The battle page pursued, behind her now.

"Stop, thief!" he called, quite an unfair accusation. She had not stolen anything. Turning around, she saw him pull out his axe and ready a throw.

Stuck in the aisle, Cinna had little room to dodge, and the axe was too heavy to catch. She grabbed the thickest book she could find and faced the page.

With a roar, the page threw the axe at her, spinning it across the horizontal plane. Cinna held the book up in front of her. With a thunk, the axe buried itself in the book, leaving her untouched.

She glimpsed the cover before throwing the book and axe onto the ground. "Thanks, *Philosophies of the Hortic Era*," she said, continuing her run to the staircase.

"No!" The battle page cried behind her. "What have you made me do to this beautiful book?"

Looking down, she did not see Yoland at his desk, a slight consolation for the mess on the second floor. She ran down the staircase two or three steps at a time, then across the stone floor of the lobby until the rug swallowed the sounds of her footsteps. She burst through the double doors of the entry and into the relative safety of the streets of Velles.

Hokuren was outside, pacing back and forth. When she saw Cinna, she said, "There you are. It's been so long, I was starting to think—"

"Run, boss!" said Cinna, putting urgency into the command.

Hokuren didn't ask questions and fell in behind Cinna. The cobblestone streets of this fancier part of Velles had light foot traffic, but they attracted stares from those they jogged by. Hokuren's outfit in particular, with its heavy coat, layers, and long boots, looked an odd choice for a run.

When Cinna had led them far enough from the library, she stopped beside a bench near a shuttered shop. The dilapidated sign welcomed visitors to Harriet's Confectioneries, but there were no sweets to be found.

Hokuren flopped down onto the bench, a hand on her heaving chest. Cinna's own heartbeat quickened, both from the exertion of the last few minutes and the buzz of what she had just pulled off. She experienced few greater thrills than escaping a chase.

"It's been some time since I ran like that," said Hokuren between gulps of air. "What happened?"

"Well, I found out what a battle page is. They're violent for librarians. Lucky for me, the Hortic Era had a lot of philosophies." Cinna ran through an animated summary of her encounter with the page in the records room and the aisle, with only the smallest of embellishments. People walking by took notice, but like all good Vellesians, they paid no mind. It was not their business.

Cinna wrapped up her story. "The battle pages saw me, boss, so I failed the mission. I tried to throw them off by telling them I'm some random urchin."

Hokuren shook her head. "A good thought, but Yoland knows who you are. Lire will put this together with the conversation I had with him and come to the correct conclusion. You aren't to blame, I should have guessed he would expect we try this." She sighed. "We'll have to be careful from now on. The battle pages may come after us, especially since you injured one of their own."

"They'll have to get in line, boss."

"Funny." Hokuren motioned to the bench, and Cinna sat down beside her. "So, how many of the book titles were you able to memorize before the battle page showed up?"

"None." Cinna indelicately reached into the front of her trousers, unfazed by both Hokuren's frown and the appalled goggle of a passerby, and produced the copy of Nyana's records. "I got it, though."

Hokuren stared at Cinna's hand and the records. "You got ink all over your hands. And didn't I tell you not to steal the record?"

"I didn't, boss," she said, peeved that Hokuren jumped to that conclusion. "I couldn't memorize it because I can't read script. But you never said I couldn't make a copy." She looked at her hands, stained dark. "The ink and I fought. I lost."

"A copy? That's a good idea."

Cinna forgave Hokuren in response to the praise.

Hokuren took the paper, avoiding touching either Cinna's grubby hand or the ink smudges on the paper. "We'll have to teach you to read script. I'll add it to the list."

"Ah, come on, boss, it never comes up," groaned Cinna.

"It just came up." Hokuren unfolded the copy of the record. "Let's see what you got." She scanned it, clicking her tongue.

"Can you read it?" Cinna asked anxiously.

"Yes, it's good enough. Your little foray was a success, even if you were found out," Hokuren said, as Cinna breathed a small sigh of relief. "A couple of these books are in the basement, where they keep the high-value books. They're usually only available under special circumstances. No wonder Nyana went right to the Head Curator."

"We can't really go back in and ask to see them, can we?"

Hokuren folded the paper up and stuck it in one of her coat pockets. "No, we definitely cannot." Cinna was silent, thinking the whole thing had been for nothing, but Hokuren continued as if she had read Cinna's mind. "Oh, you didn't do this for nothing. We are going to read these books. We just aren't going to do it at the Library of Reverie. I've got another friend for you to meet."

9

Hokuren and Cinna traversed deep into the Haven, Velles's densest residential district. The city rebuilt its walls to encompass this relatively new district several generations ago, its most recent expansion. An exercise in efficient housing, the Haven was criticized or lauded—depending on who you asked—for comprising rows and rows of similar houses laid out in a perfect grid, where color was the only character. Homeowners painted their houses wild colors to differentiate theirs from the others, leading to the district's unofficial name: the Peacock district.

Hokuren pointed out Maol's bright yellow house, fitted snugly between pink and mint green houses, to Cinna as they approached.

"This whole place always spooks me. These colors can't hide that it's so sterile," said Cinna, sneering at a nearby house with a black-and-white checkerboard pattern. "If they painted every house the same color, how would anyone would remember which was theirs? It would be like trying to find your own personal grain of rice in a paddy."

"Be nice, Maol's proud of his home." Hokuren knocked on the front door with three quick raps.

The door opened to reveal Maol Walsh, retired book-hunter extraordinaire, with crinkles in his eyes. It had been a few months since Hokuren had seen him, and she noted with dismay that he looked frailer now. He gave her a long hug. "Ah, Hokuren, my dear, it's been too long."

"I'm sorry for not coming by more often, Maol, but you know, what with one thing or another . . ." Hokuren knew it sounded trite, but she meant it.

"I understand. I had a life to lead as well when I was your age. You're here now, so come in, come in." The elderly Maol waved them into the house.

"Thank you," said Hokuren, accepting his invitation. She gestured to Cinna, who stood awkwardly at the door's threshold. "By the way, Maol, you've yet to meet Cinna, my assistant."

Maol offered his hand to Cinna, which she stared at as if it might bite before she took it. "A friend of Hokuren's is a friend of mine. You're welcome in my house."

Cinna murmured, "It's a lovely home. Great color choice." She seemed flustered, unused to being treated warmly.

"I'll put on some tea," Maol said, directing Hokuren and Cinna to sit down on his feather-stuffed couch. The home was cozy, with a small sitting room adjacent to the kitchen. "I trust you have a reason for coming beyond a social visit, but I hope you also came with a bit of time and will indulge an old man on his deathbed."

Hokuren borrowed books from Maol from time to time, and all he ever wanted in return was time spent chatting. He had suffered from acute loneliness since his husband passed away four years ago. "You're still far too spry, Maol, your mind too sharp. I see no deathbed here," Hokuren said as Maol laughed. "And of course we can stay, but we don't mean to impose."

"No imposition at all, none at all." Maol operated the teakettle in his kitchen, remaining in conversation distance from the sitting room. "I was planning on staring at the wall for the next couple of hours, but I can squeeze you in now and push that back into this evening."

"That better be a joke," said Hokuren. Maol's only reply was more laughter.

Maol brought over the tea alongside some cookies. Cinna's eyes lit up at the food while Hokuren poured for all three.

For the next hour, Maol and Hokuren engaged in light conversation while Cinna ate all the cookies with no apparent shame. Maol was interested in hearing about the goings-on in Hokuren's life, especially her cases. It had been this way since they met five years ago.

When the conversation wrapped up, Maol asked, "So, what did you really come here for?"

"You're my best hope for finding some books." Hokuren got out the copy of Nyana's record and handed it to him. "Do you have any of these on hand?"

Maol put his reading glasses on and peered at the list of four books. "In the interest of decency I shall not comment on the penmanship."

"I was under pressure," grumbled Cinna.

"This is quite the list. Do I want to know why you want these in particular?"

Hokuren demurred. "I'm sure you do, but I can't tell you until I'm done with the case."

"Hmm," said Maol, running a hand over his bald scalp, his only remaining hair a U-shape on the back of his head. "My collection contains the first three. I don't have the last one, *The Gilded Martials*, although I've read it. Never could convince its owner to relinquish it to me. A shame."

"I would greatly appreciate the three you have," Hokuren said, keeping her disappointment to herself. The only book Maol didn't have was the book Nyana had checked out on her most recent visit. "Can you tell me what *The Gilded Martials* is about?"

"Oh, a pretentious private school outside the city." Maol chuckled. "The Sanctuary of the Eclipse."

Cinna, who had been paying their conversation almost no mind, snapped to attention. "The what?"

Maol took in her sudden interest with a smile. "Ah, you know of it? Even though it's only five days' ride from Velles, few here do. They'd rather keep it that way, of course." He peered at her. "How do you know it?"

"Uh," said Cinna. "I've heard of it." She clenched her hands into fists in her lap and looked away.

Hokuren caught Maol's eye and said, "What do you know of it, Maol?"

"The Sanctuary's a private boarding school, I guess you could say. It focuses on providing a sort of martial arts training along with tutoring in the subjects of math, writing, history, et cetera. It's where the nobility sends their pampered but otherwise useless children to when they don't know what to do with them. Lots of third and fourth sons and daughters."

Cinna looked down, disquieted.

Until now, Hokuren had been unaware that the Sanctuary was an exclusive rich kids' school, because Cinna had only said she learned to fight there. The Sanctuary had not provided Cinna any of the education Maol mentioned. She had been there for ten years and yet could barely read and write before meeting Hokuren and undergoing dedicated lessons.

Cinna was reluctant to talk about her time there. But with Nyana showing interest in the Sanctuary, she might know something that would help.

"Though it wasn't always like that," continued Maol, oblivious to Cinna's discomfort. "Started hundreds of years ago. A cult built it and sealed themselves off from the rest of the world." He grinned at Cinna. "Do you also know about that? Although the Sanctuary has changed, the lack of contact with the outside world continues, doesn't it?"

"Guess so," muttered Cinna, still staring at the floor.

"Could I borrow the three books you do have?" asked Hokuren. "I can't get them from the Library of Reverie because—" She racked her brain but failed to come up with a story that stayed truthful without being incriminating. "—of reasons."

"You stole this list from the library," Maol said, a knowing look on his face.

"Yes." So much for coming up with a story.

"I figured. But it's not my business. You may borrow them, but please return them. They are originals and of great value to me."

Hokuren put her hand over her heart. "You know how I treasure books, Maol. I will take the utmost care of them."

The book collector went to his basement and returned with the three books. He held up the thinnest book first. "In my hand, I have *The History of Senara*, which is a history about the goddess Senara." He grinned. "I suppose you could have figured that out."

"I like a title that's straight to the point," said Hokuren.

"Here is *On the Nature of Souls*," Maol went on, "a book that explains what a soul is and how it interacts with us and the world. Finally, we have *Transference For the New Era*. It's also about souls, actually. Focused on the process of soul transference from one person to another." He placed all three books on the table in front of Hokuren.

"Is it possible they could do that? Magic was more powerful in the past, but that's another level." Transferring souls sounded far-fetched, even for magic.

"I don't know. I'm just an old man. That author seems to take it for granted, though."

"Thank you, Maol. I promise I will bring these back."

"I wish you luck, Hokuren." Maol glanced over at Cinna, a twinkle in his eye. "Take a cookie for the road. You seem to enjoy them."

"They're excellent," said Cinna, holding out her hands so Maol could offer the largest remaining cookie.

Bidding Maol farewell, Hokuren and Cinna returned home, where Hokuren settled into her coziest chair to read. Curling up with a book in hand and some hot tea beside her was one of Hokuren's greatest comforts. While she read, Cinna moved through a series of exercises to pass the time. Hokuren had found this distracting when she first hired Cinna, but had grown used to it.

The History of Senara was a checkout from three years ago, the oldest of the records, so Hokuren began with it. Hokuren had read about Senara in other literature before. Originally the god of nature, protector of forests and plant life, Senara created the elven race. According to the stories Hokuren had read, the Primordial Ones created both the gods and most of the animals and monsters that roamed the land. Then they created humans.

Senara created the elves based on the human blueprint provided by the Primordial Ones, which explained why elves resembled humans so closely. Senara could only change so much.

Hokuren opened the book and started reading. After a few minutes, she said to Cinna, "It says here that the Primordial Ones told Senara not to create any life as intelligent as humans." She did not need to look up from her book. Cinna, always an active listener when Hokuren spoke to her, would pay attention. "This was a problem when she made the elves. She angered the Primordial Ones."

"Were they ever mad at the god that made goblins and ogres, boss?" grunted Cinna, amid a series of one-handed push-ups.

"Goblins and ogres aren't that smart. I guess Barduk followed the rules when he made them." Although, Hokuren chastised herself, she had never met a goblin. There could be some smart ones. "Anyway, Senara created the elves and then went into hiding. She feared the wrath of the Primordial Ones, who command the demons that hunt her to this day."

"Demons?" Cinna was now doing some complicated stretches, contorting her body in ways that made Hokuren's muscles ache just watching. "And these demons have never found her? After thousands of years?"

Hokuren kept reading. "Senara is very good at hiding, apparently. The book says she hides within the souls of the elves themselves, which makes it hard for the demons to sense her."

Cinna's face was hidden within the depths of the pretzel she made of herself, arms and legs twisted to impossible angles. "I'm not buying this, boss. I'm pretty sure there's no god inside of me."

"She's in one elf's soul, not every elf. She lives within the soul until the elf passes away and then moves to the next." Hokuren rubbed her chin. "The author would prefer that Senara make herself known and guide her people once again."

"Ha," said Cinna. She now engaged in much more conventional stretching, sitting on the floor with her legs straight, bending over to touch her head to her shins. From this position, she looked over at Hokuren and rolled her eyes. "This elf doesn't need any guidance from a cowardly god like that."

"No?"

"If I were to follow a god, it would be one that faced its troubles head-on. Give me a god that doesn't run from consequences and maybe I'll listen to it." She considered for a moment. "But probably not."

"They call the elf with the soul the . . . vessel." Hokuren stopped at the word, looking up at Cinna. Anne had mentioned Nyana was supposed to be a goddess's "vessel" during her interview in the castle, though she hadn't known what it meant. Senara had to be that goddess. According to the book, the elf with Senara in their soul gained no special powers, which was why figuring out which elf had her was so difficult. But Leopold must have a reason to want Nyana to be the vessel.

"Nyana's supposed to have a goddess living in her?" Cinna was winding down, her face flushed from her exercises.

"It does say Senara likes to choose powerful or wealthy elves as her vessel."

At this, Cinna made a face and rolled her eyes. "Typical."

There was no further explanation, only a request to visit a temple of Senara for more information. The book's author was an unnamed Great Sage of the Temple of Senara atop Mount Hzarygoot, which lay six days' ride from Velles. Given the age of the book, this particular sage would have been long dead, however the book suggested that any great sage would do. The Temple of Senara was still open, as far as Hokuren knew, despite Senara's long disappearance. To devote oneself to the worship of a god that had not acknowledged you in millennia was dedication. Dedication that Hokuren preferred to spend elsewhere.

Hokuren tossed the history book aside and picked up *On the Nature of Souls*—which turned out to be dry and uninformative. She skipped most of it. Souls animated living things, giving them the spark that separated them from inanimate objects. When a person died, their soul could be reused by someone being born. The book claimed that the reused soul contained echoes of the previous people it had animated.

When Hokuren read this out loud, she added, "I wonder what echoes my soul has, and if they affect me." She shivered. "I hope not."

Cinna had completed her exercises. Now she lay on the floor, arms and legs spread out, palms straight and turned toward the ceiling. This starfish pose was, Hokuren had discovered, how Cinna meditated. If allowed, this would turn seamlessly into a nap. Sometimes, she would do this in the office, and Hokuren would need to step carefully over Cinna's limbs to get around.

Eyes closed, Cinna said dreamily, "My soul is my own. No one else can have it."

"It may not be up to you."

"If my soul came from other people and I have echoes, is that why I like pie?"

Hokuren hated the idea of being the result of other people's past lives. Everyone ought to be a new person, unrestrained by the desires and tendencies of those who came before.

Leaving Cinna to her meditation-turned-nap, Hokuren read more of the book on souls, but found little of interest. By the time Cinna stirred, Hokuren had enough of the book and placed it aside. The last book, *Transference for the New Era*, awaited, but it was late in the day. Her stomach rumbled.

Hokuren recruited Cinna to assist with dinner preparations. Where Cinna's job as assistant ended and her role as houseguest began was a line increasingly blurred. Hokuren wanted to take some time to help Cinna get her own place and a sense of independence, but that was on the pile of things to put off until they found Nyana and closed the case.

For now, Cinna made her house livelier, and Hokuren enjoyed the respite from the desolate silence she had become accustomed to at home. She was in no hurry to usher Cinna out.

Once they finished preparing dinner, they sat down to steaming bowls of beef stew. Hokuren dove in without her usual decorum, her hunger increased by the smell of the food. The beef was tender, the carrots and onions soft and seasoned. The result was worth the effort.

Cinna washed all the dishes, as she insisted on doing while she stayed at the house. Hokuren had already quit arguing over the division of labor and left her to it, heading up to her loft to change into nightclothes for the evening. She removed her earrings and opened her drawer to place them back in her jewelry box.

The box was gone. A small piece of paper lay in its place.

Hokuren's breath caught. While the pendant with her mother's image remained safe on her person, one of the items in that jewelry box, a silver bracelet, was a family heirloom, passing from mother to daughter for generations.

With shaking hands, Hokuren unfolded the paper. It read: *You may have thought you'd won, but you've only started a war already lost.*

It was signed by the Master Thief.

Hokuren crumpled up the note in her hands and stormed downstairs, where Cinna placed the last pot on a rack for drying.

"Tomorrow morning, we are going straight to Lord Doubtwell," Hokuren fumed.

"Why?" asked Cinna, taken aback.

Hokuren explained the stolen jewelry box and heirloom. She smoothed the note out for Cinna to read. Cinna's expression turned dark. "Do you believe Doubtwell can do anything about this, boss?"

Truthfully, Hokuren was unsure; she acted confident for Cinna's benefit. "Yes, but I'm not sure what he and the rest of the Watch have been doing. I can get a better read on that tomorrow if I question him."

"The Watch won't get your jewelry box back," said Cinna, with more disgust in her voice than Hokuren had ever heard. "We should take the fight to Barnaby."

Hokuren shook her head. "We aren't fighting him."

"I don't mean literally." Cinna stabbed the note with a finger. "He stole right from your house after I told his thugs I wouldn't let him get away with any more of his messing with us. We can't ignore this." She gave Hokuren her sharpest stare. "We are going to his house. Tonight."

Hokuren's head spun. Cinna wanted to escalate, when they should take time to plan. "Cinna—"

"Before you say no, I'm going to tell you why." Cinna became animated, pacing back and forth in the kitchen. "The jewelry box probably isn't even there. His house has to be the one place he can't go, right? But if he left any evidence of secret hiding spots, or whatever, that should still be there. We can't wait and let him cover his tracks. We need to strike quick as a flash."

Hokuren put her finger on her chin. She didn't expect to find much of use in his home, but the possibility that he'd left something worth finding existed.

"I think you're even angrier than me," Hokuren said, eyeing her assistant.

"If I keep letting Barnaby harass you, I'm failing as an assistant and a bodyguard."

Hokuren blew out a breath. "If we go, though, we have to do it tonight. I planned to leave for the Sanctuary of the Eclipse tomorrow."

Cinna's eyes widened, and she squeezed her hands together at the mention of the Sanctuary. "We have to go where?"

"It's the only place we can visit from the list of books Nyana checked out at the library. I'd never even heard of the place until I met you, so I can't say why she would be interested. But if there's a chance that she went there, we need to follow it up."

"Okay." Cinna drummed her fingers on her arm. "Then there's no choice but to go to Barnaby's tonight."

"Hmm," Hokuren murmured. Her ideal plans for the night included nothing but sleep and preparing to travel. It would be a long trip to the Sanctuary. She sighed. "Okay, we do this, and we talk to Doubtwell tomorrow, and then you tell me what you can about the Sanctuary while we're on the road. Deal?"

Cinna hesitated. ". . . Deal."

For the next twenty minutes, they discussed the plan. Cinna wanted to go alone, because skulking around was best done that way. They finally settled on Hokuren waiting nearby, where she could get help if things went wrong.

"You can't shut me out completely. I'm the boss, remember?" said Hokuren.

"Okay, okay." Cinna grinned at her. "But this is my specialty, so I'm in charge."

"There are limits to that, of course."

With the plan settled, they awaited the moonlit night. Hokuren took the opportunity to nap, but she was still tired when Cinna shook her awake. The dim light of the second moon, Nebulus, filtered through the windows.

Hokuren yawned and gathered herself up to get out of bed. "Let's do this."

10

Cinna resisted the urge to run ahead of Hokuren as the two of them walked to the Aviary, where Maxwell Barnaby lived, despite her eagerness to prowl Barnaby's house.

She would never say it out loud because Hokuren was the boss, but action against Barnaby was well overdue. Those days spent ogling wagons would have been better spent doing what they were about to do now. In a way, she was glad Barnaby had stolen Hokuren's jewelry box. Her pleasure at this course of action made her uncomfortable, because the theft hurt Hokuren, but it had nudged her boss toward investigating the thief.

Located on a hill in the north of the city, the Aviary was home to the richest citizens of Velles. The wealthy here lived among smooth brick walkways and streetlights with life-size bird statues atop them. Residents considered actual birds a nuisance and discouraged them through the use of cats, which wandered the area. Most of Velles's homes and tenements were similar to each other, but in the Aviary each house offered unique architecture and design.

Cinna had spent less time in the Aviary than anywhere else in Velles. Any person who did not reside there was banned entry, but the City Watch mostly enforced the ordinance on street urchins. The Watch played the role of cats, roaming with numbers to hunt any that tried to sneak in.

The Watch and the city had a point. The only previous time Cinna had gone into the Aviary was while living on the streets. She had broken into a house and stolen a valuable trinket to fence. She relished the memory, having eaten well that week.

Cinna led Hokuren into Aviary Park, the only grass field maintained in Velles. A low stone wall separated it from the main street that cut through the heart of the district. At the edge of the neighborhood, just past the crest of the hill, they stopped in a secluded area shrouded in darkness by a small grove of apple trees. They were alone in the park, the only sounds the chittering of scattering rats. Not even of the riches of the Aviary, or their cats, could fully squelch the scourge of rodents that all of Velles dealt with.

"You can wait here for me, boss," said Cinna.

"What if something goes wrong?" Hokuren always liked having a plan.

Cinna preferred to improvise. Plans went awry with enough frequency that they became meaningless, at least when Cinna executed them. But if the boss wanted a plan, she would get a plan.

"Don't come after me alone. Go find your adventurer friends." Even as she spoke, Cinna scanned the street for patrolling Watch.

"They won't be awake. I'll get the Watch."

Cinna pulled a face. "Does it have to be them?"

Hokuren huffed. "I'm aware you've had issues with the Watch in the past, but I know many of the members and still trust them."

"But if Doubtwell finds out—"

"If something happens to you, the last thing I'll worry about is what Doubtwell thinks."

"Okay, get the Watch if you like." Cinna conceded the battle. Convincing Hokuren otherwise, if it was even possible, would cost too much time.

"Don't take any unnecessary risks. Got it?"

"Got it. Don't worry, boss, this will be a cinch."

Hokuren didn't look convinced.

Cinna left Hokuren, skulking across the lush grass, the sensation of the individual blades underfoot strange but pleasant. She followed the wall, crouching to keep hidden.

Barnaby's home was of the more modest variety and close to the park. These kinds of houses, while not to the same size and splendor as the wealthiest mansions deeper in, had their own lots with individual gardens. No home in any other part of Velles boasted such.

Cinna hated to give the man any respect, but she admired the audacity of Barnaby to live among the very people he stole from.

A gap in the wall gave Cinna a spot to peek from to assess the situation. Barnaby's house was dark, as expected. She had to cross the brick walkway, well-lit and open, to reach the home. Swiveling her head up and down the street, she saw plenty of manicured landscaping, but no people. Time to make her move.

She slipped through the gap and darted over the walkway midway between two streetlamps, obscured as much as possible in relative darkness. Barnaby's garden was a patch of gritty dirt that worked its way between her toes. Not so much as a flower had been planted.

Cinna tested the windows, starting on the side of the house, hoping to find one unlocked. None were, so she slipped around to the back door. She shook the doorknob to find it locked, but at least here an accessible locking mechanism beckoned.

Aside from the jail cell door a few days ago, Cinna had not picked a lock since leaving for the Sanctuary. The lockpick still felt natural in her hand, though. She expected more of a challenge from a fellow thief, but with just three pins in the simple tumbler lock, she had it open before she had really begun. Perhaps he never expected someone would dare break into his home.

The door didn't make a sound as Cinna eased it open. Another strange decision. Squeaky doors made sneaking around more difficult. This was all too easy.

Inside the darkened house, her elven eyes saw in muted gray scale using Nebulus's meager light entering through the windows. A quick tour of the lower level revealed nothing interesting in the dining and living rooms, but a small study offered promise. Cinna padded through the open doorway and onto a large rug covering most of the wooden floor. At the desk pressed against the wall opposite the door, she rifled through papers, mostly appraisals of various items Barnaby had stolen.

Cinna jiggled the desk's only drawer. Locked. A quick check confirmed this lock served as the difficult obstacle she had expected. Cinna rubbed her hands together. Few things signaled valuables like a sturdy lock.

She stuck her lockpick in and felt the small pins inside. There were five, and she needed to adjust each to the perfect position so that the midsection of the pin aligned exactly with the shear line. The pins were touchy, fighting her, sliding out of position at every opportunity. It took longer than she wanted, but eventually the pins acquiesced and clicked as one.

Several silver coins lay spread out in the drawer, the only objects behind the lock. Having begged for coins at times in her life, Cinna had seen currency from Velles and many other cities, but she recognized none of these coins. Each had a face printed on one side, with the other side left blank and smooth.

Where were all the valuables? Puzzled, she dug through the coins to check all the unique faces. Only one looked familiar, and Cinna spent a moment before it popped into her brain. Staring back at her from the silver coin was the smug, aristocratic face of Lord Doubtwell.

Cinna palmed it, thinking Hokuren would want to see it. As she pulled her hand out of the drawer, her fingers brushed an almost imperceptible thread drawn taut. A magical alarm, and an expensive one at that.

Her stomach lurched. The owner of the alarm had known she was here from the moment she opened the drawer.

Soft footsteps approached from behind, then stopped, absorbed by the rug. Cinna's heart rate spiked, and she dove hard to her right without looking back. The unmistakable click of a crossbow firing broke the silence.

The bolt tore through the sleeve of her tunic and grazed her upper left arm before sticking into the rear wall. If she had not moved, it would have embedded in her back.

Cinna leaped to her feet and spun about to find Maxwell Barnaby with a soft magical light affixed to his brimmed hat aimed directly at her.

"Did you come for the jewelry box?" Barnaby appeared much more confident than their previous meeting. "I thought you might." He held the spent crossbow in his hand, but made no move to put another bolt in it.

"We know how this ends already," she said to him. "Give me the jewelry box and I'll go easy on you." Blood trickled down her arm from the stinging wound left by the bolt. The throbbing pain would not hinder her, but it seemed to be increasing rather than subsiding as she expected.

"Things will be different, I'm happy to say," Barnaby said, remaining still. "You didn't catch the bolt this time."

Cinna took a step toward him and suppressed a wave of nausea. Her legs felt rubbery, and her eyelids were heavy. "What—?" she mumbled, tongue thick.

"Oh, you're already feeling it," crowed Barnaby. His smile was sinister. "Ever heard of the Kharlesian toad? Even a small amount of its venom is enough to knock someone out in seconds."

Cinna collapsed to her knees and then fell down onto the rug. Her body refused orders to move and her vision blurred. She mustered her strength to stand up, but only slid across the carpet an inch or two. Her headband slipped off as she rubbed against the ground, her freed hair falling in front of her face. Soon she could no longer move a muscle. She lay facedown, fear gripping her mind as her helplessness became clear.

"Having trouble?" cooed Barnaby in a taunting falsetto. "I've never used it before, so I put much more than a small amount of toxin on that bolt to be on the safe side. I expect there's a chance you don't wake up for an entire day. And who knows where you'll be when that happens?" Cinna barely heard his words. They came from far away, like an echo from a canyon. "You and your seeker friend are the only people that can bother me. And with you out of the way, the seeker won't last long."

His boots entered her fuzzy vision. As her consciousness faded, all she could think of was how she had failed Hokuren.

Barnaby backed two steps away, cursing. "Wait, these ears—You're an elf?"

After that, Cinna's world went black.

Cinna woke up with the worst headache of her life. The dryness in her eyes made each blink feel as if her eyelids were scraping past rocks. She tried to rub them, but her arms didn't move. Her left arm, the one hit by the bolt, felt numb and unresponsive. Her right arm was stuck on something behind her. Her legs met resistance when she tried to straighten them. Nothing made sense to her scattered brain.

After a minute, the fog cleared enough for her to realize her wrists and ankles were all bound together behind her back. She could scarcely do more than wiggle back and forth.

Through her blurry vision, Cinna could tell she was still in the study. Barnaby had left her alone. Moonlight shone through the window, so although she didn't know how much time had passed, it could not have been more than a few hours. She judged it to have been much less than that, even.

Her stiff shoulders and legs complained, and she could do little to alleviate the discomfort. She spent some time assessing her bonds. The thin ropes that bound her were tight and uncompromising, digging painfully into her skin. Her questing fingers trembled as they fumbled with the rope, desperately searching for a knot to undo, only to find nothing within reach. Barnaby's ropework was impeccable.

The exertion of her failed labors left her breathless, the wound in her arm throbbing. Lying trussed up on the floor like a bundle of firewood, she could understand why Barnaby had been confident to leave her alone. But Cinna spotted a way out, one that he had not considered: the sharp corners of the rectangular legs of the desk.

Having her hands bound behind her back and attached to her ankles made things difficult, but not impossible. With purposeful wiggling, she slowly made it back to the desk and brushed up against a leg. She panted from the effort, doing her best to ignore the excruciating pain in her head.

Cinna strained to maneuver herself into position, rubbing her wrists against a corner. She told herself to avoid despairing when, after several seconds of this, the ropes remained as intact as when she'd started. If this didn't work, she would be stuck until Barnaby returned. Grunting, she pushed harder against the corner, wrenching her shoulders to their limit.

One of the thin cords snapped. Relief flooded her.

Her work was slow, blind as she was to it. Each of the thin rope's many loops needed to be cut one at a time, and her hands and feet kept getting in the way. Cinna cursed and groaned and her arms and legs cramped, but she did not quit. She would never quit.

She estimated herself to be halfway through her wrist bindings when she heard two sets of footsteps, heavy and booted, approaching the study from the outside hallway. Adrenaline flowed through her and she tried to quicken her pace, even as her energy flagged. She didn't want to be restrained when whoever those boots belonged to walked in.

"The elf's supposed to be in here somewhere." The voice, a male that Cinna didn't recognize, was right outside the closed door.

"Barnaby, you here?" A second unfamiliar voice, female and deeper than the first, called out into the house. Quieter, she said, "Damn that thief. Don't want to dig through his house to figure out where he keeps his elves."

The prospect of being taken by these unfamiliar voices kept Cinna motivated. In her current state, she couldn't have fought a kitten, let alone whoever was outside the door. Another loop of rope snapped. Her wrists were almost free.

More footsteps descended the creaky staircase. Barnaby's smarm entered the conversation. "Ah, my fine friends. Where have you been? I thought you'd never arrive."

Grouchily, the male voice said, "It's been less than an hour. We were on patrol. And we're not friends, thief."

The last rope fell away. Cinna flopped onto the rug, gasping with relief and stretching damaged muscles. Even as she felt the pins and needles in her right hand as blood flow returned, she twisted and turned to the remaining ropes around her ankles, digging for the knots.

"Just being polite. I know the score," said Barnaby. "Hey, what's your lordship want with elves, anyway? He ever say?"

"He says take the elf to the cobbler, I do it," said the male voice.

"Don't you ever wonder why?"

Cinna finished freeing herself from all the ropes, tossing them aside. She tried to stand and immediately suffered a wave of vertigo that almost made her vomit. She slumped back to the ground. Right, this would be the Kora . . . Karl . . . toad toxin.

"Don't get paid extra to ask questions," said the female voice on the other side of the door. The woman sounded irritated. "Tell us where the elf is, would you?"

Cinna had to go, regardless of her body's complaints. She tried to stand again, and this time managed that small feat. Her untamed hair fell in front of her face, reminding her that she had lost her headband. She cast a glance at the desk, where her headband and lockpick lay alongside the coin with Doubtwell's face she had pocketed earlier. Wobbling, she retrieved all three items, sticking them in her trouser pockets, and limped to the window.

The window was small, but she could fit through the opening. Cinna fumbled with the locking lever, made difficult with her vision still blurred and her numb left arm near useless.

"Sure you two folks don't want a little rum first? The elf's not going anywhere. She's a bit tied up at the moment." Barnaby laughed, but neither of the others joined him.

"I'd rather be tied up myself than share a drink with you, thief. The elf. Now." The man sounded even more annoyed than his companion.

Their conversation gave Cinna the time she needed to work the latch. It clicked, one of the most welcome sounds Cinna had heard in quite some time. She pushed the window open and hauled herself out.

"Fine, fine. She's in here, nice and packaged up for you," she heard Barnaby say as she dropped outside, closing the window and ducking beneath it as the door to the study opened.

There were three exclamations of surprise, muffled but audible through the glass pane window.

"This some sort of joke, Barnaby?" the man said, close enough to the window that his words were clear. "There's no elf here, unless you have an invisible one."

"But how? The toxin should have—She was supposed to be paralyzed. I only tied her up to make her suffer." Barnaby's confusion came through, even though the window dulled the sound. As awful as Cinna felt, sitting on the ground and pressed against the side of the house, she still found the wherewithal to take pleasure in the mental image of a dumbfounded Barnaby seeing nothing but frayed rope.

"If we don't return with the elf, it'll be you who explains it," said the woman. "And you won't be talking to the boss. You'll have to explain it to *you know who*."

Barnaby's voice pitched into a whine from right next to the window.

"We have to find her!"

Cinna pressed herself against the house, hoping she wasn't visible from inside.

"*You* have to find her. Maybe she didn't get far. Come on."

Quiet reigned once more as they left the room to head outside. Cinna needed to make herself scarce. She stumbled toward the four-foot-high fence between Barnaby's property and his neighbor's. A trivial climb for a healthy Cinna was a laborious adventure with only one functional arm and leaden legs. She toppled over the fence, crashing onto the ground in the neighbor's flower bed. Moaning, she rolled onto her back, lying on some sort of pink prickly flower and staring up at the night sky. The stars blurred together in her vision, making the sky look like smeared milk.

Cinna's exhausted body made a case for going back to sleep here. The pounding in her head rose at the same rate her will faded. Maybe Hokuren would find her here and take her back to the house. She needed to rest. Resting always healed her.

No. Checking her arm, Cinna found the area around the wound had turned an ugly dark purple color. There was a toxin. If she went to sleep here, she wasn't sure she would wake up. Even if she didn't want to, even if everything hurt, she could not stop here.

Summoning all her willpower, Cinna brought herself back to her feet, battling through a renewed dizziness. Her ears picked up boots tromping through Barnaby's dirt lot, and she risked a peek through a small gap in the fence, hoping to get a sense of who they were. When she saw them, she would have gasped if she had the energy.

The two poking around the house with Barnaby were City Watch. She caught the blue-and-gray pattern of their uniforms, her vision sharpened just enough by squinting. The situation with the Watch was much worse than she thought.

They weren't too incompetent to find Barnaby. They were working with him.

Even in her bleary state of mind, Cinna knew she needed to get away and tell Hokuren. She staggered into the street, aware enough to avoid the lights, and back into the grass field of Aviary Park. The march through the lawn was grueling, each step like trudging through a snowstorm. Her muscles sent agonizing messages of pain each time they activated.

She dragged her feet one step at a time, focused only on the next step after that.

Hokuren was not at the apple tree where Cinna had left her. Cinna allowed herself a long groan. She hoped the boss had not gone to get the Watch. They were already here.

She no longer had the stamina to walk, and no place to go, anyway. She slumped against the apple tree, sliding down the trunk. The sleeve of her tunic, already torn by the crossbow bolt, ripped further and she scraped her skin against the bark. But it didn't even register. Sleep beckoned once again, and this time she was ready to submit to its call.

"Cinna!"

It took her addled brain a few seconds to identify Hokuren's voice. Where was she? A hand touched Cinna's shoulder, the left one. She flinched, the pain searing through her.

"Help," Cinna tried to say, but it only came out as a small wheeze. Her tongue was so thick it filled her entire mouth. She was thirsty. She tried to ask for water, but all that came out was an incoherent mumble.

"You're burning up. What happened?" There was urgency in Hokuren's voice, but Cinna did not share it. She was waning, her energy spent. Hokuren wrapped her arms around Cinna, yelling something, but Cinna could no longer hear. She wanted to stay here. The grass was soft. She could sleep right now and be comfortable. Some small, shrinking part of her, the part that wanted to survive, screamed in her mind to tell Hokuren what had happened. Merely to please this nuisance, she tried.

"Toad toxin," croaked Cinna before falling unconscious.

11

Hokuren carried Cinna in her arms through the streets of Velles, moving as quickly as she could toward the nearest infirmary. There were few people about, and those that she encountered didn't offer their help. At least they didn't get in her way.

Though small, Cinna was dense. Hokuren's arms grew sore from carrying her, but she refused to take a break. She could not afford to waste a second. Cinna's light brown skin had taken on an ashen tone. She had a small festering wound in her upper arm that had purpled most of the limb. Her breathing was ragged and shallow, and her head lolled back and forth with each of Hokuren's desperate steps.

Hokuren arrived at the infirmary, one of the few places in Velles open at all hours. She burst through the doors and into the general reception, calling, "Help! I need help!"

A medic rushed in from behind a curtain. With one grim look at Cinna, he said, "With me."

He led Hokuren to the other side of the curtains, where several beds lay in a grid in a large, open space. At this time of night, most of the beds lay empty. Hokuren brought Cinna to a bed near the corner of the room, where two more medics joined the one who met her at the entrance.

"What do you know?" said another medic, her red medical gown denoting her as still in training. The other two medics wore blue, the color of full residents.

"Not much," admitted Hokuren, truthfully. She couldn't tell them where Cinna had been, but she knew very little else. "She came into my house like this. I'm not sure what happened." Hokuren recalled Cinna's last words before passing out. "She only slurred two words at me. I don't know if I heard it right, but I believe she said 'toad toxin.'"

"Get Rane," one of the blue medics said to the girl in red. She nodded and dashed toward the center of the room.

"Does that mean something? What kind of toad toxins are there?" Hokuren's knowledge, though prodigious, had a significant amphibian-poison gap.

"Rane will know," the medic said. To his colleague, he said, "Pulse low, breathing weak. She needs a potion."

"To be more specific, she needs an antidote." Another medic, speaking in clipped tones, strode over on long legs. This one, an elf, wore a white smock. The lead medic. He examined Cinna's arm, where the wound was, and touched it with a gloved hand. "Long, grazing wound. Probable cause: arrow or bolt. Yellowish stain at entry point." He looked at the other medics. "How are her eyes?"

"Pupils highly dilated," said the other blue medic. "She's an elf, Rane. Her flecks are, er, shining?" He seemed unsure, as if he had not wanted to add that information.

"Shining?" Rane leaned over to see for himself. "That I don't understand. But the rest, I do." He turned to Hokuren, his manner brisk. "Your friend has been poisoned with Kharlesian toad toxin. It paralyzes and, in large doses, kills. It appears there was a large amount, delivered via projectile." He peered at her over spectacles. "What exactly happened?"

Gutted, her voice tinged with anguish, Hokuren said, "You said a lethal amount? Is there an antidote?"

"There is." Rane paused. "It's rather pricey, however. One vial of antidote requires massaging the cheek glands of thirty Kharlesian toads. But—" he trailed off, looking back at Cinna. Her breaths were audible as she struggled to take in air.

"Whatever, I'll pay it," said Hokuren, controlling her panic. "She's dying. Please, hurry."

Rane didn't move. "I think we're already too late. The paralysis ends in the heart and lungs. The victim's heart stops and they can no longer breathe. In the time you spent bringing her here, she's likely gone past the point of no return. There's no reason to waste—"

He made a strangled sound as Hokuren grabbed his smock in her hand and wrenched him toward her. "It's not a waste," she growled. "And what do you care if I pay you right now, in gold coin?" With her free hand, she hoisted the bag of coins the prince had given her. It was meant to pay rent and cover her fees for the next several days, but none of that mattered now.

"Fine." Rane pulled from Hokuren's grasp. "You've made your point. Bynum, get the Kharlesian toad antitoxin." When the medic hesitated, he shouted, "Now!"

Bynum raced off. Rane stepped past Hokuren and pulled a healing potion from a shelf near Cinna's bed. "I assume you can pay for this, too?"

"If that's what it takes," she said.

"It won't hurt." Rane and another medic slowly forced the bright red potion down Cinna's throat, a little at a time, until Bynum returned with a small vial the size of a pinky finger, half-full of a mint-green liquid.

"That's all you have?" said Hokuren, skeptically.

"This is thirty toads' worth, yes," said Rane, smoothing his smock out where Hokuren had gripped it. "It's enough, unless she's already too far gone." Rane soaked a piece of cotton with the antitoxin and delicately dabbed Cinna's wound before pressing down and covering it with bandages.

"Well?" asked Hokuren.

Rane shrugged. "We'll know soon enough. If she doesn't die, it worked."

He and the medics drifted to other patients. Hokuren sat at Cinna's bedside. She grabbed Cinna's hand and stroked the back of it.

Although Hokuren had told Cinna that she wasn't invincible, it was still difficult to believe this was the same woman who confidently left the house earlier this evening to break into Barnaby's. In the bed, with her eyes closed, Cinna had none of that energy Hokuren knew so well. She squeezed Cinna's hand. "Come on, you say you're a great healer."

For three hours, Hokuren kept this vigil. Cinna's breathing returned to normal, as did the color in her face. Even her arm looked significantly less purple. Rane returned, and after a brief examination, grunted with approval. "She'll survive."

Relief flooded Hokuren. "Thank you," she whispered.

"Some things confuse me, however." Rane twisted to face Hokuren. "She was shot at, and tied up rather severely, as per the ligature marks on her wrists and ankles." The marks, made by some sort of thin cord or rope, were still an angry red. "Yet you say she showed up at your house, and then you carried her here?"

"I already told the other medic I don't know what happened." With Cinna's recovery now in progress, Hokuren allowed herself a flash of anger at Barnaby for daring to try to take Cinna away from her.

Rane shook his head. "I'll need to have the Watch come and interview her. Standard procedure."

Hokuren nodded. She could explain what happened to the Watch and ask to speak with Doubtwell.

Rane stood up from the bed and took two steps away, then turned back. "You know what's most interesting to me, though, as a medical professional? The amount of toxin she had in her—It doesn't matter how much time passed between the initial exposure to the toxin and her receipt of the antitoxin. That was a fatal dose the moment it entered her body. And yet—" He gestured toward Cinna.

"You must have misjudged the amount," said Hokuren, carefully. "Cinna didn't die." She did not want him to suspect Cinna's healing abilities were far greater than normal. This was more than the emulation of a healing potion.

"Perhaps," Rane said skeptically, walking away.

Another hour later, Cinna's eyes opened slowly. The flecks of blue in them glowed. Cinna brought her hands up to her head, pressing her palms against it.

"Boss," Cinna said, her voice scratchy and weak. She tried to sit up, but Hokuren placed a hand on her forehead.

"Just lie down, okay? You're going to be all right, but you need rest." Hokuren smiled. The tension in her chest eased seeing Cinna awake. There were moments when Hokuren had worried she would not see it.

"I screwed up."

"Don't worry about it, everything's fine now," Hokuren said, patting

Cinna's hand. "You gave me quite a scare at the park."

"Did I look that bad?"

Hokuren almost laughed. "Well, your arm turned purple, you bled all over yourself, your eyes were bloodshot and unfocused, you had rope burns on your wrists and ankles, and then you passed out. Yes, you looked bad." She held back a shudder. Hokuren wanted to know what happened, but that could wait until Cinna recovered. She did not need to relive it right away.

Cinna checked her arms and grimaced at the burns. She poked the bandage over the injury where the toxin had entered her body. "I feel tired."

"I should imagine. It's a good thing the medics here had an antitoxin on hand." Hokuren tried to keep her voice light, as if it was no big deal. As if she had not spent hours in panic-stricken worry. "Oh, and you needed a full healing potion on top of the antidote made from toad-cheek secretions."

"Oh." Cinna flailed if she was in distress. "A full healing potion? Plus toad cheeks? That sounds expensive. I can't afford that."

"It's paid for," said Hokuren. She had already handed over all but a few coins from what the prince had fronted her.

"Boss, no. What about the rent? I probably would have survived with my, you know, healing. I'm not worth—"

"Don't finish that sentence," Hokuren snapped. "You're worth it, and I won't hear you say otherwise. You didn't see yourself. Without the potion, you would have—would have—" She stopped, blowing out a big breath.

"But—"

Softening her voice, Hokuren said, "I can get more money. I can handle going into arrears on rent and even losing the office. I can get another office. But I can't get another Cinna. Do you understand?"

Cinna looked away, her face flushed. A silence fell over them. Finally, Cinna said, "I owe you, then. You can take it from my pay."

Hokuren sighed. She needed to remember that Cinna did not understand what it meant to be cared about. "Forget about the money and rest."

Cinna settled back into the bed, then seemed to think of something and sat up. Hokuren tried to push her down again, but this time she batted

Hokuren's hand away. "Wait. Boss, I just remembered. There's something important."

"You can tell me what happened when you've recovered."

"No." With furtive glances around her, Cinna lowered her voice and leaned toward Hokuren. "We need to go. Now. The City Watch is working with Barnaby."

"What?" Hokuren's exclamation drew stares from medics and patients alike. She bowed her head apologetically, but turned back to Cinna. Hushed, she said, "Explain, please."

"Barnaby did this to me. He had the toad toxin on a crossbow bolt. He—ugh, my head hurts." She pressed her fingers against her forehead. "But he gave me the toxin and tied me up. And then he called the City Watch in on me. They were going to take me, because I'm an elf. Plus, he had this." Cinna dug into the pocket of her trousers and pulled out a coin, which she handed to Hokuren.

"Take you where?" Hokuren's mind reeled. "To one of the jail cells? Because you're an elf?"

"To the cobbler. I cut the ropes and got out of there." Cinna gave a weak smile. "You know how I hate shoes."

Hokuren stared at the image of Lord Doubtwell in the coin and felt a pit develop in her stomach. If the City Watch was indeed collaborating with Maxwell Barnaby, then the two of them were in danger. And she had no idea who "the cobbler" was.

"I can't believe this," Hokuren said. "Are you sure?"

"I know I wasn't feeling well. But I also know what I saw. They were wearing the City Watch uniforms."

What Cinna said had the ring of truth to it, even if Hokuren didn't want to believe it. She thought about Barnaby's escape from the Watch cell. Many people within the Watch could have helped him and covered it up. Including, she thought sourly, Tarleton. Hokuren would have to consider the entire institution treacherous until she had more answers.

"Okay. So, we can't stay here." Hokuren looked her assistant over, seeing Cinna struggling to keep her eyes open. "Can you walk? Be honest."

Cinna grunted, swinging her legs over the edge of the cot. She stood up, then grabbed her head and sat back down. "I can walk, but you'll need to help me out, boss. I'm sorry."

"No apologies. But if that's the case, we need a distraction." The hairs on the back of Hokuren's neck rose. She felt Rane's gaze upon her. He had been glancing at them ever since Cinna woke up, and if they tried to leave, would surely make a scene. "Luckily, I have an idea."

Hokuren glanced around the room and spied an older patient in a bed at the opposite corner. She put a finger up to Cinna and then slipped past some medics to reach the patient.

The old woman in the bed had a heavily bandaged arm in a sling. "Can I help you?" she asked Hokuren, suspicion in her voice.

"As a matter of fact, yes." Hokuren took one of the few gold coins left to her out of her pouch. "I need you to yell and scream and say the pain is too great for a minute or two. Can you do that?"

"Why?" The old woman stared at the gold coin, licking her lips. "Ah, who am I fooling? I don't actually care. Just give me the coin and you'll get your fuss."

Hokuren placed the coin in the woman's hand and returned to Cinna. "Get ready to leave."

On cue, the old woman screamed, loud enough that everyone in the room could hear, "I'm hurt! My arm, what have you done, you butchers! It hurts!"

The acting was pitiful, but it got the job done. The old woman attracted the attention of the medical staff, most crucially the eagle eyes of Rane. As they crowded around her, Hokuren limped Cinna through the curtains and out into the daylight.

Hokuren could only think of one place to go once she got Cinna out of the infirmary. Her house and office were both out of the question. The Watch would probe both places. No, the only answer was to go to the Garrulous Squirrel. She needed people who would help her.

Seeing Cinna so lethargic unnerved Hokuren. Her assistant leaned on her as they plodded to the Squirrel. If she could carry Cinna, they would make better time. But with Cinna's death no longer pending, Hokuren lacked the strength that she had summoned to haul her assistant to the infirmary.

When they finally arrived at the Squirrel, Hokuren's adventurer friends sat alone at the only table, drinking. Before they could make a crack at Cinna's haggard appearance, Hokuren said, "I need your help. And fast."

Hokuren gave them a quick rundown, without mention of Maxwell Barnaby or Lord Doubtwell, and offered payment if they could provide a place to lie low while Cinna recovered and she retrieved a few items. She had precious few gold coins remaining, but enough to entice the adventurers.

They listened and leaped into action, refusing her money. She had thought their friendship more transactional, but that would require a reassessment.

Galina carried Cinna on her back as Krusk led them to a nearby inn called Better Than Home. The name, Krusk explained, only held true if you lived in a condemned building. Paint peeled in large swaths in the lobby, and a hole in the wall of their room looked big enough for not just one mouse but an entire phalanx of rodents to march through. But it had a bed, and as dilapidated as it was, the Watch would be unlikely to include it in their search.

"I'm fine," said Cinna when Hokuren told her to sleep. She then fell asleep the moment her head hit the pillow. Hokuren pulled blankets over her, then sat on the floor nearby.

"Thanks for letting us use your room," Hokuren said to Krusk.

"I'll have no trouble finding other arrangements," said Krusk, refusing to elaborate.

Hokuren yawned, needing some rest herself after having spent a good part of the night watching over Cinna in the infirmary. "I owe you."

"We're always here to help." Krusk lingered by the door. "Although it seems we've contributed our part. I left my beer at the Squirrel half drank and should return to it, assuming Dorben hasn't already finished it off."

"You know, you really go above and beyond for your employee," said Galina. A small smile played on her face. "I don't think I've ever had a boss that would go to these lengths were I in Cinna's shoes. Figuratively speaking."

"Cinna's more than an employee," said Hokuren.

When the adventurers left, Hokuren knelt at the bed and stroked Cinna's hair, fixing any tangles her fingers came across. Cinna's near-death had shaken Hokuren.

She remembered when Cinna came in for an interview in response to Hokuren's job posting. Though she had been thoroughly unqualified, Cinna arrived with a swagger and promised to do whatever it took to succeed. And she took her assistant position seriously. Though Cinna struggled with seeing the big picture during their cases, her infectious energy and willingness to do what Hokuren could or would not had become invaluable.

She could be difficult sometimes, but Hokuren now understood how important Cinna was to her.

Going after Barnaby had been one of those impetuous decisions that Hokuren should have known better than to sign off on. Cinna nearly died because they went after her stolen jewelry box. No number of jewelry boxes would make up for that.

Yet if she had refused Cinna's plan, she may never have known of the Watch's collusion with Barnaby.

Hokuren left Cinna to rest and took out the coin with Lord Doubtwell's face on it. This coin served as the only material gain from Barnaby's home, and its importance eluded Hokuren. She stared at Doubtwell's visage and thought back to when she'd discovered Barnaby had escaped. Something the Lord Commander said had bothered her, but she never figured out what.

Hokuren closed her eyes and recalled that day in the main office. The scene unfolded in her mind like a play, with the actors repeating their lines word for word, along with any mannerisms or gestures she had witnessed. And when she finished, she opened her eyes and knew what she had missed.

When they were first learning of Barnaby's escape and disappearance, Lord Doubtwell had not only knew Tarleton's name but also that he lived with his mother.

It beggared belief that Doubtwell would know anything about

Tarleton. He prided himself on ignoring the newer members. He had even told that mousy clerk not to bother giving her name, since he didn't plan to remember it. Tarleton, barely a year into his Watch tenure, should not have rated any attention from Doubtwell.

Not catching the slipup by Doubtwell was a mistake on her part. He had been there that night and released Barnaby. It was the only explanation. Doubtwell would have a key to the cell and could pressure Tarleton to say nothing. Putting the young man on administrative leave would get him out of the way for a bit, and who would question the Lord Commander for such a decision?

She did not know who informed Doubtwell of Barnaby's capture so quickly. They brought him in past midnight, and only Cinna knew Hokuren's plan. The most obvious assumption would be that Tarleton told Doubtwell after she left, implicating himself in the conspiracy as well. But Hokuren could not see it. Tarleton was just a boy.

A dark thought pricked her mind. If Doubtwell had indeed come to the prison that night, he may have considered killing Tarleton in order to prevent him from saying anything about Barnaby and Doubtwell's partnership. If it got out that Doubtwell was working with the city's public enemy number one in any capacity, it would be a scandal.

She wished she knew why Doubtwell would disgrace himself like this. What did the Watch, or Doubtwell himself, need elves for, and why employ the Master Thief? She pressed her fingers to her forehead. Guessing was pointless. She needed more information to make any further conclusions.

The cobbler. Hokuren fumbled in her pocket and pulled out the little slip of paper from Nyana's blank diary. She took in the picture of the shoe. "Mud Guard," she said aloud. Could this be the cobbler? Hokuren scanned her memory but could not recall a cobbler shop by that name. And after her time in the Watch, she knew almost every business in Velles.

Hokuren reeled from the potential implications. If Barnaby's cobbler was this "Mud Guard," it tied him to Nyana. Did the princess know about this elf-kidnapping scheme? If so, further investigation of Barnaby, and his strange coin, became more than indulgence. It was necessary.

Once bereft of leads, Hokuren would now need to decide which to pursue first.

Dorben and Lyriel arrived with a knock, handing over the items Hokuren had requested from her house: the books she borrowed from Maol, her sword, and some food. She was hungry, and she knew Cinna would be famished when she woke up.

"Everything was exactly where you said they would be," said Dorben, leaning Hokuren's sword against a corner. Hokuren's gaze lingered on the emblem of the City Watch engraved on the sword's hilt. Would she be willing to use the sword against her friends in the Watch, if they were in on a conspiracy with Doubtwell and Barnaby?

"Your house is being watched," said Lyriel, preempting Hokuren's question. "Some Watch members loitering around outside. There was a battle page as well, oddly enough. They were all pretty chummy." Right, in less than twenty-four hours, she and Cinna had become enemies of both the City Watch and the Library of Reverie. "It was easy to sneak past them, but I have to admit, I'm more than a little curious what you did to get them all so riled up."

"Nothing," said Hokuren, between bites of the sandwich they had brought her. "Well, something. Though, trust me, you don't want to know. Because they will come after people who know."

"We don't want to know!" Dorben waved his hands at Hokuren. "I want to enjoy my drinks in peace, thank you."

"Wait." Hokuren took the slip of paper out of her pocket again. "Do you either of you adventurers know of a cobbler named 'Mud Guard'?"

Lyriel shook her head, but Dorben said, "It does ring a bell, let me think." He tapped his foot, then brightened. "Ah, yes, bought my very first pair of boots there!"

Not expecting an affirmative, Hokuren nearly choked on a bite of sandwich. "How have I not heard of it?"

"Probably because it went out of business more than ten years ago, before you even got here." Dorben sighed. "Great boots. Guarded against mud quite well, I have to say. But the place has stood empty ever since, I think. It's a terrible location."

Perhaps not as empty as he thought. "Where is it?" Hokuren thrust a pen and paper at Dorben. "Can you draw me a map?"

"I think so." Dorben's map was simple and efficient. A hallmark of a professional adventurer. Dorben finished and backed away to let Hokuren inspect it. "Is this another thing I don't want to know about?"

"Absolutely."

When the adventurers departed, Hokuren relished the quiet again. With her sandwich eaten, she sat against the wall, resting her eyes, the book on soul transference in her hands. She needed to read it, so even though she was exhausted, she told herself to power through.

She fell asleep on the floor with the book open to the first page.

Cinna clutched her blanket when she woke up.

Her mind reached for the memories of her dreams, but it was like trying to grab a handful of water. Specifics disappeared frustratingly into nothing. All that remained was the Sanctuary of the Eclipse, and the vague, lingering sense of fear.

She returned to the waking world in an unfamiliar bed and room. She sat up in alarm before seeing Hokuren on the floor, slumped against the wall, snoring lightly. This calmed her. If Hokuren was here, Cinna was where she was supposed to be.

The events of the past day came back to her. The encounter with Barnaby, her conversation with Hokuren in the infirmary, riding on Galina's back, and being placed in this bed were all hazy memories, but they at least helped her understand where she now lay. She had the smallest of headaches, but all the physical signs of her injuries had healed.

Stretching, Cinna's hand brushed the point of one of her ears poking out from beneath her hair, and she grew anxious. She fished in her trouser pockets and recovered her headband, wrinkled from being smashed into a ball. She tugged it over her head, and when she felt her ears safely behind it, she breathed easier.

Her stomach rumbled, and she realized how ravenous she felt. A plate with two sandwiches sat beside the bed. She gobbled the first one down, the meat and cheese both of higher quality than she was used to. After a moment of deliberation, her hunger got the best of her and she ate the second one, too.

With the food gone, Cinna jumped out of bed. The wood was rough and knotty under her feet as she crept over to where Hokuren slept.

A book sat open on Hokuren's lap. She must have fallen asleep reading it. Cinna understood that—books were often boring—but the position Hokuren slept in looked bad for her neck. Worried that moving her to the bed would wake her, Cinna gently laid Hokuren flat on the ground and placed a pillow under her head. Then Cinna took the blanket off the bed and covered her. She stirred, but remained asleep.

With the boss settled, Cinna started her exercises, engaging cranky muscles not used to prolonged inactivity. Her thoughts drifted to Hokuren paying for her treatment at the infirmary. Cinna tried to imagine anyone from the Sanctuary doing that, and despite being there for ten years, she came up blank. Half of them, at least, would have helped Barnaby aim the toxic bolt at her.

Ms. Pottsdam never had the coins, and even if she did, she would never have spent that many on Cinna. She may have welcomed a convenient way to get rid of an unwanted orphan pest.

Hokuren had known Cinna only for a few months—yet she had saved her, declaring Cinna irreplaceable.

Was she that good of an assistant? Cinna knew the answer to that: absolutely not. Hokuren did all the talking and the mystery solving. Cinna's principal contributions included climbing trees, wading through mud, and eating cookies. The investigation business could survive Cinna leaving without almost nothing lost.

No, Hokuren liked her. It was a strange feeling, and she struggled to process it.

Cinna's exercises kept her busy until Hokuren woke up. For the rest of her session, her thoughts focused mainly on where best to introduce Barnaby's toad toxin to the man himself.

When Hokuren stirred, bleary-eyed, she touched the pillow and the blanket, then looked up. "Cinna, you're awake, and you seem much better."

"Good morning—well, afternoon, boss," said Cinna. "I hope you got enough sleep. I'm in great shape."

Hokuren tossed the blanket and pillow back on the bed and came over to Cinna, giving her a quick hug. Flustered, Cinna avoided wiggling away before the hug broke. She was trying to get used to Hokuren's hugs, and the boss had earned this one.

"I'm sorry. I know physical affection isn't your thing, but I'm so glad you survived," said Hokuren, squeezing her before releasing.

"It's fine. So, what are we going to do now? I know you wanted to go to the Sanctuary, but I've been thinking about Barnaby and your jewelry box."

Hokuren grinned. "Of course you have. But we should take a break from direct action against Barnaby."

Cinna decided not to push it this time. "I figured you would say that."

"My jewelry box is important to me, but we've more important things to think about. Even our trip to the Sanctuary is postponed. Because of this coin and the info you brought me, we have things that need doing. The day isn't over, either." Hokuren gestured toward the window, beyond which lay a run-down section of Velles bathed in the late afternoon sun. "There are a couple of places I want to go before we go to the Sanctuary."

"Are we going after the Watch for teaming up with Barnaby?"

"No, that too would be foolish. Like Barnaby, we need to avoid the City Watch at all costs right now."

"So, what do you want to do?"

Hokuren's wide grin made Cinna nervous. The boss only smiled like this when she thought Cinna would object to her next demand. "I'm going to make you wear shoes."

12

Hokuren procured herself and Cinna disguises from a shop near Better Than Home. They now wore hooded cloaks over sensible riding skirts and tops in neutral colors, along with standard leather boots. She picked out used items, the colors faded, which served both of her purposes: to not stand out and to keep from spending too much from her drained purse.

Her sword, strapped to her hip, was hidden under the skirts. It gave her some comfort, even if she still worried about using it against members of the City Watch.

Cinna shifted uncomfortably in her new outfit as they left the shop. "Boss, I can't fight in these. Why would you wear these skirts while riding, anyway? Trousers are much easier to move around in. Also, we look like twins."

"First off, we don't look like twins. We're wearing similar outfits, that's all. And if we get into a fight now, we've already lost," said Hokuren. "Our goal is the avoid the City Watch, because you can't fight the whole of them. Once we finish a little business, we can leave Velles for a while and you can take this disguise off."

"Fine. But do I really have to wear these?" Cinna held up one foot, gesturing to the boot that encased it. "I feel trapped in them."

"Sorry, but you'll be too easy to identify without those boots. Don't you know there are astonishingly few people who walk around Velles barefoot?"

Cinna turned away with a huff.

Hokuren put her hand on her assistant's shoulder. "So, yes, you have to wear them, at least until we get out of the city. Chin up, though. You're going to meet Fenton today."

"Who's he?" Cinna sulked under her hood, pulled close around her head so her ears remained hidden. She avoided eye contact with anyone walking by, as Hokuren requested. The more Cinna obscured her elven features, the better.

"He's a friend."

"You have a lot of those."

"Only a few. Fenton's a bit eccentric. But, and this is between you and me, he's hiding something."

Cinna looked up at Hokuren, interest in her eyes. "A juicy secret?"

"He claims to have no actual magical abilities, but can identify the properties of magical items just by viewing them." Hokuren had watched him pretend that information had "awakened" within him more times than she cared to count. "It makes no sense. I'm sure he's lying. The only thing I don't know is the extent of his abilities."

"Then why does he run a shop?" Cinna frowned. "You can make lots of money crafting magic items with a little knowledge of spells and all that."

Hokuren shrugged. "Like I said, he's eccentric. Or perhaps he doesn't want to sit around all day making healing potions and lights."

They reached Fenton's Magical Supplies and Sundries, a small shop in a run-down building on the edge of Velles's business district. A little bell rang as Hokuren pushed the door open. Fenton, the ghostly pale elf behind the counter, greeted them with a lazy drawl. "Welcome in, we've got a special on penlights today. It's a pen, it's a light, now even in the dark, you can see what you write."

"While I appreciate the rhyme, I'm not interested at this time," replied Hokuren.

Fenton squinted at Hokuren for a moment until she took off her hood, then broke into a hearty laugh. "Well, well, if it isn't Seeker Hokuren. Hard to tell with that hood. That's quite a dingy dress you've got on. How's business?"

Elves did not show their age until they approached the end of their long lives, near two hundred and seventy-five years, so Fenton's age was difficult to guess, but Hokuren thought him at least one hundred and fifty years old. His eyes, blue flecked with gray, saw far more than he ever let on. He only pretended to be a flippant layabout, though he excelled at the pretending.

She grinned back at him. "Business is fine. I'm undercover." Quick to avoid the subject of her own empty purse, she said, "What about your business? That penlight spiel moving any product?"

Fenton shook his head with exaggerated somberness. "Tragically, I'm well aware you're no customer. But I hold out hope here for your twin."

Hokuren caught Cinna's smug expression and grimaced in return.

Fenton gestured toward Cinna, and then Hokuren noticed his eyebrows rise. "Where'd you get her?" he asked.

"I didn't 'get her' from anywhere. This is my assistant, Cinna."

"She's interesting."

Hokuren didn't like the way he scrutinized her. Not leering, but examining her peculiarly. Cinna didn't seem to notice, browsing the menagerie of magical items on display. Hokuren snapped her fingers. "Hey, eyes over here. I've got an item I need you to examine. I'm hoping you can tell me what it does."

Fenton eyes flicked back to Hokuren. "I doubt it, but let's see." He made a "give it here" gesture with his hand.

Hokuren produced the coin engraved with Lord Doubtwell's face and handed it to him. "Maybe you've seen something like it."

"It's not from me," Fenton confirmed. He turned the coin over in his fingers. "The quality's too high." He looked at Hokuren for approval of the joke, but she only rolled her eyes. He waggled his eyebrows in return. This back-and-forth routine constituted most of their interactions. "Lord Doubtwell on a coin. What a shameful waste of good silver." He placed the coin on his countertop. "My analysis? I think it's a magic coin."

"Oh, yeah? So did I. I know you have more insight than the obvious. Could you please skip to the part where you turn into the competent magic-item compendium you are?"

"How could I not feel compelled with a compliment like that?" Fenton showed no additional urgency but did regard the coin anew, flipping it in the air and onto his palm. Finally, he said, "It's not a trick coin, you know, for winning a coin flip. Like heads or tails, but always heads. Get what I mean? This coin isn't balanced, but it will land on tails sometimes."

"Okay," said Hokuren, knowing that, for Fenton, this counted as getting to the point quickly.

"It's a communication device," Fenton said. "A communicoin, if you will." He flipped it back to her. She didn't see it coming and fumbled the coin, sending it toward the ground.

Cinna's hand shot out and snagged it from the air. Without speaking, she handed it to Hokuren.

"Whoa." Fenton's gaze lingered on Cinna, and he screwed up his face in concentration. "Your Cinna's fast with her hands. I barely saw her move!"

To distract him, Hokuren said, "You said this coin was a communication device. Do you mean you can talk to someone with this?"

"Er, sort of." Fenton's eyes moved back to Hokuren. "It's a way of sending a one-way message. Think sending a letter, but instead of reading a piece of paper, the recipient suddenly hears your words in their head." He scratched his chin. "It's rare these days to find someone capable of producing these. I know of no one in Velles."

Hokuren considered the coin again, staring at Doubtwell's face. "Is this a coin that Lord Doubtwell would use, then? Why is his face on it?"

"No, his face is on it because he would be the recipient. That's part of how the magic works."

"So anyone who has this could send a one-way message to Lord Doubtwell?"

Fenton's head bobbed. "Well, they could, but the magic needs replenishing. Your coin's about dead." When Hokuren raised her eyebrows in question, he said, "Communicoins are high-level magic items, but they're done in a low-level way these days, by necessity. These low-level coins can only be used two or three times, and then need to be refreshed. Used to be you could use one dozens of times before needing a little magic top off."

Hokuren had received an answer to a different question than she wanted to ask. "How do you know it's used and not replenished?"

"It would shine." Fenton shrugged. "Or something. I would know."

"Boss," said Cinna, speaking for the first time since they entered the shop. "Do you think—?"

"Yes." Hokuren knew what Cinna was going to say, and she preferred they didn't have that conversation in front of Fenton. He need not be troubled with knowledge of an alliance between the commander of the City Watch and the city's most notorious thief.

To Fenton, she said, "Thanks for the insights. It's amazing how you know these things." She let a little skepticism creep into her voice, as she always did.

"Well, you're welcome, Seeker. And what can I say? A lifetime around magic items gives you some knowledge by osmosis, perhaps." A line he had repeated to her many times. He pulled over a box of penlights. "Can I get you to stay for a penlight demonstration?"

"As much as we'd love to, we have places to be."

"Hey, remember how helpful I am if you're ever in the market for a magic item. Or a potion." Fenton dug around the shelves behind him and pulled out a white potion that resembled curdled milk. "You know, I have a real interesting one that's come in since the last time you were here. A potion of muscle soreness. That's right, it will make any muscles it comes in contact with ache as if they've been used all day. It's of good value if you have someone to prank."

"I'll consider buying something helpful to me, not harmful to others," said Hokuren, leading Cinna out of the shop with a wave at Fenton.

"I didn't like how he looked at me," Cinna told Hokuren when they had walked away from Fenton's shop.

"Neither did I." But she could guess why he'd been interested. If Cinna's healing ability was magical in nature, Fenton could potentially sense it.

"Not your fault, boss."

"But he gave us good information on the coin, and I am confident that Barnaby used it to contact Lord Doubtwell when he was in his cell." Which meant Doubtwell came to the main office that night without assistance from Tarleton. The clerk became a less likely suspect, and more likely a dead body. "Come on. We're off to see Tarleton. If we can."

Hokuren wanted to get to Tarleton's house as quickly as possible now, but had to slow down in a reversal of the usual dynamic. Cinna hobbled behind in the boots, threatening to twist her ankles with her awkward gait. It reminded Hokuren of when she was a girl and she knitted Murphy, the family dog, some mittens. Murphy would not walk normally with them on, waving his paws, every step an attempt to rid himself of the mittens. Cinna kicked out similarly, as if to fling the boots off her feet. Hokuren smiled at the memory.

"Tarleton? That night-clerk kid?" Cinna asked, catching up to Hokuren.

"I think something bad happened to him. I know I'm breaking the prince's rules by following up on this, but I can't ignore it."

"Well, boss, I think the prince said we couldn't take any other cases. This isn't a case. We're doing this for free."

Cinna sometimes surprised with devious logic. Hokuren could feel herself rubbing off on Cinna in these moments. "You're right. If the prince asks, that's what we'll say."

"By the way, you seem to really know where you're going, but I don't. How do you know—flames!" Cinna stubbed her boot into another divot in the cobblestone and nearly tumbled to the ground. As she steadied herself, she let loose a string of inventive curses against all footwear—past, present, and future. When she had two feet planted firmly on the ground again, she finished, "How do you know where Tarleton is?"

"Well, I don't. But we're going to see if he's home."

"Okay, how do you know where he lives?"

"When I was in the Watch, I memorized where everyone lived in case I ever needed someone in an emergency. It never happened that I needed to go to anyone's home, but you never knew."

"You memorized where everyone lives?" said Cinna in awe. "I can't even remember how to get back to Fenton's shop."

"We'll work on that."

Hokuren led Cinna into the section of Velles called the Haphazards. Unlike the rest of the stone-paved city, dirt lined what passed for streets here. Nothing, not even weeds, grew out of this dirt. Thousands of boots trod up and down the confusing streets of the Haphazards every day, trampling anything bold—or stupid—enough to emerge through the surface.

Scholars believed the Haphazards were where the first settlers of Velles originally built their new homes millennia ago, without regard for city planning. The buildings existed in random lots, often near one another, but never in alignment. Streets rarely ran in straight lines, instead meandering in a general direction as best they could. Dead ends were so common that signposts let visitors know when a street didn't end in one, rather than the other way around.

Hokuren marched with purpose, knowing exactly where to go despite the difficulty of navigation here. Every so often, she muttered things like, "Okay, three lefts after the gray house with the bird feeder shaped like a dragon." Hokuren pushed through late evening crowds, exhausted people returning home from their day at work. Cinna scrambled to follow her through the maze of streets. The jumble of people made it easy to get separated, and Hokuren had to monitor her assistant to make sure she didn't get lost.

After about ten minutes of twists and turns, Hokuren stopped in front of a thin one-story house that shrank back in its lot from the two taller homes on either side.

"This is it," she said to Cinna. "Tarleton's home."

Cinna stared up at the house. "What if he is, you know, dead?"

"That's why I'm afraid to knock on this door."

Gathering her courage, Hokuren walked up to the door and knocked. There was no response to the first knock, but at the second, the door opened the tiniest of cracks. "Go away, you vulture" was the welcome she received from a scratchy voice suffering from the effects of age.

Putting on her most placid voice, Hokuren said, "My name is Hokuren. I'm a private seeker, hoping to talk to Tarleton. We used to work together, although not—"

Before she could finish, the door was flung open to reveal an elderly woman with gray hair and the question-mark posture of one with a ruined back. "A City Watch, eh? Come to spit on his corpse, then, have you?" From her accent, Hokuren placed her as being from Hortham, a farming community well to the south of Velles.

Hokuren swallowed. So Tarleton was dead. And this was probably his mother. Hokuren kept her voice as calm as she could. "I'm not with the City Watch any longer."

The old woman, seething in front of her, screamed, "Old Watch or new Watch, you ain't finding Tarleton here! He's gone, and your Watch killed him!" The old woman sagged, breaking down into tears. "They killed him. Me son's gone, and no one believes me."

"I believe you." Hokuren reached into her pocket and gave the old woman a handkerchief.

She didn't take it at first, sniffling. "What did you say?"

"I'm here because I had suspicions that the City Watch had killed your son. I'm very sorry to hear my suspicions were well founded." Now the old woman took the handkerchief from Hokuren and cleaned herself up.

The anger in her was gone, replaced by a hollowness that hurt Hokuren's heart. "How did you figure?" the old woman asked. "The Watch, they covered it up like. I talked to the papers and the reporters there, snakes they were. Said to me face they wouldn't report on nothing. No interest at all."

Hokuren nodded. "*The Velles Times* gets funding from Lord Doubtwell. It's basically a mouthpiece for the Watch, I'm afraid."

"Ah," sniffled the old woman. "I don't even subscribe."

Hokuren stared into her eyes. "I can't bring your son back, and I can't promise you'll ever see justice. My assistant and I are only two small people in this world. But I can promise that if you'll tell me your story, I'll listen. And I'll do what I can. Something dark has taken over leadership of the Watch. It needs dealing with, and I need as much information as I can get."

"That's a good speech to me ears. I don't have much faith that you'll do anything, but damn if I don't think you'll try." She backed away from the door. "At least come in and we can talk proper, sitting on chairs and such."

Hokuren motioned for Cinna to follow her into the old woman's home. As they walked into the small and sparsely decorated sitting room, Hokuren said, "This is my assistant, Cinna."

"Ma'am." Cinna bowed her head.

The old woman sniffled. "Oh, I'm sorry. I'm out of sorts and have forgotten me manners. Never did give you me name. I'm Gladys. Please, sit down."

Hokuren and Cinna took their seats on the couch, a plain gray piece with cushions so threadbare that Hokuren could see the thin layer of down inside. "Thank you, Gladys. I don't wish to bother you for too long, so I'll get straight to the point. Tarleton worked the night shift five nights ago. Did you see him after that?"

Gladys shook her head. "No, I didn't. Tarleton left for work and I went to bed, on account of I never did like being awake at night. It's for sleeping, the night. When he works nights, I like to—liked to be awake in time to get him his meal when he came home. I had the food prepared and all, just a beef stew like, but he never returned."

"What did you do when he didn't come home?"

"Tarleton was never late, you understand. He knew I would worry and all if he tarried. So after one hour I was worried and after two I was terrible scared. By midday I had had enough of the waiting around. I knew something wasn't right. So I went to the office." Gladys stared at a painting of Tarleton on the wall. Three similar works hung within Hokuren's field of view. Those would be where the budget to replace the old couch had gone. "It was busy and there were a line, but I shouted and demanded to know where Tarleton was. The girl behind the counter, little mouse of a thing, told me he'd left and she didn't know."

"So, why do you think the Watch had something to do with his death?"

"I reported Tarleton missing right then, you see. Something was not right. And would you believe who shows up at me door, later that day? Why, none other than Lord Doubtwell hisself, with a man in a suit of armor, as if he's going off to battle like."

Hokuren went rigid on the couch and exchanged glances with Cinna. "Er, would you say this armor was gold by any chance?" asked Hokuren, keeping her voice level.

"Why yes, how did you know?" Gladys asked, but did not give Hokuren a chance to respond. "Well, he never said a word, but he was threatening like, you understand. Made it clear I better listen to what Lord Doubtwell says."

Hokuren's mind reeled at the revelation that Davenport had accompanied Doubtwell, but forged ahead to avoid raising Gladys's suspicion. "And what did Doubtwell say?"

"He said they heard Tarleton had been spotted at a bar, drinking too much. When he was walking home, some ne'er-do-well or something cut his throat for his coin pouch." She jabbed a finger at Hokuren, anger overtaking her grief for a moment. "And that's how you know it's all lies. That puffed-up piece of aristocratic fluff wanted me to believe me son, who never drank a drop of alcohol in his life, went and got hisself boozed up instead of coming home to the meal he knew would be there." Gladys sighed. "I know me boy wasn't the most capable, but he was always dependable. He was always there."

Gladys had loved her son, accepting him for who he was and treasuring his strengths. Hokuren shoved aside a pang of bitterness toward her father, who never presented love like this, and said, "I understand. I believe you. Did Lord Doubtwell say anything else?"

"That I should say nothing to no one. He promised to let me see the body, so I would not worry that he was lying." She looked as if she was about to cry again. "There he was, dead on a stone slab, his throat really cut..." Now Gladys started crying, and this time Cinna beat Hokuren to the punch in offering a handkerchief.

When Gladys composed herself, Hokuren said, "Did Lord Doubtwell say why he came himself, personally? Were any other members of the Watch present when you saw your son's body?"

"No," said Gladys. "Just the Lord Doubtwell and the man in the armor."

It didn't yet make sense for Doubtwell and Davenport to be teaming up. Hokuren noticed Gladys sitting expectantly for more questions. Tentatively, she asked, "I know this may be unpleasant to think about, but it could help. What did Tarleton's throat injury look like? A smooth cut, like with a knife or dagger?"

"Well, no, I know a knife cut. Used to slaughter the hogs back on the farm as a girl. This was ragged. One of me brothers got attacked by a wolf when he was six. Had this terrible claw mark on his chest. Survived, but was sickly after that. The cut on me boy's throat was like that. They butchered him." She started sobbing again.

What had the Palace Guard said about Davenport? His left hand ended in claws? Perhaps Doubtwell didn't have the guts to murder Tarleton himself, but Davenport did.

"Thank you for your time, Gladys," said Hokuren. "I'm so sorry."

Gladys sniffled and dropped her head. "There's no chance of anything being done, is there? If it's Lord Doubtwell that killed him, he's too powerful. No one would believe me if I say he killed me son."

"It's true that, at the moment, few in this city would find such an accusation credible. Yet." The strength of that final word from Hokuren moved Gladys to lift her head up. "The chances are low. Doubtwell has the power and the sterling reputation. Even I fell for it, until today. But he killed Tarleton for a reason. And if I can find this reason, and find proof, then there's a chance he'll pay for this crime."

"Don't get me hopes up," said Gladys dourly. "But seeing Lord Doubtwell, or whoever killed Tarleton, brought to justice is all I have left."

13

Hokuren's thoughts remained on Doubtwell's betrayal until she and Cinna were well out of the Haphazards and on a secluded street meant for peaceful walks that cut between neighborhoods. Small trees, only a few years old, stood in the wide road, providing a rare green presence in Velles outside of the Aviary. The sky filled with oranges and purples as the sun set.

Standing in front of a bench, Hokuren said, "Cinna, I'm mad at myself. I'm doing an awful job with all this."

"When I get angry, I like to punch something. Makes me feel better." Cinna walked up to the tree closest to Hokuren and gave it a right hook, then a left, shaking loose a few leaves. Whisper-thin and light, they floated slowly down to form a shroud around Cinna's head.

"You should try it," said Cinna.

Hokuren turned toward the bench dubiously. There was not much harm in humoring Cinna. With a yell, Hokuren slammed her fist on the wooden slats. "Agh," she said, the side of her hand exploding in pain. "I think I broke it."

Cinna grabbed the hand and pressed her fingers into the bones, making Hokuren flinch and groan. "Not broken," she declared. "Though the bench almost is. That was a stronger punch than I expected, boss. I'm impressed. Next time, I would suggest using a little less force."

Shaking her throbbing hand, Hokuren said, "I *am* less angry, but I think that's because my hand hurts."

Cinna nodded. "That's part of it, though. You get to focus on that physical pain, and soon you forget why you were mad in the first place."

Hokuren squeezed her wounded hand against her chest. "I think this is a little too big to forget, but thank you for the attempt."

"Maybe try again later." Cinna reached out and snatched several of the leaves falling around her. She opened her hands and nodded proudly at her collection, then noticed Hokuren watching her. "Just some practice. Hey, boss, by the way, did you promise the old lady that you would try to take down Lord Doubtwell?"

"I may have, yes." Hokuren rubbed her temples.

"I think we might be chewing more than we bit off."

"The saying is 'we bit off more than we can chew,'" Hokuren corrected absentmindedly. "And perhaps."

"Everything is getting twisted up and confusing to me. If Lord Doubtwell wanted to hide his friendship with Barnaby, why did he hire us to find the Master Thief?"

Hokuren had yet to consider this question. After thinking for a moment, during which Cinna waited patiently, she had an answer.

"Here's my explanation. When Doubtwell hired us to find the Master Thief, I don't think he expected us to succeed. By hiring us, he could keep any suspicion of a relationship between him and Barnaby at bay. When we succeeded, he couldn't leave Barnaby in prison, because the thief would sell Doubtwell out." Hokuren put her head in her hands. "I never thought he'd stoop to murdering a member of his own Watch, though."

"But why does he even need to work with Barnaby? And why work with Davenport?"

"You."

Cinna tilted her head. "Not me."

"Well, not you, exactly, but elves like you. Barnaby is gathering elves to bring to Doubtwell. But the Lord Commander doesn't need them. He's providing them to Davenport and Nyana. They want to find Senara's soul."

Cinna's hands went up to her ears, tucked in the hood of her cloak. "So Barnaby tied me up like a parcel to give me to Davenport?" She scratched her chin thoughtfully. "Is he the cobbler?"

"I don't believe he's taken the title, but he might be at a former cobbler's shop. We're going there next." Hokuren swallowed, fear tightening her throat. "Although I don't know where to turn if he is."

Cinna pounded her fist into her palm. "Don't worry, boss. I can take care of him."

"Not alone. If he's there, we get some help. My adventurer friends at the very least. Some of their friends as well."

"But—" Cinna cut her protests short when Hokuren crossed her arms over her chest. "I get it. So, where's this cobbler?"

A dilapidated building squatted in the southwest corner of Velles, surrounded by the prince's tax offices. The faded sign on the wall next to the front door was smeared with a dark substance, but Hokuren could make out the words "Mud Guard," complete with an identical picture of a shoe as found on Nyana's paper.

"I can't believe this cobbler didn't stay in business with all these popular tax buildings nearby," said Cinna.

"This cobbler shop is hidden without being hidden at all." Hokuren glanced around at the tax offices. Each building—she could see "Customs", "Property", and "Land" in the immediate vicinity— represented a different tax, tiny fiefdoms contributing to a common goal of collecting a piece of all economic activities with ruthless bureaucracy.

It was late enough in the evening that the district was desolate, the sun all but set. The tax people had all gone home for the day. If someone wanted to kidnap elves, they could bring them here with little worry of being seen.

Cinna circled the small building. "The windows are all boarded up, and I can't hear anything. Seems very abandoned."

"Can you get us inside?" Hokuren cast her eyes at Cinna's headband, where she knew the lockpick was hidden away.

"Can I get us inside?" Cinna repeated incredulously. "How is that even a question, boss." Cinna retrieved her lockpick and grabbed the front doorknob.

It twisted in her hand and the door swung open, the door's hinges squeaking. Cinna turned back to Hokuren and put a finger to her lips, then stomped into the shop in her awkward boots, out of Hokuren's view.

Almost immediately, she poked her head back out. "It's empty. Told you I could get in."

"Well, it was unlocked." Hokuren entered the shop, which appeared frozen in time. The cobbler's old bench and shelves were tucked away in one corner. The tools and shoes that would have once covered them were gone except for a pair of shears strong enough to cut through leather.

"Doesn't look like anyone's been here in forever," said Cinna.

Hokuren swiped her finger across the cobbler's bench, then examined it. No dust. "Quite the opposite. This place has been cleaned recently."

Cinna took a step back, then cursed as her boot caught on a gap in the wood flooring and tripped her up. "I hate these—hey, boss."

"You found something?"

Cinna crouched to the ground and stuck her fingers in the gap she'd tripped over. She lifted a trapdoor, exposing a staircase that descended into darkness below. "I found something."

Hokuren squinted, but the darkness was so pervasive she couldn't see the floor where the stairs ended. "How far down does this go?"

With her elven eyes, Cinna squinted into the dark. "Not too far, but far enough."

Hokuren didn't know how to interpret that. "We should get help."

"If there are elves trapped down there, we should get them out now. I think if Davenport was here, we'd already know." Cinna yanked her boots off and tossed them aside. "These are getting in my way." She stepped onto the staircase. "You can stay up here, if you want."

Hokuren bit her lip. Her assistant was probably right, but Hokuren still peered into the blackness with trepidation. "No, we go together."

Cinna led them down the stairs into the darkness, with Hokuren clutching her skirts. Hokuren made each step blind, slowing their progress, but they eventually reached the end. She took a step onto a stone floor.

"One moment, boss," said Cinna, and she was gone. Standing alone in the dark, Hokuren rubbed her hands together nervously, then the room lit up. Cinna stood next to a wall sconce. "Magical light down here."

"It's strong," said Hokuren, her hand on her chest, trying to keep calm. They were in a long corridor, at the end of which was a wooden door reinforced with iron. To her right, built into the wall, was a small cell similar to the ones in the Watch's main office. It was empty.

"I suppose I would have ended up here." Cinna sounded nervous and turned away from the cell, hurrying to the iron-reinforced door.

"I shudder to think of it."

The door didn't budge when Cinna yanked on the handle. "This one is locked." She dug out her lockpick and went down on her knees to work the lock. Hokuren stood nearby, watching her concentrate as she peered into the mechanism. Then Cinna's eyes went wide, and the next instant she tackled Hokuren.

BANG!

A thunderous clap detonated from the lock. They hit the ground, Cinna draped across Hokuren's torso like dead weight.

"Cinna!" Hokuren couldn't hear her own voice through the intense ringing that reverberated through her eardrums.

Cinna didn't react. Hokuren rolled her aside and found she was unconscious, eyes closed. Her chest rose and fell softly, her breathing uninhibited.

A knockout spell. Illegal in Velles, but that also described running an elf kidnapping operation. By placing herself between the lock and Hokuren, Cinna had taken the brunt of it.

Smoke spewed from the lock, growing thick near the door. Hokuren's readings of knockout spells never included mention of smoke. She grabbed Cinna under the shoulders and dragged her away from the spreading haze. Just as Hokuren worried about how far she would need to drag her if the smoke continued to encroach, the flow ceased. The cloud swirled into a small, densely packed ball directly in front of the iron-reinforced door before stretching out, taking on the shape of an undulating tube.

Hokuren's stomach flipped. This was not mere smoke.

The smoke, now gathered completely in the tube, coalesced into an enormous snake, green and yellow, several feet long and twice as thick as her leg, with a set of fangs wicked enough to puncture even a dragon's hide. The fabric of her cloak and riding skirts had never felt thinner.

Hokuren prodded Cinna. "Wake up! I don't want to fight a snake by myself!" she said. At least, she hoped she said that. Being unable to hear herself talk disoriented her. But Cinna still lay on her back, unmoving.

The snake swung its head up and down the hall, and then back at the door, as if trying to come to terms with its sudden existence.

Hokuren considered her options, her knees shaking. The ideal response would be to run as fast as possible back up to the cobbler's shop, but she couldn't abandon Cinna. She took a deep breath and pulled her sword from beneath her skirts.

The snake slithered the short distance down the hall toward Hokuren. She held the sword in front of her, hoping the snake would fear the weapon as much as she feared it. The conjured creature menaced her from just outside her striking distance. It hissed, which sounded like little more than a whisper to Hokuren's still-recovering hearing.

"Stay back," she said, her voice cracking with fear as she stood in front of Cinna, the sword trembling in her hands. Hokuren waved the sword at the snake, which maintained a healthy respect for the weapon and stayed out of its reach.

Without looking back, she said, "Come on, Cinna. Get up, please!"

The snake snapped at the sword, and Hokuren took a step back, her heart beating so hard she worried it might burst. Her boot kicked Cinna's foot on her retreat, and she felt the foot move away.

"Cinna, are you awake?" Hokuren asked, as the snake took another bite at the sword, coming closer to her with a *Snap!* that even Hokuren's damaged ears registered.

"Ugh," said Cinna, behind Hokuren. "Boss, what happ—snake!" Cinna scrambled to her feet.

"I need your help!"

The snake champed at Hokuren again, this time coming close enough to reach her hands. She moved them out of the way of the snapping jaws at the last moment.

"I'm up, I'm up," said Cinna, emerging beside Hokuren. "Distract it. I'll try to pin it down. You stab it right between the eyes."

"Uh, right," said Hokuren, trying to hold her hands steady.

The snake turned its attention to Cinna, who did not have a sword to threaten with. "Anytime now!" Cinna rocked on the balls of her feet, poised to attack.

"Right." Hokuren aggressively swung the sword at the snake. "Hey, you ugly serpent! This way!"

Its narrow pupils swung back to her, and for a moment she thought it would strike. It would be lightning quick, too fast for her to defend, and it would bite her face and—

Cinna, skirts flowing, leaped into Hokuren's vision, grabbing the snake's neck. The snake thrashed as Cinna's weight took its head to the ground. She wrapped her legs around the reptile and it, in turn, coiled its tail around her torso. While the snake's head snapped inches from her face as she held it at bay, the tail tried to pull her away. She clung to it with all her strength.

"Boss," yelped Cinna, desperation in her voice. "I'm losing this."

Hokuren steeled herself and stepped forward to reach the snake. The head shook back and forth, up and down, as it struggled with Cinna. Her tenuous grip on the snake slipped with each moment.

"Hold it still!" shouted Hokuren.

"I can't! Stab it!"

Raising the sword above her head, point down, Hokuren waited until the snake gave her an opening—There! Hokuren brought the sword down with all her strength, puncturing the top of the snake's head and driving the tip of the sword through its chin.

With a poof, the snake lost its form, returning to smoke which then dissipated within seconds.

Cinna, putting all of her effort into fighting off what was now formless air, slammed onto the floor face-first, panting. She got up to her knees. "Nice stab, boss. So, who summoned the snake?"

"It formed from the smoke that came out of the lock."

"Oh, right. The lock." Cinna went back over to it, squinting into its depths. Recognition shone on her face. "It was trapped. *I* summoned the snake."

"You couldn't have known."

"I should have noticed the trap, boss. That's my fault. Though the worst trap I've ever seen was a tiny puff of poison gas. Nothing like being put to sleep so a smoke snake could eat me." Cinna put her hands on her hips. "You have to hand it to Davenport. That's an impressive combination."

"This was a pretty powerful spell," said Hokuren, hands on her still-tender ears. The ringing had almost abated, its last remnants still buzzing in her head. "Animal conjuration. I've read about such spells, but the scholars I read said that level of spell would be impossible now."

"Well, we oughta pay some scholars a visit, because I think it might still be possible. Good news is that it's gone now."

Cinna stuck her pick back in before Hokuren could tell her to wait. Hokuren winced, half expecting the trap spell to go off again, but nothing happened beyond the lock disengaging. The heavy door opened into a room twice as wide as the corridor.

The first thing Hokuren saw was an elf, hunched and squatting on the floor, a mane of filthy white hair erratically arranged upon his head. He squealed in surprise at their entry.

"Please, help me," he whimpered.

14

Hokuren entered the basement room, moving past two side-by-side tables as she approached the old elf. Shackles had been installed on each corner of one of the tables. Hokuren shivered.

"You've got to get me out of here!" the elf said, voice quavering. "I'm almost out of water and I ran out of food two days ago. Davenport's never left me alone this long before!"

"We will try. Cinna, can you please?" Hokuren pointed at the elf's chain. He sat on the floor near the tables, one leg chained to a bolt in the wall. He appeared pallid and emaciated and his once-fashionable outfit was now frayed and threadbare. His white hair indicated he had only a few years of his long life left.

Cinna knelt by him and ran the chain through her hands before peering at the cuff around his ankle. "Boss, there's no hole. It's solid metal." Cinna frowned. "I can't pick something that doesn't have a lock."

"It's a magic lock," said the elf, morosely. "You have to know the keyword."

Hokuren gave the ankle cuff a look-over herself to confirm there was no keyhole. "I've never heard of such a spell." This and the animal-conjuration spell confirmed Davenport capable of an unknown level of magic that even the Conclave of Wizards would not claim. A frightening proposition.

"Can we try to guess the keyword?" asked Cinna, lifting the chain to her face. "Release! Hmm, that wasn't it."

The elf sighed. "I've thought of that one already."

"I'm afraid we don't have the necessary months to guess every word in existence. Is there something in here that we could use to cut you free?" Hokuren explored the room, well-lit by magical light. Loose papers covered several cabinets against each wall. Empty cages sized for small animals were scattered throughout. Nothing stood out as helpful for breaking a chain.

"No, I doubt it," said the elf, slumped over on the floor.

Hokuren skimmed the papers, covered in near incomprehensible jargon and drawings. She opened some of the cabinet drawers, finding gems and jewels of all shapes and colors. The drawers also contained various instruments and implements, including several surgical knives arranged from smallest to largest.

"I believe Julien Davenport is kidnapping elves with the assistance of various individuals. Are you one of his victims?" Hokuren didn't believe in questioning victims before freeing them. But she needed to know this elf's role here.

He looked confused, then insulted. "I'm not here because I'm an elf. I'm here for my expertise."

"Who are you?" Hokuren asked.

"Arnold Witherspoon," said the elf in a manner that suggested that should mean something. It did not.

With a meaningful glance at his chain, Hokuren said, "Forgive me for not understanding the situation. For some reason, I thought you might be here under duress. What sort of expertise are you providing?"

"I admit I am not chained here because I enjoy it. Julien has kept me here for my knowledge of soul transference, of course." He frowned. "You've never heard of me or my previous works on the soul?"

"I haven't, sorry to say." Different authors had written the books on souls that Nyana checked out. Hokuren leaned on the table nearest Witherspoon, the one without shackles. "Soul transference. Is it possible?"

"Yes," said Witherspoon, his voice a whisper. "It's possible. But unless I find Julien, he'll make a grave mistake."

"What do you mean? Tell me more."

Witherspoon sighed, shoulders slumped. "Years ago, before my hair went white, Julien came to me with an offer. You see, I have studied souls my whole life. They fascinate me because they are such an integral part of us. In fact, our lives are not possible without them. Yet they remain mysterious, their true essence tantalizingly unknown. From when I was a boy—"

"Please, Mr. Witherspoon," said Hokuren, heading off the imminent ramble. "Your lifelong interest is noted. But what did Davenport propose?"

Witherspoon groused, but continued, "My early studies on the soul focused on, well, the soul itself. However, my research was never valued the way it should have been, and I always struggled for funding. Twenty years ago, Julien offered what seemed like a golden opportunity. Enough funding for decades of research! Longer than my remaining lifespan, to be sure. But I would have to tailor that research to his preferred topic. The lost art of moving a soul from one person to another, or soul transference."

"And you succeeded?"

"I did," said Witherspoon. He avoided her eyes. "Well, in a way. I have yet to test it on people. But it seemed to work on the rats, sort of."

Hokuren leaned in closer. "That's a lot of equivocating. What happened to the rats?"

"Well, the rat that lost its soul died. That's what happens when your soul gets removed. Hard to avoid that, I'm afraid. And the other rat, the one that gained the soul, well, er, it also died." Witherspoon played with his chain, twisting the links back and forth.

"Excuse me?"

Shrugging, Witherspoon said, "I learned that one body cannot support two souls. I suspect there is a sort of, hmm, battle, you could say, that occurs when the souls meet in the body. A stronger soul might defeat a weaker one, but if they are equal, then the result is devastating."

Hokuren fingered the shackles on the table. The person giving up their soul would be guaranteed to die, potentially while bound here in this very room. She forced herself to ignore a sudden bout of nausea.

"Did you do this with any elves?"

Witherspoon's eyes widened in horror. "No, no, of course not."

"Hey, boss," said Cinna, leaning against one of the filing cabinets. "This guy only figured out a really complicated way to kill rats."

Witherspoon acknowledged this with a nod. "It's also quite a painful way to go, judging from their squeaks."

Hokuren grew much less sympathetic toward Witherspoon and his blasé attitude for his rat charges. Rats were rats, but they didn't deserve to be killed so callously.

"What purpose is this research even supposed to have?" Her voice rose in disgust. "Everyone has a soul, right? You don't need another one. Why would anyone want to transfer a soul when it kills the sender, if not also the recipient?"

"Some souls are special," said Witherspoon, meekly. "Do you know that the goddess Senara lives inside the soul of an elf? Julien told me that. He wants to put that soul into Princess Nyana. That's the whole reason for all this research."

Hokuren pulled back from Witherspoon. So that was it. She wondered how much of this Prince Leopold knew, and how much had been kept from him. The existence of a secret detention center and laboratory in the tax district, rather than the castle, suggested that the prince may have been excluded from the elf kidnapping machinations and Witherspoon's work. On the other hand, it didn't rule out his knowledge or even involvement. If this place was discovered, the prince would have plausible deniability.

There was a problem, though, with the plan to put a Senara-infused soul within Nyana.

"You'll kill one person for sure, but also kill Nyana!" said Cinna, kneeling next to Witherspoon. "Does Davenport know you're trying to kill the princess like you do rats?"

"The person who currently has Senara in their soul would die, yes," said Witherspoon. "But as I explained to Julien, not necessarily Nyana. Remember, a powerful soul should be able to beat out a weak one. Senara's soul should be the stronger one, entering Nyana's body and replacing her current soul." Witherspoon paused. "Presumably."

"Presumably." Hokuren copied his cadence and paced the elf's laboratory-prison. "It's rather dire if you've presumed wrong, don't you think? Does Nyana know this is an untested theory?"

Witherspoon stammered, "Well, I mean, not as such."

"I'm assuming she at least knows that the person whose soul she takes will definitely die."

"Uh, well, perhaps that might not have made it to her, er, as such."

"*As such*, you presented this to Davenport and he's run with it, hasn't he?" Hokuren pounded her fist on the table, eliciting a surprised gasp from the old elf on the ground. Tarleton died by Davenport's hand in order to save Barnaby from prison. Now someone else needed to die so Nyana could, what, house a goddess?

Faced with Hokuren's disapproval, Witherspoon sniveled. "I don't know. I only met Nyana a few times, before I did the testing on the rats. I don't know what she knows." He ran his hands through his white hair. "I admit, I am proud of the research I've done here, even under these circumstances. But even if I hadn't been willing, I would have done it still. You don't disobey Julien Davenport."

"He liked killing the rats, boss." Cinna narrowed her eyes.

"I assure you, I didn't enjoy that part."

"I'm not assured."

Hokuren took a deep breath and waved a calming hand at Cinna. Forcing herself to keep her voice as neutral as possible, Hokuren asked Witherspoon, "How does it work? Is there anything here that is necessary for the process?"

"No," said Witherspoon. "This was a convenient place for it, what with it being so hidden and all. But Julien has the Soul Jade and the necessary spell knowledge. He can do it anywhere."

"The Soul Jade?"

"A piece of jade cut by the giants themselves, tens of millennia ago," said Witherspoon, his voice holding a sense of wonder. "The story is that only their smiths could create such gems. Combined with a little magic, the jade can suck the soul right out of you."

Hokuren snorted. "Why would they make such a thing?"

"I can't tell you. If there were any giants left, we could ask. All I know for sure is that the Soul Jade works. On rats, at least."

"Tell me how it works."

"You say the magic spell, press the jade into a person, and take their soul. Press the jade onto another person, they get the soul. It's actually rather simple, except for the spell part. I can't do it. Only Julien could." Witherspoon grabbed his stomach. "Please, do you have a way to free me?"

Hokuren wanted to ask more questions, but it was past time to free Witherspoon. She turned to Cinna. "Upstairs there was a pair of shears. They might not be enough, but it's the best option we've got."

"Right, boss." Cinna dashed down the corridor.

Hokuren swept her hand over the room. "Does anyone else know about this? Or anything happening in here?"

"As far as I know, it's just Davenport, Nyana, and myself. And now you. Maybe others, but I don't know."

He hadn't mentioned the prince. However, if Barnaby and the Watch knew to take Cinna to "the cobbler," they must at least have some idea of what was happening here. It was possible none of them had been allowed past the door to meet Witherspoon.

Hokuren knelt down beside him, her voice low. "One last question. You said Davenport was about to make a grave mistake. Why is that?"

"Oh, well." Witherspoon struggled with the words. "I don't think I should say."

"You will, or I'll walk out and lock this door right back up." This was a lie, but Hokuren kept her voice firm to sell it.

"You wouldn't." Witherspoon held Hokuren's gaze. She narrowed her eyes. "You would." Licking his lips, he said, "Okay, okay. Well, I believe he thinks he found where Senara's soul is." He held up his hands. "Don't ask me where, as Julien never told me. But even if he has, this soul transference hasn't been tested on people. I know I said I thought it would work on Nyana, but I really believe we need to do more research."

Or he wanted to help Davenport finish the job. Hokuren considered that the more likely scenario. "Tell me, what magic is Davenport capable of?"

"I thought you'd asked your last question," he said, frowning.

"Just answer."

"More than I'm used to, for sure. He can make his voice carry, he can create images in the air, he can disappear from view and walk unseen, and more I probably don't know about. He's capable of a lot."

Invisibility would explain how he could walk through Velles with Nyana without garnering attention.

Cinna returned with the shears. "This might work," she said, crouching next to Witherspoon.

"We can't get the shackle, but the chain links aren't too thick." Hokuren ran the chain through her hands, finding what she was looking for. "This one, see it? It's got a crack in it."

"Got it." Cinna wedged the shears in the crack. She placed both her hands on the shears and pushed. Nothing happened for a short while, even as Cinna strained with effort.

"Maybe we try something else."

Cinna tensed and slammed the shears into the ground. The link finally gave out, snapping and sending a piece of metal whizzing past Hokuren's shoulder. Cinna relaxed on the ground with a sigh of relief.

"I'm free!" said Witherspoon, pulling his pant leg over his shackle.

"We can take you to the Watch," said Hokuren, before she remembered why they could not. "Well, we can get you close, anyway."

Witherspoon stood up, stretching stiff joints and muscles. "No need to trouble yourself. I thank you for freeing me, but I can handle things from here."

"If you think so," said Hokuren, letting skepticism creep into her voice.

"Yes, yes. Goodbye, and thank you for everything." Witherspoon limped down the corridor, the leg with the shackle attached not bending much.

Lifting herself to her feet, Cinna said, "Are you going to let him leave? He's behind all this soul-transfer stuff. Shouldn't we—you know?" She pantomimed several stabbing motions.

"No, of course not," said Hokuren, clicking her tongue. "For one, we aren't in the assassination business. Second, it sounds like all the research is pretty well done, and Davenport will go ahead with the transference when he finds Senara's soul, so Witherspoon's death will not stop it."

"It's just that the soul-transfer thing bothers me," said Cinna, pressing her hands together and twisting her fingers. "It feels so wrong."

"I'm right there with you. But once that chain broke, he couldn't wait to get away from us." Hokuren smiled. "Of course, we aren't going to let him do that. I believe he's eager to see the fruits of his labor pay off. So we're going to follow him. I think he might lead us to Davenport. Come on."

Hokuren stepped out of the defunct cobbler's shop to catch a glimpse of Witherspoon's shambling figure reaching the edge of the little tax district.

"Hurry, we're going to follow. Make sure we don't lose him," said Hokuren.

Cinna's eyes tracked Witherspoon. "I don't think that's going to be a problem, boss. This is going to be like tailing a slug."

Witherspoon led them on a ponderous trip through Velles. Hokuren and Cinna split up, hiding behind alleyways, doorways, barrels, and anything else they could find in the streets. They never needed to bother. At no point did Witherspoon turn around or consider his surroundings. Either he was oblivious to the potential of being followed, or he did not care.

It took the souls expert almost an hour to stumble feebly to his destination: the Scrolls of Welcoming. He entered the inn as Hokuren and Cinna observed while crouching behind a signboard several buildings down.

"What now?" asked Cinna.

"We wait. If he doesn't come out in ten minutes, we assume he's got a room. Then, we watch." Hokuren adjusted her sitting position to get more comfortable. "Settle in, we may be here for a while."

"Oh." Cinna squatted beside Hokuren, chin on her fists.

"I know this bores you, but I want to see if anyone comes and meets him here. There could be some sort of arrangement set up for Witherspoon, should he make it out of the castle. If there's even a chance he can lead us to Davenport, I'm desperate to take it."

Vitreous approached its zenith in the northern sky as one hour, then two, passed. There were few people about at the start of their stakeout, the crowds dwindling to none as time went on. Occasionally, Cinna darted through the shadows of the buildings to scope out the scene from different vantage points, though she admitted this was to alleviate her boredom more than anything.

Hokuren had time to think. Davenport seemed ready to proceed with the transference, according to Witherspoon, despite it being untested in people. His apparent interest in risking Nyana's life gnawed at Hokuren.

Her mind kept returning to the Sanctuary of the Eclipse. Given the Sanctuary's closed nature, if the elf that had Senara's soul lived there, it would explain how they had evaded Davenport's grasp for this long. Whoever had that soul would be in danger if Davenport knew their identity.

She thought about Cinna, who had left the Sanctuary six months before. Though Hokuren was not ready to conceive of Cinna as the elf in question, she could not dismiss the possibility. Still, *The History of Senara* claimed that Senara's vessels tended to be wealthy, powerful individuals. This description, which certainly did not fit Cinna, could match the expected future of the children of the elite that paid tuition at the Sanctuary.

Hokuren stifled yawns as the night dragged on. Deep into hour three, her eyes closed and she dipped her head. She jerked back and slapped herself to keep from succumbing to her drowsiness. The sting of her slap had yet to fade when someone in a blue-and-gray leather cuirass emerged into her field of view. A sword hung from their hip.

Cinna whispered, "Hey, is that . . . ?"

"Someone from the City Watch," Hokuren finished. The Watch member entered the Scrolls. She stood up, wide awake now. "Come on, I've got a bad feeling about this."

They ran toward the Scrolls and entered a small lobby, where a young woman stood behind the desk a few feet from the front door. A staircase to the right led to the next floor.

"Can I help you?" the receptionist asked, warily.

"A member of the City Watch just entered. Where did they go?" Hokuren spoke quickly, hands on top of the desk.

"A member of what? I didn't see anyone." The receptionist twirled her long hair with a finger.

Taken aback, Hokuren said, "You didn't see the Watch member who walked in right before we did?"

There was a cry from upstairs that abruptly cut off. "I'm going," said Cinna, already to the staircase before she finished speaking.

Hokuren left her to it. She turned back to the receptionist. "What about an elderly man with a limp who got a room a few hours ago? Which one is he in?"

"Don't know anything about that," the woman said, jutting out her chin.

"Boss!" Cinna yelled from the second floor.

Leaving the recalcitrant receptionist, Hokuren hurried up the stairs. Cinna waved to her from down the first long hallway on the second floor, pointing to a room near the far end. Hokuren jogged to the room, her hands going to her mouth in shock when she entered.

Witherspoon lay on the bed in a growing pool of his own blood. Someone had bludgeoned his head, which may have eventually killed him, but the slash across his throat finished him before the head trauma had a chance. His eyes bugged out, and his mouth remained agape.

"I caught the Watch as he went through the window, and I was going to chase him, but he threw that at me." Cinna pointed at a small dagger buried in the thin wooden wall. "By the time I avoided getting pierced, he was gone. I could have chased him, but I thought I should show you this instead. Shouldn't leave you here alone, anyway."

Hokuren nodded. "I appreciate that." Recovered from her initial horror, she closed Witherspoon's eyes and mouth. He deserved some dignity in death.

She averted her gaze from his corpse after that. She had seen dead bodies as part of the Watch, but she never got used to them the way some of her colleagues did. With concerted effort, she did not throw up, even as her stomach roiled.

"Now what?"

Hokuren pointed at Witherspoon's body without giving it another glance. "Search him, could you? Quickly, we don't want to be here if more of the Watch shows up."

"On it." Cinna rifled through the dead man's pockets. Unlike Hokuren, she had no reservations about touching a corpse when it needed to be done. While she worked, Hokuren went to the window and looked out. A short jump from the second-floor balcony would have brought the Watch member to the rooftop of the adjacent building. Escapes were rarely easier.

"Boss," said Cinna, bringing Hokuren back inside.

"What did you find?"

"One of those commune coins. I don't think you'll like this." She handed the communicoin to Hokuren, who found herself face-to-silver-face with Lord Doubtwell once again.

"You're right, but I'm also not all that shocked." She could see how Davenport had set Witherspoon up if he escaped. The old elf knew more than anyone about the plans for Nyana. He'd likely been told the City Watch would help him contact Davenport. But the City Watch, now merely an extension of Davenport's will, would have other instructions.

And Witherspoon, Hokuren's only lead to Davenport, was dead. She imagined Doubtwell and Davenport trading communicoin messages with each other, wishing she could send them one as well.

Hokuren flipped the coin over and over in her hand. What if . . . ?

"Boss?" said Cinna, as Hokuren mused.

"I wonder if this coin still has magic in it." Hokuren didn't know how to use the communicoin, but if Barnaby and Witherspoon could do so, surely she could.

She squeezed her fist over the coin. Closing her eyes, she focused on it. Her mind conjured the smug image of Edward Doubtwell, and everything went silent. A strange and uncomfortable tingling sensation emanated from deep within her skull. She could not move at all. Her entire body was locked down, her thoughts the only thing she had control over.

"Courtesy of the Conclave of Wizards, connection open," said a female voice, coming from inside Hokuren's head. The voice's accent had a kind of practiced pronunciation Hokuren had never encountered before. "You have thirty seconds. When I say 'start,' everything in your mind will be transferred to your other party. Start."

Everything? Scrambling, Hokuren tried to clear her mind. Of course, this only made her brain want to conjure something up, so she thought of Witherspoon's dead body. Even though it upset her, she made sure to highlight the wound on his neck.

Do you see this? I know you're behind this, Lord Commander. Focused entirely within her own mind, the words were sharp and clear. *I know who you're working with, too. I will take you down, whatever you think you're doing.*

"Connection ended," said the female voice, and the tingling mercifully ended. There was no indication Doubtwell had received anything.

"Hokuren!" It was Cinna's voice, yelling from right next to Hokuren. She opened her eyes to find concern written all over her assistant's features. "Are you there?" said Cinna, eyes wide. It was the most panicked Hokuren had ever seen her.

A strong headache overtook Hokuren, and she pressed her hand against her forehead. "Yes, I think so."

"You went into, um, a trance or something," said Cinna, calming down. "You were standing there absolutely still, and it didn't seem like you could hear me at all. It was awful."

"I'm sorry to worry you." The coin was warm in Hokuren's hand. "I think I just threatened Doubtwell."

Cinna cocked her head. "What? Oh! The coin! You used the coin?"

"I think so."

"And you threatened him?"

Hokuren sighed. "I admit, it was not the most intelligent thing I've ever done. I tried to use the coin, and suddenly there was a woman who said I was talking to him. Well, thinking to him. And my anger got the better of me."

"You got mad?" Cinna smiled. "I already told you how to deal with that, boss."

Hokuren returned a rueful grin. "My hand is still sore from the last time I took your anger-management advice."

"Well, if you want my opinion on the threat, I like it. Tell that terrible man to stuff himself straight into the fire."

The tromping of boots sounded through the window from street level. Hokuren risked a glance outside to see the tops of two helmets enter the inn. "We should leave before someone finds us here with a fresh corpse."

With one last look at Witherspoon's lifeless body, Hokuren shuddered while leaving the room, Cinna right behind her.

They returned to the front desk, walking back down the staircase. When they landed on the last step and came into view of the receptionist, she said, "There they are! The murderers!"

"How do you know there was a mur—" Hokuren clamped her mouth shut when she turned into two members of the City Watch. They stood in the doorway, blocking the exit.

"Captain Hokuren?" said the first, confused.

"Hey, it's the elf that works with Hokuren!" said the second, pointing at Cinna.

"Run, boss!" Cinna barreled into the nearest Watch, putting her shoulder into his chest and shoving him back into his partner. Both members of the Watch tumbled backward together into the street, falling into a pile of struggling limbs and curses.

Hokuren sprinted past them, Cinna on her heels. One of the Watch got his bearings enough to grab for Cinna's ankles. She danced around him, and all he got was a tenuous hold on the edge of her skirts. With a twisting jerk, she tore free, a tiny scrap of fabric all the Watch member had to show for his efforts.

He made a desperate lunge for Cinna. She kicked out, catching his chin with her heel, the crack ringing out in the empty streets. He collapsed back on the ground, groaning and grabbing at his busted jaw.

She caught up to Hokuren. "This way." They ran on the cobblestone streets as Cinna led them down thin lanes and alleys.

Hokuren scampered after her assistant, glad she had chosen skirts slit for movement. She sucked down air as the run continued, her muscles burning and an ache developing in her side. But she did not dare stop, keeping pace with Cinna as they pounded across Velles, putting distance between themselves and the Scrolls.

At first, it was not clear where Cinna was taking them. Once they reached her destination, however, it made sense. They stopped in the deafening silence of the tax district.

Safely ensconced in a dark corner between buildings, Hokuren put her hands on her knees and panted, taking deep gulps of air. "We ran . . . pretty . . . fast, I think."

Cinna, only slightly winded, said, "We ran as fast as you could run."

"Right," huffed Hokuren, between breaths.

They huddled in the corner, waiting for dawn. Nebulus, the second moon, half as bright as Vitreous, had ascended. The darker moon better fit Hokuren's mood. She shouldn't have used the coin to talk to Doubtwell.

It had been an act of frustration and would only solidify her and Cinna as targets of the most powerful Vellesians.

But if she put even the smallest drop of fear into Lord Doubtwell or Julien Davenport, she would take that as a silver lining. She meant what she'd said to Doubtwell. She would untangle this mess and expose them all.

"Seems like a good time to leave the city. The wagon rental should open right as the sun rises," said Hokuren. "We'll get one, and head to the Sanctuary."

Cinna's expression was invisible in the near darkness. "If we must."

"We made a deal."

"I was hoping you'd forgotten about that."

Hokuren leaned against the wall, her earlier exhaustion replaced with restless anxiety. Tarleton's and Witherspoon's deaths replayed in her mind. She muttered to herself, "Who else is going to have to die because of this goddess's soul?"

She hadn't wanted an answer, but Cinna gave one anyway. "I don't know, but hopefully it's not us."

15

It took five days to reach the Sanctuary of the Eclipse, and Cinna dreaded their arrival the entire trip. She enjoyed the journey, however, often walking alongside their rented wagon to avoid being cooped up within. The grass, dirt, and rocks made for stimulating surfaces to tread upon, and the fresh air was a welcome change from the aromas of the city. Cinna made Hokuren exercise when they stopped to rest the horses, refusing to accept the boss's lame protests that she did not need it.

They had both returned to their usual attire, stashing the riding outfits and cloaks in the back of the wagon with the rest of their provisions. Hokuren had been upset that Cinna had left her boots at the cobbler's, but Cinna assured the boss that she never intended to wear them again, anyway.

During travel, Hokuren held the reins and, when Cinna humored her, provided history lessons of the area surrounding Velles.

Velles's outskirts were nothing like the city itself. Wide roads connected the city to the outside world, but the nearest town of even marginal size was more than ten days' ride to the north. The grass fields around Velles gave way to a wide expanse of farmland. With the decline of monsters, eradicated by adventuring groups, the farms flourished.

The countryside was not all farms, however. Wild grasses still grew where farmers had yet to corral the soil. Pockets of forest dotted the landscape, which gave the goblins and ogres a place to live and kept them from invading Velles. And the old remnants of villages abandoned hundreds or even thousands of years ago scattered about, now overgrown.

"Look, Cinna," said Hokuren, pointing to one such settlement on their second day of travel. "Derelictia has moved in."

The abandoned village's buildings were in ruins, thick red vines tangled all throughout the crumbling stone and rotting wood.

"Is that red stuff the derelictia?" asked Cinna, the strange word difficult to pronounce.

"The vines, yes. Senara created them to break up old buildings left behind by humans, so the land can reclaim them."

But how did the vine know when people had abandoned the structures, and when they had only left for a short while, intending to return? Cinna tried to think through the question on her own, but could not come up with a workable answer. She gave up and asked Hokuren, receiving a shrug in response. None of the stories said. At least Cinna wasn't the only one in the dark this time.

They passed other wagons along the road, mostly traders or merchants on the way to Velles. They took precaution to hide their faces from these passersby, just in case, but no one paid them any mind.

On the third day, Hokuren broached the subject Cinna knew was coming. "So, Cinna, will you please tell me what happened to you at the Sanctuary?"

Cinna's chest tightened. "It's not all that much."

She looked up to see the frown upon Hokuren's face. "Will it be a problem if you return?"

Cinna tugged at loose strands of her shaggy hair. Hokuren would find out soon enough why it was indeed a problem. "Yes," Cinna said, eyes downcast.

"Come on. Sit next to me in the wagon. Let's talk." When Cinna still hesitated, Hokuren sighed. "The trip to the Sanctuary is strictly to find out if Davenport or Nyana have been there, and if so, what they wanted to find. But I need to know what we're potentially walking into. So, please."

Cinna reluctantly jumped onto the wagon, gripping the sideboards. She clambered toward the driver's box, where she squeezed in next to Hokuren. The box, meant for one person, was a tight fit for the two of them. If anyone else had asked her to sit next to them, Cinna would have declined.

"So, why are you so afraid to return?" asked Hokuren.

Cinna twisted the edge of her tunic in her hands. "I didn't leave because I wanted to. Master said I should leave and never return."

"What happened?"

"I was only allowed to be at the Sanctuary because Master wished it." Cinna lowered her head. "Master's dying, and she didn't believe her replacement would allow me to continue."

"Ah, I see," said Hokuren. "Is what Maol said true, that the Sanctuary is for noble children?" When Cinna nodded, Hokuren continued, "So then, how did you end up there?"

Cinna didn't want to talk about it. She hated to admit that part of her past and feared Hokuren would view her differently. Hokuren only knew the strong person Cinna had become. Not the weakling she used to be.

Still, she deserved the truth.

"Ms. Pottsdam died when I was ten. I lived in the streets of Velles for four years until Master came to town. She was walking through the markets when I saw her. Master had this big, fat coin purse hanging down from a thin little string." Cinna pinched her thumb and pointer finger together and held them up to her eye. "It was going to be the easiest purse snatch of all."

"But?"

"It was a trap, and I was too dumb to see it. Right as I snuck up on her to cut the coin purse, she reached out and grabbed my wrist." Cinna demonstrated by grabbing Hokuren's wrist, causing the boss to flinch and jerk the reins. The horses whinnied. Hokuren freed her wrist from Cinna's grasp.

"I get the picture, and so do the horses."

"Sorry, boss. Anyway, I tried to get free, but her grip was incredibly strong. And I was small." Cinna could still feel Master's fingers wrapped around her wrist like a shackle, tight and implacable. "I was given a choice. Go with the master to the Sanctuary, where they would give me food and shelter but I'd have to work for them. Or refuse, and she'd take me straight to the City Watch and recommend execution for attempted theft."

Hokuren startled. "The City Watch wouldn't have executed you on the whim of a random citizen."

"I didn't know that." Cinna recalled the primal fear of losing her life in that moment and shuddered. "But even so, they'd put me in a cell, wouldn't they? They'd know I was a thief, a little street rat bothering the important people. Even if they eventually let me out, they would watch for me after that, instead of looking the other way. I didn't really have a choice. I went with the master."

Hokuren was quiet for a moment before responding. "I never had to consider a choice like that. Nor did I know the Sanctuary pressed Velles's urchins into labor. Were there many of you?"

"The Sanctuary has people who prepare and serve the food, clean the rooms, wash clothes, and all that." Cinna smiled ruefully. "They were all lifted off the streets, yes. The noble children don't do any of that."

"Someone should do something," said Hokuren, her mouth a tight line of disapproval.

"Like who, and what?" Cinna shrugged. "Every urchin the Sanctuary takes is one less stealing food and fouling the streets. The thing is, I got a nice bed and regular food for the first time in my life. I never ate better, even with Ms. Pottsdam. It may not have been the best life. But the streets were worse." Cinna had spent many nights curling up in the cold, her stomach empty.

"Hmm," said Hokuren. She pressed her fingers to her forehead. "Well, so tell me. I'm guessing you weren't tutored because they didn't need their—let's call them 'servants,' to be educated. But how did you get taught their fighting techniques?"

Cinna buried her face in her hands, embarrassed by the memory of her feeble past self. "I would sneak around and watch through a crack in the wall. I wanted to learn, so maybe one day if someone grabbed me, I wouldn't have to do what they said. They eventually caught me, and the master said if I wanted to learn to fight so bad, perhaps I should spar with the students. I was just this little orphan girl and didn't know how to fight. So, they . . . they . . ."

Hokuren squeezed her shoulder. "I think I get it. They beat you up, didn't they?"

"Yeah." She couldn't look back at Hokuren, full of shame from the memories. "That's when I learned how good I was at healing myself. And the master thought it was great. The students could 'spar' with me during the day, then let my wounds heal overnight, and I'd be ready to go the very next day." Cinna gritted her teeth. "I learned how to deal with pain, too."

"That's awful." Hokuren's voice was hard with repressed anger.

"Eventually I learned what they were doing, the techniques they were using on me. And I grew up, exercised, and got stronger. Then one day, I beat one of them. Then again, and again." Cinna raised her head at this memory, one she took more pride in. "I worked so much harder than they did. They never taught me anything, but I learned it all and more."

Hokuren gave Cinna a small smile. "You shouldn't have had to do it like that."

"But I did, boss. I beat all the other students, got better and stronger than them, and they hated me for it."

"Jealousy and bitterness, then."

"I'm not supposed to come back, and I don't really want to."

"Thank you for telling me." Hokuren seemed deep in thought. "I have a much dimmer view of the Sanctuary than previously. I'm imagining spending as little time there as possible. If you want, while I go inside, you can wait in the wagon."

"No way, I won't let you go alone," said Cinna, fists clenched. "I'm not a coward. I won't hide from them."

"Of course you're not a coward. Quite the opposite, you can almost be too brave. However, sometimes you need to go where you're not welcome as an investigator. This could be good practice."

Cinna liked the sound of that. "Do you have any good stories about going somewhere you're not welcome?" Hopefully, Hokuren would let them move on to another topic.

"Do I have stories?" Hokuren stared blankly at the dirt path ahead before turning to Cinna with a grin. "I do, yes. Would you like to hear about the therapy service that was secretly a brothel? I went undercover for that one. Velles tightly controls brothels, and when I was in the Watch, we would sometimes test them to make sure they weren't doing anything nefarious."

Cinna felt her face flush. Hokuren, at a brothel? "What sort of undercover? Did you do the, you know, work?"

"What?" Hokuren laughed. "Maybe I did."

"You did?" Cinna couldn't meet Hokuren's eye. "You had"—she made a lewd gesture with her hands—"with strangers!"

"I didn't, I didn't. Don't worry. It wasn't that kind of undercover, believe me." Hokuren laughed again. "You think I would actually do that?"

"For a case? Yes."

Hokuren thought about that for a moment. "I have my limits. Would you?"

Cinna shook her head. "There's a lot I will do, but not that. Come on, we have a few days for your stories. Tell me."

"If you really want to hear them . . ."

A few stories and nights later, they reached the compound of the Sanctuary of the Eclipse. Cinna gazed upon the Center. The large building loomed imposingly over the rest of the compound from the hill it had been built upon. The roof was ringed with a series of small stone statues, said to be those of the original founders, all one hundred. Time and weather had worn down the statues' carven limbs, and a quarter of them no longer had heads.

The stone wall, standing in disrepair, surrounded the compound and blocked the view of the rest of the Sanctuary. Cinna directed Hokuren to lead their wagon off the road, far to the east of the gate.

"Why would we not go in through the gate?" asked Hokuren.

"The Sanctuary hates visitors and me especially. They'll never let us in." Cinna pointed ahead. "There's a spot where the wall's top is missing, and we can climb in."

"I'll trust your judgment," said Hokuren, tugging the reins and maneuvering the horses to the east. "What are the consequences of being caught sneaking around the Sanctuary?"

Cinna thought about it, drawing a blank. "I don't know. We never had anyone try the whole time I was there. But we won't get caught. I know the place, and I know where Master will be, unless she's dead. Then we'll improvise."

Under Cinna's direction, Hokuren led the horses until they reached a damaged section, where the top third had been shorn off in a crescent moon shape.

Cinna settled the horses with food and water while Hokuren regarded the wall. "It looks like something took a bite out of it."

"There's a story about that," said Cinna, recalling something she'd once overheard. "A monster swooped in and attacked the Sanctuary once, back when there were many trained fighters here, all masters in the techniques of the Eclipse." She pointed further up the hill, past the walls. An enormous skull, with a long snout and horns, lay among the wild grasses and flowers. "It took a bite out of the wall, but the fighters killed it with their fists, feet, and sheer willpower. The Sanctuary keeps the skull there to remember them."

Hokuren put her hand over her eyes to shade them from the bright afternoon sun and gawked at the skull. "Is that a dragon skull? Are you telling me they punched a *dragon* to death?"

"That's the story."

"Dragons can fly. Why didn't it do that instead of allowing itself to be pummeled?"

Cinna threw her hands up. "I don't know. The story wasn't full of details like your case notes."

Hokuren tutted. "I believe a dragon died there, but I remain skeptical about the rest of it."

"The techniques of the Eclipse are quite strong." Cinna shrugged. "Anyway, let's get this over with."

Hokuren looked dubious. "We're going to climb? I don't have an appropriate outfit." She picked at her beloved coat.

Cinna launched into a running start and jumped, planting a foot halfway up the wall to propel herself the rest of the way. She scrambled up and perched upon the broken barrier.

She held out her hand. "Come on, I'll help you. Oh, and take your sword. The master will respect you more if she thinks you know how to use it."

"I know well enough," said Hokuren. She hitched her sword belt around her waist.

Cinna grinned from atop the wall. "You only know enough to realize there's a lot you don't know."

Hokuren lacked Cinna's agility, but she jumped high enough for Cinna to grab her arm. Cinna struggled to pull her up.

"Help me out here, boss! Push yourself up," said Cinna, squatting and pulling with all her strength just to keep Hokuren from falling back down. Hokuren's boots slid along the side, unable to get traction.

"I'm trying," said Hokuren, her voice strained. She dangled from Cinna's grip, the sword at her hip banging against the wall as she swayed.

Finally, Hokuren's foot found a toehold, and she could assist in her own ascent. Cinna hauled her high enough that she could sit on top of the wall. From there, the two of them caught their breath and surveyed the Sanctuary's grounds.

The Center stood out ahead, requiring a crossing of the unkempt field to reach it. The barracks, the training hall, and the kitchen lay beside the Center. From her vantage point on the wall, Cinna peered around the buildings, seeing no activity.

A sense of unease settled in as the familiarity of the Sanctuary washed over her. She thought of Master and the other students. Did she want to see any of them?

The answer came easily. No.

"Everyone must be busy inside," she said, judging by the position of the late afternoon sun. "I think they're in the middle of a session in the training hall, which is perfect." She pointed at the Center. "Master will be in the big building. She doesn't do much training these days."

"It would be great to have this go nice and quick," said Hokuren.

"Now, time to go down." Cinna jumped down to the overgrown field below, landing into a roll that she popped out of. "Your turn, boss. It's safe. I'll catch you."

Slowly, Hokuren lowered herself down until she hung with her boots about three feet off the ground. Cinna was underneath, ready to help steady her.

With a deep breath, Hokuren let go. She landed, but instead of meeting the ground with both feet, only one boot hit, the second lagging behind as she kicked her leg out. She yelped, losing her balance. Cinna got under her and held her upright.

"Let's not do that again," said Hokuren.

"You fall like a brick that has bricks for legs, boss. Didn't you ever climb any buildings or trees as a kid?"

"No, I read about other people doing that in books."

"See, if you'd had to escape market-stall security after stealing produce, like I did as a kid, you'd be in much better shape for climbing up and down. Running, too."

Hokuren appeared flustered, which happened rarely. "I had a pampered childhood compared to you."

"Don't worry, I don't hold it against you, boss."

Cinna led them through waist-high grasses. She had heard from the master that the Sanctuary used to grow its own food when it was first established. But the grounds had long lain fallow and most of the land within the walls had returned to nature.

"How many people live here?" whispered Hokuren, putting a finger to her lips to request that Cinna do the same as they approached the Sanctuary's buildings.

Cinna looked up at the sun as she counted in her head. "Maybe thirty-five? There are about twenty students, then the master and the staff."

Hokuren nodded. "A lot of space here for thirty-five people."

"It used to be a lot more. Which is why most of it is now unused and overgrown. Back when this place had more people, they didn't import all their food. I thought we should start growing at least—" Cinna stopped mid-sentence and came to a halt, cupping her hand to one ear. Someone nearby was attempting to sneak up on them, but they crashed through the grasses without care, their steps louder than a herd of horses. She put her arm out to usher Hokuren behind her as she faced where the noise came from.

"Come on out, I know you're there," Cinna called.

A pale-skinned elf with close-cropped black hair wearing the uniform of the Sanctuary—a tailored silk tunic and trousers, gray with yellow trim, and black slippers—revealed herself from the thick grass. Cinna groaned.

"Francesca," Cinna said with forced friendliness. "Good to see you again."

Francesca didn't appear the least bit ashamed to have been caught. "I can't believe you would dare return, Stub Ears." She fingered the sword hanging from a sheath at her waist.

Cinna flinched at the nickname. She brought a hand up to her ear, lowering it as soon as she realized what she was doing. "We're here to ask Master a few questions, then we'll leave. It's for a case."

"Master is going to be displeased." Francesca paced in an arc that placed herself between the two of them and the Center.

"We'll be quick."

"You thought you were being so sneaky," said Francesca. "The gatekeeper saw you in that wagon, bypassing the gate and heading straight for that one broken section of wall. I thought I should be here to welcome you. And recommend you leave."

Cinna's toes curled into the soft dirt between the grass stalks, but she maintained her composure. "Speaking of stealth, was it you stomping around in the field like you were smashing grapes into wine? I don't know how you manage to be so loud in slippers."

Francesca narrowed her eyes and drew her sword. "You're not under the master's protection anymore. I don't have to hold back."

Cinna put her fists up. Even with a sword, Francesca was no threat by herself.

"Ahem," said Hokuren, beside Cinna. Francesca's eyes flicked to her, but Cinna stayed focused on her nemesis. "When do I get an introduction?" Hokuren asked.

"Now isn't the time," said Cinna. Could she not see a fight was about to break out?

As if she didn't even care about the fight, Hokuren said, "I'm Hokuren, a seeker from Velles. I'm here with Cinna to see your master. Can you please take me to her?"

"Never heard of you." Francesca pointed her sword at Hokuren. Cinna shuffled between the two of them. "Any friend of Stub Ears will not be welcome here, either."

"We have a commission from Leopold, the Prince of Velles. I simply need to ask your master a few questions, and we'll be on our way." Hokuren portrayed a serene calmness that Cinna knew the boss didn't actually feel. "And please dispense with the sword waving. I don't think you'll kill us, unless you want agents from the Palace Guard showing up here and asking their own questions in significantly less friendly terms."

"Boss," hissed Cinna. The sooner Hokuren let her tangle with Francesca, the sooner they could move on.

"I'm not afraid of the prince," said Francesca, biting out the title. "We're not under his jurisdiction."

"Enough, Fran." A boy in the Sanctuary uniform approached from behind Francesca. Tommy. He had joined the Eclipse five years ago alongside his twin sister, Tammy. They looked identical, brown-skinned humans with black hair done up in ponytails, except that Tommy was three inches taller.

"Stuff it, Tommy," said Francesca.

Tommy had heard Francesca's bluster before. Everyone had. "Your personal grudges are interfering with your ability to adjudicate the situation. Stand down and let the master decide how to proceed."

"To the fire with you." Francesca stalked away, tossing her final comment over her shoulder. "I'll go tell the master you're coming." She tried to make even this sound menacing.

Cinna mourned the lost opportunity to deal her rival the beatdown she deserved. Hokuren leaned in close behind her. "Bad blood between you two?"

"Not much." Cinna tried to sound casual, to which Hokuren responded with a raised eyebrow. "She became a student around the same time I arrived here."

"She's your age? You two are quite similar."

Cinna frowned. She was nothing like Francesca.

"Francesca is next in line to be master," said Tommy. "Though she can be a little brusque sometimes."

Hokuren hummed her disapproval, a sound usually reserved for when Cinna asked for extra dessert. "I have some doubts as to her suitability, but it's not my concern. Is the current master like her?"

"Francesca's usually not like that," Tommy offered in tepid defense of the future master. "She just really doesn't like Cinna."

"That didn't answer the question I asked." Hokuren's voice had some bite to it, a sign of irritation. "If you won't tell me, can I meet the master now and find out for myself?"

Hokuren walked a few paces before Tommy, who directed her to the master. The threat of someone so young—Tommy could not have been older than eighteen—holding a sword behind her back gave her some anxiety, but when Hokuren wordlessly caught Cinna's attention, her assistant gave a small hand signal of reassurance.

As they passed by the smaller buildings scattered around the grounds, Hokuren observed that the grasses here were shorter, but only because student and staff trampled upon them more often. Nobody had maintained the area beyond a small radius surrounding the two-story main building and the path to the gate.

The main building looked ready to be reclaimed by derelictia. Misshapen stone walls with discolorations from poor patch jobs featured prominently. A tile floor greeted them in the first room as they entered. Most of the tiles were chipped, cracked, or even partially missing. A wilted plant in desperate need of water sat forlornly in one corner of the room.

They walked through the entry into a room with a dirt floor and walls covered in what could have been bloodstains. Rake lines in the dirt suggested this room received better attention. A variety of weapons hung in a recess on the right-hand side of the room. Hokuren assumed this was a training room, but neither their guide nor Cinna offered explanations.

The wooden floor in the next room, smaller than the two previous, gleamed from a fresh wash. Two large silver candelabras on either end of the room glowed with magical light.

An ancient elf, her hair white and nearly translucent, sat on a mat in the center of the room. Hokuren knew the peculiar way elves aged into death. About one to two years before their death, which was never past the age of two hundred and seventy-five, their aging accelerated sharply, their hair losing its color until it became transparent. The lighter the hair, the closer to death.

From the looks of this elf, her remaining life could be measured in mere weeks.

Francesca had gone ahead to the master as promised and remained in the room, kneeling on a mat to the right of the old woman. This master, assuming this was in fact the master, could be so far gone with age that Francesca, the heir apparent, already had de facto rule.

Tommy directed Hokuren to a mat opposite the master and indicated that she should kneel. Her legs almost immediately complained. Tommy knelt beside Francesca. Cinna remained standing, lingering near the door.

The master was cross-legged, eyes closed. She had yet to move or show any signs of realizing she had guests. No one made a sound, and Hokuren made eye contact with Cinna for guidance. Her assistant mouthed, "Wait."

When the master spoke, it was without moving or providing any other sort of warning. "Why the fuck have you come back, Cinna?" The old elf's voice, raspy with age, nevertheless cut with biting intensity.

"She's with me," Hokuren spoke up. "I'm Hokuren, a seeker from Velles. And you must be—"

"I'm Master Shoshank, and I don't care who you are. I'm not talking to you."

Hokuren sighed. She could have finished her questions by now if everyone here did not need to express their dislike of Cinna first.

"I came here with my boss," said Cinna defensively. "We are trying to find someone."

Shoshank opened one eye. "When I said 'leave and never return' what part of that was unclear? The never or the return part?"

"I'm not trying to return," said Cinna. She met Shoshank's eye. "I would never do that."

"We can make this quick," said Hokuren. "I only need to ask a few questions."

Shoshank opened her other eye and turned her milky gaze on Hokuren. She doubted the master could see anything other than vague shapes and colors. "I don't owe you anything."

"I didn't say—"

Hokuren's rebuttal died on her lips as Cinna said, "I'll go, if it helps." She stood up and turned her back on the master. "I'll be in the training room, boss. Take your time." She stalked out of the room, slamming the door when she left.

The room was quiet once again, Francesca and Tommy waiting for instruction from Shoshank.

The master did nothing for a considerable amount of time. Finally, she emitted a short, hacking laugh. "What an irritating girl." She waved a gnarled hand at the students. "You two, leave us."

"Yes, Master," said Francesca. She and Tommy stood and headed for the door to the training room, following where Cinna went.

"Not that way."

Francesca turned on her heel. "But—"

"That was an order, not a request to open the forum for discussion."

There was a moment where Hokuren thought Francesca would disobey, as she gave Shoshank a frightening look. But then she bowed her head. "Yes, Master." She left the room through the other door, Tommy following close behind.

The interaction raised alarms in Hokuren's mind, but perhaps the master had done enough to defuse an incident between Francesca and Cinna.

When only Hokuren remained in the room with Shoshank, she waited for the master to make the first move. Shoshank's cloudy eyes stared in Hokuren's general direction for a few moments before she spoke.

"Well then. Seeker Hokuren, was it? I see Cinna has latched onto you now. She's more spunk than sense, but perhaps she has her uses to you." Shoshank chuckled. "Did you drag her out of the trash like I did?"

"Excuse me?" Hokuren's eyes narrowed.

"Like anything you find on the streets, if you keep her fed, she's hard to get rid of. You'll have to kick her out forcefully when you're done with her."

Hokuren glared at Shoshank, taken aback. She had not come here to discuss Cinna, but she hadn't expected the master to speak about her in such demeaning terms. "Cinna's my assistant and a good one. I would never want to 'get rid' of her."

"She's a handful. To be frank, I'm surprised a seeker would hire her. I expected her to resume her life as a gutter rat."

Knowing she was taking the bait, but unable to stop herself, Hokuren said, "I'm teaching Cinna, is that what's surprising to you?"

"Well, as I'm sure you know, she's not the brightest star in the sky. Loyal, which is valuable." Shoshank tapped the top of her head. "However, put a pebble in that skull of hers and you'd hear a rattle that could wake the dead. I'd have thought that a nonstarter in your business."

This was ridiculous. Hokuren gave as offended an expression as possible before remembering that the old elf probably couldn't see it. "If you think Cinna is stupid, you don't know her at all."

"I know what you're thinking. You think I don't care much for the girl." At Hokuren's hostile silence, Shoshank smiled. "You know, when I first met Cinna, she was this scrawny little waif, all skin and bones." Shoshank closed her eyes, seemingly lost in her memories. "Grabbing her wrist was like wrapping my hand around a flower's stem. I thought we could stick her with the clothes washers and get her stomach full."

"You believe you did her a favor," said Hokuren.

"She wasn't eating enough. She'd have been dead in a few more months, if that. Favor is not strong enough. I kept her alive."

"Perhaps if you had asked her if she wanted to come, instead of threatening her, I'd feel differently."

"I gave her a choice. Let her weigh the options. Although I admit I put my finger on the scale a bit."

The old elf wanted to play the role of benevolent patron, but Hokuren's doubts remained. "So you say you took her in out of the goodness of your heart. The way she tells it, you barely tolerated her existence here."

Shoshank pursed her lips. "It was a thin wire I walked with Cinna. The nobles who send their children here objected when I let her participate in the trainings. They pay, but she had no money and was here on charity." She grinned wolfishly. "I got great joy out of sticking Cinna on their pampered brats. She humiliated them on a daily basis. The shame was that I had to hide my delight."

This sounded more like the old elf had a soft spot for Cinna, even if it only seemed to be to irritate the Sanctuary's clients. "You kicked her out so suddenly. She had nowhere to go. If she hadn't come to me, I'm not sure what she would have done."

"Ah, yes. I kept her around as long as I could, but as you can see, I'll be good for nothing but fertilizer in only a few months' time." Shoshank sighed. "My affection for Cinna always had to be a secret. And I liked her much more than anyone else here. Francesca will be the master soon. I couldn't be sure what Fran and the others might do to Cinna once I'm out of the picture, so I kicked her out. And I didn't want her to come back for that same reason."

"You should tell her these things. She feels like no one's ever cared about her."

With a wave of her gnarled hand, Shoshank said, "No. Let her be done with this place and all of us. Now, apologies for trying to rile you up earlier. I was interested in seeing what kind of hands Cinna was in. Had you agreed with anything I said, I would have let Cinna know. But enough about the past. Shouldn't we discuss the real reason you came here?"

Hokuren shifted on the mat, giving up on kneeling to sit cross-legged, which was more comfortable for her aching legs. Since the old master could not see anyway, she hoped she could get away with this potential breach in protocol.

"Yes," Hokuren said. "How much did Francesca tell you?"

"Something about a commission from that puffed-up Prince of Velles." Shoshank shook her head. "You know, when I first heard you were here, I was wondering if you had come to hand Cinna over. I suppose not."

"What are you talking about?" asked Hokuren, thrown.

Shoshank tutted. "Don't take me for some fool, Seeker. You can't have brought Cinna here by coincidence."

"You're still not making any sense. I'm here because Nyana and Captain Davenport showed interest in this place. I believe they came here for a specific elf." Hokuren scrutinized Shoshank, who gave nothing away. "The question is, did they find what they were looking for?"

"That Davenport." Shoshank shuddered. "I wouldn't have tangled with him, even in my prime. He threatened me, of course, to say nothing to anyone who came by. I didn't think anyone would. But I have little to lose at this point." She lowered her voice. "We have elves in our ranks, of course, but Davenport didn't find the one he was looking for, no."

"Did he say what he wanted?" When Shoshank didn't respond,

Hokuren pleaded, "Please, Master Shoshank. My commission is to find Nyana, and I'd like to do that, but Davenport is going to do something terrible to whatever elf he finds. Their life is at risk. If you know anything, please tell me."

"You really don't know." Shoshank fixed Hokuren with a long stare, causing Hokuren to revise her opinion on the old master's sight. When Shoshank spoke again, it was in a low monotone, so quiet that Hokuren crawled forward to better hear her. "There was a story he was interested in. A man who used to be a student here went and got drunk at an establishment late at night a few weeks ago. Told stories about the people here." She shook her head. "We have a code. Never discuss anything that happens here, even when you leave. He broke it. We'll have to deal with him at some point."

"What stories did he tell?" asked Hokuren. A sinking feeling developed in her stomach. She had an idea where this was going, but wanted Shoshank to tell it.

"The one Davenport was interested in was about a young woman with the ability to heal her wounds as if she'd consumed a healing potion," Shoshank whispered.

Hokuren stared at the old elf. "Davenport came here because of that story?"

"He did. I told him that, unfortunately, the young woman had left." Shoshank examined her robe, suddenly very interested in the folds. "He offered a significant reward for information about her, but I had none to give. This old brain, you know, doesn't keep memories the way it used to."

"So you didn't tell Davenport about Cinna." Hokuren breathed a small sigh of relief.

"I didn't." Shoshank's eyes were downcast. "But someone did."

"Francesca."

"Most likely."

The pit in Hokuren's stomach returned with a vengeance, rising up to constrict her breathing. "We need to leave. She could have already told Davenport that Cinna's here." It was not much of a stretch to believe Davenport handed out a communicoin to Francesca, in case Cinna returned to her old home. She had to assume Davenport was already on the way.

"How could she do that?" Shoshank asked.

"Never mind." Hokuren stood up. "Thanks for—"

There was a shout from the training room, loud enough to be heard. "No!"

Hokuren froze. That was Cinna's voice.

16

Cinna entered the training room, breathing a sigh of relief to no longer be under Master's gaze. She padded to the weapons hanging on the wall. She would remember the precise grittiness of the dirt under her feet for the rest of her life, but the floor was not the only familiar thing in the room. Her favorite weapon, a quarterstaff two inches shorter than the others, was still here. It had not been made especially for her, but it may as well have been.

She had tried to earn the acceptance of Master and the other students. She thought that if she became stronger than all the students, and proved to them she could work hard, they would eventually respect her. That hope kept her going for all those years of lonely training, of eating by herself at mealtime, of sleeping with one eye open.

That respect never came. Cinna's improving skills only sharpened their loathing for her. For them, your family's name and prestige formed the basis of your identity. Cinna had no family; she could never be a part of their world.

Cinna hadn't told Hokuren about her nights spent in a cell when Master learned some of the students would jump her at night. The cell had been for her protection, but Cinna had always wondered why she had to be locked up and not those who beat her when they thought no one was watching.

Even now, the shame of her weakness caused her head to ache. She needed to take her mind off it.

Cinna wrested the staff from the wall and spun it about, feeling its weight. The staff was perfectly balanced. The wood was light, but solid enough that even swords barely scratched it.

She backed away from the weapons and cycled through her forms with the staff, as she had done so many times. Coming back to the Sanctuary didn't feel good, but this did. She lost herself in the motions, focusing on making the staff an extension of her body.

Cinna's flow with the quarterstaff broke when the door to the training room opened, revealing Francesca and the twins, Tommy and Tammy. They arrived through the front entrance, not the master's quarters.

Wary, Cinna said, "Leave me alone."

"Ah come on, Cinna, let's spar," said Francesca, taking out her sword. "Everyone else is still in the middle of their lessons, so we can have a good old battle, like we used to. I hope you don't mind if I use an actual weapon instead of the usual wooden sword. I think it's good to have something on the line, don't you?"

"It's not sparring if your sword is sharp," said Cinna. She glanced at the twins. "And what about you two?"

They said nothing, but spread out to encircle Cinna.

"I see," she said. "This isn't sparring, either."

"You aren't a part of the Sanctuary of the Eclipse anymore, Stub Ears." Francesca held the sword in front of her and got into a stance. "We don't have to play by the rules with you. Someone would really like to see you, thinks you can help him, and is even offering a nice reward that the Sanctuary could well use. Of course, you could just agree to wait here with us until he returns."

Cinna wasn't accustomed to people wanting to see her. "I assume you offered yourself in my absence?"

"They insisted upon you," Francesca said with a grunt.

"You'd be a poor substitute for me." Cinna twirled her quarterstaff and then held it at the ready. Her odds against all three were low, but Cinna refused to accept defeat. "You know I won't give up easy."

"Suit yourself."

Francesca swung her sword overhand, a long arcing strike that Cinna blocked by holding the staff with two hands. As soon as she deflected the sword away, she twisted to the right as one twin's fist flew past. The other twin was waiting for her, but she contorted further, bending backward to let the kick sail over her body.

"How long can you dodge all of us?" taunted Francesca.

Cinna swung the quarterstaff to keep her immediate area clear and reassessed. The twins shuffled behind her as Francesca came forward to try her luck again. She pressed Cinna with multiple swings of her sword, trying several angles. Cinna deflected them all, backing up against the flurry. The strikes from Francesca came too fast for Cinna to counter, but she didn't yet mind. Francesca was tiring quickly. She would make a mistake.

The twins stood with their swords still sheathed. The battle was now one-on-one.

With labored breaths, Francesca lurched forward, bringing her sword back and thrusting it straight at Cinna's abdomen.

Cinna spun from Francesca's blade and flicked her staff upward in a single movement. The wood connected with Francesca's chin with a satisfying thwack, and she stumbled to the ground.

"You overextended." Cinna raised her quarterstaff for a finishing strike. "You always do."

Her ears caught a faint noise, the slight shifting of displaced dirt. The twins. She wheeled around, swinging toward the disturbance, but Tammy saw it coming and ducked under the staff.

Tommy grabbed her from behind, wrapping his arms around her right arm, twisting it painfully.

Cinna cried out and tried to pry him away with her left hand, but her leverage was poor. Tammy jumped at her, grabbing a hold of her left arm and yanking it away. Now they both held her. She struggled, dropping the quarterstaff in the effort, but the twins held fast.

Francesca got up from the ground, slowly, holding a hand to her jaw. "That hurt, you flaming stubby-eared menace. I'll give you that." But she smiled. "How did you like our strategy? I knew if you thought I'd left myself open, you'd take the chance to hit me. And I figured you'd be so excited, you might forget about the other two for a second."

"Only you could come up with a brilliant plan to take the first hit with a three-to-one advantage." Cinna pulled at her arms, but it was no use. Both twins held her arms out wide with vise-like strength, leaving her helpless in the face of Francesca.

"I won't claim this to be a fair fight," said Francesca, advancing toward Cinna. "What I will claim is that reward. But first, a little fun." She reared back and punched Cinna in the jaw.

Cinna steeled herself for the attack, but her head rocked back and her teeth compressed. Francesca had held nothing back.

"We're even now," said Francesca, shaking her hand. "Although I'm afraid the ledger's going to look rather one-sided in a moment."

Tommy forced Cinna to her knees with a kick to her back. The next punch from Francesca split open her lip. The one after that cracked against the bridge of her nose, breaking it. The blows to her head left her dizzy and disoriented. She hung limply in the twins' hold, the only thing keeping her from collapsing to the ground.

"Got anything to say, gutter rat?" Francesca kicked Cinna's abdomen. Her breath left her, and she wheezed.

Francesca cupped Cinna's chin with a hand and held it up. Cinna's hampered vision made her rival's face fuzzy, even up close. "Do you remember this? Doesn't it take you back?" Francesca laughed mirthlessly.

Cinna remembered. How could she forget?

"Though you did this to us, too, you know," continued Francesca. "How many of us spent days recovering when you went overboard to prove yourself?"

The twins released her arms. Cinna flopped onto her back in the dirt, blinking up at the training room's ceiling beams with her wavering vision. Francesca pressed one slippered foot on Cinna's sternum as she pushed the point of her sword against her throat. Once again, Cinna had been reduced to the weak, small girl who had entered the Sanctuary.

"Of course, there's not really any problem for you, is there? You'll heal this all up by morning." Francesca snapped her wrist, slicing Cinna's cheek with the sword. The cut was deep enough that Cinna felt blood flow out and trickle down her face.

Cinna said nothing, taking the cut stoically. Francesca brought the sword back to Cinna's throat, the sneer on her face another thing Cinna remembered vividly.

But as Francesca played around, Cinna's vision was recovering, the world coming back into focus. There might be a moment where Francesca let her guard down.

Cinna refused to give up. She could not lose as long as she still lived. That philosophy kept her going, from the streets to every fight in the Sanctuary.

"A few more cuts like that and you'll pass out soon enough, and when you do, you'll wake up in your old cell." Francesca loomed over Cinna, the grin on her face devoid of cheer. "We've kept it warm for you. You'll be nice and safe there."

"No!" Cinna screamed, twisting under Francesca's foot, her throat pricked by the sword point. Not the cell. She would not go back to the cell, trapped like an animal.

She stopped struggling and gasped for air as Francesca pushed harder on her chest.

"I know I shouldn't, but I can't help but enjoy this," crowed Francesca.

The door between the master's quarters and the training room burst open. Cinna couldn't see who was there, but she heard Hokuren yell, "Get off her!"

Francesca took her eyes off Cinna. "Can you make me?"

This was the opportunity. Cinna had to take it now, or Hokuren might get into a sword fight she would lose.

Summoning her energy, Cinna reached up with both hands and gripped the blade of Francesca's sword. It sliced into the soft flesh of her palms, but she ignored the pain. She wrenched the sword and drove it into the foot crushing her chest. With a soft squelch, the blade penetrated deep through Francesca's instep.

Francesca looked down in horror before shrieking and falling to the dirt.

Dragging herself up into a sitting position, Cinna touched her broken nose with a bloody hand, flinching at the pain.

Hokuren appeared, kneeling next to her. "I can't believe you did that." She pressed a handkerchief into Cinna's hands and touched the cut on her cheek, so thin it stung.

"Hey, boss," Cinna rasped. The handkerchief in her hands quickly soaked with her blood. "Got a bit of a pummeling. You had great timing, though."

Francesca writhed on the ground, bawling, the sword still in her foot. The twins huddled around her, trying to calm her down so they could safely remove the weapon.

Master passed through the doorway, leaning on a sturdy cane to keep herself upright while hobbling into the chaos of the room. "What is going on in here?" she demanded, her aged voice barely audible over Francesca's wailing. Master had always been strong, but Cinna saw for the first time a frail and tired woman who had lost her authority. She almost felt sorry for her old master.

"We should go," said Hokuren.

"I was hoping you'd say that." Cinna let Hokuren help her up. She had a bit of a headache, but didn't consider her injuries major, not even her cut up palms. "I think I can get back to the wagon at least."

"Good, let's hurry." Hokuren ushered Cinna toward the exit.

"Wait," said Cinna, shuffling over to the quarterstaff lying in the dirt. She found Master's eyes on her as she picked it up gingerly, trying not to agitate the lacerations in her hands.

Master gave Cinna the slightest of nods and made a shooing gesture, mouthing silently, "Go."

Confused, Cinna returned to Hokuren, who held up her sword and pointed it at the twins. "Do not follow us," she said.

The twins stared uncertainly, still crowding Francesca's blubbering form.

Cinna stood over Francesca. "You give up and cry the moment things don't go your way. That's the real difference between us."

Hokuren and Cinna exited the Center and crossed the poorly maintained fields. Cinna's injuries caught up to her as they ran back to the broken section of the wall. The blows to the head had hurt her worse than she realized. Her body wanted to lie down and heal. But she needed to get to the wagon first.

When they reached the wall, Cinna ran up to it and jumped, but she lacked the energy needed. Her jump fell short.

"Boost me," said Cinna, panting.

"Are you okay?" asked Hokuren.

"I'll be fine once we're in the wagon. Boost me so I can reach."

"What will I do? You won't be able to lift me."

"I will," said Cinna, trying to sound confident.

"You want to leave?" said a voice from behind them. It was Tommy, standing awkwardly in the field.

"Come to finish me, then?" Cinna put her bloody fists up. "You want that reward for the Sanctuary, too? I won't go back to that cell." She was in no shape to fight, but she would go down swinging.

Tommy threw his palms up defensively. "I'm not here to stop you. I want to help you. But we need to hurry."

"I remember your help back in the training room."

The twin turned his head in shame. "I have to do what Francesca says. You know that."

Cinna sighed in understanding. If anyone showed her kindness, they became pariahs among the other students, and they saw the same treatment Cinna did, but without her ability to heal. Francesca saw to that. Tommy and the others simply did what Cinna did: survive.

"And this?" said Hokuren. "Surely Francesca didn't send you to help us."

Tommy gave her a small smile. "Francesca thinks Master sent me to get a healing potion. But Master gave me one other instruction." He strode to the wall and put his hands together around waist level. "I'll give you both a boost."

Hokuren nodded. "Let's go, Cinna."

Cinna waved Hokuren to jump up first, so she could make sure the boss made it. Hokuren stiffly jumped onto the twin's hands, yelling and pinwheeling her arms as he threw her sky-high. But she managed to compose herself in time to grab the edge of the broken wall and scramble up.

With Hokuren on the wall, Cinna lined up to do the same. "I have one request for you. Tell Francesca that if she ever leaves the Sanctuary, she should always be looking over her shoulder. I'll be out there."

Tommy trembled. "I can't tell Francesca I saw you at all."

"Fine, then. I'll write a letter."

With his boost, Cinna got more than enough height to grab the wall with ease. She jumped down and then caught a stumbling Hokuren when the boss let herself drop to the other side.

They rushed to the wagon and made quick work of hitching up the horses. When ready, Hokuren jumped into the driver's box and urged the animals on.

Cinna sat in the back. Her eyes shut of their own accord. Before she let sleep take her, she reset her nose so it wouldn't heal crooked. With that done, she found a blanket, curled up on it, and fell into a deep sleep.

Mount Hzarygoot stood high in the distant skyline, far to the southwest. The setting sun appeared to sit atop its immense flat summit. In truth, it was less a mountain and more a rather large hill, but it served as the tallest landmark for hundreds of miles, so the mountain title stuck.

Hokuren hadn't had a destination in mind once she regained control of the horses and wagon. She just wanted to put distance between Cinna and the Sanctuary. If her guess was right and Francesca had a communicoin, Davenport would be on his way. Presumably, he would come from Velles, and Hokuren had to operate under the assumption he could increase his travel speed through his magic. To return to the city risked running into him, which spelled disaster.

The History of Senara's writer was a Great Sage of the Temple of Senara on Hzarygoot. Hokuren looked back at the wagon, where Cinna now slept. Could Senara really be hiding in her soul? Hokuren had not wanted to believe it, figuring that anyone carrying Senara in their soul would know it. But perhaps Senara kept even the owner of her hiding spot in the dark.

Davenport's interest upon hearing the story of Cinna's healing ability increased the plausibility by a large margin. He might know more about Senara than anyone, given the efforts he dedicated to searching for her.

Well, anyone except for the Great Sage. If anyone could confirm Senara was in Cinna's soul, they could. The decision to go to Hzarygoot required

Cinna's input. Hokuren didn't wish to make that decision unilaterally. But until Cinna woke up, they had to go somewhere, so Hokuren had twisted the reins and directed the horses toward the mountain. She judged the distance and thought they could make it in six days, give or take a day.

She took the wagon off the road to avoid being spotted. This meant winding around existing farmland and the horses dragging their wagon through heavy grasses. It required a reduction in the horses' pace and more frequent breaks. Despite this, they managed several hours' worth of travel before the sun set.

The edge of a small patch of forest lay up ahead. Because the forests near Velles held goblin and ogre populations, travelers steered clear. The creatures didn't worry Hokuren too much. Tales of goblins and ogres, whispered among the Vellesian populace, told far too sinister a story. It was unlikely that goblins wore the skin of humans and elves as pants, for example. That would be impractical.

However, the stories also said goblins sometimes attacked wagons for their supplies. These seemed much more plausible.

Hokuren ventured as close to the forest as she dared, then stopped for the night and let the lathered horses rest. She jumped into the back of the wagon, cursing when she realized Cinna's wounds had been left undressed for the entire trip. The swelling in Cinna's face had reduced considerably, and the deep cuts in her palms had already half healed, but they were dirty.

Hokuren washed the wounds, then wrapped them in gauze. During the effort, Cinna stirred, but did not awaken. When Hokuren finished, Cinna wore two white mittens made of bandages. She would complain when she woke, no doubt about it, but her wounds would now heal cleanly.

Satisfied, Hokuren wrapped Cinna into her blankets and lay down next to her. Sleep came fast.

She awoke in the morning when Cinna prodded at her with one of her makeshift mittens. Hokuren was immediately alert. "What is it? Something wrong?"

"Can you remove these? I can't get them off," said Cinna, squatting next to her and waving her bandaged hands. "I want to make breakfast, but I think I need fingers." She turned to look behind her, and Hokuren followed her gaze to a pile of spilled oats on the wagon's floor.

Visible bite marks dotted the bandages in front of Hokuren's face, and she imagined Cinna trying, but failing, to gnaw at them. Now sure there wasn't any danger, Hokuren yawned and unwound the bandages on Cinna's hands. "Sorry, but I wanted your cuts to heal well."

Cinna sat patiently while Hokuren finished removing the bandages and then inspected her hands. No evidence of the cuts from the previous day remained.

"I can't get over how fast you heal," said Hokuren, mostly to herself. A knot formed in her stomach. This was why Davenport searched Cinna out. Could he sense it happening? She chided herself for the thought. Fear of him made her willing to believe almost anything.

Cinna jumped out of the wagon and began setting up a fire. Hokuren cleaned up the spilled oats and joined Cinna outside.

Gesturing to the surrounding grasses, Cinna said, "I have no idea where we are. We seem to have missed the road. Is this what happens when I'm not awake to direct you?"

"A bit of a scenic route," said Hokuren, twisting one of her braids.

"Something wrong, boss?" Cinna asked, picking up on Hokuren's nervousness.

"About where we are going," said Hokuren. "We should talk."

"Did you learn anything interesting from Master? I may have been too busy getting ganged up on by Francesca and the twins."

"You could say that." Hokuren took a deep breath, unsure if she should ease Cinna into her new revelation or dive right into it. She elected the latter. "I learned who Davenport's interested in. He knows—"

"Shh," said Cinna urgently, cutting Hokuren off with a finger to her mouth. She scanned the trees to the south of their wagon. In a low whisper, she said, "Someone's watching us from the forest."

Hokuren peered into the dense foliage, an impenetrable mosaic of brown and green. She couldn't see or hear anything out of the ordinary. "Are you sure? Davenport?"

"Yes, I'm sure. No, not Davenport," said Cinna, focused on the forest. "They're right th—get down!"

Before Hokuren could even register the words, the twang of a bow pealed from the direction of the forest. The next thing she knew, Cinna held an arrow in front of her.

Her brain finished processing what her eyes had seen. Cinna had snagged the arrow from the air right before it hit Hokuren's chest.

Cinna glared at Hokuren, the arrow still hovering directly next to her buttoned-up coat. "I said 'get down,'" Cinna said, her voice neutral, "not to stand still and get shot."

"Cinna," said Hokuren, releasing the breath she'd been holding. "You can catch arrows."

"I told you I could." Cinna looked back at the forest. "We should really do something about whoever shot this."

Hokuren scrambled for an explanation. "Goblins," she said. "Where there's one, there's supposed to be many. They can use bows and arrows. I think."

Cinna played with the arrow in her hands. "Too big for goblins." She called out to the forest, "Hey! Only cowards hide and shoot! What kind of coward are you?"

In silent response, a figure emerged from the forest, tossing their bow aside. Hokuren had no trouble recognizing the white-and-black armor.

A battle page headed straight for them.

17

Cinna sized up the battle page as he approached. "It's one of the librarians. Get my staff, please, boss, while I stare at him. It's important to show we aren't afraid." After a moment, Cinna felt the wood of the quarterstaff in her hand.

"Sorry to sound like I'm repeating myself, but don't underestimate a battle page," said Hokuren.

"I'm familiar with them. But he won't leave us alone, even if we get away. We shouldn't run from problems we can take care of now."

She walked out to meet him. So close to the forest, the ground here was lush with grasses similar to what covered Aviary Park. The difference was in the variety of wildflowers that tickled at her feet.

The battle page stopped roughly ten feet short of Cinna, and she followed suit. They stared in silence at each other until the page broke it first. "Gabriel sends his regards."

The confusion must have shown on her face, because he added, "You met Gabriel in the Library of Reverie. His eyesight is still recovering from the face full of ink you so ungraciously delivered to him."

"Oh. I didn't know his name." She shrugged. "Why did you follow us here?" She racked her brain for questions Hokuren would ask while sizing up her adversary.

The battle page's white armor covered most of his body, giving him decent protection from quarterstaff strikes. His face, uncovered by his helmet, stood out as his only real weak spot. He also had eight or nine inches of height on her, and at least a few dozen pounds of weight. She hoped his armor made him slow.

"You must be brought to justice, of course," he said piously, clasping his hands in front of him and opening his palms, emulating the opening of a book.

"You followed us all the way out here for copying a record?" Though she put some skepticism in her voice, she could appreciate the commitment.

"There's more to my doggedness than a simple record. You made a mockery of the Head Curator with your theft and you left a fellow battle page with a humiliating injury. And, most grievously, you put a book in the path of an axe and ruined it. We cannot allow that to go unpunished. Our honor is at stake."

"Put a book in the path of an axe." Cinna scoffed in an emulation of Hokuren. "What a phrase. It was one of you lot who threw the axe. If you weren't prepared for the consequences, you shouldn't have thrown it."

The page scowled. "You have a choice, you know. If you and the seeker put shackles on yourselves, and submit of your own accord, you have my word I'll deliver you untouched to the City Watch for judgment of your crimes."

"Bad deal," said Cinna. "Even if I were willing to accept that, I don't trust you. If I hadn't snagged your arrow, my boss would be dead already."

"That was a neat trick, catching the arrow." He made a show of looking her over. "Maybe there's more to you than meets the eye. Under better circumstances, I'd ask you to teach me how to do that."

Cinna doubted he would have the courage to risk getting shot with arrows repeatedly until he had the skill learned. "That was a good shot from that distance. Maybe I'd ask for archery lessons in return."

A small smile played upon his face. "I was aiming for you."

"Oh. Never mind, then. I already know how to miss my target."

"Seems we're at an impasse." The battle page unhooked his hand axe from his hip, gripping the leather-wrapped handle. "Last chance to go quietly."

"No one wants to believe me, but I'll always go down fighting." Cinna held her quarterstaff with both hands and raised it in a defensive position.

He walked closer. "My opponents often go down, fighting or not," he said. Then he pushed off with one foot, coming at her fast. The blade of his hand axe tore through the air. Cinna dodged to the right, pivoting behind him. She thrust her quarterstaff toward the back of his helmet.

The page ducked to avoid it. While she was faster than he, the difference was much less than Cinna would have liked, considering his armor and size advantages.

Cinna hopped backward to stay out of range of the next axe swing. It came too close for comfort.

Feinting left, Cinna drew his attack that way before jumping to the right. His swing opened a small window, and she brought the quarterstaff up and thrust it straight into his face.

The page turned his head so that his helmet caught the blow, near his ear. He groaned, staggering. She swung the staff overhand, following up, trying to keep the advantage.

But he recovered more quickly than she expected and put his arm up to block the staff. He lashed out with the axe and Cinna had to twist awkwardly to avoid it. He swung again, and she skipped away. Off-balance now, her back to him, she could not elude his follow-up punch.

The gauntleted fist hit Cinna's back, just to the left of her spine. She cried out and fell to the ground, losing her grip on her quarterstaff. Pain stung her lower back, but she kept her bearings enough to roll through the grass, away from the page. He slammed his armored boot into the ground, narrowly missing her head.

Cinna crawled from him, getting to her feet. They stared at each other for a moment, a pause in the fight. She tried to ignore the pain spreading up her back. Then the ground shook.

Boom.

Cinna didn't dare take her eyes from the page to look toward the thudding coming from the nearby forest.

Boom.

Slightly louder now, the noise caused the page to risk a peek, so she did as well. There was rustling in the branches and leaves, but nothing out of the ordinary.

BOOM.

Cinna exchanged glances with the battle page.

Something was coming.

BOOM!

The biggest ogre Cinna had ever seen burst from the forest into the grassy field. The creature had to be at least fifteen feet tall. He—and Cinna knew he was a he because his far-too-small loincloth waved with each stride, removing any doubt—had muted blue skin and a massive brow. Like all ogres, not a single hair grew on a body both corpulent and muscular. He raised his meaty fists, each twice the size of her head, and bellowed so loudly her eardrums popped.

He had his eyes on their wagon, where Hokuren had hidden during her fight with the battle page. Cinna felt her stomach clench. The ogre took another step, his eyes on the horses. They whinnied and stamped their hooves in distress.

"You!" barked the battle page. "Distract it!"

He ran off toward the ogre. It was rather bold of him to assume they would team up to deal with this creature, but Cinna agreed with the strategy. The only problem was she had no plan for how to distract this giant. With his immense size, the ogre could easily ignore her diversions.

The battle page looped behind the ogre, axe in hand. Cinna ran over to her quarterstaff, snatching it up without slowing down. The ogre continued to lumber toward the wagon and horses, and she scampered to catch up. She grimaced at the sight of his bit swinging back and forth like the pendulum of a cheeky brothel's clock.

"Hey!" she yelled as she got close. The ogre didn't acknowledge her shout. His sunken eyes, big as plates and with pupils black as night, were only somewhat more pleasant to view than the thing behind his loincloth. She lifted her quarterstaff in one hand like a javelin. It would take quite a shot, but if she aimed it right, she would have her distraction.

When she reached throwing range, she stopped, wound up, and launched the quarterstaff. Her throw was off, and the end of the staff hit his cheek, below his right eye. Still, it had the desired effect. He seemed to see her for the first time and swung his body toward her.

Cinna hoped the page could do something with this distraction. She saw him behind the ogre, stalking it but keeping his distance. She backed away as the ogre stomped toward her. The battle page rushed up to it, swinging his axe and slashing the back of the ogre's leg.

Screeching, the ogre swiped at the page, but his clumsy swing caught only air as the page hurried to his other leg and cut him there, as well. The ogre couldn't catch him, but the page's cuts seemed too small to bring the ogre down quickly enough. He might tire before the ogre did, with all the running to stay ahead of the creature's long arms.

She watched the ogre swat at the page like a sloppy drunk waving at a mosquito, his size making his movements slow and deliberate. He shuffled his legs ponderously, trying to swivel enough to strike the battle page. It gave her an idea. She scurried over to the wagon. "Boss!" Cinna called when she approached. "Get me some rope!"

Hokuren, poking her head out from within the wagon, said, "Get in! Our horses could outrun that ogre, I suspect."

"No," said Cinna. "That battle page could have let it come after me, but he didn't."

Hokuren looked up at the wagon's canopy, and then said, "I understand." She rummaged through the wagon and came up with a coiled length of thick rope.

Cinna took the rope. It was heavy. She hoped it would be enough. "The ogre's hungry for horse. If he starts after you again, leave."

"I'm not leaving you."

"I'll catch up to you. But if the horses get eaten, you'll lose your deposit."

Before Hokuren could object further, Cinna bolted from the wagon and back to the fray. Thick streaks of crimson blood trickled from several wounds on the ogre's legs. But the page's steps to avoid the furious ogre's fists had slackened, and the ogre missed by less with each violent swing.

"Librarian!" said Cinna, her gait made awkward by the weight of the rope on her shoulder. "Help me with this!"

Panting, the page dodged another swipe from the ogre, his face puzzled for only a moment before he understood.

They met beneath the ogre's tree-trunk legs, and Cinna handed the battle page one end of the rope. "You run right, I'll go left," she said, barely pausing to evade a stomp from the ogre's enormous foot that would have crushed her flat.

The ogre's next punch caught the rope the page was holding. Slow to release the rope, the page tumbled, and the ogre dragged him along the ground before he came to a halt.

"Move!" Cinna yelled. The battle page struggled to his feet, his movements too sluggish. The ogre's fist caught him cleanly with a sickening crunch. He landed several feet away, unmoving. The ogre beat his chest as he roared, gloating over his victory.

Cinna cursed and redoubled her efforts, trying to push the image of the page's broken body from her mind. The ogre seemed to realize what she was doing and tried to lift his legs out, but she had revenge for the page on her mind. With grim determination, she pulled the rope taut around each ankle to immobilize the ogre before going for both his legs at once.

The ogre raged and swatted at her with increasing intensity as his frustration rose. She dipped around every attack.

Failing that, the ogre grabbed for the rope around his legs, which proved to be his undoing. He tried to shift his legs to better reach, but the rope tightened up. The ogre tripped, crashing to the ground, waving his arms and screaming in anger. The ground shook with such ferocity that Cinna stumbled, and the resulting sound reverberated against the forest, shaking the trees.

While the ogre squealed and thrashed, Cinna ran to where the battle page had landed, finding his hand axe near his crumpled form. She stalked back to the ogre, fingers tightly gripping the axe's handle.

He was pulling at the ropes around his legs. Cinna rushed in, swinging the axe. She danced around the ogre, slicing at his head, neck, shoulders, and anywhere else she found herself as she dodged his panicked arms. Not long after, he started to whine.

Giving up on fighting Cinna, the ogre thrashed at the ropes. He roared and ripped with brute strength, but not before she had landed several more cuts. The axe was a heavier weapon than she was used to. Her arms burned with the effort, but she kept up her harassment until the ogre clambered to his feet.

Cinna faced him, ready to swing the axe again, but the ogre had had enough. He shambled back into the forest, disappearing into the thick canopy of trees.

Breathless, Cinna tossed the axe on the ground, massaging cramping fingers and arms. She left the shredded rope, retrieving only her quarterstaff before trudging back to the wagon. A bleak sense of melancholy settled in as she climbed onto the wagon's back and stared out at the battle page's lifeless form.

She felt Hokuren's hand on her shoulder. "He was going to kill us. He nearly killed me."

"I know. Yet he died helping us survive." When he had died, he had been her ally. Theirs was not meant to be a permanent alliance, but he could have run off and let the ogre storm their wagon, cleaning up any mess left over.

"Can we do something for his body, at least?" Cinna asked. "It seems wrong to leave him like that."

"I agree with you. But I don't think we have the tools to bury him."

After a bit of discussion, Hokuren suggested they respectfully burn his body, and Cinna accepted that as good enough. To wrap him, they took some extra tarp that could be used to make repairs to the wagon's cover.

"Wait," said Hokuren. "Search him."

Cinna found little except for a few pieces of gold, which she left on his person. It didn't feel right taking them, even though he would no longer have use for them.

"He travels light," she said.

"No communicoin," said Hokuren. "He wouldn't have been able to report our current direction to the Head Curator. He wasn't here on Davenport's behalf."

"He followed us because I ruined a book. I only ruined it because one of them threw an axe at me."

They rolled the page up in the tarp, set up a bonfire, then stood over his body as the flames crackled around it. Heat blasted them from both the fire and the sun, which now loomed overhead. Cinna moved her headband down her forehead to soak up the sweat on her brow. She had no idea how to respect a dead person and told Hokuren the same.

"I haven't honored a corpse like this since my brothers' funeral," Hokuren said quietly. "I said a few words then, but they were my brothers. You don't have to do anything. Thinking about him is good enough, if that's all you can do."

Cinna wanted to ask Hokuren more about her brothers, but Hokuren had a faraway look in her eyes. Cinna decided to leave the boss alone. Instead, she closed her eyes and thought about the battle page. She didn't know anything about him, not even his name. But he had been a good fighter, and in a different world she might've shaped him into a valued sparring partner, better than anyone she ever had at the Sanctuary.

Hoping that was indeed good enough, she opened her eyes to find Hokuren watching her. "Are you all right?" Hokuren asked.

"Of course," said Cinna. The punch that killed the page replayed in her mind, and she shook her head to clear it. "There's only one problem to come out of this, isn't there?"

"What's that?"

"We're going to get blamed for his death, aren't we?"

Hokuren tapped her chin. "I think they may add it to the list they have on us, yes."

Confused, Cinna said, "List? We haven't killed anyone."

"At the very least, we stepped in it pretty good with Witherspoon. It would not surprise me to learn that Doubtwell used our presence at the murder scene to pin his death on us." Hokuren nodded at the page's corpse. "Likewise, when this page doesn't return, and it's discovered he was after us, it will be easy to assume we killed him, too."

Anger roiled in Cinna. "That's not right! We didn't kill either of them!"

"In Witherspoon's case, it's my fault for giving Doubtwell the opportunity."

"You're a lot less upset than I am," growled Cinna.

"Not really, actually," said Hokuren, still radiating calm. "But you're angry enough for both of us."

Cinna watched the fire die out, still fuming. The boss taking the blame for Witherspoon's death would be unfair. The Watch had killed him. Cinna herself practically witnessed the deed.

Hokuren doused the smoldering remnants with water. "Come on, the ogre made a scene and we've been here long enough. We should keep moving before anyone shows up here with questions."

While Hokuren worked the horses and led them away from the forest,

Cinna sat on the back of the wagon and observed the charred remains of the firepit as it grew smaller and smaller until she could no longer see it at all.

Cinna napped the rest of the morning away. When she woke, the sun sat at its zenith and the wagon had stopped once again. She exited the wagon to find Hokuren brushing the mane of one of the horses while it foraged in the grass. This time, Hokuren had stopped far from any forests.

"Let me," said Cinna, feeling guilty for sleeping during their travel since the Sanctuary. "I've done nothing for a while."

"It's fine." Hokuren picked small leaves out of the horse's hair. "I enjoy this. I wanted a horse growing up, but my father said we didn't have the space for one." She sighed. "He was right about that, of course. Though I couldn't accept it at the time."

Cinna watched Hokuren finish the job, then lay out food and water. "Boss, bit of an unrelated question to current events. Do you think Francesca and I are the same?"

"Do you?" Hokuren raised her eyebrows.

"Not exactly. I guess, in some ways." Cinna paused. "While I was at the Sanctuary, I wanted to win every fight there. I still do. But beating Francesca and making her cry didn't feel as fulfilling as I remembered."

"You know what I think?" Hokuren wrapped an arm around Cinna. "You're not the same. The Sanctuary is her entire world. You've seen more since you left. You know better."

"Do you think it's because I've spent so much time with you?"

Hokuren laughed. "I get the sense that staying at the Sanctuary can arrest development. It's good you got out. I like to think a little of my maturity has rubbed off on you."

Cinna watched the horses replenish themselves. A few minutes passed, during which Hokuren fussed with her coat buttons, a sure sign she was nervous—just as she had been before the battle page interrupted them that morning.

"Oh yeah," said Cinna, recalling their conversation. "Weren't you going to tell me what you learned from Master at the Sanctuary?"

"Right, yes." There was something like pity in Hokuren's expression. "Did you find out who Nyana and Davenport came to the Sanctuary to find, boss?"

Hokuren did not answer immediately. A sense of dread developed in Cinna's mind the longer the silence stretched. Finally, Hokuren said, "Cinna, you were the one they were searching for."

"Me?" Cinna's voice rose to a squeak.

"You." Hokuren took a deep breath. "Davenport thinks you're Senara's vessel."

Cinna laughed. "Come on, boss. That's impossible."

"If you think about it," said Hokuren, carefully, "it does make some sense."

"It doesn't." Cinna crossed her arms. "I'm as likely to be the next Prince of Velles as I am Senara's vessel."

"Please hear me out." Hokuren put her hands together in a pleading motion. This was serious, and it was time to take it seriously.

"I'm listening."

"Let's start with your healing ability. It's special, and precisely the kind of thing I would expect from someone with the power of a goddess in them."

Cinna shook her head vigorously. "Couldn't I just have a really robust, um, constitution?"

"Sure, it's possible," said Hokuren, charitably. "But you know how I've remarked about the flecks in your eyes shining? I've been thinking about that, and they only do that when you've been injured."

"So you think that's evidence?"

"I don't know. But it's something."

Cinna didn't reply, mulling it over in her head. She didn't want it to be true. Being Senara's vessel sounded like too much responsibility.

"Okay, my next point," said Hokuren, filling the silence. "Davenport's been seeking Senara for a long time. It's difficult to tell exactly when he showed up, but he seems to have arrived in Velles more than two decades ago, according to Witherspoon's account. Not long after you were born."

"Coincidence."

"Perhaps. Yet he's never found you, even though he's been searching for elves and you didn't try to hide from him. Why not?"

Cinna tried to think of an answer. "Because I'm no one worth looking into?"

Hokuren shook her head. "Every elf would be worth looking into, from his perspective. But you're partly right. I'll tell you why." She ticked her points off on her fingers. "One, Ms. Pottsdam registered you as a human with the city when she took you as her ward. Whether that was a mistake on her part, or wishful thinking, it meant that even if Davenport checked on every elf in that registry, he'd skip you. Two, you've worn that headband since you were young, haven't you?"

Cinna's hand went to her ear. "Honestly, I don't remember not wearing one."

"Right. So it wouldn't have been easy to see you for an elf, even while you were on the streets." Hokuren ticked off a third finger. "Three, you got holed up in the Sanctuary. The rules about discussing others in the Sanctuary were eventually broken, but only after you'd left." She put her hands down, evidently done with counting. "If any elf could have evaded him for this long, it seems like it would have to be you."

Cinna felt a wave of panic rush over her. "No, boss, please, it can't be me. There are so many better choices." Surely, if Senara lived in her soul, she wouldn't have let Cinna suffer like she did her entire childhood.

"For your sake, I hope Senara is not in your soul. But you should find out the truth." She stared straight into Cinna's eyes. "Davenport is trying to track you down. And he scares me. He's a killer, and he's capable of magic that isn't supposed to be possible anymore. If you have Senara inside of you, he'll take your soul and give it to Nyana. The soul transference might kill her." Hokuren squeezed her eyes closed. "It will definitely kill you."

"If this is true, I need to get rid of this goddess." Cinna grasped Hokuren's coat sleeve. "Any ideas on how to do that?"

Hokuren held up her hands. "We don't know for sure you have Senara riding around in your soul. But if we can prove you don't, we might be able to get him to leave you alone."

"But how can we even confirm it?"

"I want to take you to the Temple of Senara at the top of Mount Hzarygoot. It made mention of a certain ritual that could be performed there. Here, look at the verse yourself." Hokuren rifled through her bag of books and flipped through pages until she found the appropriate passage in *The History of Senara*. "Right here." She handed Cinna the book, pointing to a short poem.

> *If you believe the god of elves inside*
> *In Temple, great Senara built, confide*
> *The sage, adherent, your devoted guide*
> *The hidden one, Senara, verified*

Cinna read the passage, scratching her head, then read it two more times before handing the book back to Hokuren in frustration. "I can barely read normal words, boss. Please don't give me poetry."

Hokuren put the book away. "What it means is that the sage of the temple has a way of knowing if Senara really is in your soul. I'm wary, because I don't know anything about the Temple of Senara or these sages. But I also don't know if there's any other way to find out."

"I see." Maybe the temple people could get rid of Senara, if she really had taken up residence in Cinna's soul. "Okay, boss, let's do it."

"Are you sure?" Hokuren knelt across from Cinna. "I'm pushing you for this, yes, but I want this to be something you agree with. Don't say yes because I'm asking."

Cinna had to grin at this. "Boss, of course I'm only saying yes because it's you asking. I trust you. So I'll do it."

"Okay, then." Hokuren gave her a small smile in return. "Whatever the answer is, I'll be right there with you. You're not alone."

"Thanks, boss."

Cinna helped Hokuren clean up and get the horses ready for the next leg of their journey. She looked up and saw Mount Hzarygoot in the distance. When she squinted, she thought she saw a building at the very top of the short mountain. Answers to her questions might lie inside.

If Senara was in her soul, and the sage could talk to her, Cinna might get to ask the goddess who her parents were. If Senara could tell her that, it would make playing host to the goddess worth it.

And knowing that Hokuren would be there made this choice even easier. For the first time in her life, she was not alone.

18

Hokuren guided the horses and wagon to the base of Mt. Hzarygoot early on the sixth day after leaving the Sanctuary. Switchbacks carved into the side of the mountain served as the path leading from the trailhead to the summit. Wide and well maintained, the trail's condition suggested the Temple of Senara was important enough to warrant the upkeep.

The mountain's name came from an old, forgotten language. Nearly every scholar agreed that "goot" meant "mountain," but no one could come to a consensus on what "hzary" meant. Various theories had been offered by scholars, from "the flat-topped" to "upon the sunrise," but the most popular interpretation remained "tall."

This trip had little to do with Hokuren's goal of finding Nyana to complete her commission, yet if Senara was indeed inside Cinna, she might have a way to lure Nyana to her. Though the irony was not lost on her, Hokuren pursued this course only for Cinna's sake. Protecting Cinna took precedence above all else, even the prince's commission.

Hokuren spent the day urging the horses up the switchbacks while Cinna performed her exercises in the wagon. Left alone with her thoughts, Hokuren ran through the list of many enemies they had accumulated over the course of the past few weeks. Barnaby, Lord Doubtwell, Okumak Lire. Perhaps the entirety of the Sanctuary of the Eclipse save Shoshank. Davenport and even Princess Nyana had to be considered, although she had never met either of them. As she looked up at the layer of clouds that lingered above the mountaintop, she wondered if they were soon to add the sage of the Temple of Senara to that list.

It would be a nice reversal of fortune if they could find an ally here.

They needed more than a full day to crest the mountain while giving the horses sufficient rest. The summit turned out to be the rim of an enormous water-filled crater. A building sat upon an artificial island of pontoons in the center of this caldera lake.

"I'm glad we don't have to swim," said Cinna, preparing a rowboat tied up to a pole at the edge of the lake, where they left the horses and wagon. "Boss, take your sword."

Hokuren was startled. "This is a temple to a goddess. We aren't going to get into a fight." If you couldn't feel safe at a place of worship, then where could you?

"Things have gone sideways for us enough that as the bodyguard, I can't allow us to go anywhere without a proper weapon." Cinna hopped into the boat. "We don't know what's in that temple, but if it's more Senara soul-obsessed loons, we'll want some protection, I think."

"What about you?" Hokuren gave Cinna's quarterstaff, propped up in the wagon, a meaningful look. "Aren't you going to bring a weapon, then?"

Cinna pointed to each of her fists and feet. "I'm bringing four."

"Oh, very clever."

Hokuren retrieved her sword and clambered into the boat. While Cinna rowed, Hokuren gazed down into the water. It was deep enough the sunlight dissipated before hitting bottom. "I wonder how this lake formed. I've read that eruptions can leave behind a crater, but I had no idea they could be this big."

"Maybe the acolytes dug it out," said Cinna. "Doesn't look like there's much else to do up here."

The temple itself was plain and dominated the tiny island. A smattering of rocks and bushes lined the short path from the dock where Cinna tied the rowboat. White paint covered spotless walls, bright in the sun that shone through the clouds. A staircase led up to a set of green double doors, painted with a circular white moonflower, its petals cupped as if in bloom. As Cinna and Hokuren approached, these doors opened to reveal a woman in a brown robe.

"Pilgrims, welcome!" the woman called down. "We don't get many here, so this is a special occasion."

"Thank you," said Hokuren. Turning to Cinna as they ascended the stairs, she muttered, "Are you ready for this?"

"No." Cinna was staring into the temple beyond the woman. "But I don't think I'll ever be, so we might as well go."

The woman who had spoken came down the staircase. "Have you come to worship at the altar of Senara?" Hokuren regarded her smile and found it surprisingly genuine.

"Actually, no," said Hokuren. "We have no interest in that."

Her smile fell. "Well, then, why are you here?"

"Is there a sage in we could talk to? I'm not really interested in repeating myself. I assure you, our request will be of interest to them." Hokuren saw the woman close off, like Yoland had, her eyebrows falling and her forehead creasing, so she added quickly, "Unless they no longer value information on the location of Senara."

The woman's mouth hung open for a moment. "I need to check with the sage."

"The Great Sage Lady Lasca will see you shortly," said a bald elf who had referred to himself as the "Sageyon," or servant of the sage. An intricate image of a moonflower dominated the back of his black robe.

Hokuren and Cinna now sat cross-legged on pillows in front of a long, low table in a private room. Cups of tea had been presented to them and placed on the table, where they remained untouched. The room had no windows, but was illuminated by magical lights in candles that resembled more moonflowers.

Paintings of moonflowers were all that adorned the walls of the room. *The History of Senara* mentioned Senara's favorite flower was the moonflower, but the temple took that to a rather obsessive extreme.

Left alone in the room, neither Hokuren nor Cinna spoke. Although

Cinna refused to admit it, her silence and the way she wrung out her tunic told Hokuren that her assistant was nervous. And Hokuren's own nerves increased as minutes ticked by. She picked at the stockings on her feet, having had to remove her boots. Afraid to be parted from them, she had carried them into the room and stashed them in a corner.

After an interminable amount of time, the door opened, and a tall, thin elf entered. Her robe had several layers and colors and, of course, featured a moonflower on the back. It wrapped tightly around her body; she did not walk in her tight stockings so much as she shuffled. Large earrings with moonflowers painted on them hung from the tips of each of her long ears, bowed down from the weight. They looked uncomfortable, if not outright painful.

The Sageyon followed her in, bowing and presenting her seat, as if she needed direction. "Presenting Lady Lasca, Great Sage of the Hzarygoot Temple of Senara!" he said, his voice much too loud for the size of the room.

"Apologies for keeping you waiting, esteemed guests," said Lady Lasca, bowing as deeply as her robes allowed. Her voice was not quite unfriendly but willing to consider the idea, at odds with the words of welcome. "I was not expecting company today. I require some time to put myself together."

"We appreciate you seeing us unannounced." Hokuren stood up to bow, hearing the intended rebuke. "The info we carry is rather delicate, and we did not want word to reach anyone else before we met with you. I'm Hokuren, a seeker from Velles. And this is my assistant, Cinna."

When her name was called, Cinna stood up, bowed as she had for Prince Leopold, then sat back down. Good enough.

Lady Lasca nodded and lowered herself to the ground, her robes making this an arduous task. She needed to bend precisely to reach a kneeling position at the table. The effect was like properly refolding a map.

"Is there a kind of tea more to your liking?" Lady Lasca asked once she had completed the complex sitting procedure. Her gaze pointed at the two full teacups on the table. "I have a pleasant herbal mix that can help ease tension."

Sitting back down to mirror the sage, Hokuren said, "I'm not sure we're much in the mood for tea."

"Please give it a try." Lasca beckoned the Sageyon. "Two cups of tea from my personal collection, please."

"Y-yes," said the Sageyon. His eyes met Lasca's for a moment and there seemed to be a wordless exchange. Then he bowed. "I will return."

When the door closed behind him, Lasca glanced at Hokuren. "Now it's just us. I hope that will put you more at ease."

"Thank you." Hokuren suspected the sage did not care if they drank the tea or not. "I like your earrings," she said. She would make the sage bring up the subject of Senara's location. "I didn't know moonflowers were so important to Senara before coming here."

Lady Lasca's smile was practiced. She seemed in no mood for small talk. "Yes, I think we can say that if moonflowers hadn't already existed, Senara would have made them." She adjusted herself, perhaps already uncomfortable in her kneeling position. "Now, I understand you claim to know where Senara is. While it is a little insulting that a human would know what we elves do not, I will entertain the idea that you indeed do. How did you even know she was missing?"

"Well," said Hokuren, not wanting to say too much, "we're tracking a missing person, and over the course of our investigation, have discovered the belief that Senara hides within the souls of elves. Is that actually true?"

"Yes." Lady Lasca closed her eyes. "Senara is a powerful god, and one we owe everything to as elves. She comes and goes as she pleases, and we have all become used to it." Her eyes opened. "But if we could find her, we would love to be able to talk to her. Even once."

"Why does Senara live in souls, though?" Hokuren put her finger on her chin. "The book I read suggested she was hiding from the Primordial Ones, who wish to punish her for creating the elves. Is that also true?"

"The stories we have from Senara tell us this, yes." Lasca lowered her voice. "I think there's more to it than that."

Intrigued, Hokuren asked, "What makes you say that?"

The sage seemed excited about the opportunity to present her views, her eyes lighting up. "I think Senara did something far worse in the eyes of the Primordial Ones. If the problem was creating elves, why haven't we all been wiped out?"

"Interesting." Hokuren hoped Cinna, who studied the tea in front of her while making no move to drink it, was paying attention. "Do you believe Senara hides within the soul of an elf?"

"Yes," said Lasca. "Her *crime*"—the sage put sarcastic emphasis on the word—"was so great she's had to hide for all these thousands of years." She straightened her back, and her tone turned formal once again. "Do you know where she is?"

"If you were to find Senara, what would you do?"

Lasca scowled for the briefest of moments, losing what little patience she had. "Are these questions necessary?"

"Before I tell you, I need to know what your plans are."

"We'd talk to her. What else would we do?" Lasca's eyes, ice blue with bright pink flecks, bored into Hokuren, challenging her with this question. "She's been absent from us for hundreds of years." She snapped her fingers. "Tell me where you think she is, or I'll be forced to assume this is an elaborate prank."

Hokuren took a deep breath. It was now or never. "I think your god is here in Cinna." Cinna tensed, her hands forming fists.

Lasca's eyes widened. "Her?" She threw Cinna a disdainful glance. "I always thought Senara would choose someone more . . . appropriate."

Cinna stood up. "What is that supposed to mean?"

"Someone who takes care of their appearance, for starters. Perhaps someone well-to-do, tall, stunning." Lady Lasca sniffed. "Senara is known for beauty and poise. Her influence over her vessel would make them in her image. They could not possibly end up as dirty as this girl."

Hokuren had tried to get the bloodstains out of Cinna's clothes on the trip up, but with no soap to work with, she could only do so much. And there had been no place to bathe along the way.

"Someone like you, perhaps, is what you are saying?" said Hokuren.

"Well, the thought occurred. I have been serving Senara for more than one hundred years in my role as the Great Sage. I feel I would be a natural vessel, should my goddess require one." Lasca lifted her chin.

"Maybe Senara doesn't like snooty shutaways," said Cinna, still standing.

Lasca narrowed her eyes.

Hokuren sighed. "Lady Lasca, if you could put your condescension aside for a minute, I believe there's stronger evidence for Cinna that doesn't involve her appearance at all. Cinna has a spectacular healing ability, as if she's constantly under the effects of a healing potion." Lasca's eyebrows went up, which Hokuren took as encouraging. "There's another reason, but you may not find it convincing."

"Try me," said Lasca.

"Cinna is being pursued by someone named Julien Davenport, who has been searching for Senara for quite some time. And he believes Senara is in Cinna, as well."

Lasca seemed to think for a moment. "I know him."

"Really?" Hokuren wasn't sure how much of the outside world reached this isolated temple.

"A dangerous man, but one with keen insight. Let me look in her eyes."

Cinna grimaced, but said, "Fine."

Kneeling by Lasca, Cinna presented her face to the Great Sage. Lasca cupped Cinna's chin in her palm and held her gaze for several seconds. Neither of them blinked, and Hokuren couldn't tell if Lasca was using some sort of magic or if the two of them had unconsciously turned this into an impromptu battle for dominance.

Then Lasca reached out with her other hand and pinched Cinna's arm with her long fingernails, twisting and slicing the skin open.

"Hey!" shouted Cinna, pulling her arm away. A bead of blood bubbled from the wound.

"What are you doing?" asked Hokuren, angry on Cinna's behalf.

"Look into my eyes again," said Lasca. Cinna glared daggers into Lasca, but Hokuren saw what Lasca saw. The flecks in Cinna's eyes glowed softly.

Lasca released Cinna's chin. "I will do the test," she said, quiet excitement in her voice. "The goddess could very well be here."

"What are you going to do?" Cinna blotted the blood on her arm with a handkerchief.

"I will do little but monitor." Lady Lasca drew a small vial from a pocket buried within the many folds of her robes and examined the contents, a milky yellow fluid. She shook it, which did nothing to make it appear less revolting. "You will drink a simple potion that I have prepared for this moment. The active ingredient is the extract of the seed of the twinnova plant."

Cinna put her hands up. "Oh no. Are you crazy? I'm not doing twinkle."

Hokuren had never partaken in twinnova, a powerful hallucinogenic known as "twinkle" among both its adherents and its detractors. Users reported having the most vivid dreams they had ever experienced. Some believed the dreams carried messages, but others left so frightened after their first experience they panicked at the mention of the drug.

"I assure you, this will not be the typical twinnova experience," said Lasca, her gaze on Cinna as she held the vial up. "Only Great Sages such as myself learn the spell that changes the twinnova. You will enter your soul and meet Senara." She pointed at Cinna's chest. "If she's actually in your soul, of course."

"How does it work?" Hokuren was curious about what would happen and, although she would never say this out loud, more than a little jealous that Cinna would get to try it. Twinnova experiences were taboo in Velles, but the idea of evocative dreams tantalized her.

Lasca gave Hokuren a coy smile. "Magic." Hokuren made sure Lasca saw her frown at the nonanswer. "I don't know how it works. I only know what I am to do."

"I'm going to visit my soul?" asked Cinna.

"You have a special opportunity. Few get the chance to project their consciousness into their own souls." Lasca breathed deeply. "It can be life-changing, even if you don't meet Senara."

"You speak from personal experience, don't you?" said Hokuren. "Is this dangerous?"

"The only danger is learning truths about yourself you weren't willing to acknowledge." Lasca closed her eyes. "The soul contains everything that makes you *you*. Even the things you would rather didn't."

Cinna scoffed. "I'm good with who I am. I don't have any truths I can't handle."

"If you say so." Lasca shrugged. "You would know better than I."

Hokuren turned to Cinna and saw the fear in her eyes that she could not hide with her bravado. "Cinna, if you don't want to do this, I understand."

Cinna swallowed hard. "No. I'll do this. If only to get everyone to stop thinking I'm some god's vessel, I'll waste an hour lying around in my soul. But"—she pointed at the vial—"do I really have to drink this yellow stuff?"

"Would you prefer it entered your body through a different orifice?" asked Lasca, shaking the ugly liquid in front of Cinna.

"No."

Cinna was directed to sit at the table, Hokuren next to her. "We should know she's met Senara by her body language," said Lady Lasca. "Now, let's not delay."

Lasca handed Cinna the vial. Cinna opened it and took a sniff only to recoil and stick out her tongue. "This is foul." She gagged. "Where'd you get the main ingredient, the temple latrine?"

Lady Lasca's lips were a thin line. "To think Senara chose you as a worthy vessel. It's not designed to be appealing. Just drink it."

Taking a deep breath, Cinna turned to Hokuren, who put on her most reassuring face.

"I'll be here," she told Cinna.

"Here goes." Cinna threw her head back and downed the contents of the vial. She immediately began choking and gasping. "It tastes terrible and it burns," she said, her voice hoarse. Before Hokuren could react, however, Cinna's eyelids drooped and her head lowered. She collapsed, and Hokuren directed her fall as she lost consciousness.

Hokuren arranged Cinna so she lay on her back with her head on Hokuren's lap. Her face showed no signs of distress, and she was breathing normally. "Was it supposed to be that fast?" Hokuren asked Lasca.

"Yes, that's normal." Lasca leaned over Cinna, her head close to Hokuren's. They both watched for a sign, though Hokuren didn't know what that would look like, exactly.

"Do you know when—"

"No," snapped Lasca. "It could be any point in the next hour. Quiet."

Hokuren took the hint and didn't ask any further questions. They sat in silence. At some point, the Sageyon returned and sat down against the wall near the door. The tea he had been sent to get joined the previous tea, all of it ignored.

Cinna stirred after fifteen minutes. Hokuren thought she was waking up, but she was not. Instead, she let out a low moan, and then her eyelids shot open. Her blue flecks outshone the brown of her irises.

"What's going on?" Hokuren asked, concerned.

Lady Lasca whispered a prayer. "She's here."

Cinna stood in a lush forest, clad only in a loose yellow cotton dress covered in hand-painted images of blueberries. Vibrant greens stretched in every direction, with sunlight streaming in through gaps in the overhead tree canopy. The moss under her bare feet was soft and damp.

She pulled the knee-length hem of the dress out to get a better look. It resembled a dress she wanted when she was six or seven years old. During a rare excursion into the market with Ms. Pottsdam, she had seen the dress in a seamstress's stall. Cinna loved blueberries, even at that early age, and asked Ms. Pottsdam if she could get the dress. But her guardian dragged her along, explaining that such a dress would be wasted on a scrawny little girl who almost never left the house, anyway.

The dress she now wore. She did not remember putting it on or, for that matter, entering a forest.

What did she remember? Drinking one of the most foul substances she had ever swallowed. Then being here. Everything in between was missing. Maybe there was nothing in between. Was this her soul? She would not have thought it would be so tranquil.

It was also possible this was a hallucination brought on by the twinkle, a cruel prank played by Lady Lasca. She was not in her soul at all, but some sort of dream that made her wear a dress from her childhood memories.

Her hands went up to her ears. Not even her headband survived the trip into the soul, or wherever she was.

Cinna surveyed the area, unsure of how to proceed. Absolute silence reigned in this forest, and every direction seemed as appealing as the rest. She would need to pick a direction and start walking. If this was her soul, and Senara was here, Cinna would need to find her. If Senara was not here, well, she had nothing more pressing to do at the moment.

The moss quickly became Cinna's new favorite surface to walk on. It squished underfoot, and with each step she squeezed out cool water that tickled her toes in a most pleasant way. As she walked, she gawked at the intense colors of the flowers on all the plants. They bloomed in such contrast to the drab grays and browns that made up much of Velles. The flowers looked healthy; she could not find a single blemish. The leaves were enormous, big enough to wrap around her like a blanket if she wished.

Streams of clear water flowed gently around her, pooling in tiny ponds. Cinna bent over one to stare at her reflection. She looked ridiculous in the dress, like an overgrown child. Cutesy buttons styled like blueberries connected the dress to thin shoulder straps, and she had almost forgotten that some of the blueberries on the dress's fabric had little smiley faces drawn on them. All she needed now was a lollipop and anyone who saw her would ask if she needed help finding her mommy. How embarrassing.

The silence of the forest became eerier the longer she walked. There did not appear to be any other animals, or even insects. After about ten minutes, she came upon a small clearing dominated by a large tree stump in the center. Someone sat upon the stump, obscured by the sun, which was now directly behind the figure. Cinna lifted a hand to block the sunlight and get a view of the person. She had not noticed the sun was setting.

"Ah, my little Cinnamon," said a melodic, feminine voice, coming from the person on the stump. "We meet at last."

"Who are you?" Cinna wished she could get a better look at the person. "I can't see you."

The figure seemed to turn around and glance at the sun. "Oh, I see. Well, it was dramatic, I think, but I suppose it's also terribly annoying." The figure clapped her hands, and the sun disappeared in a blink of an eye. Just as quickly, it returned to the sky above their heads. "Is this better? Now do you know me?"

Unsettled, Cinna looked up at the sun, then back at the figure on the stump. Now visible as more than a silhouette, she was a striking woman with angular features and a tall, robust figure. She had dark green skin, emerald pupilless eyes, and a long, flowing mane of brown hair. Bare feet poked out from a pearl white dress that ended at her ankles.

"I can see you clearly, but I don't know any people with green skin."

The woman laughed. "You're funny, Cinnamon. You know who I am."

"Don't call me Cinnamon." She had let it go the first time, but could not the second. "And no, I don't. Unless—Senara?"

The woman had her hands up in mock surrender. "I forgot how touchy you are about your name." She smiled. "I am in fact what you feared: Senara, goddess of the elves and passenger of Cinna the elf." She inclined her head. "I thank you, my vessel, for allowing me shelter in your soul until the end of your life."

19

Cinna regretted her choice to sit on the ground as she struggled to comprehend the goddess in front of her. The dampness from the moss seeped into her blueberry dress.

"I'm hallucinating, right? This is just a twinkle-induced nightmare."

"I assure you, dear Cinna, it is not." Senara waved her hand, and an image of Cinna lying unconscious on the floor inside the Temple of Senara flashed into existence. It was as if the entire room had appeared in the forest, complete with her body plus Hokuren and Lasca.

Cinna's head was in Hokuren's lap, worry clouding the boss's features. Lady Lasca, licking her lips in anticipation like Cinna would for a slice of pie, stared at her from her position at the end of the table.

Senara snapped her fingers, and the image disappeared. "Welcome to your soul. As you can see, I've made some improvements over the past twenty-four-odd years." She reached down to pat the mossy floor. "You like this, right? I made this specifically for you to walk on."

Cinna turned from where the image had been, her mind far from the moss. "Was that me? Am I dead?"

"Of course you're not dead." Senara laughed softly. "If you were, we would definitely not be having this conversation."

This was real. Cinna's heartbeat quickened. "You're in my soul. It's true then. I've got to tell Hokuren."

"You will get the chance. But since you're here, I think we should talk. Don't you have anything you want to say to me?"

"I do," said Cinna, rounding on Senara. Goddess or not, Cinna refused to be fazed. "Leave. I didn't ask to be your vessel and I don't want to be."

Senara's face remained placid, but irritation flashed in her eyes. "That's not—Why do you keep adjusting your dress?"

Cinna stopped pulling at the dress. She hadn't even realized she was doing it. "It's wet." She averted her gaze. "And I feel stupid in it."

"Stupid?" Senara's surprise appeared legitimate. "I thought you would appreciate the chance to wear it. I always thought it heartbreaking that you couldn't have the dress when you first saw it. You wanted it so badly. Those smiling blueberries would have been adorable on little kid Cinna." She put a thoughtful finger over her mouth. "Though they're also cute on the current Cinna."

Feeling her face flush, Cinna said, "I'm not cute and I don't want to be cute. I'd like my regular outfit back. What did you do with that?"

Senara wagged her finger. "Cinna, this is your soul. You aren't really here, and neither are your clothes. What you think of as *you* is merely a projection of your consciousness. And I, as a resident here in your soul, can project you as I see fit. I used to meet with my vessels in the nude, but so many were uncomfortable that way, I stopped. Would you prefer that?"

"No," huffed Cinna. She looked back down at the dress and a rare feeling of nostalgia washed over her. She could at least wear it while she visited her soul. To please her younger self, of course.

"So now you want to keep it. See, a little introspection can do wonders." Senara's lips quirked upward in amusement. "Now, I'm sure you have a lot of questions—"

"When can you leave?"

"Please don't interrupt me when I'm speaking." Senara cleared her throat. "And the answer to that is never. Well, I can leave when you're dead. Which, from your perspective, is the same thing."

"What do you mean?"

"I cannot leave because that's part of the deal. Once I enter your soul, I become so much a part of you that you cannot survive without me. But I've helped you, Cinna. It isn't a completely one-sided relationship."

"I didn't make any deal or ask for your help."

"Well, you got it. Now, let's start at the beginning. So, I—"

Cinna interrupted again. "Where are my parents?"

Senara was no longer smiling. Her tone turned harsh. "Listen. I let you get away with it the first time, but this time I'm annoyed. When I said 'I'm sure you have a lot of questions' that was not an invitation to blurt them out the instant they appeared in your mind. It was to acknowledge their existence and to indicate that I will, over the course of our discussion here, answer them naturally." She leaned toward Cinna. "Now, apologize."

Attempting to tamp down her anger with only mild success, Cinna wished Hokuren were here. Hokuren kept her cool, most of the time, and helped keep Cinna from lashing out as well.

"Fine, I'm sorry," Cinna grumbled.

"That was the least believable apology I've heard in thousands of years, but I also know this is very difficult for you, so I will accept it, nonetheless." Senara held up two fingers. "But that was interruption number two. Go for three and I'll eject you from your soul and you can live without any answers from me."

"Please, continue," said Cinna, straining not to show frustration. She could not ruin this opportunity to get answers. Hokuren would never forgive her.

"You know, most elves are thrilled to have me in their soul. To them, it's an honor." Senara returned to her serene smile. "I must say, it's almost refreshing to meet someone who feels aggrieved. Now, do you know the story of how I created the elves?"

Cinna tried to remember what Hokuren had told her when she read from *The History of Senara*. "You made them slightly different from humans, but no one knows why."

"Humans have so many flaws. I wanted to do what I could to fix them."

Thinking of Hokuren, Cinna said, "Not all of them."

"Trust me, even your Hokuren. The Primordial Ones did a good job building humans from scratch, but I knew I could do better." Senara clasped her hands primly in her lap. "I spent thousands of years studying everything that made humans work. It was fascinating. You wouldn't believe how the body truly functions. Tiny particles, invisible except under extreme magnification, responsible for giving instructions on creating proteins and . . ." Senara paused. "Sorry. This is all going to be too complex for you."

"I know what proteins are," said Cinna, a touch defensively. "They're in meat."

"Adorable," Senara said, laughing.

"You think I'm an idiot," grumbled Cinna. People constantly belittled her for not knowing things she had never been taught.

"Do I?" Senara appeared to consider it. "No, I don't. You have a very direct way of thinking that sometimes prevents you from seeing how things connect. If the world is a forest, you focus intently on one tree at a time."

Cinna didn't understand what Senara meant, but also didn't want to admit it, so she stayed silent as Senara continued.

"Keep thinking about that. Anyway, I came to understand how the Primordial Ones made humans and even how I could make changes to improve them." Senara waved her hand, and several naked elves dancing around a campfire appeared in a space near to Cinna. "Clothes were unnecessary. The elves I made were not ashamed of their bodies. They lived in the forests and they would dance and sing and frolic and make friends with the animals. Very wholesome, but of course it didn't last."

The elves, Cinna had to admit, appeared to be having a good time. She walked over to them, but they did not react.

"They can't see or hear you," said Senara. "They're merely images I created."

Cinna watched them circle the fire. Their bits bobbed up and down realistically enough, for images. "The Great Sage said you committed a crime when you made the elves."

"She's right." Senara smoothed out a small wrinkle on her dress.

"What?"

"I'll get to that in a moment. I could not make all the fixes I wanted when I molded the first elves. But I enhanced their lifespan, postponed most of the worst aspects of aging, and added the ability to see in the dark. Oh, and I changed the ears to make them longer and pointier. A personal preference."

"Not long enough, sometimes," muttered Cinna.

If Senara heard the interjection, she ignored it. "I wanted to get it right the first time, so I took every precaution and didn't change as much as

I wanted. And would you believe that I got it absolutely perfect? No mistakes, the first elves." She let out a long sigh. "But they met up with humans. It took millennia, but you see the result. They put on clothes made of fabrics, moved to cities, lost the ability to communicate with animals, and now they're pointy-eared humans that live longer." Senara looked wistful. "Not what I wanted, really."

"Did you really think they would dance naked in the forest and talk to birds and squirrels forever? That sounds boring." When Senara stared at her icily, Cinna said, "I'm just being honest."

"I suppose you're right. The elves did find it boring compared to the cities the humans built. A goddess can dream, though, can't she?" Senara rose from the stump, pacing. "Going back, though, to those first elves. Everything I did worked perfectly, and I was ready to start work on the next iteration with even more enhancements. But the Primordial Ones found out what I was doing much sooner than I anticipated. Their agents, the demons, marked me for death."

"I don't get it." Cinna scratched her head. "Why? What was the great crime?"

Senara leaned toward Cinna, whispering, "Keep this one quiet, dear Cinnamon, but the demons want to kill me because I made elves not to coexist with humans, but replace them."

"What?" Cinna was dumbfounded. "But humans and elves live together. They even make babies together sometimes."

"An unbelievable pity, and not at all what I planned." Senara pouted.

"Plus, Hokuren's been better to me than anyone else, including every elf." Cinna stared down Senara. "No wonder the Primordial Ones want you dead."

Senara put her hand to her chest. "Whose side are you on? I don't think I deserve to die. I've come to terms with the fact that elves and humans will live together as equals, even if I didn't expect or desire it. Alas, the Primordial Ones are rather unforgiving."

"Okay, so how come you live in my soul? You're a god. Don't you have lots of god powers? Couldn't you kill those agents?"

"I have"—Senara cleared her throat—"'god powers,' I suppose you could say. But not the kind that are much use against demons. The fiends were designed by the Primordial Ones specifically to kill gods. But I'm here because I had a plan for survival. When I made the elves, I made a little space in their souls for me, should I need to take advantage of it. If I'm in an elf's soul, the demons cannot track me down easily. Souls like yours are the only worthwhile hiding spots I have."

Cinna asked the question that bothered her the most. "Why me, though? If any elf soul will work, and lots of elves want to have you in their soul, why not one of them?" She thought of Lady Lasca, who would be ecstatic to host Senara. "I heard you usually take over the souls of the well-to-do, the beautiful." Cinna gestured at herself. "That's not me. I'm an orphan. I have no money, I have few skills, I'm small, sloppy, barely able to read—"

Senara held up a hand. "Please, I know your story, and I'm quite familiar with who you are. I've watched your entire life."

"I'm not saying this to make you feel sorry for me. If you can choose anyone, why—" Cinna stopped. "Wait, my entire life?"

"You seem to be operating on the assumption that I only recently entered your soul." Senara's eyes shone with something close to regret. "The truth is that I've been your passenger since you took your first breath on this world. I joined your soul the moment you were born. It wasn't supposed to be like this, but it was."

Cinna felt surprise, then wondered why that should be so surprising. Entering a soul right at the start of a life made as much sense as anything else. "You never talked to me. You let me live a life of poverty."

"Most of my vessels never know I'm inside them. They live normal lives, and when they pass on, I move to the next. The Great Sage did not lie to you about that potion you drank. It's the only way to give your consciousness the ability to enter your soul like this and speak with me. I specifically barred myself from having any control over your thoughts and memories, nor can I 'speak' to you from inside your soul. I don't want that level of control, because I'm afraid I would abuse it. I didn't *let* you do anything."

Cinna thought back to Senara's earlier words, something else bothering her. This felt like an interrogation, and Hokuren had taught her a thing or two about those. One of the lessons was to focus on strange, out-of-place statements and tease them out.

"What did you mean by 'It wasn't supposed to be like this?'" Cinna asked.

Senara seated herself on the stump, staring down at the moss. "This is going to be the least fun part, Cinna. I had a whole life set up for you. You were going to live with a wonderful couple." She waved her arm. An image of a house appeared in front of Cinna. It was small, but charming, with an oversized roof and a big front door. "They were good elves, kind and generous, but childless despite years of trying. With their small farm, they worked hard but had a comfortable life. You would be born, dropped off with them, and they would raise you into a quiet, peaceful life. Which is precisely what I wanted."

Cinna's mind reeled. "But that didn't happen. I ended up with Ms. Pottsdam. She was human and wasn't kind and didn't live in a nice farmhouse. What about my parents? My birth parents? Why couldn't I stay with them?"

Senara didn't look up at Cinna. "That would not have been possible, for one excellent reason. I sincerely hope you accept that and don't demand further explanation." Now she turned to Cinna, a sad smile on her face. "I think we both know you won't accept that."

"I won't."

"I want to be clear. You won't like this, and I think it would be better for you if you didn't know. If you still want to know, I promise I'll give you the absolute truth. But the truth can be worse than a nice little lie."

Cinna folded her arms over her chest. "They're dead, aren't they? Just tell me, I can handle it."

"We shall see," said Senara, sighing. "First, a short quiz. Elves give birth to elves, like humans give birth to humans. But what about the first elves I created? How were they born, do you think?"

Cinna didn't answer at first, thinking about it. "Um, the same way everyone else is born? A woman gets pregnant?"

Senara gave Cinna a patronizing smile, like a parent whose child claimed it rained because a god cried. "But what if there are no women to become pregnant? How do you create the first elf?"

"I don't know," said Cinna, frustrated. This didn't have anything to do with herself. "You laid an egg? This is obviously some sort of trick question. Did you magic them into existence, or can you stop making me guess?"

"You're about to find out. I am going to show you your birth." Senara weaved her hands through the air again.

"No thanks." Cinna had a general idea of what childbirth entailed. It didn't sound like the kind of thing she wanted to see. "Can we go to the moment right after I was born instead?"

"Hush," said Senara. The goddess closed her eyes and began chanting in a language Cinna didn't understand. The forest around them disappeared, and all Cinna saw beyond Senara was a black void. Senara changed the very nature of the world of her soul.

An enormous plant with a single white bud almost half as tall as Cinna appeared in front of her, a small circle of grass surrounding it. The bud was closed tight. Beyond the grass, black void stretched infinitely in every direction. "This is a moonflower," Senara said. "Although I made some extensive modifications."

At first, nothing happened, and Cinna wondered why Senara stared at the plant so expectantly. Then, bulges appeared on the bud, as if something inside struggled to get out.

"Here it comes," said Senara, excitement in her voice.

The moonflower bud lowered to the ground and opened up. Spilling out among a sea of translucent fluid was a brown-skinned newborn with stubby, pointed ears.

"What is this?" said Cinna, disgusted. "Why did you show me this?"

"Cinna," said Senara gently. "Has this not sunk in yet? This is you. You being born." When Cinna looked back at her, stunned, Senara said, "Like every new soul I've created, you were gestated within a moonflower."

Cinna felt like retching. "I can't believe it. I don't believe it." Senara kept silent as the infant lay on the grass alone, crying. "You're telling me I don't have parents. My search for them will always be for nothing. Because I came from a flower." The pit in her stomach grew until she turned aside and threw up. "A flower! How is this even possible?" she choked out.

"My 'god powers.' They allow me to manipulate plant life in wondrous ways that no one else, not even any other god, can do. Aren't you impressed?" Senara gave Cinna a smile, but seeing her expression quickly dropped it. "You're the first new elf soul I created in many thousands of years."

Cinna stared at the wailing infant, despair clouding her head. "How can I tell Hokuren that we don't need to search for my parents anymore because they're a stupid plant?"

"You don't have to tell her." Senara shrugged. "Make up a story. I told you that you didn't want to know. But now that you do, you should probably see the rest."

"The rest?" said Cinna. She fought the urge to cry like the baby. Senara would not want to see her tears, anyway. "What more could there be?"

"Well, you should know what happened to what was supposed to be your adoptive family. It may explain some things."

The infant—Cinna struggled to think of it as herself—was now joined by two creatures that bounded into the scene of Senara's making. Wolves. One wolf seemed to act as a lookout while the other carefully used a piece of cloth in its mouth to swaddle the infant. Cinna didn't know much about the way wolves cared for their cubs, but this didn't seem like typical wolf behavior.

"Pets of mine," said Senara. "While their paws and claws make them less than ideal nursemaids, someone had to feed and shelter you until you reached your new home."

Cinna said nothing, dismayed. More than once, students at the Sanctuary had told her she must have been raised by wolves to get a rise out of her. She could only imagine what they would say if they found out they had gotten it right. Too wrung out to react further, Cinna watched as the wolf delicately bit the infant's swaddling and carried it away.

The scene shifted around her, blurring before returning to focus. The wolves were walking through the forest. Now the wolf held a basket, inside which was the sleeping infant. It was bigger, indicating some time had passed. The wolves arrived at a small farm, heading for a house in the distance that was the same charming one Senara showed Cinna earlier. Senara had a troubled look on her face as the scene played out.

Cinna almost asked where the wolves got the basket, but feared the answer would be that they wove it themselves.

The front door of the house burst open with enough force to knock it off its hinges. From within stepped a massive figure clad from head to toe in golden armor. Cinna recognized him, even though she had never seen him before.

"That's Julien Davenport, the Captain of the Palace Guard," she said to Senara. "Why is he—"

Senara hushed her, gesturing for Cinna to watch.

Davenport strode onto the walkway leading from the house, blood splattered upon his armor and dripping from the clawlike fingers on his left hand.

"*THE CHILD WON'T BE FAR.*"

The words filled the air, causing Cinna to wince. It was a loud, deep, distorted voice that never modulated.

"*FIND IT.*"

It was like the soldiers at the palace had said. Cinna twisted her head, but his voice remained inescapable.

The wolves had stopped when Davenport bashed open the door, then started slowly backing off.

Cinna glanced at Senara, who had been unfazed by the voice. "Davenport killed my adoptive family? Why?"

Senara's mouth was a long, thin line, but she remained silent.

Davenport strode across the field outside the house with a quickness that should not have been possible in heavy mail. For all it impeded his movement, it may as well have been made of the same cloth as her blueberry dress.

Other soldiers were with Davenport, filtering in from around the field. They wore the garb of the Palace Guard. "Captain!" one yelled. "The wolves!"

Davenport's helmeted head turned to where he was pointing. As Cinna had heard from the interviews with the Guard, she could not see into the darkness of his visor.

"*GET THE WOLVES.*"

But the wolves were too fast, disappearing into the dense forest. The soldiers could not even mount their horses before the wolves melted away, and the horses would be useless in the thick brush.

"*THE INFANT WAS ALREADY INSIDE, YOU SAID.*" Davenport's

helmet pointed at a trembling guard beside him.

"Y-yes, Captain, I thought—"

He never got a chance to finish his explanation. Davenport's right hand swung out and grabbed him by his neck, lifting him off the ground with all the effort of picking up a small toy. Davenport threw the guard against the side of the house hard enough to break the wooden siding. The guard slumped to the ground like a rag doll.

"*THEY'RE HEADING FOR VELLES.*"

The remaining guards stood to attention and pretended they hadn't watched him murder one of their own.

"*I WILL FIND THAT CHILD.*"

"That's enough," said Senara. The room went dark, ending the scene. The forest and tree stump that had previously been there returned.

Cinna took a moment to gather herself. She felt sick, even after already emptying her stomach, and overwhelmed. She put her hands on her head and squatted on the ground.

"Yes," said Senara, after a prolonged silence. "That is Julien Davenport. Or, I should say, that is the demon who goes by the name of Julien Davenport. And the so-called 'Palace Guard' are its charmed thralls. Though, as you have seen, they aren't completely under its control all the time."

"That was going to be my home." Cinna's voice caught. "I may have been born in a flower and raised by wolves, but I still could have had parents. I could have had a home."

Senara frowned. "Well, saying that the wolves raised you is giving them entirely too much credit. Ms. Pottsdam raised you. These wolves simply made sure you survived the first few weeks. You know, feeding you their milk, changing your swaddling, keeping you safe and clean."

Cinna shot a glare at the goddess. "Close enough." She stood up, her legs weak. "Tell me, what's under that armor?"

Senara thought for a moment. "It is a formless blob that takes over the object it inhabits from the inside. That suit of armor protects it, and this demon is rather clever. By appearing as an armored human, it can hide its true identity. With magical charm, it can make anyone who meets it believe it's human."

"So you need to break through that armor to get at the demon inside." Cinna wondered if demon blobs could be killed. Surely, if they were alive, they could also die.

"Yes. Although the demon cannot truly be killed," said Senara, as if reading Cinna's thoughts. "It can be incapacitated. Such incapacitation could last centuries, even."

"It would be all it deserves." The area the farmhouse had been had returned to a jungle of trees and moss, but Cinna could still see the image of it in her mind. "How did I end up with Ms. Pottsdam? Was that the backup plan?"

There was only sadness in Senara's laugh. "I didn't think anything would happen. The only 'backup plan' I had for the wolves was to take you to Velles and leave you on a doorstep. And you know the rest."

Cinna snorted. She didn't know what she wanted. An apology? It would be pointless. The demon had really ruined everything. "Are you going to take me over like the demon did that suit of armor? Don't you think you two have similar strategies?"

"Of course I'm not," said Senara, offended. "I am merely a passenger in your soul. I will not and cannot 'take you over.' But I do offer some services you may already be aware of."

"Hokuren thinks my healing ability is because of you."

"Yes, I can direct the unconscious parts of your body and run them at maximum efficiency. Your eyesight and hearing are perfect. Your muscles and stamina are robust, your reflexes are second to none. And of course, your immune system, mostly responsible for healing, is much more effective under my direction. Do you remember that toxin that abominable Mr. Barnaby gave you? If I hadn't done everything I could to keep you alive until you got that antidote, you would have died in his house."

"I suppose I owe you thanks. But does that mean I didn't earn my skills?"

Senara regarded Cinna levelly. "You had to put all that work in yourself. I only provide the means to make your training and skills as effective as possible. My typical vessel cannot catch arrows, believe me."

Cinna sighed with relief. Her skills were more than just the work of the goddess. "But wait. If you created my soul, why are my ears so short?"

"I know your ears bother you, and I wish you wouldn't obsess with them. No one cares, except when they know they can get under your skin." Senara brushed her hair back to reveal her own ears, the same stubby shape as Cinna's. "The answer is that I only gave you the same ears I gave to all elves originally and which I gave myself. They were much shorter in the beginning. The elves themselves elongated them, over the course of thousands of generations. Consider it a kind of evolution."

"Couldn't you have let me fit in better with the elves alive now?" groused Cinna.

"Honestly." Senara rolled her eyes. "I was trying to survive, that was low on the priority list. Back to your original question. I need to keep you alive, especially with the demon so close by. If you died, I would have to leave your soul and lose its protection. The demon would immediately know where I am and come to kill me."

Before Cinna could respond, Senara's head snapped up. She raised one finger and closed her eyes.

"Senara?" said Cinna. There was no response from the goddess. She sat rock still, as if her mind had gone to some other place. Cinna waved her hand in front of Senara's face to no effect, then settled back onto the wet moss to wait.

After a few minutes, Senara's eyes opened. "We have trouble."

20

"What are you doing?" asked Hokuren as acolytes filed into the room, led by the Sageyon. She felt the weight of Cinna's head in her lap as she received only silence from the temple denizens. "What is going on? Tell me!"

"Senara is here," said the Sageyon, his voice reverential.

"Praise be the moonflowers," said the three acolytes that had entered with him, in unison.

Lasca sat at the end of the table, her eyes closed and her visage serene. One hand was clenched in a fist. When she opened her eyes, she placed the contents of her hand on the table.

It was a silver coin.

The hairs on the back of Hokuren's neck prickled. She peered over at the coin, and the image of a helmet, face behind the visor obscured, stared back at her. It could only be a Davenport communicoin.

"Did you call Julien Davenport here?" Hokuren tensed and shook Cinna, wondering if it would be possible to wake her from her drug-induced unconsciousness. Cinna remained still.

"Years ago, he promised me the opportunity to be Senara's vessel, should I find the current one." Lasca wasn't looking at Hokuren, and it wasn't clear that she was even addressing Hokuren. She looked straight ahead, a lilting quality to her voice. "Finally, the goddess will be where she belongs, within the soul of one of her great sages."

"You fool," said Hokuren. "He's already promised the soul to Nyana."

Lasca glanced at Hokuren as if remembering she was there. "He was just using her and the prince for their resources, and acknowledged me as Senara's rightful vessel."

This called into question everything Davenport had told Witherspoon about wanting to stick Senara within Nyana. Hokuren stood up, positioning herself between the acolytes in the room and Cinna's prone form. "He's lying to at least one of you, and I think there's a good chance he's lying to both of you. Are you aware that attempting a soul transference will more than likely kill you while it certainly kills Cinna?"

"A risk I'm willing to take," rasped Lasca, licking dry lips. "Davenport assured me—"

"His assurances are worth nothing. I spoke to his so-called souls expert. Not once in his soul transference tests did he accomplish anything but kill both transfer partners. I'm not sure what he's planning to do, but I'm increasingly sure it doesn't involve putting Senara into your, or anyone else's, soul."

Lasca wrung her hands in front of her. "You can't tell me that wretched urchin girl should still get to be Senara's vessel. After I spent my entire life in devotion to her." She nodded at the Sageyon and he and the three acolytes advanced on Cinna. "I don't care what you say, I'm going through with it. With all the time I've devoted to Senara, she'd never let me die in the process of taking her on into my soul. Now, step aside."

Without thinking further, Hokuren removed her sword from her hilt and pointed it at the acolytes. They stopped, uncertainty etched in their features.

"You would dare pull a weapon in this temple to our goddess?" Lasca unfolded herself and rose, teeth clenched in fury.

"You would dare threaten to murder your guest?" said Hokuren, keeping her voice sharp to hide her anxiety rising over the prospect of having to use the weapon. "Does Senara have any thoughts about that? And you would dare think that I'd just stand by and let you?"

"How precious," said Lasca. She made a series of hand gestures at the Sageyon, who turned and left the room. The three acolytes remained, lurking outside her sword range, spreading out in the room. "You're not the only one with a sword here, by the way. Ours will be here shortly. And we outnumber you. So, what's your next move, seeker from Velles?"

Cinna ran over and punched an acolyte in the stand-off with Hokuren in Senara's magic image, but her fist went straight through his face.

"I already told you, this is an image. They're not real," said Senara, as Cinna tried again with a kick, her foot sailing through the apparition.

Cinna clenched and unclenched her fists. "I should be there to protect Hokuren. Instead, I'm here blabbering with you while she has to protect me. That's not how it's supposed to work."

"Patience, please," said Senara. "I feel your frustration and trust me, you'll get a chance to blow off some steam in a minute, but we need to finish our talk first."

"No!" shouted Cinna. "I'm needed there."

"Recall that you are under the effects of a powerful sedative, which still has far too long to go before its effects wear off. I am aware of the need to wake you up early, and I am doing everything I can to achieve that, but it takes time."

"Go faster."

"Your body is a complicated set of processes, too complex to describe in the limited time we have here, and I cannot—" Senara paused beneath Cinna's seething stare. "The point is, we have some time in which we can do nothing but talk. Your human friend will have to hold out until that time."

"What do we need to talk about?" Cinna sighed. Everything happened on the goddess's terms, she had come to discover.

"Well, the demon is on its way to the temple. You have a few days to escape—if it was in Velles, it can speed its travel but will still require three days at a minimum to arrive. But if you've been paying even the slightest bit of attention, you should know that it arriving while you are as well results in both our deaths. You need to run. Go far away, where it will never find you."

"Hold on. I don't run from my problems." Cinna gave the goddess a grim smile. "I'm not you."

"There's a reason I'm still alive." Senara's voice harshened, her emerald eyes an unending blackness. The skies overhead filled with foreboding dark clouds. Lightning struck, setting a tree ablaze, and the resulting thunderclap reverberated in Cinna's skull. Growing to three times her original size, Senara loomed over Cinna.

"Don't be foolish, elf child of mine." Senara's words crashed down, harsh as the thunder and lightning. "The demon is a creature of the Primordial Ones, its entire body covered in a special armor. You have no way to penetrate it. It wants to kill me, and to do that, it will kill you. It will use the Soul Jade, and you will suffer horrible agony in your final moments."

Cinna tilted her head to stare up at the goddess, planting her feet deep into the moss in defiance. If these magical tricks were supposed to make her cower, they failed. With as much dignity as she could muster in her blueberry dress, she said, "I won't be running."

A second lightning bolt struck, closer this time, bringing another monstrous thunderclap. The clouds sundered, thrashing thick sheets of rain onto Cinna. Within moments, her hair was plastered to her head and her dress clung to her skin. As if standing in a waterfall, she could not look into the crashing rain above.

Still, over the din of the cascading rainfall, she shouted, "I will not run!"

The rain stopped, and the skies cleared. Cinna shook her head, sending water in all directions. Senara returned to her original form, her eyes a clear green once more.

"Usually that little routine gets me what I want." Senara pouted, her voice now remarkably soft compared to what she was capable of. "You're a stubborn one, Cinnamon."

"I won't budge." Water dripped onto the moss from Cinna's head, fingers, and the hem of her drenched dress. She felt like a drowned rat, and imagined she looked like one, too. "You want me to live in constant fear, passively waiting for the demon to hunt me down? Never."

Exasperated, Senara said, "I want you to run away so we both live, fear or not. I've taken the liberty of coming up with some options. Trebello has a wonderful climate, and it's located far across the Sea of Expanse. It's a bit chilly in the winter, and somewhat uncomfortably authoritarian, yes, but so is Velles, really, so you'll barely notice—"

Cinna ignored Senara's earlier demands not to interrupt her. "I'll never be able to truly hide from it, though. It knows who I am now. It will find me." Senara said nothing, so Cinna rolled on. "I'm right, aren't I? There's no good option available, but the only one I'm willing to do is to face this head-on." She gestured at the image in front of her, where Hokuren now faced down two acolytes armed with swords in the only sword fight Cinna had ever seen in which none of the participants wanted to make a move. "If it's coming to the temple, then I can end this right here."

Senara sighed theatrically. "Please understand, you're not prepared to deal with a demon. Hokuren has a sword that will do nothing to its armor and you have even less. At the very least, you cannot hope to take it on in the temple, surrounded by acolytes who will further hinder you."

Cinna begrudgingly agreed that the temple was not the right time and place for the encounter for one reason: Hokuren. She couldn't bear to see Hokuren killed as collateral damage in a battle with Davenport. But Hokuren could come up with a plan, and Cinna could get her showdown on her terms, not the demon's.

She stared at the image, taking in each of the acolytes' faces. Her enemies. They had numbers, but most of them were nonthreatening. "Okay, so to get out of the temple, we'll have to deal with all these acolytes."

"I'll help with that. I have an unusually strong connection with Lasca. Perhaps because this is my temple, and she really has been as devoted to me as she claims." Senara squinted at the image, peering at the coin on the table. "I think I can emulate one of those communicoins. I felt the magic when Lasca used hers. By the way, if you see Fenton again, tell him I find the name charming."

"What are you going to do?"

"Shh, you'll know. I'm almost ready to wake you, but allow me to impart one more piece of knowledge upon you. It's difficult to build a temple on an island at the top of a mountain. The wood brought here had to be light. Its walls are thin."

"So?" Cinna scratched her head.

Senara raised her eyebrows, but Cinna still didn't understand. The goddess sighed. "So if the front door isn't an option, make yourself a back door."

"Oh, I see."

"All that's left to do is wake you up and hope you can escape with your life." Senara folded her arms over her chest. "I will keep the sedative in the twinnova potion at bay as long as I can. However, at some point I will have to allow it to work its way back in past the blood-brain barrier where it bonds with receptors and—" She seemed to notice Cinna's impatient glare. "Right, right. I forget no one knows about any of that. In Cinna terms, it means you'll be alert for a few hours before the remaining sedative will take effect and put you back to sleep until it's gone."

"Got it," said Cinna. She barely listened to Senara's droning about the sedative, focusing on the situation in the temple.

"Now, my little Cinnamon. When you wake, focus on the immediate and get out alive. And then after, perhaps consider my proposal to flee from the demon."

Cinna ignored her. "Wake me up." She was still watching the image. "I'm coming, Hokuren."

"Goodbye, Cinnamon."

In one moment, Cinna stood next to Senara and heard her say goodbye. In the next instant, she lay on her back, staring up at a sword slicing through the air.

Hokuren swept her sword in a wide arc to keep the acolytes at bay. She didn't consider herself great with the weapon, but these acolytes seemed to have never used them before. Their greater numbers kept things at a standoff.

Before she could think about leaving, she would need Cinna to wake up. There was no way out Hokuren saw that involved carrying Cinna out of the temple. Luckily, her assistant woke before Hokuren considered more drastic awakening techniques.

"Cinna, you're awake!"

Cinna groaned, holding her head. "I'm a little woozy, boss," she said. "It's like my head is stuffed with cotton."

Lasca, still standing to the side, said, "What are you waiting for? Take her—" She froze, eyes glassy. The acolytes exchanged glances. It was as if she'd entered a communicoin trance. Only the coin was still on the table and not in the sage's hand.

"This is good, boss," whispered Cinna. She got to her feet. "I think."

"Davenport is here!" said Lasca, her voice exuberant. "We must meet him at once! The rest of you, with me." Lasca shuffled as quickly as possible in her restrictive robes. "We'll lock these two in the room for Davenport to deal with. That sword won't be much use against him."

"Davenport?" Hokuren's blood ran cold as the acolytes filed out behind Lasca, obeying her command without question. The two with the swords backed up, ready for one last desperate attack, but Hokuren found herself unable to move. "Here, already?" she squeaked.

The door closed and the lock was engaged, leaving Hokuren alone with Cinna in silence, save the fading socked steps of Lasca and her entourage.

"That flimsy lock wouldn't hold me for even a minute, but we're not going that way." Cinna had pressed her palms against the back wall, pushing against it. Then she put her ear up to the wall and knocked at a few different places.

"But the only exit is the front door, and if Davenport is there—" Hokuren shook with fright. It didn't seem as if Cinna was acting with enough urgency for the situation. "What are you doing?"

Cinna stopped her bizarre study of the wall and laid a steadying hand on Hokuren's shoulder. "Davenport isn't here yet, boss. Lasca has been misled. We have time to make our escape." She pointed at the back wall. "We're getting our own private exit by bashing up these thin walls."

Hokuren stood dumbfounded. "I suppose now is a bad time to ask how you know all this." She raised her sword. "Attack the wall?"

"As hard as you can."

Hokuren gripped the sword with two hands and heaved it upwards and behind her head before bringing it down on the wall with an overhand smash. Paintings of moonflowers crashed to the ground and wood splintered. Her sword burst through the wall, stuck after opening a slit. Cracks formed around the small hole.

She yanked the sword, but it wouldn't budge.

"Great start, boss." Cinna spun into a kick just beside the sword, breaking the wall further and freeing the sword. "Again."

Together, it took only two more sword swings and three more kicks to create an opening large enough for them to slip out of. The back of the island was a quick hop down.

"They'll see us if we take the boat," said Cinna, looking out over the water.

"We don't have a choice to cross the lake," said Hokuren.

They crept along the perimeter of the temple, needing precious few steps to reach the front. Lasca's fiefdom was tiny. Perhaps no wonder she wanted her time spent here to lead to something as grand as becoming Senara's vessel.

"Where is Davenport?" Lasca's voice, audible once Hokuren could see their boat, cracked. "Senara said—she told me he was here. Did she. . . lie?"

A genuflecting acolyte made placating gestures at Lasca. "Great Sage, I'm sure there's an explanation."

Cinna mouthed, "The boat." They slinked towards the craft, still tied up to the dock. This exposed them to the sage and her acolytes, and it didn't take long for Lasca's confused glance to turn to malice.

"How did they escape? Stop them!" Lasca's shout rang out over the still mountaintop air.

"Run!" Cinna dashed to the boat, reaching it before Hokuren. She unwound the rope tethering the boat to the dock with frantic motions.

Hokuren slashed her sword, cutting the remaining rope and freeing the boat. "Get in."

Cinna didn't need to be told twice. She leaped in and then helped Hokuren to the far bench. The temple disgorged four acolytes, some armed with bows and arrows. With an oar in hand, Cinna shoved the boat off into the water. She handed the other oar to Hokuren before facing the acolytes that lined up at the end of the dock.

"Need you to row, boss."

The first arrows whizzed past Hokuren's head. "Okay, rowing." She wished Cinna had let her have both oars. As it was, she had to alternate rowing on the left, then rowing on the right, to keep their course reasonably straight.

The archers fired a second volley. Cinna held the oar up and spun the blade out to smash the arrows in midair. They snapped, splashing into the lake in pieces.

Seeing this, the archers placed their bows aside, and for a moment, Hokuren thought they had already given up. She crossed that idea off when they, along with other acolytes, piled into the other two rowboats and cast off in pursuit.

Cinna sat down and put her oar into the water. Without a word, they synchronized their strokes—Hokuren to the left, Cinna to the right—to propel the boat. The acolytes, for all their lack of skill with swords and bows, rowed with clinical precision and despite Hokuren's and Cinna's efforts began narrowing the gap their head start had provided.

"We need to row faster," said Hokuren.

"Or we let them come to us and I whack them with this oar," said Cinna.

There was a faint rumbling from below.

The acolytes had a brief period of infighting on the subject of continuing the chase. They did, but with trepidation.

"Should we be concerned?" Hokuren couldn't see more than a few feet into the water beneath them.

Cinna joined her in peering down into the depths. "I don't think so."

Almost halfway across the crater lake, there was another rumbling, this one much louder. An enormous shadow dwarfed their boat from within the water, as well as the two acolyte boats. And it was getting bigger.

"Now I think we should be concerned," said Cinna.

"We may need to brace for impact." Hokuren surprised herself with how calm she sounded.

"We should hit it with—"

Cinna didn't get a chance to finish that thought. The shadow breached the water directly beneath them with alacrity, lifting their boat well above the water and throwing it up into the air. Hokuren fell away from the boat, and for a few long, terrifying seconds, tumbled freely. She caught a brief glance of a massive whale-like creature breaching the lake's surface, its huge snout open to reveal rows of curtain-like teeth.

She spun and now glimpsed Cinna, who oriented herself into a dive as she fell. Cinna shouted something at Hokuren, but she couldn't hear it over the leviathan's deafening splash as it returned to the water.

The acolytes and their boats had been tossed up as well, and Hokuren might have found their flailing in their oversized robes amusing were she not doing the exact same thing.

With the grace of a sack of flour, Hokuren hit the lake. Her back took the brunt of the force, stunning her. She sank and held her breath as she tried to coax her unresponsive muscles to work.

The world around her grew dark as she descended further. She flexed her arms and legs, but her lungs ached. The last breath she took had been short.

She thought this was the end, blackness creeping into the edges of her vision, until arms grabbed her and hauled her back to the surface. Her head crested the water and she took a grateful gulp of air. Pieces of now-ruined rowboats floated around her. The acolytes were bobbing in the water, closer to the temple.

Cinna, holding onto Hokuren, popped her head above the surface as well. "Are you okay, boss? I told you to make yourself as skinny as possible."

"Even if I heard you, I don't have any idea what that means," grouched Hokuren. Her heavy coat and boots made even staying afloat challenging, and if Cinna let her go, she wasn't sure she wouldn't sink again. "We need to get to land before that... whatever it is returns for round two."

"The whale thing helped us out." Cinna nodded toward the edge of the crater lake. They had been thrown in the right direction, at least, closer to where they left their wagon, but a daunting swim remained. Cinna, seeing Hokuren's struggles, said, "Hang on, boss."

"What are you going to—"

Cinna took a deep breath and dove underwater, swimming under Hokuren. She felt Cinna's hands push her from behind, legs kicking. Cinna guided Hokuren to the shore more quickly and safely than Hokuren could have swum herself.

They crawled out of the water and onto the shore. Hokuren panted, winded even though she did not swim the last part. Even the indefatigable Cinna seemed exhausted, her face drawn, as she stood up and pulled Hokuren to her feet.

Hokuren looked back toward the temple. The leviathan had resurfaced, a shiny black curve visible over the surface of the water. The acolytes had swam to the temple—which could not have been an easy feat in robes—and, with no more boats at the dock, were rather stuck. They would need to wait for the next visitor to take a boat from the far end of the crater to have an exit, or complete a grueling swim.

For a moment, she thought perhaps the leviathan worked to protect them, but dismissed the thought as impossible.

"Let's put some distance between us and the temple." Hokuren shed her soaked coat, buckled her sword belt around her waist, and readied the horses. Cinna jumped into the back while Hokuren urged the horses into as much speed as she dared while going downhill on a mountain switchback.

After a few hours, during which Cinna maintained a close watch on their rear to see if the acolytes followed, Hokuren pulled the wagon into a flat area off the trail, meant for resting travelers. "It's getting dark," she said. "The horses are spent, too. Let's hide this the best we can."

They could do little to obscure the wagon. Vegetation was light even this far down the mountain, and while they did cover the wagon with some excess tarp, that only made it look like a wagon covered in tarp. Hokuren hoped the acolytes of the temple didn't have another boat stashed elsewhere near their temple.

"As long as we can get off this mountain before Davenport shows up, I think we're in the clear," said Cinna.

The tension in Hokuren's shoulders eased. "We can't be too careful, but I do agree."

They shared a small meal of salted meat and bread outside the wagon. Cinna ate without her usual gusto and stared blankly into the middle distance.

"You were right about the sword." Hokuren hoped for a quip from Cinna, something along the lines of "I told you so," but received nothing but a small, disinterested nod. "Are you all right?" Hokuren asked, now concerned.

"I'm fine, boss. You know me." Cinna's usual bravado fell flat, however. Hokuren had never heard her so down.

"Of course you would say that. But it's rare that you aren't interested in eating." When Cinna said nothing, Hokuren continued, "You took that potion so you could meet Senara in your soul. Did you?"

Still, Cinna said nothing. She stared at the floor, leaving Hokuren at a loss as to what to do. Obviously, something had happened, but Hokuren couldn't help without knowing the problem.

"You don't have to keep it all inside," Hokuren said. Cinna bit her lip, a nervous tic Hokuren had never seen from her. "Whatever happened, please, let me help you."

Cinna got up and walked a few steps away from Hokuren. "I—" Cinna paused for some time, her back to Hokuren. "I'm—" Hokuren heard the warble in Cinna's voice and realized that she was doing something Hokuren never expected to see.

Cinna was crying.

Before Hokuren could react, Cinna slumped to the ground, kneeling, burying her head in her hands. Her sniffles grew louder and transformed into uncontrollable sobs that echoed off the side of the mountain.

Hokuren walked over and knelt behind Cinna. Gently, she wrapped her arms around Cinna's torso, pulling her close to envelop her. At first, Cinna seemed to stiffen, but Hokuren whispered, "It's okay. Let it out." Cinna relaxed into Hokuren's embrace.

They sat like that for a while, the soft sounds of Cinna's cries all that broke the quiet of the mountain. Finally, she exhausted herself, falling asleep, held up only by Hokuren's grasp. Careful to avoid waking her, Hokuren willed strength into her own weary body and carried Cinna to the wagon, laying her down under a blanket.

Even in sleep, Cinna's face remained troubled. Hokuren dried the still glistening tears and snot from Cinna and sat beside her. Whatever she had experienced, helping her navigate through whatever she had been told was the least Hokuren could do for her now.

21

Cinna slipped from the wagon into the early rays of sunlight, careful not to disturb the still slumbering Hokuren. Birds chirped nearby in the tranquil morning.

Her face flushed with embarrassment as she thought about the previous evening. If she had ever cried before, she had been so young she could not remember it. She learned to hold it in, never show her pain. Not when Ms. Pottsdam died. Not when she almost starved to death in the streets of Velles. Not when the Sanctuary used her daily as a punching bag.

But the previous night, for reasons she had yet to figure out, she had not held back.

The rest area had space for a small fire, but the trees here were short, their branches little more than twigs. It required a good amount of effort for Cinna to scrounge up enough of the pathetic sticks to get the fire going. Once she had collected as many as she could hold, she had an epiphany. She had cried because Hokuren cared in a way no one had before.

Ms. Pottsdam would slap her if she misbehaved, or drag her by the arm if the old woman felt she was lollygagging during a shopping trip. But Cinna missed out on hugs, hair tousles, and gentle praises—all the affections of childhood. When Hokuren held her, she had felt comforted for the first time in her life.

Cinna didn't know how to tell Hokuren that.

Using the motley assortment of wood she collected, Cinna managed a fire to heat her usual concoction of water and oats. The porridge soon bubbled in its pot, but she was not yet ready to pull the dish from the flames. The warming oats were a welcome distraction from her thoughts.

Hokuren awakened and emerged from the wagon to cross the now twig-free ground. "Cinna," she said as she approached. "Are you feeling better?"

"I'm fine," said Cinna, her eyes on her spoon stirring the porridge. She was not fine, and she knew Hokuren could tell. But claiming to be fine was always going to be her reply. "I'm sorry about last night. I don't usually do that."

Hokuren put her hands on Cinna's chin, guiding Cinna's face toward her. "Please don't say that. You did nothing wrong, except to hold everything in for so long. When you bottle everything up inside you, eventually you burst." Cinna remained silent, no good response coming to mind. Hokuren released her and continued, "I'm the one who needs to apologize. I shouldn't have brought you to that temple. I didn't realize how determined they would be about getting hold of Senara."

"You couldn't have known. And, despite that, I'm glad you did, boss." Cinna thought back to her conversation with the goddess. "Senara told me a little lie was better than the truth, but I disagree. I can face this truth, even though . . ." she trailed off, already feeling like she had said too much.

She braced herself for Hokuren to ask about that truth, but Hokuren said, "Did your cry help you feel better? It really can be cathartic."

Cinna nodded. "I appreciate you hugging me. It was . . . nice." The words came out halting and stilted, but she meant them. They were just hard to say.

"I'm glad." Hokuren put her hand on Cinna's arm and squeezed. She peered into the pot of porridge, grimacing at the contents. "This seems well past done. Maybe we should eat before it congeals?"

They ate in silence, Cinna taking her time with her share. While eating, her encounter with Senara weighed on her mind, much as she tried to avoid it. No parents. She had to tell Hokuren.

When all the food had been consumed and the cooking materials cleaned and packed, Cinna summoned her courage. "Boss," she said, and Hokuren looked up expectantly. "If you still want to know what happened, I want to tell you."

"Of course." Hokuren seated herself upon a rock jutting out from the dirt. "Whatever you want to tell me, I'll listen."

Cinna stood in front of her and started from the top, from the moment she woke up in her soul. She told Hokuren everything she could remember, acting out scenes to jog her memory. When she reached the part about being born from the moonflower, she struggled, but kept going with a small encouragement from Hokuren. Finishing with the moment she returned to consciousness, Cinna felt drained all over again.

"That was a lot to take in," said Hokuren, looking overwhelmed herself. She had listened patiently, never interrupting, as Cinna went on. She knew Hokuren would remember everything, and she hoped the boss would have some insights that she could not come up with herself.

Hokuren gave Cinna a sympathetic smile. "I can understand why that made you so upset. But however you were born, you're still you. It doesn't affect anything about who you are, and I sincerely hope you won't let it."

Cinna stared at the little trees, and neither she nor Hokuren spoke. All the talk about herself exhausted her, and Senara had provided information on more important topics that deserved discussion.

"So, about Julien Davenport."

"Ah, yes. What was it you called the demon? The agent of the Primordial Ones?" Hokuren tapped her finger on her chin. "Well, I had reason to suspect Davenport was something other than human, although I didn't guess demon. Do you remember the stories about him we got from the soldiers in the palace?"

"The voice thing is real, boss. Davenport being a demon explains those stories. As well as the lack of underwear."

Hokuren smiled. "And the lack of underwear, yes." Her smile disappeared. "But, also, that demon has been searching for you since the moment you were born. And this confirms what I had already suspected after what Lasca told me. Davenport never intended for Nyana to receive Senara's soul."

"What does that mean, boss? And why has it been playing at Captain of the Palace Guard?"

"The theory is simple," said Hokuren, getting up from the rock to pace the camp. She had taken control of the conversation, which suited Cinna.

"As Captain of the Guard, the demon would have plenty of power and influence to search for you. It would earn the prince's favor by promising to find the current vessel and transfer the soul to Nyana, its rightful owner. It could have told the prince many stories about Senara and her powers."

"Well, Senara is responsible for my healing, as you said." Cinna frowned, playing with a rock on the ground with her toes. "I guess that's a power."

"But the demon's work with Arnold Witherspoon was all a ruse to keep Nyana, and the prince, believing that was what it wanted to do." Hokuren closed her eyes. "That's why it didn't care that Witherspoon hadn't figured out the full soul-transference process. It only wants to kill Senara, and that means killing you. Now, the tricky part is how do we prevent that from happening?"

Cinna stood up straight and thrust out her chin. "I want to fight it. I'm not running."

She expected Hokuren to talk her out of it, like Senara, but Hokuren said, "I'm actually happy to hear that. It means you're still you."

"Really? That's all you're going to say?"

"Normally, I would suggest caution. But something Senara said to you comes to mind. Give me a moment to collect my thoughts." Hokuren lowered her head. Her lips were moving, but no sound came out, something she occasionally did when working through a case or a puzzle. Cinna had come up with a theory: Hokuren's brain moved so fast she couldn't hold all her thoughts at once, so she had to speak them aloud to free up space.

She had yet to ask Hokuren if this was actually the case.

Hokuren abruptly raised her head. "She said that if you died here, the demon would sense her leave your body."

"So?" Cinna had almost forgotten to include that line of Senara's when retelling the story to Hokuren, thinking it irrelevant. In that scenario, she would be dead and no longer able to care.

"Hmm, consider: The demon knows who you are. As a vessel intended to hide Senara, that makes you less than ideal. If you went somewhere far enough away that the demon could not sense Senara if she left your body, somewhere like, say, Trebello, I think it's likely she uses the opportunity to find a new vessel."

Cinna shuddered. "But she knows that would kill me. Would she do that?"

"From a purely pragmatic standpoint, she almost has to," said Hokuren, crossing her arms over her chest. "As long as you remain close to the demon, she cannot leave your body, so she has a vested interest in keeping you alive. If you go somewhere far away, her interests lie opposite." She stood up, putting her fist in her palm. "We have no choice but to fight the demon head-on in order to save your life." She grinned, shaking her head. "That sounds more like your line than mine, but it was fun to say."

"It's what I want to do, anyway, so I like this logic." Cinna's shoulders sagged. "But I don't know how to actually win a fight against a demon. Senara said I couldn't punch through its armor, and I'm worried she's right."

"She is, but that's why I'm here." Hokuren tapped her head. "I've got an idea percolating already. I don't think Senara is thinking creatively enough. It's not quite fully formed, but let's talk about it on the way back to Velles. We have several days. By the time we get there, we should have it all figured out." Hokuren began taking the tarps off the wagon. "Help me wrap these back up. There's no time to waste."

"Wait," said Cinna, deflecting a tarp Hokuren tossed at her. She wanted Hokuren's help, but she couldn't drag her into what was most likely a doomed situation. "Boss, when it comes time to fight it I can't ask you to come. It only wants to kill me."

Hokuren dropped the tarps and laughed, which made Cinna wonder what was so funny. "You think I should let you go off to your death by yourself? I care about you too much. I'll do whatever I can to see you come out of this alive."

"It's not that I think you don't care." Cinna tried to form the words, but found herself hesitant. "I— "

Hokuren walked right up next to Cinna. "Why not ask me if I want to come or not?"

"Because I don't want to have to see you die," said Cinna, more forcefully than she wanted.

Hokuren said nothing for a long time, to the point that Cinna wondered if she had angered her somehow.

"I don't want to hear about your death and wonder if I could have done something." Hokuren stared straight into Cinna's eyes with an intensity that Cinna couldn't meet. "I love you, Cinna. You're my family now. I abandoned what family I had, and I probably shouldn't have. But I won't do it again. And damned if we aren't going to figure out how to beat this demon together so we can live the rest of our lives in peace. Neither of us are dying. What do you say?"

"Got it," Cinna whispered. Love? Family? Once again, Cinna found herself at a loss for words.

Hokuren's eyes softened. "Good. Now, I think we've dawdled here long enough, don't you? Let's get these tarps put away and the horses hitched up."

Hokuren spent a majority of the return trip to Velles working over the plan to deal with the demon. Sometimes she ran through it in her head, sometimes she bounced ideas off Cinna. Ideas that sounded so good in her head exposed their flaws when spoken out loud.

And Hokuren wanted to give Cinna a distraction from her constant ruminations on her encounter with Senara. When they descended the mountain, Cinna stayed morosely quiet in the back of the wagon. As the trip went on, she pulled out of her gloom to discuss the plan with Hokuren.

According to stories from the adventurers Hokuren had read, demons were powerful creatures that would take over humans and use their bodies for their enigmatic purposes. She had not heard of anything inanimate, such as a suit of armor, being the vessel of a demon.

Demons knew magic and enthralled people to influence their decisions and actions. Despite the danger they posed, demons had one glaring weakness: their innards. In one adventurer's report, these were described as "purple goop," and they were surprisingly fragile. Demons created a protective shell to hide within, different for each one, that must be penetrated. A direct strike to the purple goop caused a breakdown, rendering the demon incapacitated. This incapacitation could last centuries. The adventurers often recommended sealing the demon in a tomb, so that when it inevitably recovered, it remained trapped for eternity.

Adventurers also recommended that only the brave, experienced, and stupid attempt to fight a demon. Hokuren counted herself as none of those three, but her desperation should count as compelling a reason as the rest.

With her information at hand, Hokuren had a scheme to both encounter Davenport and incapacitate it. The protection this demon had chosen, the golden armor, posed an issue, but she figured she'd come up with a way around that. And while she did not have the money to fund the building of a tomb, a suit of armor functioned like an anchor in water. The bottom of the sea served as almost as good a resting place.

Her plan required three things: adventurers, a potion, and a ship captain who was brave, experienced, and stupid enough to agree to her plan. And she knew just the man.

A single member of the City Watch, not one that Hokuren recognized, ran Velles's western gate the morning they reached the city nearly two weeks after they had left. They donned their cloaks to keep their faces hidden. The Watch member waved them through without issue, not even bothering to ask them to put their hoods down. External threats had been rare for so long that the city's security had grown quite lax.

Hokuren returned the wagon and horses, receiving her deposit back. This money would be crucial to the plan, because the people she needed found gold most enticing.

With that done, Hokuren and Cinna continued to their next stop.

"Aw, this place again?" said Cinna, outside of the Garrulous Squirrel, as if Hokuren had not told her multiple times they would come here.

"This place again."

Hokuren entered the bar to discover it completely empty, not even a bartender in sight. Hokuren hoped her adventurer friends had not gotten an actual job while she traveled outside of the city.

Two flyers were pinned side by side to the otherwise empty Job Board. When Hokuren read them, she put her hand on her temple and massaged the sudden headache that came on.

"Wait a minute," said Cinna, on her tiptoes and peeking over Hokuren's shoulder. "That's me."

The portrait of Cinna, though crude, showed her shaggy hair and headband, making it easy to identify her. The word "WANTED" hovered over her image. Below that, a declaration naming her the Master Thief that had been "terrorizing" Velles for months. Hokuren's head spun thinking about the amount of the reward for bringing Cinna in alive.

"I'm not the Master Thief!" Cinna, having read the actual words on the posting, pulled it from the board. "They're lying."

"Yes, unfortunately," said Hokuren, growing incandescent with anger as she reread the second flyer. "And they're lying about me, as well."

Pinned next to Cinna's wanted poster was a second, with a slightly better drawing of Hokuren centered on it. This one named her the murderer of Tarleton, Arnold Witherspoon, and someone named Rafael. This last one must have been the battle page done in by the ogre.

Calling her "extremely dangerous," the poster offered a smaller amount for her capture, "dead or alive." She tore it from the board, most furious to be blamed for Tarleton's death.

Cinna judged both portraits, peeking over at Hokuren's. "Why are you drawn so much nicer?"

"The Watch's sketch artist is more familiar with me. Give me that." Hokuren took both postings and crumpled them into balls, the action therapeutic. "I'm sure there are more of these around the city. We have our disguises, but we should still be careful. Keep your hood up. I wish you'd kept those boots I got you."

"I'm glad I didn't."

Hokuren pulled out a posting of her own, one which she had made during rest periods on the trip back. There were no pictures, as neither she nor Cinna had any artistic skill. It read:

JOB
Come down to the docks at dawn tomorrow for a **BIG JOB**
All adventurers welcome and **ALL** will be **PAID IN GOLD**
There will be **DANGER**, there will be **GLORY**
Come if you have the **SKILLS** and **GUTS**
Signed, Mysterious Patron

"This says a lot, but nothing at all," said Cinna, scratching her head after reading it.

"Adventurers love vague, trust me. This job could be anything, and that's much more interesting than a job that's obviously one thing." Hokuren ushered Cinna out of the bar. "Now come on, no time to waste. Off to the next stop."

The sun hit its midday high as Hokuren led Cinna back to Fenton's Magical Supplies and Sundries. Hokuren and Cinna entered Fenton's shop. Fenton, head down in the midst organizing bottles full of colored liquids, said, "Welcome, we have a special on—"

"We don't want penlights," said Hokuren briskly. "But we are in a bit of a hurry."

Fenton lifted his head and beamed at her. "Well, well, if it isn't my favorite customer who has more murder victims than items purchased from me." He gestured at Cinna. "And her assistant, Velles's notorious Master Thief. What a pair of criminals you two are."

"I'm not a thief!" Cinna, heated, raised her fist. Then she put the fist down. More softly, she said, "Well, I'm not the Master Thief."

Hokuren put a hand on Cinna's shoulder to calm her down as Fenton's smile stretched ear-to-ear. "It's not true," she said.

"Of course it's not. Hokuren the Seeker is too much a paragon of justice to turn into a sloppy three-time murderer. As for you, Cinna, I recall one of the Master Thief's calling cards the City Watch released had our illustrious thief claim his shoes were as silent as snowflakes." He pointed at her feet. "Yet I see you wear no shoes. Ergo, you can't be the Master Thief."

"Ergo, that's right! Boss, he could be a seeker, too."

"I'd make a terrible seeker," said Fenton. "I can't even find a customer most days."

"If you've had your fun, I need your help," said Hokuren to his amused face. "But I don't need any information from you today. I'm actually interested in buying something."

Fenton's eyebrows rose. "Oh? I always thought goblins would fly before you'd make a purchase."

"Get an umbrella, it's raining goblins outside. I need to buy a potion. One that can dissolve gold."

Fenton's eyebrows went up even higher. "That's a pretty rare potion. It requires a fair amount of magic to create." He leaned on the counter. "I'm afraid to inform you that I'm fresh out."

Hokuren nodded. She had been expecting this. She leaned on the counter from the other side, putting her face right up next to his. In a low voice, she said, "You're the only one I can turn to. I need one bottle. And I know you can make it."

Fenton said nothing, and the two stared at each other, noses almost touching. It was the magic shop owner who broke first, leaning back and laughing. "We better quit these high-intensity stares. It's bad for our eyesight."

"I mean it, Fenton. Anything you can do. Our lives depend on it."

Fenton shrugged. "I wish I could help you, but I can't—"

"Don't lie to me anymore," said Hokuren, polite but firm. "You aren't as useless as you want everyone to think you are."

"Ah, Hokuren, that's the nicest thing anyone's said to me all week. But I'm afraid that I am, in fact, quite useless. I can't even move this penlight product, despite coming up with a number of inventive marketing strategies. So many unsold boxes!" He put the back of his hand to his forehead and pretended to swoon. "I just may go under!"

She had expected this distraction attempt as well. "You know all about magic items, no matter what they are. I've pretended to buy that story for your sake, but I need the real you." She touched her hand to her chest. "Nothing discussed here will ever leave the room. You have my word."

Fenton's detached smile showed the tiniest of cracks. "Nothing here will be of any interest to anyone outside of this room."

"Fenton." Hokuren put her hands on the countertop. "You can make the potion, can't you? You're capable of magic. Not just detecting it. Using it."

The smile on Fenton's face finally broke, and his tone harshened. "This is a dangerous accusation you're making."

Hokuren didn't budge. "You want to know what clinched it for me? That potion of muscle soreness you tried to sell me last time."

Fenton waved his hand. "Oh, that. I find things here and there." When she only scoffed in reply, he filled the silence. "Are you trying to suggest I made that abomination of a potion? Ridiculous."

"Who else would?"

"Come on," said Cinna, jumping in to cajole Fenton. "Can't you help us out? We have a demon to kill."

"A demon?" He sounded intrigued and less surprised than he should have. "Seeker, what kinds of stories do you tell this gal of yours?"

Hokuren groaned and said, "I didn't exactly want to tell you, but it's the truth." Now that Cinna had blurted it out, Hokuren had no choice but to run with it. "What do you know about Julien Davenport? The Captain of the Palace Guard?"

"The captain of the—wait." Fenton's brow furrowed. "The gold armor. Are you intending to do what I think you're intending to do to him?"

"Davenport's not human." Hokuren watched his reaction closely. She decided to mix in a little lie, for Cinna's sake. "It's a demon hunting the goddess Senara. It thinks Senara is in Velles, and it's going to get aggressive. We have to kill it, because no one else will. And getting past that armor is step one."

Fenton took a deep breath. "Well, no point in pretending anymore, I suppose. I don't know how you figured out Davenport is a demon, but if I was wearing a cap, I'd tip it right now."

"So you already knew." Hokuren's eyes narrowed. "And you told no one."

Fenton spread his arms wide. "And who would believe me? I start saying things like that, and the only one that takes me seriously is the demon, who shows up one day and—" Fenton made a throat-slashing gesture.

"I'll accept that. But now do you see why we need you? One potion of gold dissolution, in order to defeat a demon that haunts our city. We need to get past that armor. I know you're capable." When it looked like Fenton was about to protest again, Hokuren put up a finger to keep him quiet. "Don't waste my time telling me you aren't. I know it as much as I know your penlights are junk you'll never sell."

There was a long silence. Finally, Fenton said, "I underestimated you, Hokuren. I thought you were one of the brighter people in Velles, but I still underestimated you. I genuinely thought you bought my act. Can I ask, was I hamming it up too much? Should I rein it in?" He pointed at Cinna. "Did she figure it out, too?"

"No," said Cinna. "I thought you were just eccentric."

"Thank you for the prompt answer." Fenton put his hand on his chin thoughtfully, then snapped his fingers. "You're a tough negotiator, Hokuren. Against my better judgment, I'll admit that I can make your potion for you. Because I think that demon should be vanquished. And even though you forced me to admit my secret, I still like you. But I have one condition."

"I'm listening," said Hokuren.

"First, let's get started on that potion. Join me in the back, would you?" Fenton unlatched and opened up part of the counter. He waved for them to head behind the curtain as he switched his sign to "Closed" and locked the door.

Behind the curtain, Hokuren found herself in a closet-sized room with a hole in the middle of the floor. A ladder led down into a dark, underground stone bunker the same size as Fenton's tiny shop upstairs.

"This better not be where you kill people," said Cinna, climbing down the ladder with a suspicious look on her face.

Fenton laughed, shining one of his penlights down so Hokuren could see where she stepped. "Don't worry. The only thing I kill is my revenue streams."

When Hokuren finished climbing down, she found herself next to a wooden table, the only furnishing in the room. Around the walls of the room were boxes full of what Hokuren discovered were empty bottles, vials, and flasks. Jugs of water squatted in one corner.

"Welcome to my true business." Fenton flashed his arms all around the small space. "Fenton's Illicit Magic Station."

22

Hokuren stood at the table in the center of Fenton's underground lair, with Cinna by her side. Neither she nor Cinna had bathed in over two weeks, and the lack of airflow in the stuffy little room caused this to become rather obvious.

Fenton bent over the opposite end of the table, fidgeting with a vial in one hand while flipping through a thick book with the other. If he noticed the smell, he played the courteous host and did not acknowledge it.

He paused in his work to address Hokuren. "So, first, my condition. I know there's more than altruism behind your desperate need to kill that demon. If it wasn't personal, I bet you'd do what I've been doing and stay out of its way." He gestured at Cinna. "It's got to do with her, doesn't it?"

Hokuren hesitated. He had probably already figured it out, but she didn't want to give it away. "You feel something in her, don't you? I noticed last time I was here, but I wasn't sure what you were reacting to."

"There's something inside her, but I can't tell what it is." He tugged at his chin. "Let's see. You said the demon is hunting Senara. Let's assume that's true, although not everything you told me was. You want to kill the demon. I think you're too smart to volunteer to kill a demon unless you felt you had no choice. Everything would only add up if that was Senara right there in her soul."

Worry shone in Cinna's eyes. She glanced at Hokuren. "Is it okay if he knows?"

"I think so." Hokuren glared at Fenton. "If you tell anyone, anyone at all, I'll—"

Fenton put his hands up. "You've nothing to worry about. I don't side with demons. And you could ruin me if you blab about magic spells to the wrong people. I think you'd be willing to do so if I acted first."

"I would."

"Right." He smiled, getting back into character. "I would never betray my customer's trust. Good thing you're about to become one, finally. One potion of gold dissolution, coming up."

With a pair of tongs, he tried to lower the vial into a flask, but the opening was too small. "Hmm. As I expected," said Fenton, murmuring something to himself as he placed the vial on the table and studied the book. "You would have to ask for one of the more difficult potions to produce. Pro bono customers like you always do."

"I'm planning to pay for this one," said Hokuren. "What's the problem?"

Fenton traced a few lines in the book with his finger. "Gold doesn't dissolve easily. You actually need to mix two potions. There are a couple of different acids that, together, have the right combination of effects to make it happen." He picked up the flask and set it aside. "But the process is quite slow."

"How slow?"

"Let's just say that if you poured such a potion on our demon friend, it would have time to make tea, do some light reading, and then kill you ten times over before it even realized something was wrong."

"Not ideal." Hokuren put her hand on her chin. "I really need it to be faster than that."

"Fast enough we can avoid dying even once," Cinna interjected.

"Bring me a bottle, would you?" Fenton waved in the direction of a stack of boxes.

Hokuren collected a bottle from one of the boxes and handed it over. Fenton grabbed a handful of wires from another box and began folding them into various shapes. "So we need to make two potions, each of those acids. And they can't mix until you're ready to use the potion."

"But even then, it won't help us, will it?"

Fenton smiled, showing his teeth. "It will, if we also hasten it with an auxiliary spell."

"This is too complicated." Cinna stared at the wires.

Fenton followed her eyes and handed her a wire and the vial. "Complicated? Magic often is." He motioned to the wire in her hand. "Can you bend this around the vial for me, please, Cinna? Around and around, try to cover the whole thing if you can."

Cinna, happy to have something to do, got to work, sticking out her tongue as she pressed the wire against the vial.

"I've heard of them, but I was also under the impression they were no longer possible." Recalling the animal-conjuration spell at Leopold's castle, Hokuren demurred. "At least, impossible if you aren't an ages-old demon made by the forces of creation."

Fenton put a finger to his lips. "Shh, remember when I swore you to secrecy? This is part of the reason."

"But, how? Everyone knows magic has weakened. That's why the auxiliary spells don't work anymore. The wizards in the books I've read are quite clear on this."

"There's your problem, trusting in books written by the propagandists. Magic hasn't 'weakened,' Seeker," said Fenton, placing the last shaped wire on the table. "It hasn't changed at all. We have."

Hokuren's jaw opened, and she consciously closed it again. "Wait, what are you saying?"

"Everyone forgot the words." He flashed more teeth. "Well, almost everyone did."

"So, we could still create healing potions that regenerate limbs, or cast fireballs and lightning bolts or teleportation spells. But we don't, because we forgot?" Hokuren put her fingers on her temple. "How could that have happened?"

"Well, saying we forgot is deceptive. Much like most wizards are." Fenton arranged his variously shaped wires into the bottle. They seemed to form some sort of basket on the bottom. "The Conclave of Wizards decided generations ago that there were too many people capable of shooting off fireballs or teleporting whenever they pleased. You know magic spells are requests made in the Old Language, right? We beseech the Primordial Ones to grant us the spell."

"But is it really the Primordial Ones that answer?" mused Hokuren. Senara told Cinna that the Primordial Ones had removed themselves from the world.

"Your guess is as good as mine. It's not important, as long as someone answers." He crouched down to view his wire basket from a different angle. Pleased, he continued, "The power of the spell depends upon how exact your pronunciation is. So the wizards made up stories about the decline of magic and began a long process of spreading mispronunciations of magic spells. And now, after hundreds of years and many generations, the spells everyone knows are the weakest versions of those spells, and only wizards within the Conclave are any the wiser."

Hokuren was stunned into silence. Then she narrowed her eyes at Fenton. "If no one outside of the Conclave knows this, how do you?" The realization hit her before she could finish the sentence. "You're—"

Fenton put a finger to his lips. "I was. Like you, I ditched the organization that I joined as a young adult when I became disillusioned. And, also like you, said organization has a substantial bounty for my corpse."

Still working the wire around the vial, Cinna piped up. "Wait, which organization?" She whipped her head between Hokuren and Fenton. "What's the Conclave?"

"The Conclave of Wizards," answered Hokuren. "They claim to be magic's shepherds."

"Though they're more akin to jailers than shepherds," said Fenton.

"And becoming an owner of a magic items shop?" said Hokuren, eyebrows raised. "Not exactly the most inconspicuous occupation for a former wizard."

Fenton tapped the wires in the bottle, pleased. "You're right, but I couldn't leave magic behind. I take precautions. Now." He clapped his hands together. "How about we get you this potion, eh? You've got a demon on your hands. That's enough to deal with, don't you think?"

Hokuren nodded. "Fine, but please discuss it with me further someday. I'm too curious."

"I'll keep it secret, also," said Cinna. "No one would listen to me, anyway."

"A shame, truly," said Fenton. He took the vial from Cinna. The wire, now wrapped around the entire vial, served as a protective sleeve. "Now, the reason I asked you to join me here. I need your help. I need to borrow your energy." Fenton held his hands out.

"I need my energy," said Cinna, pulling back from him.

"I need it more." Fenton placed the vial into the basket of wires in the bottle. "I'll be asking for three spells at once here. Two different acids and the hastening auxiliary spell. It'll be exhausting, and my energy alone may not be sufficient. And if it's not, the spells will fail."

"How does it work?" Hokuren agreed with Cinna's reticence. Although she knew spellcasting required energy, she did not understand the exact mechanics.

"The brain is the muscle when it comes to spells." Fenton tapped her head. "I need your brain power. We'll be focusing and thinking hard about the spell. You may find this surprising, but thinking can be exhausting, just like physical activity."

Hokuren crossed her arms over her chest. "I don't find that surprising at all."

"Well. Please?"

There was nothing for it. "This is our request. We should help how we can."

"If the boss wills it," said Cinna. She looked down at her chest. "Hey, Senara. I know you can hear me. Give us some of your brain energy, why don't you? This is for your benefit, too."

"Can she hear us?" Fenton asked, his curiosity genuine.

"She knows things the boss said, at least. I assume she's always listening," said Cinna, poking herself in the chest. "Is this where the soul is?"

Fenton cleared his throat. "Come on, let's do this. All we need to do is hold hands."

Cinna, never a fan of physical contact, put her hand out to Fenton with trepidation. He took it, and Cinna's grip on Hokuren's hand tightened.

Fenton closed his eyes and took a deep breath. "Keep holding hands, no matter what happens," he said. "We cannot break contact with each other until it's done. When the spell is working, you might feel a little pain. Don't panic, it's quite normal. Now, I'll begin."

"Pain?" said Cinna, narrowing her eyes at Fenton. "You're not allowed to hurt Hokuren."

"It'll be okay." Hokuren was not nearly as confident as she sounded.

Fenton's lips came together, and he started murmuring the spell in the Old Language, the language of the Primordial Ones themselves. Notoriously difficult, the language comprised a complicated series of tonal shifts and sounds unlike any known language. Many people found listening to spells uncomfortable, but to Hokuren it had an obscure beauty. The words came from another world, perhaps the only thing humans had left to connect themselves to the beings that created them.

As Fenton continued to read aloud from a tome in front of him, an ache appeared in Hokuren's head, near the base of her skull. Unlike a normal headache, it was as if something had crawled inside her head to squeeze various parts of her brain.

When it started, the pain was merely uncomfortable. As time went on, its intensity grew excruciating.

Next to her, Cinna struggled as well. Her legs were shaking, and she gulped down breaths with increasing desperation. Hokuren wanted to tell her to stick with it, but her head burned with an all-encompassing agony. The only word she could form was a gasping "Fenton!"

"Hold on, almost there," Fenton said, his own voice strained. He no longer spoke the spell, but it was still in progress. Lights of all colors popped in and out of existence like a series of silent, ethereal fireworks, leaving behind colorless liquids in the bottle and vial.

Just when Hokuren's will faded and she was ready to break the hand-holding circle to escape the throbbing in her mind, the pain disappeared. Only the echoes remained, a phantom horror. She felt drained and put one hand on the table to support her rubbery knees while wiping the sweat from her brow with the other.

Cinna collapsed to the ground on her hands and knees, her whole body shaking. Hokuren gathered herself enough to kneel next to her. "Cinna, what's wrong?"

"My head," Cinna grunted.

"What's wrong with her?" said Hokuren, alarmed, shooting an

accusatory glare at Fenton.

He bent down as well. The ghostly magic-shop owner managed to appear two shades paler than normal. "I think I underestimated how much energy would be required for this one. Been a while since I did an auxiliary spell, and neither of you have any experience with magic. The more you use your brain for spellwork, the stronger it is. You two are like babies trying to crawl for the first time."

Hokuren helped Cinna to lean against the wall even as her assistant let out a low, constant moan and pressed her hands against her skull. "How come she's doing so much worse than me?"

"Well, the spell was failing, actually." Fenton looked embarrassed. "Our energies, even all three of us, weren't enough. I think Senara might have indeed shared her own, helping it succeed, but that much energy flowing through Cinna's unprepared body will leave her feeling a little sick. It'll pass, but probably not fully until tomorrow."

"Sorry boss," said Cinna, still panting. "I'm good . . . help me up." She tried to stand, but cried out and stumbled back to the ground.

"Don't push yourself." Hokuren guided Cinna back to the wall.

All three of them sat on the floor and rested weary bodies for several minutes. Eventually, Fenton stood up. "Want to see the result of all this exhaustion?"

Hokuren struggled to her feet, a slight lightheadedness all that remained of her ordeal. Cinna remained sitting, her eyes closed and head drooped into her chest. Hokuren let her nap.

"The potion of gold dissolution only works for a short period when these two acids are mixed together," said Fenton, pointing at the liquids in the bottle and the vial. "Be careful with it. The wire Cinna wrapped around the vial will cushion the glass so it won't break easily, but it isn't foolproof. When you're ready, shake it vigorously to break the vial and mix the acids, then break the bottle against the gold of the demon's armor to melt it away." He cocked his head. "Assuming the demon hasn't anticipated this move and come up with some sort of countermeasure."

"My hope is that it doesn't see this coming. After all, no one can make this potion anymore, right?" Hokuren picked up the bottle and studied it. The vial rolled in the basket formed in the bottle's bottom. "Not bad," she said, nodding with approval. "Thank you, Fenton. Uh, how bad would it be to get this acid on our clothes or skin by accident?"

"It's a potion of gold dissolution. It dissolves gold. Nothing else. Not even silver."

"So, we never actually talked cost. How much do you want?" The coin purse weighed heavily in her coat pocket, but she would need as much as possible for the rest of her plan.

He waved a hand. "I knocked your endearing assistant out for naptime, and Senara contributed more than I did, I think. It's on the house."

"Come on, I was prepared to pay."

"And while I appreciate that, I'm turning you down." He gave her a wan grin. "You already pledged not to tell people where you got it. But if they find out, at least don't tell them I didn't charge you for it. Can't have people thinking this is a charity shop."

"I owe you, then." Hokuren held the potion tightly. She could let nothing happen to it before her planned showdown with Davenport.

An hour passed. Hokuren sat with Cinna on the floor while Fenton bustled in his shop above. He returned by the time Cinna woke up. She claimed to be fine even as the strain in her expression told a different story, but there would be no point in telling her to take it easy.

Fenton had regained his color. Hoping he was well enough for more magic, Hokuren pulled out the communicoin imprinted with Lord Doubtwell's face that she had retrieved from Arnold Witherspoon's corpse.

"Fenton, is there magic left in this coin? Can I use it to contact Doubtwell?"

He stared at the metal a moment, then gave her a slight tip of the head. "You have enough for one contact. Though I don't think you can just tell Doubtwell those murders he pinned on you were some misunderstanding."

"Worth a shot, right?" she said, grinning. That was not the plan, but she didn't have the energy to explain. "Thanks again, Fenton. If we survive, I hope I can make this up to you."

"If you survive, I'll want to see if I can get your luck to rub off on me."

Hokuren left Fenton's with one last gift: a shoulder bag to hold the fragile potion bottle, wrapped in an old coat for cushioning. She adjusted the bag's strap until the fit felt good, then said to Cinna, "To the docks."

Cinna put her hand against her forehead, shading her eyes against the midafternoon sun, and looked toward the east, where the city ended and the Sea of Expanse began.

"I'm hungry," she announced.

Hokuren's stomach rumbled in agreement. "We'll eat at the docks."

Walking to the docks meant an hour passing through the flat topography of the city's business districts to reach a steep slope down to the waterfront. A wide cobblestone street flanked by small trees provided the only access for the hundreds of carts that delivered goods between the city and the merchant vessels at port.

When Hokuren was freshly arrived in Velles, she remarked to her superior officer in the Watch that the city would be unable to get anything from the docks if the streets iced over. The officer laughed. Velles never froze, he told her. And in her ten years here, she had never seen him proved wrong.

Quiet reigned at the docks, a symptom of the late hour. The sun hung low in the sky, and the ships in port had been unloaded in the morning and loaded back up in the afternoon. Only a few straggling containers, still to be worked by tired dockworkers, lingered. The sailors would be in their favored dock-level bars, every one of which had nautical names like the nearby Tease My Oyster.

Hokuren used some of her precious coin to purchase grilled swordfish skewered with onions and peppers. The fishmonger charred the outside too much for her taste, but at least the inside was rich with fishy flavor.

"That was delicious!" said Cinna, having inhaled her skewers before Hokuren's were even prepared.

"Thank you, my lady," said the fishmonger, a stout man with a beard who smelled like raw fish.

When he handed Hokuren her skewers, she gestured at the ships docked behind her and said, "Lots of ships in today."

"Oh, yes." The man bobbed his head up and down when he spoke. "Busy one today. You missed the excitement. A crate of cucumbers fell into the sea." He grinned. "I said to them, I said, that water's so salty that they should leave it in there a while and sell some pickles."

Hokuren chuckled appreciatively at the joke and took another bite of her swordfish. Swallowing, she said, "Do you know if the *Flying Porpoise* is docked?"

"Ah, yes, that adventurer ship." The fishmonger nodded. "Right over there." He pointed to the last slip on the docks. Small and fast, the *Porpoise* had three masts that rose high into the air. The name of the ship was painted in red letters over black treated wood.

Hokuren thanked him and walked with Cinna down the docks, finishing her skewers. The wood planks under their feet bent and wiggled, badly in need of repair, and Hokuren trod lightly, hoping with each step that the planks wouldn't break.

"Okay, we need to find Captain Tulip. He'll be in a bar at this hour." Back when Hokuren was in the Watch, Tulip had been accused of running contraband tea. She had cleared his name, and kept up an infrequent friendship with the adventurer. She took in the sight of the setting sun. "I'd like to do it before dark."

"Because you don't want to walk on these docks in the moonlight?" asked Cinna, her eyes on Hokuren's deliberate steps.

"No. Well, yes. But also, I don't want Tulip to be too drunk when I talk to him." She glanced over at Cinna, whose face was drawn with fatigue, the results of the earlier magic spell persisting. "Do you remember what we discussed during the trip back to Velles, about what to do during the negotiation with him?"

Cinna nodded. "Of course, boss. I'm ready."

The first three taverns they walked into failed to produce Captain Tulip. They drew stares from the clientèle made up entirely of sailors, merchant marine, and dockworkers.

The fourth bar, Canals & Crews, was packed, its long tables full of boisterous drunks. Smaller tables featured groups playing dice and card games. A young man with a lute played from a stage in one corner, but neither his voice nor his instrument carried over the din of yelling and laughing. Cinna remained at the entrance, pressed against a wall and watching Hokuren, having pledged to intervene if things got messy.

Hokuren sidled over to the bar and squeezed in between impatient patrons demanding their next pour. She could slither through the crowds looking for Tulip, but bartenders always knew their regulars. It was faster to ask.

A bartender with a mustache that drooped over his lip like a sedated caterpillar pointed to her. Shouting to be heard over the ambient racket, she said, "Do you know where I can find the captain of the *Flying Porpoise*? Captain Tulip?"

The bartender laughed and nodded over at the dice tables. "Big hat," the bartender said, leaning over so Hokuren would hear him.

Hokuren placed a silver coin on the bar. If she ever needed information from this bartender again, she wanted him to remember she paid for her info.

She slipped through the crowded tavern to reach the dice table the bartender had indicated. The "big hat" was white and encircled by a floppy brim several inches wide. A human, his skin tanned and leathery, wore the hat, which had the word "CAPTAIN" stitched into the front.

Only Captain Tulip would wear such an ostentatious hat. As Hokuren approached, Tulip lost a round of dice and stood up angrily.

"The sea take your loaded dice," he bellowed, loud enough that Hokuren could hear him over the noise. "I'm done."

The other men at the table hooted and jeered as Tulip stepped away and walked right into Hokuren, who had meant to get in his way but did too good a job of it. She toppled backward, landing on her rear.

Tulip leaned down to offer a hand. "I do apologize. I left in a huff and forgot to check for lovely ladies before stalking away from my dice game like a boorish simpleton."

"It's fine," said Hokuren, accepting his help to stand back up. She paused as her throat tightened when she remembered the potion of gold dissolution in her bag. She fumbled through the bag with her hand and breathed a sigh of relief when she felt her precious cargo still intact.

Refocused on the captain in front of her, she said, "Actually, I came over to speak with you, if you're free." She had to yell to be heard.

"Oh, well, well." Tulip tipped his hat and smiled at Hokuren, revealing a set of large white teeth. He eyed her up and down, then recognition flashed across his face. "Hokuren the Seeker." He bowed, chagrined. "My apologies. It's been a while."

"I have a business proposition. Can we talk outside? I'm tired of yelling."

"Business? At this hour? Fine, yes. I can entertain the idea of work."

A few minutes later, Hokuren sat on the edge of the dock, Cinna to her left and Tulip to her right. Their feet dangled over the water, which lapped softly against the dock structures.

"Beautiful night. Feeling a smoke," said Tulip, sighing with satisfaction. He reached into his jacket, navy with brass buttons, and pulled out a small packet of tobacco. He rolled it up with expert fingers, stained brown. "Offer either of you one?"

"No," said Cinna, shaking her head emphatically. "Those are disgusting."

Hokuren elbowed her. They needed him. "Be polite," she hissed. To Tulip, she said, "No, thank you."

The captain struck a match against a plank and lit the end of his cigar. "The little lass is right. Filthy habit I've got." He took in the water that stretched endlessly to the horizon. "Doesn't matter how much water I see, I never tire of looking out over it."

"It certainly is beautiful," said Hokuren, who said what she thought the captain would like to hear.

"I could see getting tired of it," said Cinna, who said whatever she wanted to say.

Tulip turned toward Cinna, then broke out into laughter. "The view's not for everyone. So, tell me about this business proposition." The captain eyed Hokuren with interest. "I won't lie. I need work."

His desperation was music to her ears. Hokuren took a deep breath. "I will warn you, it will be dangerous and unconventional."

Captain Tulip gave his deep laugh again. "My dear lady, my crew and I are adventurers! Dangerous and unconventional is all we do. Now, what is it? Last time I heard a job was going to be dangerous, I had to kill a so-called giant squid. Bugger was barely the size of the little lass there."

"Doesn't mean it wasn't dangerous," said Cinna, shooting the captain a disdainful look.

"Well, in this case it did. One harpoon shot was all it took to put fried calamari on the menu."

"I assure you, this is much more dangerous," said Hokuren, steering the conversation back on track. "I need a boat tomorrow morning, bright and early. And your crew. We'll meet up with some other adventurers I'll hire and all sail out to the open ocean."

"Sounds good so far." Tulip gave his cigar a long puff.

"If things go as I expect, the Palace Guard and City Watch will chase us on their ship."

"Hmm, less good."

The captain seemed reticent, but Hokuren barreled on, wanting to get it all out there as soon as possible before reeling him back in. "I expect they'll use the *Ceaseless Pursuit*. It's the fastest ship the Watch owns, though it isn't as fast as yours." She swallowed. "There will also be a demon aboard. We will need to fight the Guard and Watch, incapacitate the demon, and toss it into the sea."

"Nope," said Tulip, slapping his knees and standing up. "I know I said I needed work and wasn't afraid of danger, but I'm not stupid."

Hokuren stood up and grabbed the arm of his jacket. Maybe being completely honest had not been the right move. "Please, wait. You're the only one who can do this."

"Listen, lady, you're talking about committing several crimes against the prince and city right in front of his personal guard and the organization that runs all of Velles's prisons. And going on about a demon as well?" Tulip shook his head. "You've turned crazy. Normally, I like crazy, but even I have my limits."

"The Palace Guard and City Watch are both in the hands of the demon," said Hokuren, desperately. "If we defeat it, we will break the spell it has over them. There's no prison if we succeed."

Tulip paused, massaging his chin. "There's a demon with its hooks that deep into the city? How do you know all this?"

"I'm a seeker. I've been investigating an unrelated incident and discovered the demon that threatens us all." Hokuren put up her finger. "And don't forget, you still owe me."

"A fine time for you to call that in, Seeker." Captain Tulip scowled, but he didn't walk away. He wavered, and they still had a chance to get him on board. She looked down at Cinna, still sitting on the docks, kicking her feet absently. It was time for her to act out her part of the performance, but she had evidently forgotten.

Hokuren nudged Cinna's back with the toe of her boot.

"Oh!" Cinna jumped up and in an exaggerated voice said, "Forget it, boss. This friend of yours is no adventurer. I've seen cowards before, but usually their bellies aren't such a—hold on." She paused, searching for a word. "Oh yeah. His belly is a vibrant yellow."

"Where is this coming from?" Tulip glared at Cinna, then Hokuren.

"He hears 'demon' and he gets afraid," said Cinna, ignoring the captain, speaking to Hokuren. "You're a seeker and my last job was urchin and we're going to fight it, but the adventurer captain won't? Pfft." She turned her back on the captain with a huff. "Let's take our bulging bag of coins to someone with a spine that hasn't gone to, uh, atrophy, that's right."

Captain Tulip snorted. "I wasn't born yesterday, little lass. I see what you're doing, and I'll tell you right now, it's only going to work if that bag of coins really is bulging."

Hokuren brandished the coin purse that the prince had given her and counted several gold pieces, holding them out in her hand. "This is for now, to guarantee your services. You'll get the second half once we're out on the water."

Whistling, the captain eyed Hokuren's hand. "That's half?" he asked, incredulous. "That's more than I got for the last three jobs combined."

"It's a demon," said Hokuren.

The captain grinned. "You're crazy, but you've got yourself a deal. I'll help you beat your demon." He wagged a finger. "But only because I owe you. I'll say no next time you have a demon problem."

"Thank you." Hokuren handed him the coins.

He counted them out, then bit one with a frown. "Don't know why I do this. I can't tell genuine gold from fake just by biting it." He shook hands with Hokuren, and then patted the bag of coins, nodding at Cinna. "Still think I'm a coward?"

Cinna was unawed. "It took a lot of coins to buy you a spine."

Tulip laughed his big laugh. "You've got a tough one here, Hokuren. Now, if you'll excuse me. I need to gather the crew and ready for departure tomorrow morning." He bowed. "See you then, bright and early."

Hokuren and Cinna stood together on the edge of the docks, watching Tulip stroll to the *Flying Porpoise*, cigar smoke trailing in his wake.

When he was well out of earshot, Cinna said, "How did I do? I forgot some of my lines, but luckily I wrote the big words on my hand." She held her hand up to Hokuren.

The words "vibrant" and "atrophy" were written in scrawling block print on Cinna's palm.

"You did great."

Cinna grinned. "Maybe I could join one of those acting troupes." She paused. "Well, now what?"

"We're as ready as we'll be," said Hokuren, watching the *Flying Porpoise* bob in its slip. Her stomach tightened at the thought of encountering the demon tomorrow. Her plan was nearly set, and all that remained was execution.

Hokuren stared wearily at the uphill climb back to the neighborhoods of Velles. "We need a place to stay. Someone might recognize us even at a dump like Better Than Home."

"Don't worry, boss. I know just the place," said Cinna. "I guarantee no one will find us. I used to sleep there when I lived on the streets."

"If you think it will work." A bit of tension melted from Hokuren's shoulders. Then it flared right back up, and she cast a glance at Cinna. "How . . . clean is this place you slept in?"

Cinna grinned. "Not very, but at least there weren't many rats. It's safe, though, I promise."

"Hmm," grunted Hokuren. Cinna's place sounded dubious, especially since she didn't know what number of rats Cinna considered "not many." But when Hokuren tried to come up with a better option, she drew a blank. "It's our only option. Take me to your secret hideout."

23

Hokuren followed Cinna through the broken stone streets of the most run-down neighborhood in Velles, informally known as the Dregs. The buildings crumbled from repairs pending indefinitely, and storefronts sat empty, their signs long since faded. The tenement buildings were in poor enough repair that they offered little more appeal than the streets. Both adults and children huddled under blankets at the late hour.

"We're almost there," said Cinna, keeping a brisk pace while deftly skirting chunks of stone and the broken glass from shattered windows, forcing Hokuren to hustle to keep up. Hokuren's previous excursions into the Dregs had been official visits as a member of the City Watch. As one of the few who had even attempted to respond to complaints and requests from the area, she wondered if anyone still did now.

Cinna stopped near an alley with a dead end. "Let's make sure no one's watching," she said in a low voice. Pretending to rifle through Hokuren's shoulder bag, which held the invaluable potion of gold dissolution, Cinna kept her eyes on the quiet streets around them. Hokuren saw no one, but that didn't mean they were alone.

"Okay." Satisfied, Cinna ducked into the alley, and Hokuren followed right behind.

"Please don't tell me we're sleeping in this alley." Hokuren gagged at the pungent stench that only grew worse the farther in they walked. Some sort of brown liquid covered most of the ground, and swelling trash heaps lined the end of the alley. Hokuren pinched her nose with her fingers, but she still tasted the fetid air on her tongue.

"Here we are." Cinna put her hands on the wall on the right side of the alley. The surrounding buildings blocked all but the slightest slivers of Vitreous's light, and none of the sparse streetlights reached into the alley. Envious of Cinna's elven ability to see in the dark, Hokuren saw only the outline of her against the wall.

Cinna's shadowy form began ascending. "We're climbing?" asked Hokuren. "I don't see any ladder."

"There's no ladder, boss," said Cinna, scaling the wall with impressive speed. When she reached the top, she hauled herself up and over, then poked her head back down at Hokuren. The moonlight illuminated Cinna's expression of pride from the roof.

Hokuren felt the wall where Cinna had started, shivering as her fingers touched something unidentifiably slimy, and eventually found small holes in the stone. The holes were only big enough for one, maybe two, fingers or toes. None of them appeared to accommodate boots as thick as Hokuren's. Not that she had any intention of free-climbing this building.

"I can't go up this," she whispered up to the roof, the sound carrying in the alley's silence.

Cinna untied the rope belt from around her waist and threw one end down. "I know. Grab on, and I'll haul you up."

"This is too dangerous. Let's find someplace else." Hokuren touched the end of the rope Cinna had tossed down. It seemed too thin to support her weight.

"Boss, we already agreed there is no other place. Didn't you say we needed some place where no one would find us? This is it! My secret hideout. No one but me knows about it. And no one but me can climb it because they all wear boots like you."

"I didn't know your secret hideout would be on a rooftop." Hokuren grabbed the rope with both hands. "Fine, fine. Pull me up. Don't drop me."

"I won't," promised Cinna. "Not on purpose. Hold on tight. Before you know it, you'll be up here."

"Did you know I have a slight fear of heights?" Hokuren's palms already felt sweaty and her boots still touched the cobblestones. "It mostly manifests when I'm dangling from a rope high above the ground."

"You'll be two stories up at most. No big deal."

Hokuren felt the rope tighten and swallowed her disagreement as she was lifted into the air. Above, Cinna grunted as she hauled Hokuren up. Taking Cinna's advice to an extreme, Hokuren not only didn't look down, she didn't look anywhere, closing her eyes until Cinna said, "You're here, boss."

Hokuren opened her eyes to see the flat rooftop. With Cinna's help, she pulled herself up, glad to be on solid ground again.

Solid rooftop, anyway.

The barren roof had one feature of note: a small structure built following the original construction. "The secret hideout is in here," said Cinna, pointing to the structure. "Used to be storage, but whoever stored things there is long gone." She stamped her foot on the roof, gesturing below. "I think there used to be some sort of shop using the building, but it's been empty as long as I've known about it."

"This isn't bad, I guess," said Hokuren, walking toward the door to the small structure. "But are you sure no one will check the rooftops?" She feared the Watch finding out they were in the city and spending the night canvassing for them.

"No one cares about the Dregs. They won't come here," said Cinna, a touch of bitterness in her voice. "But anyway, we aren't going into that door."

There was only one door, leaving Hokuren confused. Cinna rounded the structure to the opposite side and removed the bottom wooden panel from the siding. "It's in here, the hideout," Cinna said, presenting a small cubbyhole.

Hokuren bent down and tried not to show her disappointment. It was about three feet high and only long enough for people as small as Hokuren and Cinna to lie down. An old, lumpy mattress covered most of the floor, tattered blankets and pillows strewn over it. The space would be cramped for one person, let alone two.

"It's cozy," said Hokuren, because that was more diplomatic than comparing it to a coffin.

"I can tell you don't like it," said Cinna, a little deflated. "You wanted to be safe. I built this myself. See?" She pointed around at the door to the little structure. "There's an old chest up against the wall inside. I cut the back out of that chest, and that's what we'll sleep in. You can only see this place if you pull this panel off, and who's going to do that?"

Hokuren nodded. "You're right, this is as safe as possible." She crawled in, worming her way to the far wall. Cinna followed suit, dragging the wooden panel behind her. With a bit of maneuvering, she slid it into place.

They lay side by side in total darkness. Up on the roof, with the sun down, Hokuren felt chilled and tried to cover herself with some of the ratty blankets. A lump in the mattress below her right shoulder blade made her position uncomfortable, but she didn't have enough space to avoid it. After several failed attempts to shift the lump, she sighed and let it press into her back.

"How is it, boss?" asked Cinna. There had been no rustling from her direction. But, as Hokuren had found, Cinna could sleep pretty much anywhere and in any position. Hokuren, used to a decent bed every night, had struggled at points during their trip to the Sanctuary to sleep in their wagon. She felt a pang of longing for her big, comfortable bed back at home.

"Great," Hokuren deadpanned.

"Oh, good. I thought you would find it tough to sleep on."

"Did you really sleep here, back before you were at the Sanctuary?"

"Almost every night. Especially if I managed to get some food. It was safer to be here than down in the streets of the Dregs. I was a little girl, easy to steal from." Cinna spoke frankly, no sadness in her tone.

Hokuren let that sink in. She thought of her childhood bed in Fondence, where she spent every night under warm blankets and never had even a hint of danger to avoid.

The silence was long enough that Hokuren thought Cinna had fallen asleep, but then Cinna spoke up again. "Are you still awake?"

"Yes."

"Um, I wanted to say something about what you said after we left the Temple of Senara." Cinna's words were halting.

"I'm listening."

"Well, I'm not good at this, but I was thinking about what you said, and you're really important to me. I don't have a birth family, but now I have you and I'm happy." Cinna paused for a moment. Hokuren's heart swelled while waiting for Cinna to finish. "I'm scared about tomorrow, because I don't want to lose you."

Hokuren felt around beside her until she found Cinna's calloused hand, grasping it and intertwining her fingers with Cinna's. "I'm afraid as well, for the same reason," said Hokuren. She felt Cinna squeeze her hand back. "But we've got our plan, and we can beat this demon. And once we do, you'll be free to do whatever you want."

"I want to stay with you." Cinna released Hokuren's hand, shifting on the mattress. She was invisible in the total darkness inside the little cubbyhole, but Hokuren could feel her breath. "I will be the best assistant you've ever had."

A tightness in her throat that Hokuren hadn't even realized she held relaxed. Even though she doubted Cinna would leave, hearing Cinna say it was a relief. "You already are, and then some. In fact, if—*when* we beat this demon, I want to give you a promotion."

"A promotion? What would that be, lead assistant?"

"You're the only assistant already. Think bigger. You won't be my assistant at all. I want you to be my partner in the business, fifty-fifty split."

Cinna gasped. "Boss, I don't deserve that!"

"Sure you do. You're resourceful, and I think your strengths are a perfect complement to mine. Don't you think so?"

"Hmm," said Cinna, as if mulling it over. "Can I still call you boss?"

Hokuren laughed. "If you want."

"Then I accept."

Shivering, Hokuren said, "Congratulations."

"Are you cold?" Cinna shuffled around. "I think there are more blankets, but they've all been chewed through." She paused. "I did say there weren't many rats, but that didn't mean none."

"I'm trying not to think about who did the chewing. Yes, it's a little chilly up here." Hokuren gathered up more of the blankets, but they did little to warm her.

"I could try something." Cinna pressed against Hokuren, wrapping her arms and legs around Hokuren's body. Her head tucked up on Hokuren's shoulder. "I hope this is okay." There was an unusual vulnerability in Cinna's voice. "I can warm you up. This is like when you gave me that hug, right?"

"It's perfect," said Hokuren, feeling much warmer already. She put her own arms around Cinna's back. Wrapped up with Cinna, the lump in the mattress no longer bothered her.

Cinna quickly fell asleep, her soft, rhythmic breathing granting Hokuren a sense of calm. She reached into her shirt, pulled out her necklace, and opened the clasp on the pendant.

"Mother," she whispered. Hokuren rarely talked to her mother's image, because she didn't believe there was anyone to hear her, but on this night, she made an exception. "If you were here, would you accept the risk I'm about to take tomorrow? Or would you try to talk me out of it?" She patted Cinna's back. "I'd like to think you would understand."

She fell asleep thinking this was a wonderful way to spend her last night, if that was what it turned out to be.

"Boss, time to get up."

Hokuren woke to Cinna's jostling. Her silhouette, and the predawn twilight behind her, greeted Hokuren's sleepy vision.

"It's now or never." Hokuren crawled out of the tiny space and stretched her achy arms and legs.

"I'm ready to kill a demon." Cinna met Hokuren's eyes, and they nodded at each other. They could only incapacitate the demon, but Hokuren elected not to correct her.

There was nothing left to say. In comfortable silence, Cinna lowered Hokuren back to the ground with her rope belt, then clambered down. They made good time returning to the docks, stopping only once to pick up fruit for breakfast at a small stall. The apples and bananas they purchased sufficed, as Hokuren's nerves left her with little appetite.

When Hokuren brought out the small package of blueberries she had purchased, Cinna declined.

"No, boss," she said, waving her hand at the bag. "These are special. They're for when we've won." She grinned. "Something to look forward to."

The docks bustled with activity as the sun peeked over the horizon. Goods in containers of all shapes and sizes were being loaded onto merchant ships in harbor, which would leave by midmorning in order to open up slips for incoming traffic.

A group of four people stood amid the chaos, the dockworkers giving them a wide berth. Hokuren picked out Galina's war hammer as she descended the hill to the docks before she could make out the adventurers' faces.

As she approached, Hokuren picked up a spirited conversation among the adventurers. They were boasting to each other about their previous endeavors. The air was rife with exaggeration.

Lyriel noticed Hokuren first, when she and Cinna were slipping past dockworkers rolling a crate. "Yep, it's Hokuren. Dorben, pay up," she said.

Dorben grumbled as he dug through his coin purse. "I would have sworn Hokuren would never actually make a posting."

"The 'Mysterious Patron' arrives," said Krusk, with a wave. "I think I prefer Hokuren, myself."

"So, you went back to the Garrulous Squirrel yesterday," said Hokuren, by way of greeting. "But no one else did?"

"You should have posted this elsewhere. Only idiots go to the Squirrel," said Galina.

"You'll be perfect then, and I think you'll suffice. With Captain Tulip's crew, we should have enough." Hokuren saw Tulip and his crew on the deck of the *Flying Porpoise*, readying the ship for sailing. She caught Tulip's eye and waved him over. "That is, if you're as good at adventuring as you are pounding the streets for leads."

"This isn't going to be more of that, is it?" Krusk eyed her warily.

"No." Hokuren gave the adventurers the same explanation as she had Tulip. At the word demon, their eyes lit up.

"You're asking a lot of us if you're hiring us to kill a demon for you." Lyriel's voice was full of excitement.

"I'm not actually. Cinna and I will handle the demon. I'll need you and Tulip's crew to keep the Guard and Watch busy."

"And how can we trust you are going to do it?" Krusk scoffed. "No offense, Hokuren, but I know you. You're no adventurer. You couldn't kill a rat in a basement. A demon is far beyond your ability."

Krusk's words resonated with Hokuren. She had faltered so many times when the situation became dangerous. But this time, she would not. Squaring her shoulders, she said, "I have a plan and I have Cinna. And if that's not enough, I'll have the rest of you to help."

Galina stepped forward, twirling her war hammer. "This may kill us all." She and the others nodded at each other. For a moment, Hokuren thought they would back out. Then Galina said, "We haven't had a job with any real danger in years. Been feeling mighty bored lately. A demon, you swear it?"

"A real demon!" interjected Cinna, rushing up to Galina before Hokuren could respond. "It's made of armor, and it knows all sorts of magic." She waved her hands around, wiggling her fingers, even though she knew magic wasn't done that way. "And it wants to destroy Velles!"

Cinna winked at Hokuren, who hoped none of the adventurers caught that.

"Destroy the city? Even better! We'll be damn heroes. The blood's already flowing!" Galina glowed, her war hammer resting on her shoulder. "Count me in."

"Count us all in," said Dorben. "If there's a demon, as adventurers I don't think we have any choice but to join. There's hardly anything to do worth writing about anymore, but this is our chance to inspire a tale or two."

Hokuren handed them coins from her purse, dispersing the promised pay. She gestured to Tulip, who had stayed on the periphery of the group while they made their decision. "Everyone, this is Captain Tulip. He'll see you aboard the *Flying Porpoise*, then I'll tell you the rest of the plan."

The *Flying Porpoise* floated in the Sea of Expanse, waiting for Hokuren's next move. Velles's docks remained in sight, although far enough away that the people looked like ants scurrying up and down.

The adventurers sharpened and shined weapons and armor. Hokuren was impressed by how formidable she found them. Krusk held a staff with a long blade at the end. Lyriel had a longbow carved with runes, and even Dorben seemed dangerous wearing a bandolier of daggers across his body.

Cinna stood next to Hokuren, near the stern. "I don't like those coins, boss," said Cinna, narrowing her eyes at the Doubtwell communicoin in Hokuren's hand. "Wizards control magic, and I don't trust them because I don't know who they are."

"I need to do this. We have no way to contact Davenport directly. But Lord Doubtwell surely does."

Cinna grunted at the coin. "Let's get this over with."

Hokuren closed her fist around the coin, focusing on it with her eyes shut, as she had done before. That uncomfortable tingling sensation returned, as well as the feeling of being disconnected from her body, but she concentrated on the message she had prepared for Doubtwell.

The same female voice as last time said, "Courtesy of the Conclave of Wizards, connection open." She received the warning about having thirty seconds to send her message. "Start."

Hokuren was ready the moment the voice stopped talking. *You and Davenport want Cinna? You want Senara? Come get—*

An explosion of pain overcame her, as if daggers had stabbed through her eyeballs and into her brain. She wanted to cry for help, but her paralysis was so complete she couldn't even move her vocal cords. A voice, deep and rich, entered her mind.

"*WHERE IS THE ELF?*"

The pain was so intense, she couldn't even think coherent thoughts. Images of the ship, the Velles docks and sea, the adventurers and crew, and Cinna floated in and out of her mind. The images stopped cycling and settled on Cinna, standing on the deck of the *Flying Porpoise*.

"*THERE.*"

Hokuren writhed with agony. Nonsense went through her mind, swirls and spirals on a blank background.

"*TELL ME WHAT YOU HAVE PLANNED.*"

Please, stop, she thought. It was all she could think, over and over again.

The pain stopped as quickly as it had arrived.

Hokuren opened her eyes to find she lay on the deck of the ship. Her body felt clammy, and sweat beaded upon her brow. The crew and adventurers gathered around as Cinna knelt beside her, holding the communicoin. Looks of fear and concern darkened each of their faces. Hokuren's hand, which had previously held the coin, was covered in scratches. She pressed her other hand to her forehead.

"What happened?" she rasped.

"This coin," said Cinna, pinching it between her thumb and forefinger as far away from her body as possible. "I told you. It's evil. I'm never letting you use this again."

"If the little lass hadn't pried your hand open and ripped that coin from you, no telling what would have happened," Captain Tulip said, standing above her. "You looked terrible, worse than any case of seasickness I've seen."

Hokuren gathered the thoughts in her mind. That voice had interrupted her message to Doubtwell. "Cinna, did you hear Davenport speak when you, er"—she glanced at the surrounding crowd—"saw him at the temple?"

Cinna nodded. "Deep, terrible voice."

"Hmm. I think the demon interrupted my message to Doubtwell. Perhaps it can even monitor all messages sent via the communicoins. It knows we're here."

"That's what we wanted, right?"

"Yes, although I was hoping to come out of it feeling a little better." Hokuren tried to stand, taking Cinna's offered hand. Her legs felt like jelly, but she stayed upright, trying to present as much strength as she could to the rest of the ship.

"You don't look well," Lyriel said. "I think you should sit down."

So much for projecting strength.

Hokuren waved her off. She addressed everyone, her voice scratchy and her throat dry. "The demon is coming. If you've ever seen the Captain of the Palace Guard, Julien Davenport, that's it. It wears a suit of golden armor, impossible to miss. When it gathers its forces and they get on a ship, that's when we'll lure them out to sea."

Grunts of acknowledgment emanated from the assembly. They scattered, and Krusk gave her a pat on the shoulders.

Cinna still held her arm out in front of her, but had moved to the edge of the ship, holding the coin over the water. "We should get rid of this," she said. "I hate it."

"It could come in handy," said Hokuren, but there was no feeling behind it. Everything in her body, from her head to her toes, ached. She could not imagine trusting the coin again. "Fine, let it go."

Cinna launched the coin into the water, and they both watched it flip through the air before landing in the gentle waves with an inaudible splash.

"Good riddance," Cinna said, dusting her hands.

Hokuren monitored the docks as she gradually recovered, sitting on a box against the wall of the cabin, shaded from the sun. The crew stood ready to hoist the sails when Davenport made his appearance. Cinna squatted next to her, fussing like a mother hen until Hokuren told her it was more important to watch for Davenport.

Finally, she saw it. The glint of golden armor marching down to the waterfront, distinguishable even at the great distance the *Porpoise* floated from. A group of Palace Guard and City Watch trailed behind it, blobs of red and yellow and blue and gray, respectively.

The rest of the ship had seen it, too, judging from the sudden silence aboard the *Flying Porpoise*. Even the jocular adventurers turned grim with the demon now in sight.

"Get ready to go," said Hokuren to Captain Tulip. He gave her a terse nod and motioned to his crew, who settled into their positions.

The demon was but a speck in her vision, and to it the *Porpoise* would look like a toy boat in the midst of endless water. Yet as the hairs on the back of her neck tingled, she had the odd feeling that it stared straight at her.

As Hokuren expected, the demon and its entourage loaded onto the City Watch's vessel at the docks, the *Ceaseless Pursuit*. Doubtwell had named it, hoping it would remind criminals they were never safe from the long arm of the law, even at sea. Thinking of the Lord Commander, she wished she could make out whether he or Princess Nyana were in the group boarding the vessel.

When the Watch ship left the dock, Hokuren said to Captain Tulip, "Go."

"Look alive, you scallywags!" shouted Tulip. "Lift the anchor, open the sails! Let's show those demon thralls what real sailing's about!"

The sailors responded with a group "Hurrah!" and, working with remarkable efficiency, had the anchor lifted, the sails open, and the boat on the move in mere minutes.

To Hokuren, Tulip said, "I expect this demon of yours knows you got something planned."

Hokuren didn't take her eyes off the *Pursuit*, which had set a course to follow the *Porpoise* into the deep waters of the Sea of Expanse. "It has existed for an unfathomable amount of time. I don't expect it to think much of us. To a demon, we're a pack of rubes, barely worth a second thought."

Tulip leaned in close. Under his breath, he said, "Been listening to these adventurers you hired. Might be they are a pack of rubes."

"They don't have to be much more than that to fight off the Guard and Watch. We have one trick up our sleeve that I doubt it will be expecting." Hokuren patted her shoulder bag.

"If you think so." Tulip rose to his full height. "In a few hours' time, we'll let them catch us, and we'll see if you're right, or if we're all dead."

24

Cinna locked her vision on the *Ceaseless Pursuit* as it chased the *Flying Porpoise*, a constant reminder of what she and everyone on the ship had signed up for. The golden armor of the demon wasn't visible. It was possible he stayed below deck.

In the hours at sea, Tulip had aimed the *Porpoise* at a storm cell, claiming chaos could only help them against the regimented forces of the Palace Guard and City Watch. Hokuren agreed with him.

The first few raindrops hit the ship. "We're far enough out to sea," said Hokuren to Captain Tulip. "Can you slow us down?"

"We'll be doing so once we hit this storm," Tulip said, holding a nearly spent cigar.

Hokuren huddled with Cinna under cover as the rain beat against the quarterdeck and the winds whipped the sailcloth overhead. Waves crashed into the ship, tossing Hokuren up and down. She held onto Cinna to stay upright.

Tulip gave assurances that they were in no danger of capsizing, which only served to put the idea into Cinna's head, then yelled orders to his crew.

One of the sails, straining against the winds, broke free from the mast and collapsed onto the deck. Crew scrambled to gather up the sail as a wave slammed into the ship, sending seawater onto the deck and forcing Cinna to fight to keep her balance. The sailors struggled to control the sail, the white canvas flapping erratically until they finally corralled it.

"What's happening?" Hokuren shouted to be heard over the storm.

Tulip grinned, taking one last puff on the dying embers of his cigar before tossing it into a bin of filthy water. "Exactly what I wanted. We sure look inept and out of our element in this puny storm, don't we?"

The *Ceaseless Pursuit*, which had not sabotaged its own sails, made up distance as the *Porpoise* floundered.

Cinna could make out the individual Watch and Palace Guard on the deck. Among them was Lord Doubtwell, standing behind the collected soldiers in his snugly fitted plate cuirass. It took her a minute or two of watching to figure out what she found so unnerving about everyone except Doubtwell. They did not fidget, rock back and forth, or even so much as turn their heads. They stood straight, unmoving, as if frozen in place.

"The demon's control of them must be near complete," Hokuren said, her voice shaking.

When the ships were only a couple hundred feet apart, the Watch and Guard lowered into a slight crouch, moving in creepy synchronicity. A small few, acting independently, twirled grappling hooks and prepared to draw the ships together.

Davenport's golden armor gleamed even in the rainy darkness as he appeared on deck. Its faceplate, black as night, scanned the *Flying Porpoise* before settling on Cinna. She felt something—she could not call it eyes—on her. An icy chill ran down the nape of her neck, but she stared back in defiance.

The scene of the demon walking out of the house, the blood of the couple meant to adopt her dripping from its claw, replayed in her mind. She gritted her teeth. He would finally pay for that.

Lyriel ran up to the edge of the ship next to Cinna, longbow in hand. "I can end this right now," she said, nocking an arrow.

"No!" shouted Hokuren. But before either Cinna or Hokuren could stop her, she shot at the demon.

The runes on Lyriel's longbow glowed white as her arrow released. Improbably, despite the pitching of both ships in the storm, she hit her target. The arrow plinked against the gold armor of the demon's helmet and bounced harmlessly onto the deck. The demon stood still, unfazed, then raised its clawlike hand and pointed at her.

As one, all heads on the deck of the Watch ship turned to face Lyriel, who scrambled backward. "Hey, what are they doing?"

"I hope she'll be okay," said Hokuren.

"She's taking attention off us. That's good to me, boss," said Cinna.

The demon spoke, the voice filling the eardrums of everyone on the *Porpoise*. Cinna clapped her hands over her ears, but that did nothing to mute the sound.

"*BRING THE ELF TO ME. KILL THE REST.*"

With that pronouncement, the demon returned below deck, out of sight.

"It's baiting us," said Hokuren.

"It'll work, too." Cinna scanned the faces of the Watch and Guard. "Know any of them? The Watch?"

"Yes." Hokuren stared out grimly. "Many of them."

The two ships grew ever closer, with the *Ceaseless Pursuit* swinging in order to get parallel with the adventurers' ship. Cinna tugged Hokuren's shirt. "Let's get back, boss."

"Right."

Cinna led Hokuren away from the Watch ship, letting the adventurers and Tulip's crew take position to lead the defense. The crew, armed with swords, spears, and crossbows, arrayed themselves along the deck.

As they passed Galina, the adventurer said, "Something's not right about those people on the ship."

"The demon," said Hokuren. She glanced at Galina's war hammer. "Remember what I said about not killing them. They don't know what they are doing."

Galina was stone-faced. "They've been ordered to kill us. No promises."

The *Ceaseless Pursuit* pulled up alongside the *Flying Porpoise*, its deck only a few inches lower than Tulip's ship's. Watch members threw grappling hooks, catching the gunwale. In unison, the Watch and Guard grabbed the ropes and pulled to bring the two ships together. They then tied the ropes to anchors to keep the ships bound.

The enthralled servants of the demon jumped from the ship to the *Porpoise*, and the battle began.

Amid the chaos, as metal clanged against metal and yells and screams filled the air, Cinna dragged Hokuren out of the fray. One of the Palace

Guard came for her, sword drawn. Her quarterstaff brought him down with a single blow to the head. While he charged at full speed, eyes empty of life, he did not attempt to dodge her attack or defend himself.

It unnerved Cinna.

The rain made the deck of the *Porpoise* slick, exacerbating the effects of the ship pitching in the storm. Cinna needed every bit of her balance and dexterity to stay upright, the wet soles of her feet tractionless on the drenched wood. As they navigated from the fight, Hokuren nearly slipped twice, only avoiding crashing to the deck because Cinna grabbed her and steadied her.

Cinna caught a glint out of the corner of her eye, toward the stern of the ship. There, poking out between spokes of the ship's wheel: a bolt in the crossbow of Maxwell Barnaby. He wore the uniform of the City Watch, and she had missed him among the group of boarders.

"Barnaby," Cinna hissed, pulling Hokuren behind her. Barnaby aimed the bolt right at her. The wheel was close, but not close enough for her to get to him before he hit the trigger. His hand shook when she turned to face him, so he steadied it against the spoke. She couldn't see it, but she had to assume he'd applied his precious toxin to this bolt, too, making catching it risky.

Barnaby fired the crossbow. Cinna flicked her quarterstaff at the bolt. It clattered to the deck, and the boot of a crew member, backing up as she used a spear to fend off two frenzied palace guards, snapped it in two.

Terror filled Barnaby's features. Unlike the others who had come over from the *Ceaseless Pursuit,* he was not enthralled.

When Cinna took a step toward him, Barnaby turned and ran for the *Pursuit*.

"Boss," said Cinna. She grabbed Hokuren's hand, clammy and slippery with nerves and rain, and gave chase. They passed one of Tulip's crew on the ground, a Watch member on top of her. Both of them had lost their weapons and wrestled, each trying to choke the other. Without slowing down, Cinna kicked the Watchman in the back, twisting him enough that the crew member could get the upper hand.

Cinna dragged Hokuren through the battle, adventurers and crew clashing with the invaders. She dispatched a couple of palace guards with swings of her staff to clear a path. Another jumped in front of her, sword raised. Galina's war hammer slammed into his side and sent him sprawling. Hokuren yelped in concern, but Cinna nodded in thanks as Galina moved on to find more targets.

"We need to jump!" said Cinna when they reached the gunwale, the unmanned grappling hooks keeping the two ships a couple feet apart through the upheaval of the storm. Barnaby was already on the *Pursuit*, climbing the ladder built into the main mast. She wiped rainwater from her eyes, dripping down from her soaked headband.

Hokuren nodded, but then gulped and shrank back. "Cinna, I can't—"

"You can!" urged Cinna. "Come on!" She pulled Hokuren, and they each put a foot on the edge of the *Porpoise*. Cinna grabbed her hand. "Three . . . two . . ."

"No—"

"One!" They jumped together, Hokuren behind Cinna, landing on the deck of the *Ceaseless Pursuit* in a heap. Cinna rolled and popped up to her feet in time to see Lord Doubtwell lumber over, sword over his head. He headed straight for Hokuren, who still struggled to get her bearings.

Cinna dashed in front of Hokuren, quarterstaff in hand, and blocked Doubtwell's swing. He kept applying pressure, sneering. Cinna kicked his breastplate, and he tumbled onto his back. She looked up at Barnaby, still climbing the mast.

"Go!" said Hokuren, taking her sword out.

"Ha!" Doubtwell rose to his feet. "We both know you're not nearly as capable as me in swordplay."

Cinna glanced back at Hokuren. "Boss—"

"We can't let Barnaby shoot from up there." Hokuren put her sword up, facing Doubtwell. "You're the climber. I can keep this old bastard busy."

Cinna didn't waver. She had to trust Hokuren would hold out. Without any more delay, she dropped her quarterstaff and ran to the mast. Barnaby, not an adept climber, labored as he neared the crow's nest.

As she ascended the mast, Barnaby paused underneath the crow's nest, resting against the ladder and loading another bolt into his crossbow. They made eye contact, and Barnaby nearly fumbled the bolt as he tried to work too quickly with hands made slippery by the storm.

"Oh no, you don't," Cinna said under her breath. She jumped from the ladder and grabbed hold of the sail's rigging, intending to have the sail obscure her as she climbed. Gripping the tar-covered ropes, slick in the pounding rain, made for perilous climbing as she hauled herself up.

A bolt ripped through the sail, narrowly missing her leg. The Master Thief was firing blindly. She smiled. He feared her.

"Missed me!" she yelled.

Barnaby muttered curses as Cinna reached the top of the sail. His boots pounded the ladder as he finished climbing.

"I can't believe you actually were the elf Davenport wanted to find." Barnaby had made it to the crow's nest. His voice was pitched high, with an unstable cadence that didn't sound like the Barnaby she had encountered before. He sounded frightened, but more than that. Insane. "And I let you get away. Do you know what sort of punishment Davenport gave me for that? Do you know?" His voice cracked.

Cinna couldn't muster sympathy for him. But if he wanted to blabber, she could use this to her advantage. Carefully, she shimmied back to the ladder that led up into the crow's nest, trying not to make any noise that could be heard over the crashing of the rain.

"But all I have to do is bring you alive. Barely alive, even." Barnaby giggled as Cinna readied herself to leap up into the crow's nest. "Then I can make up for my mistake. Get Davenport off my back, maybe return to some semblance of a normal life. Even—"

Cinna popped her head up into the nest and stared right at the point of a crossbow bolt. "Ah flames," she said, ducking back down. The bolt whizzed past where her head had been and hit the mast with a plink.

"Missed me again," she crowed, rising back up. She met the butt of Barnaby's crossbow as it struck her in the forehead above her right eye.

Reeling, Cinna cried out, her head exploding with pain. She lost her footing on the ladder, slipping into a stomach-lurching free fall. She reached one hand out and grabbed a rung of the ladder without thinking, every ligament in her shoulder screaming in pain as she arrested her fall several feet from the crow's nest.

She shook her head, trying to clear the fuzziness in her brain. Climb.

She had to get up before Barnaby readied another bolt. She forced herself to put her hands and feet back on the ladder and climbed once more.

When Cinna reached the crow's nest again, she heard the soft click of another bolt being loaded. She leaped up into the nest, greeted by Barnaby's wild eyes. The bolt lay askew in the stock, improperly loaded. Barnaby saw it as he aimed the crossbow and backed up to the edge of the nest against a waist-high railing.

The blood dripping from the gash on her forehead stung her eye. With no more taunts on her tongue, Cinna stayed focused on Barnaby, waiting for his next move.

"Stay—stay back. How did you survive again? Why can't you *die*?" Barnaby took the bolt out of the crossbow and threw it at her. She sidestepped it with ease. It sailed off, its final destination the sea.

With this, Barnaby seemed to give up. He hung his arms and head. "I must stop you, but I can't."

Cinna approached, watching him. This was some sort of ploy. She bet herself that he would swing the crossbow again when she got near.

She won the bet. Barnaby's eyes shifted and he swept the crossbow with a vicious backhand once she was in range. Ready for it, Cinna ducked and rose into an uppercut that crashed into his jaw.

Barnaby collapsed onto the floor of the crow's nest, releasing his crossbow, the weapon clattering beside him. Cinna picked it up and hurled it into the sea far below. Then she knelt down next to him.

"I hate you," he groaned, spitting at her rain-soaked cheek.

She wiped the spittle away with the back of her hand, mostly for effect. "Feeling's mutual." She removed her rope belt and tied an end around one of Barnaby's ankles.

"Hey, what are you . . . Hey!" Barnaby struggled to a sitting position.

Cinna paused in her work to shove him into the railing, then scuttled to the ladder and tied the rope's other end to the top rung.

She returned to Barnaby, who was trying to untie the rope from his ankle. "Knock that off," she growled, tackling him and wrapping an arm around his neck.

Sputtering, Barnaby said, "What are you doing?"

Cinna answered by dragging him to the opening in the crow's nest.

Barnaby realized her scheme and increased his efforts to fight her off. But she held fast and dragged him to the hole, dazing him with a punch. One final shove pushed him into the opening.

Barnaby screamed as he fell face-first, then shrieked with agony as the length of rope went taut around his ankle and stopped his fall. "My ankle," he blubbered, hanging over the deck of the ship.

"Stay here until I'm finished with the demon."

"You can't leave me here!" Barnaby shouted as Cinna left him there.

Sliding down the ladder as fast as she dared, Cinna worriedly scanned the deck for Hokuren and Doubtwell.

Hokuren stared down Edward Doubtwell as Cinna climbed up to deal with Barnaby, standing an arm's length apart from him. Rain fell in sheets around them.

"Hokuren," said her old Watch commander. He kept his sword down. Rainwater flowed down his helmet and platemail in tiny rivers. "What are you doing here? The demon is unstoppable. Even I knew well enough not to fight it."

"Why stop me, if I'm doomed to failure?" she asked, trying to regulate her tone. A rush of hatred flowed through her. This was Tarleton's killer, as much as Davenport may have been the one to actually commit the deed.

"I know we've had our differences, but I don't want to see you throw your life away," said Doubtwell, his patronizing words further inflaming Hokuren. "I can offer you a position in Davenport's new regime."

"Regime?" Hokuren choked on the word.

"We just have to get that god out of your little elven assistant there." Doubtwell nodded up to where Cinna had climbed. "We'll depose Leopold, and the best man for the job of running Velles takes over." He jerked a thumb at himself.

"You?" Hokuren snarled. "The Watch has fallen to new lows since you took over."

"So take over its leadership. After all, we'll need a new commander once I'm prince. I promise you free reign to run the Watch however you want, in pursuit of justice or whatever it is you believe." Doubtwell held out a gauntleted hand. "You believe the Watch could do a lot of good? Give up Senara's vessel, and you'll be able to help so many more souls."

The thought of betraying Cinna made Hokuren's stomach ill. "I'd never debase myself by accepting such an offer." She raised her sword, her grip so tight on the hilt that her nails dug into her palms. "You and your demon will never get your disgusting hands on Cinna for any price."

"The elf girl, invaluable? Difficult to believe. There are plenty more street urchins we could provide so you can keep playing savior, if that's what it takes."

Hokuren put as much venom as she could into her words. "You don't believe it because you only care about yourself and imagine everyone else is the same as you. You know nothing about Cinna and me."

Doubtwell sighed and raised his sword, getting into a fighting stance. "I promised Davenport I would stop you and bring her to him." His lip curled. "You think you're so superior to me, but sword fights have always knocked you down a peg or two."

Hokuren mirrored his stance. What she knew of sword fighting had been taught by instructors at the Watch. At Doubtwell's insistence, they instructed recruits on the methods and styles favored by the Lord Commander himself. She readied herself. "I won't lose to you."

Doubtwell swung first, a ponderous overhead swing that Hokuren jumped back from. She did this a few more times, never truly threatened. Age had done him no favors.

"Fight me like you mean it, Hokuren." Doubtwell thrust his sword at Hokuren. She twisted away, then parried his next strike.

"You killed Tarleton!" she cried, swinging the sword with two hands at Doubtwell. He was surprised, and her sword slammed into his breastplate. The plate dented, but held.

Doubtwell coughed, wincing at the blow. "Unfortunate that the boy had to go." He grinned at her. "Really, it was your fault for bringing the Master Thief to him."

This hit too close to home. "Damn you." Hokuren swung again, her sword crashing into his helmet. It deflected this shot, too, but dazed Doubtwell, sending him stumbling. "You could have made up a story!"

"He promised he would keep quiet, but he was lying." Doubtwell shook his head, regaining his footing.

"It wasn't necessary!" Hokuren swung again, wild. This time, Doubtwell blocked her, pushed her sword back. He kicked with his thick boot, hitting her stomach and sending her to the deck. She lost her grip on her sword and it clattered away.

Doubtwell marched toward her in no particular hurry, his figure hazy in the rain. "Davenport said it was necessary, Hokuren. He is not someone to argue with."

Hokuren scrambled backward on her hands and feet, stomach clenched from the pain of the kick. She could not see her sword, nor any sign of either Cinna in the crow's nest above. With Doubtwell in control of the fight now, she wasn't sure how much longer she could hold out.

"Coward!" she shouted. "You've always taken the easy way, never willing to fight for anything worth fighting for."

Doubtwell was near her now, and she had backed up against the mast. "I've done very well for myself that way." He lifted his sword over his head. "Now, you won't need to worry about what I have done for much longer."

Hokuren pushed herself further against the mast, then her hand felt something. A piece of wood, smoother than the planks of the deck.

Cinna's quarterstaff.

She barely had time to register it before she held it up in front of her and blocked Doubtwell's erstwhile killing blow.

Doubtwell stepped back, not expecting her to defend his attack. Hokuren jumped to her feet and pushed the end of the staff into his belly. The plate blocked this as well, but she kept pushing and sent him back to the deck. He released an "Oomph" and dropped his sword.

Hokuren strode over and picked it up. Doubtwell flailed his arms and legs, like an upturned turtle, struggling to get to his side so he could get back up. One leg lashed out and kicked Hokuren's calf. By reflex, she stabbed at the leg with his sword.

The point buried itself in his thigh. He howled and clutched at the wound even as Hokuren removed the sword. In shock, she threw the blade aside. Blood flowed from his leg at an alarming rate.

"What have I done?" she asked, mostly to herself.

"Boss!" Cinna climbed down from the mast toward her. She had a nasty gash above her eye, but had no other obvious injuries. "Nice job with the old guy."

"I stabbed him," said Hokuren, horrified. The Lord Commander lay on the deck, clutching at his bloody leg, his chest heaving up and down. He was silent, eyes closed.

Cinna grabbed Hokuren's shoulders, turning her away. "You did what you had to."

"He's going to die." Hokuren felt sick, resisting an urge to hurl on the deck. "I didn't want to kill him. Not even him."

"We have to take care of the demon," said Cinna. "That's the only way this stops. We can save him, but only then."

Hokuren faced the battle still raging on the *Porpoise*, the clash of metal ringing out through the storm. From where she stood, it was difficult to tell who was winning. Many of the Guard and Watch had fallen, but there were more of them, and the numbers on the other side seemed to have dwindled.

She took a deep breath. "You're right. This was my idea, and I need to see it through." She picked up and sheathed the nearest sword, which had been Doubtwell's. "Come on, it's down below."

"Maybe we can catch it by surprise." Cinna retrieved her quarterstaff and trotted to the stairs leading down into the ship.

Hokuren took one last look at Doubtwell, then followed close behind.

Cinna descended into the darkness of the hold, skulking down the stairs, keeping her footfalls as light as possible. Hokuren undid her work, finding the squeakiest part of each step without fail. Holding her quarterstaff close, Cinna expected someone, either one of the Palace Guard or the demon itself, to jump out at her at any moment.

The stairs first let off midship, where the remnants of a card game were visible on the table. She wondered if today's crew had abandoned the game before Davenport had activated its control over them.

One more set of stairs beckoned, leading to the bilge. Candlelight flickered from beyond the staircase. As Cinna continued down, the air turned dank and musty, and the wood beneath her feet was damp and water-logged. Water from the rainstorm above dripped around her. A few drops leaked on the top of her head through cracks in the ceiling, but she was so thoroughly soaked from the storm that they were no bother.

When she reached the bottom of the stairs, she turned left to find several boxes strewn about. Sitting upon one of them was a blonde-haired woman who Cinna didn't recognize until the drawing of Princess Nyana from weeks ago came to mind. The princess wore a well-tailored, yellow silk dress that was far too fashionable for the dinginess of the bilge.

Across from her, its back to Cinna, was a suit of golden armor. The demon. Could it be this easy? She motioned to Hokuren, who reached her hand into the pack.

The plan was for Cinna to distract the demon and engage it long enough for Hokuren to throw the potion of gold dissolution at it.

Cinna felt a rapid movement behind her. As she turned around to find the source, sharp claws raked diagonally across her back, from shoulder to hip. Her back felt as if it were on fire. She waved her quarterstaff behind her. There was a clang, but her quarterstaff seemed to meet only air. She glanced back toward the boxes. The demon was still there, unmoved, as well as Nyana, a smile of amusement on her face, of all things.

Hokuren grunted and flew into the staircase, an invisible force shoving her backward. Her back hit one of the steps and she gasped, falling into a heap.

"Hokuren!" Cinna dashed toward where she lay. The four slashes on her back burned with every movement. Even her Senara-powered pain tolerance was no help.

Before she made it to Hokuren, something that felt like an elbow struck her in the abdomen with enough force to double her over. The impact knocked the air out of her. Another force—a fist?—struck her in the back, causing the flaming slashes to produce an altogether fresh pain, and she fell face-first onto the soggy floor of the bilge. She struggled to her hands and knees and was rewarded with a kick to the ribs, hard enough that she heard the cracking of broken bone. The kick propelled her across the bilge, where she landed several feet away, rolling close to where the demon and Nyana sat.

Every breath felt like a stab to the chest. Blood soaked what remained of the back of her tunic and blended with the dirt and mold on the floor of the bilge. She knew she needed to get up, but energy failed her. In her mind, she begged Senara to dull the pain. Her back remained on fire, but at least the pain in her chest eased a small amount so she could breathe.

Cinna glanced up from her position on the floor to see Davenport's armored figure materialize in front of her, blood dripping from its clawlike left hand, just like she had seen at the farmhouse of her intended adoptive family.

Invisibility. The Davenport sitting across from Nyana faded away, an image like what Senara was capable of. Feeling foolish and badly tricked, Cinna willed herself back to her hands and knees. She checked over at the staircase, where Hokuren lay, still not moving.

"*SO THIS IS SENARA'S VESSEL. AT LAST.*" The demon mercifully lowered the intensity of its voice. "*YOUR TRAP BECAME MY TRAP.*"

The demon rushed toward her with jarring speed and grabbed her by the front of her shirt. It lifted her off the ground, then slammed her back-first into the side of the bilge. She cried out, the pain excruciating, as the demon pressed her against the slimy, rotting wood. She punched and kicked at the arm holding her. She may as well have been attacking an iron beam.

"*DON'T STRAIN YOURSELF, VESSEL.*"

The demon increased the pressure of its fist, pushing into her chest, cutting off the flow of air to her lungs. She saw black as she struggled to breathe.

"Hey," said Nyana, standing up. "Knock it off." For a moment, Cinna thought Nyana was coming to her rescue. "You've already won. Anyone can see that. This torture adds nothing. Let's get it over with already and take that soul from her."

So much for that.

Writhing in pain, Cinna panted out, "You've won nothing yet."

"*I AGREE.*"

The demon slammed her against the wall again. She coughed, tasting blood in her mouth.

"Enough!" shrilled Nyana, anxious. "You'll kill her before we get Senara, you maniac. The sooner we take her soul, the sooner Senara can be where she belongs. In me."

Cinna laughed, a hacking bark that caused her rib to stab her over and over. With as much strength as she could muster in her voice, she said, "That won't happen. This demon will not give you Senara. It's going to kill her."

"What?" said Nyana as the demon slammed Cinna again. This time, the back of her head bounced off the wall, making her dizzy and her vision blurry. She would not last much longer. But she had Nyana's attention, and she couldn't give up.

"Don't you know who this is?" Cinna slurred.

"If you're going to tell me it's a demon, save your breath, street rat. I've known for years."

"*YOU CAN SEE THERE IS NO POINT TO THIS.*"

Cinna's tongue felt thick, and she had a strange sense she was floating away from her body, but she pressed on. "This demon screwed you, princess. Its job is to find and kill Senara for the crime of creating the elven people." She sucked in a painful breath, groaning. "It'll never put Senara in you. It never meant to."

"Is she telling the truth?" Nyana scowled up at the demon's helmet. When she received no response, she said, "She's telling the truth, isn't she? I suspected, but all the bullshit we did, the people we killed, the years spent looking for this girl. It was all for me to get Senara. I—I thought that, in the end, you'd do as you promised."

The demon paused, inscrutable. Finally, it spoke. "*I WILL KILL SENARA. AND THEN I WILL LEAVE.*"

"But what am I supposed to do?" demanded Nyana, stamping her foot on the ground. Then she stopped, and her eyes widened. "Wait. The Soul Jade." She rummaged through a pack on the floor of the bilge. "Let me have Senara until the day I die, then you can—"

"I WILL TAKE NO SUCH CHANCE."

Cinna shot a bloody grin at Nyana, who recoiled from her. "You'll get nothing, princess."

Hokuren regained her senses, moaning as she struggled to sit up, her hip in pain and not working quite right. Groggy, she watched in horror as Davenport smashed Cinna against the hull of the ship. She coughed up blood. Nyana stood next to them, furious over something. Hokuren couldn't make out the words.

Cinna had a maniacal smile on her face even as she dangled in the demon's grasp. She said something to the demon, Nyana, or both, which further agitated Nyana. The princess thrust a finger at the demon's visor. Whatever her relationship with it, she clearly had no fear of it.

If Hokuren didn't do something quickly, Cinna would die. Perhaps even before the demon got around to using the Soul Jade on her.

Hokuren reached for the potion of gold dissolution in her pack and felt a sharp prick. She jerked her hand back, blood welling from a cut on her palm. Her stomach dropped. She opened the bag and peered into it in the relative darkness of the bilge, then moaned.

Her crash into the staircase had broken both the bottle and the vial. One of the broken pieces of glass had cut her. The potion of gold dissolution now soaked the bottom of her bag, near useless.

Ignoring the blood on her hand, she pressed her palm against her forehead. She could not stop the demon. She could not save Cinna.

No giving up. Hokuren studied the bag again. The glass and wires were strewn inside, as well as the old coat. The last item caused Hokuren to release a gasp of excitement she did her best to stifle.

The blueberries. They were wrapped up in a thin bag damp from the potion of gold dissolution. Hokuren checked inside and found them coated in the potion. They were her only hope. She gripped the package and wobbled to her feet, wincing at the pain in her hip. She limped toward

Davenport.

Drawing closer, she could hear Nyana screaming at the demon about the Soul Jade and Senara, distracting it. Neither seemed aware of her approach. She summoned all the courage in her body, down to the bones.

"Davenport," Hokuren said in her most commanding voice. "There are two of us."

Nyana, her face pinched with frustration, glanced over at Hokuren. "What do you think you're doing?"

"Hokuren, leave," rasped Cinna.

Hokuren ignored them both, focusing on the demon. It did not move to face her, but she had the sickening sensation of invisible eyes being turned on her.

"YOU ARE NO CONCERN OF MINE, HUMAN."

"Oh, but I am." Hokuren drew Doubtwell's sword from her sheath with her free hand. "My concern is how many holes I can punch into that obnoxious armor of yours." She hoped the demon's invisible eyes couldn't tell how badly her knees shook as she attempted to keep up her air of confidence.

Nyana rolled her eyes. "You can't be serious." She stared at the package. "Are those *blueberries*?"

Hokuren had to convince the demon to turn around so she could hurl the berries right into its face. With the open visor, it was the best option.

"I'm not going to let you kill her," said Hokuren.

"YOU CANNOT STOP ME."

It turned around, holding Cinna's limp body in the air.

Hokuren feinted with the sword. The demon reacted as she wanted, swiping with its claw to block the blade.

Without waiting, Hokuren threw the package of blueberries at the demon, aiming for the visor. The bag tore in midair. A few dozen blueberries, glossy with gold dissolving acid, hurtled toward Davenport, striking him across the face of his helmet.

The demon screamed, a noise so terrible it brought Hokuren to her knees, hands clamped over her ears. It dropped Cinna, who fell to the floor with a thud. Several holes developed in the gold of its helmet. A purplish goo squeezed out in the shape of noodles.

"WHAT HAVE YOU DONE!"

The roar of the demon's voice paralyzed Hokuren. Flailing, the demon slammed its claw into the hull, snapping the wood. Water trickled into the bilge through a small crack. The pressure of the sea quickly turned this into a stream.

Hokuren shook free of the demon's hold and crawled to Cinna, who lay motionless. From the corner of her eye, she caught Nyana fleeing up the stairs and out of the bilge. "Cinna! Get up!" Hokuren cried.

Cinna's eyes fluttered open. "Boss," she said, barely audible over the screams of the demon. "There's an awful noise."

The demon's arms covered where its helmet used to be, now almost completely dissolved. This had been a mistake, as residual potion seeped onto its gauntlets. Purple goo seeped out from new holes and dripped onto the floor, sizzling as it dissolved the wood.

The volume of the demon's screams reached deafening levels. It backed away, trying desperately to rub the potion away, but this only spread the acid further.

Hokuren helped Cinna sit up as puddles of water formed near the hole. "Can you get up? There's a leak. The ship will sink."

Cinna rolled over and pushed herself onto her knees. "Have to... finish it..."

Hokuren shook her head. "This will be good enough. We need to get you to the others for medical attention."

"No," said Cinna. She reached a hand out to Hokuren. "Pull me up." She sounded stronger. Hokuren had to marvel at Cinna's healing ability. She pushed the thought of this being Cinna's body giving her one last gasp out of her mind.

The demon, still shrieking in fury, punched another hole in the bilge, this one even bigger than the first. More water gushed in. Already it pooled up over Hokuren's boots.

"We need to move."

"Boss, your sword." Cinna let Hokuren help her to her feet, then stalked over to where her quarterstaff lay in the rising waters. Each step Cinna took was pained and deliberate. Blood soaked nearly every inch of her clothing. Cinna took a deep breath, then gasped and grabbed for her side. She lifted the staff.

"What are you doing?" Hokuren checked the twin holes in the bilge, anxiety building in her gut. "Let's get out of here!"

Cinna lurched back over to Hokuren. "No. Together, strike it." She pointed at the demon, which had slowed down and now stood still, as if in disbelief. For the first time, Hokuren had a good look at what was under the helmet.

She suspected she would spend the rest of her life wishing she had not.

It was a purplish-black, gooey simulacrum of a human head, deformed by the acidic wounds inflicted upon it. Its "eye" was a large purple mass, darker than the rest, that resembled decaying eggplant.

The demon emitted haunting sounds, like a sheep bleating from deep within a canyon. Hokuren's eyes burned and her throat went dry.

Cinna held her staff up high. "Boss." Hokuren nodded, and Cinna counted them down one more time. "Three . . . two . . . one!"

She charged the demon, side by side with Cinna. She thrust her sword out, aiming for the dark purple. Her sword hit at the same time as Cinna's quarterstaff. The sword and the staff penetrated the gooey eye with a stomach-turning squish.

Then Hokuren felt a wave of pressure and her world went black.

When Cinna opened her eyes, she expected to be in the afterlife. But as she stared up at the turgid wood of the bilge's ceiling and felt the pain from her injuries, she came to understand that she wasn't dead.

Her feet were wet, and she sat up painfully to investigate. She lay across one of the steps of the staircase. Her legs dangled off the edge of the stair, submerged up to the ankles in water. This confused her until she saw the two holes in the bilge. The rising water lapped higher and higher, climbing the stairs.

What remained of the demon knelt in chest-high water in the center of the bilge. The exposed "head" of goop was now black and solid, like dark-colored chalk. The butt of Cinna's quarterstaff and the hilt of Hokuren's sword poked out from this substance. Whatever happened now, Cinna felt secure that they had dealt with the demon.

Hokuren.

In a panic, Cinna searched the room for her, then sighed with relief and felt a little silly when she found her lying on the step right above. She crawled up to Hokuren, who was still unconscious, but breathing.

Cinna stared up the two flights of stairs leading back to the deck. Everything hurt, particularly her back, which still burned as much as it did the moment the demon had slashed her. Her broken ribs brought a lancing stab of fresh pain with each breath.

"Okay, Cinna, get it together," she said to herself. No matter what shape she was in, the situation did not allow a rest or pause for thought. "You need to get to the top deck, that's all. Someone will help from there." Hopefully the adventurers had not been wiped out by the Guard and Watch.

Cinna maneuvered Hokuren onto her back. Then she tried to stand, but her legs and back refused.

"Senara, if you've got anything left in there to help me get this done, please," Cinna pleaded, gasping from pain. "The demon's gone, and I want some appreciation. Help me and Hokuren out of here, and I promise not to give you a single 'I told you so' about saying I couldn't kill that demon."

As if Senara had heard her, Cinna's body found some final reserve. She stood up, Hokuren draped over her shoulders. She took one step and hauled Hokuren up. Her back burned so badly, it was as if she carried Hokuren on exposed bones. Her legs shook and barely held her up. The staircase spun and wavered in her unsteady vision. She felt ready to pass out at any moment.

But still she moved on.

Another step. She looked up. Just fifteen more. Maybe fourteen? No, sixteen. "Hokuren," she said, still talking to herself. "Next time I want to fight a demon, talk me out of it."

Cinna focused on each individual step. Before she knew it, she'd reached the hatch leading to the deck. She threw it open and staggered out into sunshine, squinting at the brightness. The storm had passed.

The *Flying Porpoise* was still connected to the *Ceaseless Pursuit* with grappling hooks, but the *Pursuit* now floundered inches below. There was activity on the *Porpoise*, with crew, Watch, and Guard all administering or receiving aid.

Cinna waved and yelled at them. Captain Tulip was the first to hear her, and she heard shouting as he rallied some crew to assist.

Before they could arrive, though, Cinna coughed violently, her ribs painfully jabbing her, and she passed out once more.

25

Hokuren entered her office, greeted by a pair of filthy bare feet propped up on her brand-new desk.

"Cinna—"

"I'll take the pie here, boss," said Cinna, leaning back in the chair behind the desk and holding out her hand.

With a disapproving click of her tongue, Hokuren snapped her fingers and pointed down. "Didn't we agree no feet on the desk? They're not what I want a potential client to see when they first walk in."

Cinna swung her feet to the floor, grumbling something about why they even had the desk then. She accepted her slice of pie from Hokuren, an unusually sweet breakfast. Hokuren felt like celebrating. Prince Leopold had finally agreed to see them to present their final payment.

"So, when are we going to the castle?" asked Cinna, right before cramming a thick bite of pie—blueberry, of course—into her mouth.

"Soon. Wadsworth will bring the carriage around." Hokuren pecked at her slice of pie.

She was going to speak to Prince Leopold and Nyana. She hadn't seen either in the three weeks since she and Cinna defeated the demon in the bilge of the *Ceaseless Pursuit*.

After the battle, Hokuren had woken up in her bed after sleeping for an entire day, Cinna by her side. The adventurers had brought them both there and nursed them back to health. Nyana, under the escort of the surviving Palace Guard, had already returned to the castle.

"How's the hip?" Cinna asked, licking pie filling from her lips.

"Better every day." Hokuren grimaced as she sat on the edge of the desk. Her hip tightened if she didn't move it, but her limp became less pronounced as time went on. "Your back still good?"

"I don't feel a thing." Cinna finished her pie before continuing, "I bet the scars make me look tough. It's too bad I have to cover them."

Cinna had recovered quickly from her broken ribs and punctured lung. However, the slashes on her back caused by the demon's claws had left scars, the first that had ever developed on Cinna's body. Hokuren suspected not even Senara could fully heal those demonic wounds.

"Do me a favor and don't pull up your shirt in front of the prince."

No one had emerged from the battle unscathed. The adventurers suffered injuries of their own. A few of the Palace Guard and City Watch, reckless in their enthrallment, could not be saved.

Hokuren had recurring nightmares of Cinna, gashed and bloody, hanging limp in the demon's grasp. She hoped those would fade away, like the hip injury.

She had been waiting for the prince to send for her to provide her final payment. In the interim, Hokuren had testified against both Edward Doubtwell and Maxwell Barnaby. She admitted to the Watch's acting commander that she didn't know the extent to which Doubtwell or Barnaby had been enthralled by the demon, and what, if anything, they had done of their own free will.

Doubtwell had been stripped of his position in the Watch and his nobility, but thus far had evaded any jail time, with Tarleton's death attributed entirely to Davenport. In Hokuren's mind, the former Lord Commander got off easy, and it left a sour taste in her mouth.

Barnaby was admitted to prison as the Master Thief, where he would languish for years. He had revealed the location of Hokuren's stolen jewelry box when Cinna threatened to visit him daily until he did.

Wadsworth arrived with his carriage as Hokuren took her last bite of pie. She locked up the office and entered the carriage with Cinna.

At the castle, the guards escorted Hokuren and Cinna up to the fifth floor without fuss, not even requiring her to fill out a form. But Hokuren's danger sense went off when the guards retreated without a word before she entered Leopold's reception room, leaving them alone.

"Be alert," she said softly to Cinna.

Cinna nodded and took point, tiptoeing to the slightly ajar door. She opened it slowly to reveal a room, dark except for the sunlight streaming in from a window on the far east wall, the magical candles snuffed out.

"It's empty," whispered Cinna, poking her head past the door's threshold.

Certain something was wrong, Hokuren entered with trepidation. "Hello?" she called out. "Prince Leopold?" Every step of her boots on the stone floor echoed in the massive room. Cinna crept silently beside her in a crouch, head swiveling back and forth.

In the back of the room, tucked away where the sunlight couldn't reach, rested a desk twice the size of the one Hokuren now owned in her office. Cinna tapped Hokuren's shoulder and made a motion toward it, telling Hokuren with a hand to wait. With her silent footsteps, Cinna snuck behind the side of the desk, then jumped out into view of anyone potentially hiding behind it, fists at the ready. But she quickly dropped them.

"Boss," she said, her voice giving nothing away. "You should see this."

A sense of dread settled over Hokuren as she hurried over, intensified when she saw what Cinna pointed at. Prince Leopold's lifeless body lay on the floor, his throat slashed in a way eerily similar to Witherspoon's. She gagged.

"Need me to check it out?" asked Cinna.

Hokuren waved her aside. "Thank you, but I can do it." She swallowed audibly and knelt at his body, mindful of her hip. The cut on his throat was neat and clinical. His peaceful expression suggested his death had been quick. Either someone he trusted had caught him unaware, or the prince had been unable to believe he would fall victim to an assassination.

The blood around Leopold was wet, and Hokuren followed a trail that started near to his current position. Someone had murdered him here, near the desk, and it had happened recently. Well timed for her arrival at the castle with Cinna.

"It's a setup," said Hokuren, staying calm.

"And just when our names got cleared," grumbled Cinna.

"Hello, ladies," said a familiar voice in the doorway. Hokuren recognized the voice, despite having heard it only briefly in the bilge of the *Ceaseless Pursuit*.

Nyana.

Cinna emitted something like a growl at the sight of the princess. Nyana entered the room alone, not a single guard with her.

"Princess Nyana," said Hokuren, putting an arm in front of Cinna. "I have some bad news. We found your father. He's dead."

She gauged Nyana's reaction. The princess's expression did not change. Her placidly neutral expression did not match her cold, calculating eyes.

"My poor father." Nyana walked over to the high-back chair that Leopold had sat in during his previous meetings with Hokuren and Cinna. The chair faced away from Hokuren. She could no longer see Nyana once the princess sat down.

Cinna, her eyes slit, stared daggers into the back of the chair.

"He never could truly appreciate how much everyone disliked him," said Nyana from the other side of the chair. "Most of all myself. Please, come sit down."

Hokuren remained in place. "I suppose you're the new prince, then."

"I suppose I am," said Nyana, as if contemplating it for the first time.

"I can't help but notice you don't seem upset."

"That's because I'm not." The disembodied voice sighed. "Having this conversation with someone standing behind me is difficult."

Hokuren nodded at Cinna, who followed wordlessly to sit with Hokuren on the couch opposite Nyana. The princess—the prince—wore a grim smile, along with a fiery red dress that went all the way to her ankles and white heels.

"Shouldn't we be informing the acting Watch commander that the prince has been murdered?" Hokuren asked. "I think he would want to know."

"We'll get to it," said Nyana, waving a disinterested hand. "Not much to be done now. A few more minutes won't mean anything. First, we need to determine who will take the blame."

"The murderer," said Cinna. "Obviously."

Nyana laughed mirthlessly.

Hokuren put her hand on Cinna's leg and shook her head. "Let me do the honors of being direct. You found us with the freshly dead body, and you meant to frame us."

"Oh, quite forward." Nyana's cheeks dimpled in amusement.

Cinna jumped up from the couch. "Oh no, not again. Not more bad drawings of my face posted around the city."

Hokuren coaxed her back onto the cushions. "If she simply wanted to frame us, she would have come here with the Palace Guard." Hokuren turned toward Nyana. "I think our new prince wants to negotiate. We have something she wants. Is that right?"

Nyana crossed her legs. When the new prince sat in the chair, Hokuren saw much more authority than she had from the old one.

"I want to make sure you don't go around claiming I was a willing participant in Julien Davenport's illegal activities." Nyana made a show of examining her nails, then peered over them at Hokuren. "The blame's all his. Let's keep it that way. I want you to tell the Watch I was enthralled, just the same as anyone else."

"Were you?" countered Hokuren levelly.

"It would be best if I was, officially," said Nyana. "You understand."

Hokuren looked at Cinna, who stared at Nyana with absolute contempt. "Before I agree to anything, are you still hoping to take Senara from Cinna?"

"Oh, my, I wouldn't think of it." Nyana fluttered her eyelashes innocently. "Firstly, I can't. The Soul Jade is at the bottom of the sea with the demon, and even Witherspoon is dead. Even if I wanted to, I can't take Senara from her." She leaned forward in the chair. "But with Davenport removed from the situation, all I really needed was my father—my adoptive father," she corrected herself, "out of the picture."

"You'd better leave me alone," snarled Cinna. "I remember how eager you were for Senara, even though you knew that would kill me."

"We've all done things we regret," said Nyana, her mischievous tone only inflaming Cinna further. "Don't I get any credit for saving your lives?"

"You didn't save us!"

"Wait, Cinna." A puzzle piece fell into place, an unanswered question that had irritated Hokuren since the bilge. "Nyana, you dragged us to the staircase after we subdued the demon."

Nyana brushed her hair from her face. "You were going to drown. Of course, I wasn't sure you'd survive, but I gave you a chance, thinking you would be useful to me if you agreed to my terms in the end."

"So what happens if we don't agree to keep silent?" Hokuren asked, interrupting another of Cinna's responses.

"I tell the Watch you killed the prince, and within days you are executed."

Hokuren studied her face. This was no bluff, and worse than that, the new prince would see little resistance. "And if we do?"

"I tell the acting Watch commander that my father had a heart attack." Nyana grinned. "He hid it well, but his heart was never strong."

"Heart attacks rarely slice open throats so clinically."

"Once again, you have conflated the truth with the official story. They aren't the same."

Hokuren's stomach rolled. So that was the deal. Let Nyana get away with regicide and patricide both without the complications of being charged with the crime. There really was no choice, though. She opened her mouth to reply when Cinna stood from the couch.

"We don't care who's in charge of Velles," said Cinna, beating Hokuren to the punch. "Run the city. It doesn't make any difference to us. But before you keep making threats, remember your demon friend did the same." She leaned over Nyana, causing the latter to blanch. "It's gone and we're here. Consider that before putting our backs against the wall like it did."

Cinna had not raised her voice. Nyana fluffed her dress, more unsure than she had been at any point in the conversation with Hokuren.

"Give us the pay the prince owes us for finding you," Hokuren said, standing up next to Cinna. "Drop any pretense of claiming we committed a murder that we definitely did not commit. And I'll tell the authorities the truth: I cannot prove whether or not you were enthralled."

It sickened Hokuren to offer the deal, and she suspected she would need a long time to come to terms with it. However, she had learned from Cinna that sometimes you did what you needed to do to survive, no matter how bad you might look doing so.

Nyana considered for a moment. "In the end, Davenport did not take you seriously enough as a threat. You going off to sea was obvious bait, and I told that demon not to take it. But in its arrogance, it thought it was invincible. And until it met you, it was." She smiled in a way that reminded Hokuren of the drawing of her, where the smile did not reach her eyes. "I will not make the same mistake it did. Fine, you'll receive your payment. You did, after all, find me."

Hokuren had one more pressing question in her mind. It was not the most important one, but she had to ask it. "Why did you go along with Davenport's plan? Didn't you ever think that it was just using you? That there was no way to survive a soul swap?"

"My father told me from the time he adopted me that I was meant to have Senara in my soul. He had this idea in his head that Senara would give me omnipotent powers that he could use to extend Velles's reach to other cities up and down the coast. I went along with it, because I intended to use it for myself, and not him."

"He was so wrong about the powers," muttered Cinna.

Nyana nodded at Cinna. "Yet the fool died never realizing it. When I returned without Senara, my father went ballistic, threatening to disown me and ensure I saw none of his inheritance, including Velles. I'd lose everything." Nyana lowered her voice conspiratorially. "With no more Davenport on my side, I had no choice but to kill him."

Hokuren shook her head. "There's always a choice. You pick the ones you think can live with."

Nyana shrugged. "You'll receive your payment at the security desk." She smiled with the same insincerity her portrait artist had captured. "Satisfied?"

"Yes." One last lie to the new prince.

"Then we are done. See yourselves out, and may our paths never cross again."

Nyana proved true to her word. An attendant at the security desk delivered the payment to them—increased fourfold from what they had been owed.

Wadsworth drove her and Cinna back to the office. In the carriage, Cinna stared at her toes.

"What are you thinking about?" Hokuren asked.

Cinna raised her head. "Ah, boss. You know how Nyana and I were both orphans? And she got adopted by the prince and became the heir to Velles, and I got adopted by Ms. Pottsdam and became a street rat?" She frowned. "What would you think if I told you that if I had to option to go back in time, I wouldn't trade lives with her, because I wouldn't want to turn out like her?"

Hokuren wrapped an arm around Cinna and hugged her close. "I think I understand it."

The carriage arrived at the office. Wadsworth bowed to Hokuren. "I fear we may not meet again for some time. Please take care, Seekers Hokuren and Cinna."

"Goodbye, Wadsworth," said Hokuren. "And thank you for the rides."

Wadsworth waved farewell and started the horses back to the castle. Hokuren felt betrayal in her return wave, having said not a word of the prince's death to him. She wondered when he and the rest of the castle staff would learn of the prince's "heart attack."

A few minutes later, she sat cross-legged on the floor across from Cinna, a significant pile of gold coins between them. Neither of them spoke as they took in the sight of the money. Finally, Cinna broke the silence.

"I haven't seen this much money since the time I broke into the Sanctuary's vault."

There were enough gold coins to pay not only the rent in arrears and the remaining balance of the new desk and door repair, but at least another couple months' rent forward and even a new sign that included Cinna's name.

Hokuren's face twisted with disgust. "This money is dirty. We know Nyana killed Prince Leopold, and we're doing nothing about it."

"We were in a bad position, right? But now Nyana thinks we'll leave her alone." Cinna made a fist and aimed it in the general direction of the castle. "We don't have to."

"I don't think she'll keep her word and leave us alone, either," said Hokuren. "As long as we remain here in Velles, we'll need to watch our backs. Even if she's telling the truth about being uninterested in Senara, the new prince has to be considered more our enemy than friend."

"We can handle her." Cinna brushed some coins into her hand and poured them back into the purse. "And one day, maybe we can see her brought down."

Hokuren nodded. "One day."

Cinna and Hokuren spent the rest of the day plotting what to buy with their new windfall. Hokuren preferred sensible things like chairs and replacements for the weapons lost to the demon. Cinna, on the other hand, suggested a baking oven so they could make their own pies.

"Cinna, that's not a business expense." Hokuren waved the idea away, but she smiled.

Near closing time, when they were about to head home, the doorknob turned, surprising both of them. Hokuren tensed, wondering if Nyana had gone back on her deal and had sent the Watch to arrest them and take her money back.

The door opened to reveal a small elf girl wearing a heavy green silk dress threaded with gold.

"Um, hi," the girl said, shyly looking down at the floor. "You're a seeker, right? I want to hire you."

A customer. They had not seen one since taking the Nyana case all those weeks ago. Hokuren tried not to sound overeager. "We're seekers, yes. I'm Hokuren, and this is Cinna."

Cinna waved at the girl, who returned the gesture nervously.

The girl stammered, "Well . . . my mommy gave me money . . . We need your help."

Hokuren placed a finger on her chin and considered the girl. Why might someone send their child to ask for help? Her mind went straight to trouble in the child's home, so she crossed the office and knelt to the girl's height. "Go ahead and tell me what you need, and I'll tell you if I can help."

Cinna leaned closer to the girl, doing a poor job of holding back her excitement for the details of a new case.

The elf girl looked back and forth at them, then again stared at the floor. "My cat's missing."

Hokuren sighed, but Cinna put her fists on her hips, standing proudly. "You've come to the right place, kid. Hokuren and Cinna Investigations, where finding pets and princesses is our specialty!"

Acknowledgements

Firstly, I'd like to thank some critique partners that helped highlight some pain points with the early draft of this novel all the way through: RJScribbe, Temari, Jeffh and Ferallian

Special thanks to Natalie, Jesse and Becca for their help in beta reads. Your insight and time spent reading early versions of this novel were instrumental in shaping it into its final form. Thank you!

Thanks to my editor, Kyra Rogers, who caught and helped me correct a great many of my worst mistakes. Any remaining errors are the fault of the author.

Thank you to the Regional Authority: Ethan, Daniel, Jeff and Sheila. The first version of Cinna existed because of our game together, without which this novel never gets started.

Thank you to the Exeggcutors: Malia, Stars, Milton, Pat and Kaido. You all helped mold Cinna and Hokuren into the duo they are today.

Thanks Mom and Dad for your love and support.

About the author

Quinn lives in the Pacific Northwest and spends time each day either writing or thinking about writing. Other activities include playing Dungeons & Dragons, walking around the neighborhood, and reading as many other books as possible.

Along with Columbo, who takes on a dual role as lead writing assistant and very affectionate cat, Quinn is excited to present *Cinnamon Soul* and share future novels starring Cinna and Hokuren with the world.

Visit quinnlawrencebooks.com to sign up for Quinn's newsletter and get a free short story starring Cinna and Hokuren delivered right to your email inbox.

Email: quinnlawrencebooks@gmail.com